Love Untold

www.penguin.co.uk

Also by Ruth Jones

Never Greener
Us Three

Love Untold

Ruth Jones

bantam

TRANSWORLD PUBLISHERS
Penguin Random House, One Embassy Gardens,
8 Viaduct Gardens, London SW11 7BW
www.penguin.co.uk

Transworld is part of the Penguin Random House group of companies
whose addresses can be found at global.penguinrandomhouse.com

Penguin
Random House
UK

First published in Great Britain in 2022 by Bantam
an imprint of Transworld Publishers

A CIP catalogue record for this book
is available from the British Library.

ISBNs 9781787633872 (hb)
9781787633889 (tpb)

Typeset in 11.25/15.25 pt Sabon LT Pro by Jouve (UK), Milton Keynes
Printed and bound in Great Britain by Clays Ltd, Elcograf S.p.A.

The authorized representative in the EEA is Penguin Random House Ireland,
Morrison Chambers, 32 Nassau Street, Dublin D02 YH68.

Penguin Random House is committed to a sustainable future
for our business, our readers and our planet. This book is made
from Forest Stewardship Council® certified paper.

For my beloved mum, Hannah Jones,
who gives so much joy to this world.

PROLOGUE

February 1968

She is huddled into the corner of a shelter on Aberavon Promenade, wrapped in layers to protect herself from the cold. The wind is icy, though nothing can cool her excitement. She pulls back the cuff of her navy leather glove to reveal her wristwatch. It is still early, too soon yet to worry that he won't come. Though that is, of course, a possibility. She has no way of knowing his intentions. She only knows he'd clutched her note firmly in the palm of his hand. And she is here, as she'd said she would be.

'I brought an umbrella, though the rain's held off.'

She recognizes his voice in an instant.

And she turns.

And there he stands.

'Come and sit down,' she says nervously. 'I've brought a flask.'

She pours them two coffees from the Thermos.

'We should have done this eighteen years ago.'

'Better late than never!' she jokes, trying to cover up the painful memory of that horrific night.

The grey Welsh waves are crashing on the shore beyond and the promenade is deserted bar two passing dog-walkers, heads down against the cold and unaware that this most precious of overdue reunions is taking place just yards away from them.

2022

1

grace

'You all right there, love?'

The man wasn't someone Grace recognized. Must be a tourist. The dog looked unfamiliar too – was it a schnauzer?

'Yes, thanks!' she called back cheerily as she strode into the water, hoping this was enough reassurance to send him on his way, but he hesitated.

'Are you sure you're safe doing that?' he shouted.

Uh-oh, Grace thought, *a responsible citizen.* She fought the urge to tell him where to go and began cutting through the water with a steady, well-paced breaststroke. The sea was calm today. How she loved the swimming out – her own infinity pool, the Irish Sea stretching for miles before her, brimming with possibility. The number of times she'd thought, *What would happen if I just kept going?*

She could hear shouts now from the shore, a woman's voice this time. 'Excuse me! Helloo? I really think you ought to come back, y'know, dear.'

Oh, bugger off! she thought, and carried on sturdily scooping back the water with her arms.

Most weeks she swam at least three times, usually in her outdoor pool but sometimes in the sea, for a treat. She'd done it ever since moving to Dylan's Quay fifty-four years ago. When she told people she swam regularly in the sea they didn't believe her; when she told people she had her own pool they assumed she must be very rich; they assumed Spanish villas and mosaic tiles and sun-loungers. But Grace's pool was a free-standing canvas and metal-framed affair – a deeper, wider version of a kiddies' paddling pool, like the rugby players once used after a game. It was an ugly utilitarian construction that took up the bottom half of her garden, but she loved it and it kept her fit. Which at the age of eighty-nine was no small feat.

Reaching her usual end point – a big bell-shaped buoy, striped red and white – she stopped and trod water for a few seconds. She took in the beauty of the vast ocean and caught her breath before flipping on to her back to float. In just over two months she'd be turning ninety. Ninety years of age! 'Ye gods,' she whispered, staring up at the cloudless summer sky. 'When did that happen?'

Nobody answered except a disgruntled skua passing overhead who looked down and screeched at her with contempt. Grace lay there for a minute, supported by the ocean, allowing the water to lap gently against her skin. This was the best place in the world for solving problems and working things out. And for several days now, she'd been mulling something over: an issue which just wouldn't go away. If she went ahead with her idea, it was going to cause such trouble. And yet if she didn't . . . she would never forgive herself for not trying. It was tempting to opt for an easy life and just forget the whole thing. After all, it wasn't too late – she hadn't discussed it with anyone else: John knew nothing of it, nor did her granddaughter, Elin.

Grace winced at the thought of telling *her*.

She turned on to her front and began swimming back, dismayed to see that a welcome party had gathered on the shore. The man with the schnauzer had been joined by a likely wife and two sons. The wife walked towards the water's edge, followed by the man, their arms outstretched in fear. *Iesu Mawr, they're going to try and help me.*

And sure enough, as Grace took her last couple of strokes, the two-person rescue team waded into the water up to their knees and reached out to grab her, one on either side. 'Don't panic,' said the wife as they yanked Grace on to the sand. 'We'll soon have you safe and dry.'

Grace didn't as a rule fit the Grumpy Old Lady stereotype: she was generally polite and tried to respect others, no matter how different their world view may be from hers. But the one thing she could not tolerate was being patronized. And although she knew *intellectually* that these kind holidaymakers believed they were doing a good turn, she couldn't hide her annoyance. 'GET OFF ME!' she snapped, and pushed the wife a little too hard, sending her flying on to the sand.

'It's all right, let's just stay calm, shall we?' said the man.

'I think she must be . . . y'know.' The wife got up and dusted herself down, making meaningful eyes at her husband.

'You think I must be what?' asked Grace, in a louder voice than she'd intended, but there was water in her ear. She turned her head on one side and gave it a few swift taps, trying to dislodge the fluid. Grace knew this would simply add to the wife's assumption that she was in the company of a batty nonagenarian.

'WHERE DO YOU LIVE, DEAR?' shouted the wife, slowly and emphatically.

Grace responded at the same volume and speed. 'ABOUT FIVE MINUTES' WALK FROM HERE, DEAR.'

'Aw, she's just taking the mick now, Lyn,' the man whined.

'Dad, can we get ice-creams?'

'Yeah, go on, Lyn,' said Grace. 'Bugger off and buy your sons an ice-cream.' She pulled her portable changing room – essentially a long, home-made towelling poncho – over her head, and began to disrobe. Lyn appeared to be torn between staying put or joining her family, who were now bored with the whole pensioner-rescue thing and heading off up the beach. It was Grace who helped her decide, smiling inanely she whispered, 'I'm completely starkers under here now, Lyn. D'you fancy a gander?' The woman needed no more encouragement, turning on her heel and stomping off, the sand impeding her steps. 'Honestly, you try to help some people!' she mumbled indignantly.

Grace laughed to herself as she pulled on her knickers and bra with well-practised ease, her head poking out the top of the poncho as she dressed quickly underneath. She'd always said that when she reached ninety, if she made it that far, she hoped she'd be able to walk without a stick and fasten her bra. She'd surpassed that ambition, for sure: as well as her swimming, she still did twice-weekly yoga, could easily climb the steep hills of Dylan's Quay, and drove to Aberystwyth once a month. The staff at Cadwallader House – a local residential home very close to her heart – never tired of saying, 'Grace Meredith, you're a phenomenon, and an inspiration to us all.'

She rubbed her head with a towel, combed her hair and gathered her things. Licking her lips, she savoured their saltiness before slathering them with lip-salve. She loved the feel of her skin after sea-swimming – it invigorated her, made her feel alive, which these days she didn't take for granted. Reaching the top of the beach steps, she sat on the brightly painted bench, caught her breath and surveyed the view – Dylan's Quay, her beloved home town for more than five decades. There was no other place like it on Earth.

Unzipping the side pocket of her little rucksack, Grace retrieved the greetings card she'd been carrying around with her for the past two days and stared at it for the umpteenth time. The picture on the front was taken from a painting of the Brecon Beacons – a winter view with snowy peaks and crisp, stark lines. But it wasn't the picture that held Grace in its thrall: it was what was printed on the back of the card. That name.

Shutting her eyes for a moment, she drew breath. It was no good. The thought just wouldn't leave her alone. It had plagued her, given her sleepless nights, and she needed to share it with someone else, get a fresh perspective. Much as she dreaded doing so, she would have to talk to John. And thrusting the card back into her rucksack, Grace began striding up the hill.

2

elin

A two-hour drive east of Dylan's Quay, Grace's fifty-one-year-old granddaughter stood in her Cardiff kitchen, staring at a Post-it-covered breakfast bar. Each pink square bore the name from a guest list that Elin Matthews held in her hand. She was currently debating where to position an elderly cousin and a much-loved family friend. 'Just put them next to each other, for God's sake!' said her husband, Greg, exasperated that yet another Sunday morning was being taken up by this damn party planning. 'I don't see what the problem is!'

'The problem, Greg,' said Elin, equally exasperated, 'is that politically the two of them are poles apart. And the last thing I want at my grandmother's ninetieth is out-and-out geriatric fisticuffs!'

Of course, the *real* problem had nothing to do with the seating plan. The *real* problem was that the party was to be a surprise. And the reason it was to be a surprise was because Grama Grace had said categorically that she didn't *want* a damn party. 'A load of fuss and nonsense over a silly old woman like me!' she'd grumbled.

Elin had told her she was being mean and even ungrateful. 'But people want to celebrate you, Grama Grace. Don't deny them the chance to do that!'

'Well, they can do it in the comfort of their own homes,' Grace had retorted. And the subject was well and truly closed. Or so Grace had thought.

But Elin – as usual – felt she knew better, and that her grandmother was just being frustratingly humble. 'She'll love it on the day!' she had said, annoyed when Greg raised a doubting eyebrow in response. And ignoring the tiniest of niggles that perhaps the party *might* be a mistake, she had thrown herself into planner mode. Which, of course, she was delighted to do, seeing as organization – aka *being in control* – was Elin's happy place. Admittedly it had been easier said than done. Deciding on an afternoon tea party was no problem. Even finding the venue was straightforward – the Brookfield Hotel in Dylan's Quay on 2 September – Grace's actual birthday.

It was just the guest list that was proving to be difficult. Since the original plan had been drawn up, three of the guests had died – understandable, seeing as they were in their nineties. And whenever Elin thought she'd finalized the list, she'd remember someone else from her grandmother's past who she'd like to invite. Then there were the locals in Dylan's Quay, like the window cleaner or the street sweeper: Grace would talk to absolutely anybody, and felt that absolutely anybody was her friend. How was Elin meant to prioritize those friendships?

It would have helped, of course, if she'd enlisted the help of John, who to all intents and purposes was Elin's step-grandfather. But John would undoubtedly have spilled the beans and told Grace of the plan: there were no secrets between those two, after all.

'What are fisticuffs?' sixteen-year-old Beca asked her parents. She'd been loitering in the kitchen after breakfast, grateful for any distraction from her Geography revision. Even the boring details of who sat where at her great-grandmother's birthday tea were more interesting than glacial landscapes.

'"Fisticuffs" is an old-fashioned term for fighting,' said Greg with a smile. 'And your old-fashioned mother, as usual, is being overly cautious.'

'No I'm not! I just want everyone to have a nice time, that's all!'

Greg kissed his wife's head as he passed her en route to the dishwasher, carrying Beca's empty cereal bowl. 'I know you do, sweetheart. But this party is starting to take over your life. *And* mine, come to think of it.'

'*And mine*,' mumbled Beca.

'Erm . . . excuse me, young lady!' said Elin in a tone Beca knew well. 'The only thing that should be taking over *your* life right now is tomorrow's GCSE.'

Beca rolled her eyes.

Returning her attention to the table plan, Elin sighed with frustration. She was allergic to asymmetry. She liked things to be balanced, neat and ordered, and these two stray invitees were bugging her.

'Look, just shove 'em anywhere,' said Greg. 'Preferably on a table full of skinny guests so there's more elbow room. I'm going for a run.'

'Please be back by two, Greg. I need you to test Beca on Water Supply and Consumption. She'll only shout if I do it.'

'I don't *need* testing!' moaned Beca, who hated the way her mother interfered with her revision. Mainly because she wasn't really doing any and didn't want to be caught out.

'Let's not waste time arguing, Bec,' said Elin, trying to keep the irritation out of her voice. At all costs they must avoid arguing today. Beca only had one exam left and then they could all relax.

'See ya!' shouted Greg, and the front door slammed.

But Elin didn't reply. She was too caught up in a world of party planning and Post-it notes.

3

grace

As residential homes went, the exterior grandeur of Cadwallader House belied its more functional, clinical interior. Nestled safely on the highest reaches above Dylan's Quay, with grounds surrounded by firs, it boasted thirty-two bedrooms which gazed out either at the coast or back into the hills. Formerly the country residence of a local benefactor and shipping magnate, the house had been bequeathed to the community in his will and for the past twenty years it had been a well-run, friendly, council-owned residence, specializing in care for the elderly. Everyone who visited would comment on the vast floor-to-ceiling windows overlooking the town and the West Wales coastline beyond. Through these vast glass panes, soul-uplifting light flooded the rooms, compensating for the not-so-uplifting utilitarian furniture, the handrails and stair lifts and safety grilles – ugly but necessary.

Grace had been visiting Cadwallader House for over three years. She knew virtually every resident personally, but two of them were particularly special: her darling John, of course, and his younger sister, Cynthia, aka Cissie. They'd known each other a lifetime, and for so many years she'd felt they were indestructible. But, of course, they weren't. Time was bound to take its toll eventually on one or all of them. It was Cissie who'd moved to Cadwallader House first, her mind having taken her to such extremes that the only way forward was full-time care. What a heart-breaking decision that had been. Grace and John had continued living together for another eighteen months until John's deteriorating balance began to lead to more and more falls. Reluctantly at that point they'd decided he should go and join Cissie. It was reassuring for Grace to know that they were both being cared for, of course. But their departure had left a gaping hole in her home. She missed them more than she would ever admit. And it was why she'd become such a regular fixture at Cadwallader House – visiting at least once a day. Even during Covid, Grace would take her daily exercise in the form of a walk – striding up to Cadwallader House, where she would stand in the grounds and wave at them through their individual bedroom windows. When life returned to some semblance of normality and she was allowed back inside the building, the staff would frequently ask her when she was going to move in. But Grace would always smile and politely decline the offer. She knew that John was torn: on the one hand, he'd love them to live under the same roof again; on the other, he adored the fact that at eighty-nine his *annwyl* Grace still thrived on her independence. Cissie, bless her, had no opinion on the matter. Not any more.

This afternoon Cissie was in her chair by the window, looking out, chatting to herself in the made-up language only she understood. It was a happy room, this. John and Grace had done their best to brighten it up with boldly coloured cushions and throws, fresh flowers and scent diffusers. Framed photographs filled the walls and shelves with bygone smiles: stolen moments from Cissie's past and happier days from her long life. One such photo was a black-and-white shot, taken at her wedding to Syd when Cissie was barely twenty. But she no more knew Syd's face now than that of Grace or John.

Today the carers had dressed her in purple, a bonny dress that had once fitted her properly but now swamped her ever-diminishing build in swathes of fabric. And on her tiny feet were the home-made socks that Grace had knitted her for Christmas, tucked inside fur-lined slippers. Despite the summer warmth outside, Cissie's shrinking body still fell prey to the cold, even on the hottest of days.

'She's had her nails done today,' said John, pulling up a couple of chairs. 'Haven't you, beaut?' And his sister smiled back at him, her face still pretty and her eyes still shining, despite the disease that permanently resided inside her head, distancing her more, day by day, from the world she'd once inhabited.

'Let's have a look, then,' said Grace, admiring Cissie's manicure. 'Oh, there's posh! You put me to shame!'

'And she bought you something from the WI stall, didn't you, Ciss?' said John, reaching under Cissie's chair and pulling out a gift, wrapped in pink tissue. He placed it in Cissie's lap, hoping she'd make sense of his actions and give the gift to Grace. But her brain could not process the task he'd set and she pawed at it gently.

'Oh, thank you, cariad!' said Grace, playing along and carefully taking the gift. Cissie watched as Grace unwrapped it, revealing inside the layers of delicate tissue a headscarf patterned with copper-and-yellow-coloured squares. 'Wow!' Grace exclaimed, taking the scarf and wrapping it around her head. 'Very Audrey Hepburn, don't you think?'

And Cissie gasped with delight, before uttering one of her very rare coherent responses: 'Pretty, pretty.'

John squeezed Grace's hand.

They stayed for over two hours. The care assistant brought them tea and slices of home-made cake also purchased from the WI, and then Grace put on the CD of fifties classics that always made Cissie smile. It was their routine now, and one which gave both her and John a short-lived but precious relief from the pain of losing Cissie to that inaccessible world. The transformation when she sang along was indeed a joy to behold. Almost instantly, Cissie would join in with Elvis Presley or Frank Sinatra or whoever was up first on the track shuffle, articulating the lyrics with such clarity that sometimes Grace wanted to say, *Is it an act, all this? Are you just pretending?*

*

John walked her to the door and partway down the drive, though he was much slower on his feet than Grace, tentatively relying on his Zimmer frame.

'Come on, Captain Tom.' Grace firmly believed the less mollycoddling of seniors, the more apt they were to stay mobile – after all, she herself was a case in point.

'Beca's last exam tomorrow, John.'

'*Duw*, she's growing up fast, isn't she, bach?'

'Yes indeed.' Grace's voice faded. Should she tell him?

As usual, he could read her mind. 'Right, come on, Grace Meredith. Out with it.'

'What?' asked Grace, though she knew feigning ignorance was pointless. He looked at her, waiting. She took a deep breath, shut her eyes and told him.

'I think I've found Alys.'

Her voice was shaking and John remained silent as he took in the news.

'She's living in *Brecon*, John. Eighty-odd miles away. Can you believe it? I presumed she'd be abroad, or worse than that, I thought she might—'

'Whoa, slow down, beaut. You're going too fast for me now.'

Grace took another deep breath and steadied herself before calmly recounting how she'd received a little thank-you from Dolly Hughes earlier in the week.

'Dolly Hughes?'

'From yoga. Rescues greyhounds.'

'Oh yes. Go on.'

'Well, I'd done some dog-sitting for her when she had her cataracts done and she made me a bara brith to say thank-you and sent it with this.'

Grace reached into her rucksack and pulled out the Brecon Beacons card.

John took it from her and stared at it for a few moments. 'You've lost me now, bach,' he said.

'Turn it over. Look at the back.'

He did so, revealing a plain printed sticker that read, *Arcadia Gallery, Brecon. Taken from a painting by local artist Alys Meredith.*

'Doesn't mean anything,' he said eventually, handing back the card. 'Could be anyone.'

'But Alys always loved painting hills, didn't she? And it's unusual to see "Alys" spelled like that, isn't it, the Welsh way?'

'Not really, love. We are *in* Wales, after all.'

'Anyway,' she paused, unable to look him in the eye. 'I'm thinking of getting in touch.'

'No.' The word was out before he'd had time to think.

Then he reached out and took her hand, his voice steady and direct. 'What she did to you, Grace. And to Elin – it was awful.'

'It was also thirty years ago,' Grace countered, and there was a steeliness to her voice which he'd rarely heard before. 'I'm nearly ninety, John. And Alys is my daughter!'

'Little Beca thinks the woman's dead! Doesn't even know she's *got* a grandmother.'

Grace shook her head. 'Well, that's what Elin wanted – I had to respect that, didn't I?'

'Oh, Gracie, Gracie . . .' This whole subject was obviously upsetting John a lot more than she'd anticipated.

'Look, you're right,' she said, softer now. 'It's probably not my Alys, and even if it is, she's unlikely to reply—'

'You've already written to her?'

'Not yet,' she whispered.

'Don't, Gracie. *Don't!* Why set yourself up for all that pain?' And his usually calm demeanour was disturbed, tears moistening his kind eyes.

She sighed. Maybe he was right.

'I take it you haven't discussed all this with Elin?' he asked gently.

'Of course I bloody haven't!' said Grace, a tad of hysteria creeping in at the prospect. 'She'd go ballistic.'

'Well, it's not often I agree with that granddaughter of yours,' he smiled, 'but I think she'd have good reason on this occasion.' And he hugged her to him, reassuring her with a kiss as she inhaled his decades-old, familiar clean smell of Brylcreem and Palmolive soap.

'I love you, John.'

And John replied, as he always did, in Welsh: '*Caru ti 'fyd*, Grace.'

4

beca

'DON'T MAKE ME HAVE TO COME UP THERE—'

Beca made a bet with herself as to what her mother would shout out next.

'—WE'RE LEAVING IN FIFTEEN MINUTES!'

Almost right, Beca thought. She'd just got the time wrong, expecting *five* minutes leeway, not fifteen. Still, this was good news. A whole ten minutes more in bed. Beca shut her eyes and pulled the duvet over her face. She should really have been leaping out of bed – desperate for today to be over, eager to be free of school at last. But the thought of sitting at a desk in a hall full of silent, scribbling sixteen-year-olds, staring at a paper full of questions that she would never be able to answer, made Beca Matthews feel nauseous. By lunchtime she would have handed in her nineteenth exam paper and failed her nineteenth exam. She knew this, without a shadow of a doubt.

The kids in the year above her still bemoaned the fact that they couldn't take *their* GCSEs last summer *because of the Covid*. Or 'Corvid' as Mrs James Art pronounced it – her Valleys accent turning the pandemic into a classification term for ravens and magpies with a single stretched vowel. Beca thought the year above were deluded: why would you *choose* to sit exams, for God's sake? She'd have given anything to do the whole thing on coursework – though as her mother was so fond of pointing out, 'It wouldn't make any difference with you, Beca, you don't put the work in *either* way!' She tried to think of a time when her mother had congratulated her, rather than berating her. It'd happened a few times, of course – the woman wasn't a monster, after all. It's just that praise wasn't her default position.

She had *definitely* been proud when Beca passed her grade one piano. And two, three and four. And when she got a distinction in her grade five, Beca had witnessed her mother actually weep. *Weep.* The joy didn't last long, of course, because when it came to sitting grade five theory, Beca had monumentally failed. And then her mother had let out that awful, disappointed sigh she'd mastered so well. 'But I'm no good with all that stuff,' Beca had whined defensively. 'Music theory's as bad as Maths!' Big mistake, as this had only prompted her mother to play the same-old-same-old song, *You're no good at Maths because you refuse to listen!*

It wasn't that. Lessons simply outwitted her, that was all. She couldn't fit the logic together in her head. Her mother had sent her to all sorts of specialists and psychologists over the years, trying to get to the root of it. Was it ADHD? Depression? Dyslexia? Asperger's? As if a label would somehow solve Elin's frustration. As if finding an adjective to describe her daughter's failure at pretty much *everything* would provide them with the missing link, the key to unlock the issue.

'Maybe she hasn't got an *issue,*' her dad had ventured during one of her parents' many whispered discussions that they thought Beca couldn't hear. 'Maybe she's just . . .'

'Do *not* even think about saying it, Greg!' her mother had snapped.

'What?'

'Our daughter is not . . . *thick.*' She'd spat the last word as if it had been *psychopathic* or *murderous.*

'I was going to say *artistic,*' he'd mumbled.

'She's had the bloody tests! She's not autistic and you know it!'

'Calm down, Elin, I said *ARTistic*, for Christ's sake.'

21

And then a row had ensued, where her dad put forward his case in defence of his daughter – that she painted beautiful pictures, that she could play the piano and she could draw. So what if she couldn't solve a quadratic equation or tell you who Winston Churchill was. She was an artist!

In that moment, Beca had loved her dad for describing her so, even though it wasn't true. She wasn't bad at art, for sure, but she was hardly Van Gogh.

'For God's sake, Beca, you're not even dressed!' her mother screeched as she barged into Beca's doze-dream and swiftly opened the blinds. 'I despair of you, I really, really do. Now COME ON!'

As Elin pulled off the duvet, Beca screeched back, as she did most mornings, 'That's abuse, that is! It's an infringement of my human rights!'

'Uniform. Now!' And Elin picked up the navy skirt and polo shirt abandoned on the floor since yesterday and hurled them at her. 'I'm not leaving this room until you've put it on.'

'Weirdo.'

'You can call me what you like, Beca Matthews. You have a responsibility to finish these exams and finish them you will!'

Ten minutes later, they were sitting in Elin's Skoda estate heading towards St Stephen's High. They had taken this journey together every school day for the past five years. Beca had never missed a day of school – she had a perfect attendance record. This wasn't due to any sense of commitment on her part – it was due entirely to her mother's determination. 'We have to set an example, Beca,' she'd said on many occasions, always with an apologetic smile that beckoned Beca to see things from her mother's perspective and come onside.

Because Beca's mother was Mrs Elin Matthews.

And Mrs Elin Matthews was Head Teacher of St Stephen's High.

*

22

Being the daughter of a head teacher brought along its own particular brand of downside. No one dared gossip or share secrets with the Head Teacher's daughter, for fear of being reported; and no one dared call at the house of the Head Teacher's daughter, because it was also the house of the Head Teacher. So the best and safest option was to avoid the Head Teacher's daughter altogether. Beca was used to it by now. This state of friendlessness had accompanied her throughout her high-school life. It was not that anyone was mean to her – that was the *upside* of being who she was – but they treated her with a kind of distanced respect. She was acknowledged but never included. Smiled at but never laughed with. And that's just the way it was.

The truth of the matter, though, was that Beca actually liked being on her own. It wasn't that she disliked the other girls in school – or the boys, for that matter. She just found them all a bit . . . samey. They dressed the same, liked the same music, had no actual opinions – none that were exciting or controversial, anyway. So she didn't really feel as if she was missing out. Beca knew she was different. But why was different *bad*? She could get so much more done on her own: on her own, Beca could immerse herself in the world of a book. Or play the electric piano in her room. Hour upon hour, headphones on, neither of her parents ever hearing what she was playing but always assuming it was classical. Because the music rack displayed works by composers she knew her mother loved – Mahler, Mozart and Brahms. And if either parent were to pass the bedroom door or peep in, all they'd see and hear was Beca's fingers pounding the keys with velvety thuds, navigating flats, sharps and arpeggios with dexterity and speed. And they'd congratulate themselves that their daughter was such an accomplished classical pianist. But what Beca was *really* playing was far from classical: what Beca was *really* playing was completely improvised, as she lost herself in the notes and the key changes. Eyes closed, she'd let the music transport her to a world only she knew, losing all sense of time, and only stopping when her mother gently tapped her on the shoulder to ask if she wanted lasagne for tea. This would disturb her from her semi-hypnotic state and bring her back to the boring present-day of her life.

'You're sure you don't want me to drop you by the hall?' Elin asked gently.

'No, you're all right,' Beca said, clambering out of the car. 'Cheers, Mum.'

The one demand Beca had made of her mother in exchange for agreeing to accept a lift to school was that she drop her off two streets away – the thought of anyone witnessing her leave the Head Teacher's car made her blush to her roots. 'What difference does it make?' Elin had asked at first. 'It's not like it's news to anyone that you're my daughter!' But for Beca this was a deal-breaker.

Just as she was closing the door, Elin stopped her. 'Becs?'

'What?' Beca knew what was coming and she watched as her mother struggled with emotion.

'I do, y'know . . .'

Beca looked around to check no one was listening, anxious to put distance between herself and her mother's car. 'Mum, I've got to go,' she mumbled, shutting the door.

'Good luck! Do your best!' Elin called out.

Beca swallowed hard. She preferred it when her mum was cross with her or disappointed. It was far easier to deal with Angry Mum than Sad and Needy Mum. She knew that her mother meant well and that she berated herself for being an inadequate parent far more than she'd ever let on. As Beca headed in the direction of school, she didn't turn round for fear of seeing her mother's face, forlorn and anguished. Elin beeped her horn as she passed and Beca raised her hand in a half-hearted wave.

Reaching the main gate, Beca looked at the tired buildings, the kids all identically clothed tootling in different directions like a thousand busy ants, heading this way and that, bustling with noise and hormones and energy. And she felt liberated. Because this was a milestone, albeit a secret one right now: this was the last time she'd ever have to walk through this gate. She had no idea what she was going to do after today, or where she was going to go. The only thing she *did* know was that she wouldn't be coming back here in September. Or ever again, for that matter. She just had to work out how to break the news to her education-obsessed mother. Because whatever Beca's next step turned out to be, it was guaranteed not to win Elin's approval.

5

elin

When she arrived home that evening, Elin presumed the house was empty. Calling out to Greg, then to Beca, she was met only with silence. She'd phoned Beca earlier to see how the Geography exam had gone. All she could glean from her clammed-up daughter, monosyllabic as usual, was that it *went okay,* before she disappeared behind the excuse of a bad signal. It would have been nice to celebrate with Beca tonight – it was the end of a stressful few months for them both, the end of a chapter really. There'd be sixth form starting in September, of course, so Beca's schooldays weren't over yet. But finishing GCSEs was a milestone in her daughter's young life.

Elin shuffled off her high heels, rubbed her aching feet and berated herself for not wearing sensible brogues. It was just that a court shoe was so much more in keeping with how a head teacher should look. She picked up the mail en route to the kitchen – a lot of junk which she slung into the recycling. She sighed – such a needless waste of paper. But in amongst all that was a slim cardboard box bearing the logo *Party Time Printers.* She let out a little yelp of joy – the invitations for Grama Grace's ninetieth had arrived! Ooh, good, she was looking forward to opening those. There was also a parcel for Greg. She gave it a little rattle and smiled affectionately. More of his beloved supplements. Poor guy was obsessed with the need to battle time, trying desperately to stop it in its tracks.

Catching sight of her reflection in the wall mirror, Elin did a quick spot check: she was still looking good for her age, fair play. The highlights in her shoulder-length auburn hair added to its vibrancy, and her complexion was fresh and creamy. Even after a hard day's work. Elin was blessed with full lips and bright eyes and although age had not forgotten her when it came to handing out crow's feet, she didn't mind. It was natural. And she prided herself on never having had Botox or fillers – God forbid she would ever go down that road.

Opening the French doors that led on to the decking, she let in the warm June air, shut her eyes and inhaled. This evening she could allow herself to relax a little and indulge in a guilt-free gin and tonic. Gin was strictly an occasional treat because Elin believed that treats, like anything in life, needed to be earned. She measured out a single shot and poured it over the ice and lemon in a pristine crystal glass before topping it up with tonic. Greg never understood why she had to measure the gin. 'Just guess! Pour the bloody stuff in!' he'd say, confounded once again by her cautiousness. But Elin knew to her cost that alcohol needed to be respected.

Outside on the decking, Elin flopped into the capacious garden chair, put her feet up and turned her face towards the evening sun, still quite high in the sky – it was midsummer, after all. '*Iechyd da*,' she whispered in a solitary toast to herself, savouring a sip of the fresh, zesty drink that sent a welcome tingling through to her fingertips. Then with a small kitchen knife she slit open the cardboard box that sat in her lap and carefully retrieved its contents: a neatly wrapped bundle of sixty invitations. Printed on rose-coloured card and framed with ivy:

You are invited to
GRACE MEREDITH'S

SURPRISE

90TH BIRTHDAY PARTY

on September 2nd 2022, at 2pm
at The Brookfield Hotel, Dylan's Quay

But PLEASE REMEMBER IT'S A **SURPRISE**

GRACE MUST NOT FIND OUT ABOUT IT!

RSVP itsasurprise@widenet.com

Or

23 Elm Tree Avenue, Lakeside, Cardiff CF23 3SX

AND REMEMBER, **MUM'S THE WORD!**

Had she gone over the top by repeating the word 'surprise'? Now that she looked at it objectively, the invitation did sound a bit . . . well, *bossy*. Greg would no doubt have something to say about it. But she'd rather be thought of as a domineering grand-daughter than have the whole project jeopardized. She put the invitations carefully back in their box. She'd send them all out tomorrow. Sitting back and feeling proud of herself, Elin took a deep breath and relaxed.

But her peace was soon disturbed by the sound of two male voices coming from next door's garden. The house had been empty for almost a year, since the death of her elderly neighbour Mrs Latham, and had been on the market for several months, so Elin had grown accustomed to nobody living there. Someone new must have bought the house. She got up and made her way to the party wall. 'Hello?' she called out tentatively. The voices stopped.

'Yes?' came the impatient reply.

Elin couldn't see much through the abundance of foliage but could just make out two figures on the other side of the wall – an Asian man with greying temples and a small, neat moustache, about the same age as her, was standing with a younger white guy, in his thirties maybe, with long sandy locks. The younger man wore a sleeveless T-shirt that shamelessly showed off his biceps. Which he undoubtedly used a lot, judging by the weighty hedge-trimmer he was holding.

'Hello, I'm Elin,' she said. 'Welcome to the neighbourhood! Sorry, I can't really see—'

'My name is Sunil Chakrabarti,' said the older man, polite but very formal. 'I'm just making preparations. We shan't take up residence for some time.'

'Oh,' said Elin, thrown by the fact that she couldn't really see who she was talking to. 'So what's your moving-in date?'

'I'm not at liberty to say, I'm afraid. Sorry, but I really have to get on. Time is against us.' And with that he resumed talking to Mr Biceps, who she thought possibly gave her a friendly nod of apology, though it was difficult to tell through the foliage.

She headed back to the house. How intriguing! Greg would find out more. He was a much better detective than she was and also far more sociable. Before she knew it, Mr Chakrabarti would no doubt become a family friend.

Her mobile buzzed.

Managed to grab court @ David Lloyd. C U @8 ish?

Elin wished Greg wouldn't abbreviate like that. It was so . . . teenage. The man was fifty-two, for God's sake. She was about to reply when another message came in on her book club's Whats-App group.

Don't forget ladies – get together's been changed to tonight not next week. See you later bookworms, Joan x

Oh God, she *had* forgotten. Bloody hell.

Her first thought was not to go. She'd only just sat down and now she'd made a start on her gin she couldn't drive, she'd have to walk. She texted Greg back:

**Forgot Book Club! Sorry! Pick me up from
Joan's at 10 if you can. Thanks.**

Right. Better change. And grab the notes she'd made on tonight's book. It was called *He Kills in Blue* – a Jack Danfield thriller about a murderous American cop. Not the best book Elin had read, to be honest. Highly predictable and very derivative – and strangely Joan's choice *again* this month, but Elin couldn't complain: the women in book club were nice enough and she'd felt honoured they'd asked her to join. She did find it frustrating though that they were mainly interested in devouring brownies, guzzling prosecco and discussing fantasy casting. Morgan Freeman and Colin Firth seemed to be shortlisted for every book, though Benedict Cumberbatch had been featuring a lot lately. *Why can't we just discuss the damn book?* Elin would think, though she was fighting a losing battle on that one.

As she walked across the landing, Elin heard a familiar sound – the soft, velvety thud of fingers on a muted keyboard. Ah, so Beca *was* home. She knocked on the door out of courtesy, though she doubted Beca would hear her, shoulders hunched over the piano, headphones on and lost in her own world. Elin was loath to make Beca jump, to spoil the peace her daughter was clearly enjoying, but as she turned to go the velvety thudding abruptly stopped.

'Alrigh'?' said Beca, having sensed her mother's presence and pulling off her headphones.

'Well, I bet *someone*'s a happy bunny!' said Elin with a smile, trying to sound jolly.

'Yeah,' mumbled Beca, looking nothing like a joyful rabbit.

'Nice break for you now before we have to start thinking about A levels. I was wondering whether—'

'Mum, don't! Seriously, just . . .' Beca looked forlorn. 'You're always moving on to the next thing. You never stand still.'

Elin nodded. 'Sorry. You're right. Let's enjoy today's achievement first.' There was an awkward silence. 'I've got book club tonight, otherwise we could have celebrated. D'you have any plans?' She regretted the question as soon as it was out of her mouth. Of course Beca wouldn't have any plans. She didn't have any friends.

'Nah. Gonna FaceTime Grama Grace and then I might get a pizza.'

Elin rustled in her bag for some cash. 'Here we are – my treat,' she said, handing Beca a twenty-pound note.

'Thanks.'

'And don't forget when you're talking to Grama Grace, don't mention—'

'Don't mention the bloody party! Yes, I know, Mum, you don't have to keep saying it.'

Elin smiled sheepishly, aware of her control-freakery. An awkwardness descended between them once again before Beca put her headphones back on and returned to the keyboard. The invisible wall of things unsaid had once again defeated Elin, leaving her separated from her little girl, as it so often did. Swallowing down a sob, she retreated to the sanctuary of her en-suite bathroom and turned on the shower.

6

beca

Beca's usual pizza outlet was closed due to family bereavement. So she'd have to try somewhere different. After her mother left for book club, she hauled herself off her bed and set off on the ten-minute walk to Bellamy's Italian Palace. The name was far too grand for what it was: a cheap and cheerful pizza takeout that made a fortune selling overpriced slices of pepperoni deluxe to hungry teenagers. Two boys she recognized from school were waiting in front of her in the queue. They ignored her, of course, too caught up in their own world to notice anyone else and in very high spirits, probably induced by vodka or some other substance. It was just banter between them but they were loud and showing off and the girl behind the counter scowled at them. 'Keep it down,' she shouted, 'or I'll 'ave you barred!'

Beca bit her lip to stop herself smiling. The counter girl's Cardiff accent was really strong, and her 'barred' sounded like 'baa-aahed'. As she boxed up the boys' order, she turned to Beca with as much warmth as a bowl of cold porridge and asked what she wanted. 'An' don't ask for a slice, 'cos we're sold out. It's whole pizzas only or you can sling yer hook.'

'A Slim Jim with extra chillies,' said Beca quickly, adding a fearful, 'please.'

Counter Girl nodded, and silence ensued.

Beca tried reading the name on Counter Girl's badge: *Soozi*. She thought what a cool spelling it was of an otherwise plain name. But then, to be fair, 'Soozi' did exude cool. Clear black skin, bleached braids twisted up high on her head, the sides of her hair still dark and cut close to her scalp; she wore no make-up, but a row of studs adorned her right ear and she had a silver sleeper through her left nostril. *I bet she's got her tongue pierced*, Beca thought. Soozi was wearing latex hygiene gloves, but through their opaque whiteness Beca could see her nails were painted vibrant orange.

'Take a photo, it'll last longer!' Soozi barked when she noticed Beca staring. And turned back to her dough.

Beca blushed at being caught out, but she was fixated on the way Soozi tossed the soft white floury ball back and forth, changing its shape in the process, transforming it within seconds into a flat round base. With well-practised ease, she flung it down on the counter, splattered a dollop of thick tomato sauce in the centre and spread it out uniformly to the edges. Then she grabbed a handful of grated mozzarella and dropped it from a great height on to the base, before sprinkling chopped ham, herbs and chillies on top of the cheese. The whole process was like a carefully choreographed dance. And with one swift action she scooped up the raw pizza with her paddle, slammed it into the oven and hooked the door shut. 'That's five seventy-five,' Soozi sighed, pulling off her latex gloves and holding out her hand for the cash. Beca handed her the twenty and Soozi gave her fourteen pounds in change, depositing the twenty-five pence change in a jar on the counter. 'Cheers for the tip,' she said. Beca frowned but was too shy to complain about the enforced gratuity. 'I'm savin' up, aren' I?' Soozi said, by way of explanation. 'For my tour.'

'Backpacking?'

'Gigs,' she said. 'I'm a singer.'

'Oh. Right.'

And that was the end of the chat. They waited in silence as the pizza baked, Soozi wiping down the surfaces before deftly constructing a takeaway box in a matter of seconds. She must have been working there a while, Beca thought.

When the oven eventually pinged, Soozi pulled out the sizzling pizza, neatly flipping it on to the counter. Then, pizza wheel in hand, she cut it into six before sliding it into the box. 'Enjoy,' she said as she handed it over. 'Oh, and do us a favour, turn the *Closed* sign round on your way out, I'm off for a fag.'

From somewhere unexpected, Beca suddenly asked, 'Why d'you smoke if you sing?'

Soozi, halfway out to the back, stopped in her tracks and turned. 'What you say?'

'Wrecks your vocal chords. And your breathing.'

She was met with a thunderous stare. But Beca held her ground. 'You're not gonna disagree, are you?' she challenged Soozi, whose face suddenly softened and broke into a smile.

'No, I ain't,' she said. 'Now piss off and shut the door behind you.'

Back at the house, Beca sat on her bed, phone in one hand, pizza box in her lap, and FaceTimed her Grama Grace. She loved the fact that she had such a modern-thinking great-grandmother who embraced technology. They'd been FaceTiming every Friday for the past two years.

'So how was it?' asked Grace, sipping a mug of tea.

'Absolute disaster,' replied Beca, relieved that she wasn't met with any patronizing consolations. There were no *It-won't-be-as-bad-as-you-think*s or *You'll-surprise-us-all-you-wait*s. Instead Grace said, 'Well, it's only what you expected, isn't it, bach? And at least you'll never have to open another damn geography book again.'

'True,' replied Beca.

Grama Grace was very much a graduate from the school of no-nonsense. She didn't faff around. And for that reason Beca firmly believed that Elin's surprise party was going to be a big mistake. Grace didn't suffer fools and if she said she didn't want something, she bloody well meant it. Beca feared her great-grandmother was going to be extremely pissed off that Elin had gone against her wishes. Should she warn Grama Grace of Elin's party plans? Just so that it wasn't too much of a shock, so that she could be prepared? But what if Grama Grace lost it and started railing at Elin? Elin would never forgive Beca for spoiling the whole thing. Of course, there was always the danger that someone else had already let the cat out of the bag. Someone from Dylan's Quay, maybe. Because Grama Grace wasn't herself tonight. She was distracted.

Deciding to risk finding out, Beca ventured near the subject without specifically using the word *party*. 'How you feeling about turning ninety?' she asked nonchalantly, unable to look at the screen in case she gave herself away. Grama Grace was extremely perceptive, even through a cloud of pixelation. A string of melted pizza cheese dropped languidly back into its box as Beca tried to catch it in her mouth.

'Haven't given it much thought, bach. Still over two months to go.'

Beca pushed her luck further. 'Maybe we could take you out for lunch or something? You could come to Cardiff, or—'

Grace interrupted her. 'What do you know about your actual grandmother, cariad? About Alys.'

This was a bolt from the blue.

'Erm . . . not a lot,' said Beca, her mouth on fire from the pizza chillies. She never really gave her mother's mother a second thought. She'd died when Elin was younger, she knew that, and Beca's dad had said she was a bit of a hippy. Though Beca had no idea how he knew, seeing as he'd never met the woman.

Grace smiled sadly. 'But does your mother ever mention her?'

'No . . . but then again, nor do you.'

'Only because it upsets me.'

Beca felt guilty. She'd heard it said time and time again that teenagers didn't really take much notice of stuff going on around them. Maybe this was true. She'd never had a grandmother so she didn't miss having one. And after all, Grama Grace fulfilled that role, didn't she?

'Mum thinks of *you* as her mum, doesn' she? And I've just always gone along with it. Anyway, how comes you're askin' about Alys all of a sudden?'

Grace sighed and started to say something, but then stopped herself. 'Oh, nothing.' She smiled and changed gear. 'Probably been on my mind with this ol' birthday coming up. You're right, bach. Maybe we should go for a little lunch somewhere. Something simple. No fuss!'

Oh God, thought Beca, envisaging Elin's pink Post-it-note table plan. *You are gonna go mental, Grama Grace.*

7

grace

As a rule, Grace wasn't prone to low mood or anxiety. She put this down largely to the benefits of staying active, the invigoration she enjoyed from her wild swimming and the natural resilience she'd developed as a result of what life had thrown at her over the years. But tonight . . . oh, tonight was different. After FaceTiming Beca, she'd felt more out of sorts than ever and had ordered herself off for an evening walk. She'd called in on Neeta at the café, who was clearing up after a tourist-packed day of trade. As usual, sixty-one-year-old Neeta had tried spoiling Grace with home-cooked fare, presenting her with a large piece of carrot cake and a mug of hot chocolate.

'Have you even heard of diabetes?' Grace asked, staring at the excessive portion.

'Oh, go on with you,' said her friend. 'You'll outlive the lot of us, you will. Anyway, I made that myself – don't be so rude.'

Neeta had been friends with Grace since opening the café in 2010 and they were completely at ease with one another. Neeta loved to talk. Usually this didn't bother Grace, who enjoyed putting the world to rights as much as the next person, but tonight she didn't seem to hear anything Neeta said.

When she left the café she wandered down to the pier and

gazed out at the ocean. The sea was choppy with an offshore wind that sent sets of waves majestically crashing on to the sand. She breathed in the salty air, seeking a nourishing calm from its ions. But even that didn't work. Should she head up to Cadwallader House and see John? Would singing with Cissie settle her soul? It was nearing nine o'clock now, though, and the chances were they'd both be in bed. 'Oh, stop your moaning,' she said to herself, and a passing seagull squawked in agreement as Grace turned for home.

Taking her shoes off was such a relief. She'd been on her feet too long and now they were starting to swell and ache. For a moment she considered dusting off the foot spa she'd been given by Elin and Greg two years previously. But even doing that seemed too arduous a task. She sank into the comfort of her favourite armchair and let out a weary sigh. On days like this she really felt her age, and that wasn't good. Probably best to have a little rest and then do some yoga before bed. That'd help. How she loathed feeling old. John always said that one of the things he most loved about her was her relentless drive. But sometimes she worried she'd set the bar too high: that she could *never* be negative, *never* admit to anxiety or fear of what was to come. In reality she knew she was living on borrowed time, of course she was – even if she was lucky enough to make it to a hundred, that would still only give her just ten more years. Ten years! They could get swallowed up in a heartbeat.

Strangely, fear of death wasn't the heaviest weight that pressed down upon her when she was in one of these rare anxious moods; after all, *once you're gone you're gone!* Grace herself would be blissfully unaware she'd died; she wouldn't know she was gone, of course. That would be the sorrowful burden placed upon those left behind. And all her affairs had been put in order long ago, so there was nothing to worry about on that front. No, it was the fear of losing others that plagued her most, fear of losing those who'd trodden life's path with her for longer than she could remember.

And Alys.

To the outside world, her daughter didn't exist. Talking to Beca tonight had brought this home to her again, and her conversation with John had reminded her of Elin's wishes: to erase the memory of Alys Meredith from their family history. To behave as if she had died long ago. And that's what they'd done. That was the story they'd given out for years. Only John knew the truth. And Cissie – when she had still been in possession of her mind. Grace knew it was easier for Elin this way. And to her own shame, it had sometimes been easier for her, too. Out of sight, out of mind. Except privately, this could never be the case.

Because she thought about Alys every single day – sometimes just fleetingly, a passing memory – usually an unhappy one. And then on other occasions, like tonight, she'd feel the pull, the natural, biological mourning for the loss of her child. Seeing Alys's name on the back of that card had ignited a tiny flame of hope. And try as she might to extinguish it, the flame just wouldn't go out.

She knew that John was right. That to attempt to contact Alys at the Brecon gallery would at best result in no reply, and at worst result in anger and chaos being revisited upon them all. Elin would never forgive her. And Beca would probably be traumatized – Grace would effectively be bringing a dead grandmother back to life! Yes, John was probably right, and having been her rock for so many years, she felt superstitious about ignoring his advice now. But the draw was so strong.

The last time they'd seen Alys had been in 1992.

Since then, Grace had written her dozens of unsent letters. Writing them was the nearest she had ever come to therapy. Sometimes the letters were just newsy, sometimes they were covered with tears and filled with anger at how Alys had behaved.

Sometimes they didn't get further than *Dearest Alys*. They were never intended to be read. Often she wondered about burning them. After all, once she was gone they'd be there for all and sundry to digest, and did she really want to inflict all those private feelings on John or Elin or whoever cleared out her house in the wake of her death?

Hoisting herself up out of the chair with the requisite *Oof* – something she'd started doing of late, and which she'd always vowed never to do – she headed to the bureau in the corner of the living room and unlocked the top drawer. Inside was a Manila box file where she kept all the letters.

She took a clean sheet of heavy cream paper and unscrewed her fountain pen. Then, settling back into her chair, she began to write.

Dearest Alys . . .

8

alys

The lunchtime meeting of Alcoholics Anonymous was held in the side room of the Baptist hall. It was always a popular meeting and well attended, and today was no exception: the room was packed. Seventy-year-old Alys Meredith inwardly preened at the prospect of her large attentive audience. She looked around at the gathered crowd whilst the chairperson ran through the Twelve Steps and Twelve Traditions of AA, before asking if anyone had any announcements. A big woman with a candy-pink streak in her otherwise lank brown hair put up her hand and complained to the room that people were being a bit selfish with the biscuits. 'So please ration yourselves to no more than two each, and then everyone gets a look-in.'

'Thanks, Jess,' came the chorus response.

Alys thought Jess could do with rationing herself to *no* biscuits, judging by the size of her. But this was unfair, of course. Not all women were blessed with her figure and good looks, after all. On the other hand, not all women put in the effort like she did. It was true that her genes had played a big part, gifting her with elasticity in the skin, a strong bone structure and a well-proportioned figure with flesh in all the right places. And for this she thanked her Higher Power every day. But a Higher Power could only do so much. The rest required grit, determination and an almost constant attention to her appearance: the subtle (and expensive) highlights in her hair, the good-quality make-up – without which she would never be seen in public – not forgetting the low-carb, high-fat diet, generously supplemented with non-alcoholic kombucha and green tea. But her most powerful weapon for success was Dr Deepak, her cosmetic surgeon, who lived in Chennai and who gave Alys a hefty discount on her bi-annual procedures, in exchange for 'a little loving' on the side. Her trips to India were explained away as visits to an ashram for spiritual rejuvenation, and so far she hadn't been found out. Although Alys was technically seventy years of age, she was only fifty-nine if anyone asked. She'd been fifty-nine for the past three years. She should probably think about having a sixtieth birth-day party when she turned seventy-one.

'Without further t'do, I'll hand over to Alys, who's agreed to share her experience, strength and hope with us tonight.'

'Thanks, Paul,' she beamed at him, then took in the room, pausing for effect before announcing, 'My name's Alys and I'm an alcoholic.'

'Hi, Alys,' came the group response.

And so began Alys's performance – for that's how she viewed her AA shares these days. She knew the script off by heart. She started by telling the room she was now thirty years sober, *one day at a time, by the grace of God*. Then she'd talk about her first experience of alcohol at the age of five – a sip taken from the brandy bottle in the medicine cabinet of her childhood home in Neath, *which made me feel all glowy and warm and I thought, ooh, I like this!* – before moving on to her final 'drunk' in 1992, when she woke up in the doorway of a well-known Birmingham department store at 3 a.m. She kept the details hazy. This was especially important in front of a roomful of alkies, she thought, who at any point could turn back to booze and start mouthing off about her personal business.

Where family was concerned, Alys firmly believed in adopting a need-to-know policy, selecting the parts of her life story that suited her image – an old hippy artist who believed in peace and love and a sober life, who liked to be thought of as wise and humble, experienced yet vulnerable, spiritual but fun. Nobody knew what really went on inside her head – even her Higher Power wasn't completely in the know.

'By the age of seventeen I'd perfected the art of topping up the vodka bottle with water and the brandy with weak tea, just so I could feed my ever-growing addiction – which I know you lot will all understand.'

Murmurs of recognition flitted around the room and Alys went on to finish her drinking story: she told them that she didn't see her mother for several years before she died, and that she didn't go to the funeral, but felt that being sober was the best way to honour the woman's memory. She finished by talking of her love for AA and how it had saved her, the importance of staying connected, of meditating every day, of trying to help other alcoholics, and most importantly of being scrupulously honest.

Her story was indeed steeped in truth.

But it was also littered with lies.

She'd omitted to tell them she had a fifty-one-year-old daughter.

She'd failed to say that her eighty-nine-year-old mother was, so far as she knew, still alive.

And she'd conveniently missed out the bit about having a sixteen-year-old granddaughter.

Need to know basis, she thought. *Need to know.*

It had been several years since Alys had 'killed off' her mother. It meant she never had to discuss her with people in AA – or anyone else, for that matter. And for the most part, Alys could believe the lie that her mother was dead. There'd been a phase some years previously when curiosity had got the better of her and she'd started looking on Facebook. She'd checked out all the community pages associated with Dylan's Quay and, after much research, had discovered a local yoga group with a photograph featuring a Mrs Grace Meredith from Swn-y-Môr. Alys had signed up under a false name and begun checking in a couple of times a year. It was through the yoga group that she found out about Elin's wedding – 'Congratulations to our stalwart member Grace Meredith, whose granddaughter Elin was married at the weekend. Here's Grace in her rather fetching rig-out and hat!' Then, in 2006, she'd discovered that the same stalwart member of Dylan's Quay yoga had also become a *great*-grandmother, after the birth of baby Beca. That was a tough one. And she decided after that to stop checking on Facebook. What was the point? It only put her through more pain. And it would be much kinder to herself to stop looking. To live in blissful ignorance. Well, maybe not blissful.

Despite years of self-development and self-forgiveness, Alys still couldn't shift the shame she felt at her behaviour in the past. Towards both her mother and her daughter. That despite being given several chances to change and mend her ways, she'd stupendously succeeded in failing to do so. Every time. She felt such a behemoth of guilt at what she'd done that she'd decided there really never could be any going back. There were only so many times a fatted calf could be killed, after all. And so the best thing for Alys had been to detach herself permanently from her family, put it down to the hand that life had dealt her and make the best of the here and now. Because all she'd ever brought her mother and her daughter was misery. Some relationships were just never meant to be. And now it was simply too late.

Of course, if she sat and thought about it for long enough, Alys would sink into a vat of self-loathing at what a monumental fuck-up she was both as a daughter and a mother, and consequently as a grandmother, too. Which was why whenever any thoughts of her family crept inside her head, she always banished them instantly. No. She was alone in this life. End of. And she was doing okay. Dealing with the here and now, and the recent though not unfamiliar problem of finding herself a new home.

*

Over the years, Alys had lived all over the country, flitting from one town to the next and never putting down roots. But this last place had been fairly long-term by Alys's standards. An abandoned one-bedroom flat above a bookie's on Brecon high street, where she'd squatted for almost two years. She'd had magnificent views of the Beacons, access to a little communal art studio down the road and a weekly indoor market where she could set up a stall giving Tarot readings. And, of course, there were the regular AA meetings at the Baptist chapel hall. Yes, she could easily have stayed there for good, seen out her twilight years ensconced within its homely four walls. But the absent landlord, who had been living in Kuwait, had decided to turn up three days previously. He'd actually been rather civilized about the whole thing, even offering her a proper rental agreement at the going rate. She suspected he may have been worrying that she'd invoke her squatters' rights – something she probably would have done had she been younger. But in truth she couldn't be bothered. Instead she packed her things and left. She'd stayed a couple of nights at a hostel, before putting out feelers in the AA meetings, hoping someone might offer up a sofa or a bed. The real story didn't feel dramatic enough to garner sympathy, so Alys made up a tale about her boyfriend turning nasty, leaving her no option other than to flee. She did a very convincing job of describing him and bringing him to life, and because nobody had ever been to Alys's home, nobody could dispute what she said.

'All that time you were living with him and we never met the chap once,' said a regular member of the women's AA group.

'Ha, count yourself lucky,' said Alys, quick as a fox. 'I should've left him long ago, the guy didn't have a shred of kindness in his soul.'

'So what did you see in him?' asked the woman, not suspiciously, just out of genuine curiosity.

'What he lacked in compassion,' countered Alys, 'he made up for in the sack. The man was insatiable, my dear. Which at my age is no small thing. Excuse the pun.'

Lying came easily to Alys. In fact, she enjoyed it. Her fantasy life was so much more interesting than her real one.

At the end of today's meeting, several people thanked her for her 'inspirational' share and two women asked her if she would become their sponsor. She told them she'd think about it, explaining that she already had a 'sponsee', the lovely Kirsty J., and she didn't want to overstretch herself by taking on too much. She tried not to show it, but Alys was thrilled to be asked. It gave her some sense of purpose, the joy of being needed.

Kirsty was waiting patiently for Alys as the congratulators dispersed. Usually they both went for a coffee after the morning meeting, where Kirsty would unload and they'd do some work together on the Twelve Steps. 'I've had an idea,' she said now, beaming. 'And I think you're going to like it.' Kirsty handed Alys a piece of notepaper bearing an address. 'I'll pick you up tomorrow morning at ten,' she said with a glint in her eye.

One thing Alys had in common with Kirsty was that she, too, loved a bit of drama. 'Oh, okay,' she said, smiling like an indulgent parent. Though secretly feeling intrigued.

9

beca

The noise in the kitchen of the Dog and Fox reached decibellic heights at lunchtimes. The continuous clank of pans, thrash of plates and metallic crash of cutlery were all thrown together in a heady cacophony of shouts and banter from the staff – those cooking and those serving. And then there was the heavy *ker-thunk* of the two-way doors that separated the kitchen from the dining room. Every time they opened, they let in the boisterous bonhomie of the customers as they set about their top-notch pub grub and relaxed with copious glasses of wine. Orders came in fast and furious, and it appeared to be a lottery as to whether any food would materialize. Yet somehow it always turned up on the serving hatch as requested. Yes – the kitchen of the Dog and Fox operated like an olive-oiled and complex machine. And Beca loved being one of its cogs. She was a quiet cog, admittedly – never contributing to the deafening soundtrack of restaurant service in full flow, keeping herself to herself and observing it all from her very own dishwashing corner.

Getting the job had been a stroke of sheer *right-time-right-placeness*. With the exams behind her, she'd known she'd go out of her mind staying home all day. Lockdown had put her through that hell already, and she didn't want a repeat. So she'd printed off a CV of sorts – listing her scant achievements: grade five piano and a 1,500-metre swimming badge – and headed off on the hunt for a job.

The Dog and Fox had been the fourth place she'd tried that particular June morning. When she'd entered the dining area, no one was around, but *someone* nearby was having an argument. She couldn't understand what they were saying – was it Italian? Spanish? It didn't really matter, as whoever it was had come storming out from the kitchen, pulling on their jacket and almost knocking Beca over in the process. A few seconds later, an angry man who looked about the same age as her dad only with more hair came out from the kitchen and headed for the bar. Beca had stood stock-still as she watched him pour a shot of whisky, knock it back and sigh. He seemed completely unaware that Beca was in the room and, unsure what to do, she decided the best option was to sneak out as quietly as she'd come in.

She'd only taken three steps towards the door when she heard a gruff voice say, 'What d'you want?'

Beca felt like she'd been caught stealing or trespassing. 'Umm . . . I was looking for a job, but it doesn't matter,' she mumbled and continued her escape.

'Can you wash dishes?' asked the man, a slow smile dispelling his frown. And she realized that he probably wasn't that angry after all.

His name was Jonty. He gave her a quick demo of the monster industrial dishwasher and left her to her own devices.

Her first shift hadn't been a huge success – she'd ended up washing most of the pots by hand. But Jonty had asked her back for a second go, nonetheless.

It was now past mid-July and she'd been working there for four weeks. It hadn't taken long for her to master the dishwasher, learning to load and unload it with slick efficiency, relishing the clouds of steam that escaped when she lifted open the cumbersome steel door at the end of each four-minute cycle. Her skin was going to be amazing at this rate with all these dishwasher steams.

She wished she was working tonight as well: she was going to be at a loose end at home. And she'd already got a weekend trip to Dylan's Quay with her parents ahead of her. It was a family trip they always took the weekend school broke up for summer. Of course, she was looking forward to seeing Grama Grace and spending two days by the sea. It's just that her mother always made such a fuss about going: insisting on an early night in readiness for the two-hour journey the next day and wanting to get there before midday.

Beca signed out on the till and Jonty wished her a good weekend. 'Make sure you come back!' he called after her and she blushed when he added, 'No one washes dishes like you do!'

Passing through the lobby of the pub, she heard a familiar voice in the deserted lounge bar.

'But you can't just drop me in it like this, Jez . . . I don't care! You got your priorities all wrong . . . No! I CAN'T USE BACKIN' TRACKS 'COS I HAVEN'T GOT THE RIGHT SYSTEM, HAVE I?? . . . Oh fuck off, Jez, you're a knob.' Silence.

Beca peeked around the door of the lounge and her suspicions were confirmed. It was the girl from Bellamy's Italian Palace. She'd recognize that delightful 'Diffian drawl anywhere.

'Aww, WHAT NOW?' the girl snapped.

'It's Soozi, isn't it?' Beca asked warily.

'Who wants to know?'

'You served me a few weeks back, in the pizza place?'

'So? What d'you want, a medal? Now piss off. I'm in the middle of.'

Soozi turned back to her phone and began frantically searching through her contacts. But Beca didn't move, fascinated by the angry, wild energy exuding from this girl who could only be a year older than her, two at tops. She looked different out of her pizza gear – her hair was down now, still in braids, still bleached blonde. And instead of the generic Bellamy's Palace uniform, she was wearing blindingly pink hot pants that set off the beautiful black skin of her long, lean legs, which filled Beca with envy. It

49

was the height of summer and Soozi was wearing platform boots – that surely required a shedload of confidence. As did her black leather crop top, edged with fake diamonds. Soozi's toned arms suggested she must work out a lot – though some people just naturally looked fit, Beca supposed. Feeling completely self-conscious in comparison, she pulled at the cuffs of her long-sleeved T-shirt as if to hide her own pale, slightly doughy arms.

Suddenly she found the courage to speak. 'What's up?'

Soozi's frown disappeared and she looked all at once softer and more vulnerable. 'I been let down, haven' I?' she mumbled, and Beca thought how like a sulky toddler she sounded.

'How come?' asked Beca, brave enough to approach and sit down.

'I'm singin' here tonigh', aren' I? – look!' She pointed agitatedly at the blackboard, which announced TONITE – SOOZI COLE – 8PM. 'Only been giggin' a few months and my fuckin' keyboard player's walked. Back to square fuckin' one.' She kicked a bar stool and it toppled to the floor.

Beca went over and picked it up. Her heart was pounding – she never *ever* took risks like this. 'Got any sheet music?' she ventured.

'What?'

'The songs you're doing tonight. You got any music?'

''Course I have,' Soozi snapped again.

'Pass it here, then.'

The changing-room facilities in the Dog and Fox left a lot to be desired. In that essentially there weren't any. Jonty said the best he could offer was an unused staff-toilet-recently-turned-store-room. Considering what Beca had seen so far of Soozi's temperament, she was surprised that the pizza-chef-turned-singer didn't object. She just wheeled her big case in through the door, shoved it on top of the lav, unzipped it and took out a portable mirror. She then proceeded to top up her make-up whilst Beca stood watching, mesmerized.

As far as Beca was concerned, Soozi was the epitome of cool. And a unique kind of cool, at that: not copied or stolen or borrowed. Just self-generated, pre-possessing. Soozi Cole was completely at ease in her own skin. So settled, yet hungry to conquer the world. And she was beautiful. Beca could really see that now, as she was granted the chance to legitimately stare. How she yearned to be like Soozi, to bottle that allure, to exchange who she was – dull, clumsy Beca Matthews – for something much brighter, more sophisticated, more *majestic*, like this stunning creature before her, who was meticulously gluing a diamanté false lash along the base of her left eyelid.

'You're not wearin' that, are you?' Soozi barked, breaking the spell of Beca's adoration.

Beca suddenly felt very self-conscious, pulling at the hem of her Dog and Fox work shirt and anxiously rubbing at a grease stain. 'It's all I got,' she mumbled. 'And I can't go home and change, there's no time.'

Soozi sighed, and with her left eye firmly shut began riffling through the voluminous case. She pulled out a couple of tops and threw them at Beca. 'One of them'll do.'

Beca opted for the 'quieter' option – a black halter-neck with long sleeves and purple fringing. The other one was a definite no-go – a leopard-print vest that left zero to the imagination. Beca pulled on the black top, praying it would fit.

'Looks okay,' Soozi said approvingly. 'D'you want me to do your make-up?'

'What? No!' Beca replied, terrified. 'I've never worn make-up in my life.'

'Fuckin' weirdo,' Soozi laughed.

By ten that evening, the lounge bar at the Dog and Fox was hot and full, people mesmerized by the rich, velvety sound of Soozi Cole, steeped in soul, deep-rooted and startling in its power. Her encore was a stupendous rendition of Des'ree's 'I'm Kissing You'. It was only a pub audience – no more than forty people – but they went wild when Soozi took a bow. The broad Cardiff accent of her speaking voice belied the breadth and universality of her singing voice as she muttered humble thanks into the mike – 'Cheers, crackin', tidy.' Beca sat at the piano, forgetting that she, too, had been part of tonight's performance, clapping along with the rest of the crowd in appreciation of the singing. But then Soozi turned to her and with a sweep of her arm demonstrated her thanks, inviting the audience to join in with applause. Beca, predictably, blushed to her roots.

When the gig was over, Beca made her way back to the 'changing room', took off her borrowed top and put her old work T-shirt back on. It felt like she was coming down to earth with a huge bang. The magic was over. And it *had* been magical. She folded Soozi's top and placed it by the mirror, wondering whether to write a note – should she leave her number? Maybe Soozi'd like her to accompany again? But then was she being pushy, thinking that? Anyway she didn't have any paper or a pen. She spied Soozi's lipstick, unlidded, plum purple, lying naked with the brushes and powders, and thought for a moment about using it to write a message on the mirror. But then that would be a bit weird, wouldn't it? A bit, sort of – intimate? And also probably annoying – Soozi would have to wipe it off and the lipstick would be wrecked. No. Best just to leave it. She'd surely be coming in here in a minute? Beca waited – five minutes, ten minutes – and then a text from her mother came hurtling into her world.

Very early start tomorrow, remember!!

She sighed. She'd have to go.

At the bar, Soozi was crowded round by fans – mainly men telling her how incredible she was and asking if they could buy her a drink. Beca decided to bow out gracefully. It was half ten now – her mother would be going mad. She waved to Soozi, but Soozi didn't see, so Beca sneaked out of the pub and began the walk home. It was a beautiful evening – balmy and full of promise.

Suddenly a voice – 'O! Jools Holland! Hang on a mo!'

She looked behind her to see the cumbersome sight of Soozi Cole attempting to run in her big platform boots.

'You look like that Miranda Hart!' Beca shouted, smiling.

'Fuck off,' came the reply, not unkindly.

When Soozi finally caught her up she was breathless. She held out her hand and leaned against a lamp-post until the wheezing stopped. Then she reached into the pocket of her hot pants and pulled out some cash. 'Sorry it's only a twenny.'

Beca hesitated.

'Well, take it, then, before I changes my mind!'

'But I didn't want paying.'

'Don't be a knob. Go on.'

Beca took the money and Soozi nodded her approval. And then this remarkable entity ambled away, far more gracefully than she'd arrived. Before disappearing around the corner she turned and shouted, 'You was really good, y'know!'

'Cheers.'

'Saved my sorry ass, if truth be told.'

Beca smiled. And Soozi was gone.

Her phone buzzed. Predictably, it was her mother.

Where ARE you??

She quickly texted back that she was on her way, and headed off with a spring in her step.

10

alys

The two women were stood in the living room of Kirsty's holiday cottage, which nestled at the foot of the Brecon Beacons. 'Everything's written on the laminated card,' Kirsty said, 'but you know you can just call me if you get stuck.'

'This is so kind of you,' said Alys quietly. 'You've got me out of a real hole.'

Kirsty laughed, her eyes brimming with happy tears as she took Alys's hands. 'Oh yeah, right, and like you've never pulled *me* out of any holes, have you?'

It was true that as Kirsty's sponsor Alys had certainly helped her. The younger woman had been an emotional wreck when she'd first walked into an AA meeting six months previously, so Alys had taken her under her wing. She'd listened and comforted, guided and cajoled, citing tough love as part of the whole alcoholic-recovery process. But Alys couldn't deny that the relationship was mutually beneficial. It hadn't gone unnoticed by her that Kirsty turned up to the dingy church hall meetings in a flash silver Mercedes. Or that her shoes were designer, as were her clothes; or that her nails were always perfectly shellacked and her hair exquisitely coiffured. Kirsty was certainly one of the classier kinds of alcoholic. And Alys had a keen eye for class. And for money. She was drawn to it. Probably because she couldn't manage to generate it herself. And sometimes, having wealthy sponsees came into its own. Especially now, when she had found herself homeless – again.

Done out in Farrow & Ball and furnished tastefully, the cottage could fetch at least a grand a week in rentals. And here was Alys, being offered it for free. 'It's just until I get sorted,' she repeated for the umpteenth time, unable to believe her good luck.

'Listen,' said Kirsty. 'Douglas is always on about putting it on Airbnb or some such, but I'm not interested. It's always been a little sanctuary for me or for my friends, and now it's yours. For as long as you like.'

You might regret saying that, thought Alys, but instead said, 'Thank you, angel.'

Kirsty really had saved her bacon. Though to be fair, this was just how Alys lived her life. Had *always* lived her life. She was no stranger to floating from one place to another – an ageing, nomadic hippy, waiting to see where circumstances took her next.

'It's the least I can do for you,' Kirsty kept saying. And who was Alys to deny her sponsee the need to be helpful?

'Kirsty,' she said nervously, striking whilst the younger woman's generosity was hot, 'there's something else. And I feel really embarrassed asking . . .'

But Kirsty seemed to have read Alys's mind as she took out her Gucci purse and handed her a wad of notes. Alys blushed and whispered a thank-you. 'Listen,' said Kirsty firmly. 'Money is the least of my worries, I'm lucky on that front.'

'I'll pay you back! I've got a buyer for another one of my paintings and—'

Kirsty waved her hand dismissively before taking out a silver-grey credit card. 'I also want you to have this.'

Alys felt momentarily dizzy. 'What? No . . . I can't, I—'

'It's my secret card. Douglas doesn't know I've got it and I never use it. The pin is 3011.'

Alys stared at the plastic oblong in her hand, brimming with opportunity. 'You're too kind,' she mumbled. And meant it.

'Just helping a fellow alcoholic,' said Kirsty proudly. 'Isn't that what AA is all about?'

After settling in, Alys decided to venture to the Co-op on her bike. She had no intention of using Kirsty's credit card and every intention of paying back the cash. But it was nice to know she had a bit of back-up, should she need it. Alys's grocery requirements were basic – vegetables and eggs, some cheese, maybe. Seeds, nuts and berries – that would keep her going for a while. She locked up her bike and went in.

As she picked up a basket and wandered down the fresh-produce aisle, the thought landed with a bang – *I could buy a bottle of whisky now. And no one would be any the wiser.*

Alys had often wondered if part of the reason she no longer drank was because she simply couldn't afford it. Given the choice, would she think twice before embracing a champagne lifestyle? Probably not. Having been sober for thirty years now she never walked down the booze aisles out of habit. But today the Jameson bottle was shouting at her from five paces away – *Buy me! Drink me!* She shook her head to dislodge the thought, promising herself to get to the eleven o'clock meeting the next morning. These moments of weakness were a rarity, but Alys knew better than to let them linger, because if she *were* to drink again, life would get very, very messy. Alcohol had cost her much more than money, after all.

At the end of the booze aisle was a modest collection of books, greetings cards and basic stationery. Alys hadn't bought herself a book in a long time. The thought of sitting out in Kirsty's little garden with a mug of tea and a gruesome thriller was quite appealing. And a paperback was hardly an extravagance – even with someone else's money. She selected something suitably trashy – *He Kills in Blue* – reading the blurb on the back and deciding it'd be an easy read. She put the book into her basket and headed to the checkout, where she relented and made a contactless payment using Kirsty's card. *I could get used to this*, she thought.

11

grace

'IT'S SOOO GOOD TO SEE YOU, GRAMA GRACE!' screeched Elin as she stepped inside her grandmother's double-fronted house that looked down over the bay. It was aptly named Swn-y-Môr – which translated as Sound of the Sea. Elin immediately threw her arms around her grandmother, almost toppling the pensioner off-balance.

Grace had seen Elin like this before – edgy, hyper-happy, putting on an act. And it didn't bode well. 'Ooh, there's a hug and a half!' she replied, winking at her great-granddaughter over Elin's shoulder. Beca smiled back shyly and blushed.

'GOD, YOU ARE LOOKING SO WELL!!!' Elin continued on high volume. 'Let me look at you!' She stood back, surveying Grace as if checking a small child in a Halloween costume, before issuing a swift order to Beca under her breath. 'Give your great-grandma a cwtch, then!'

Beca duly obeyed.

'Hello, cariad,' said Grace softly as she kissed Beca on the forehead.

'Hiya.'

'Now, I won't look at you and say you've grown,' said Grace to Beca, 'because I know these days how sensitive all that is, with body-image dysmorphia and what have you.'

'Tell me about it,' Elin chipped in and tried to digress, but Grace ignored her and carried on.

'So I won't say that, but I will say you look more beautiful every time I see you, bach. And that old FaceTime doesn't do you justice!' She enveloped Beca in her arms before announcing, 'Let's have some tea, is it?'

'I'm gonna lie down for a bit,' said Beca, reverting to her eight-year-old self.

'Beca! We've only just got here . . .' Elin objected.

But Grace overrode her. 'Of course you can, cariad. Go you.'

Elin feigned annoyance and followed her grandmother into the kitchen. She launched into a catalogue of complaints about 'teenagers today', but Grace stopped her in her tracks. 'Never mind all that, Elin Matthews. Sit yourself down on that settee and tell me why your husband's not with you.'

At which point, Elin promptly burst into tears.

'God, what is *wrong* with me!' Elin was still sobbing ten minutes later and Grace handed her a fresh handkerchief from the dresser drawer. 'Thanks.' She blew her nose vigorously and let her grandmother rub her back.

Grace wished they all lived closer. She worried about Elin a lot. Especially in recent times. She was so independent-spirited, which wasn't a bad thing in itself, it's just that her granddaughter was in danger of being *so* independent, of bottling everything up to such a degree that eventually an explosion was inevitable. Such a quiet little girl she'd been. Unsurprising, given what she'd had to endure in her tender young life. But she had never seemed to shift that persona, never seemed to allow herself to relax. At uni, she'd had a couple of nice friends, though they had disappeared off the scene a long time since. And she'd not been short of admirers – but they had all been 'nice' boys, Grace thought. Responsible and sensible and a little bit dull. And Elin had never rebelled in any way, shape or form. She'd even waited till she was twenty-one before she'd had her ears pierced. If it wasn't so tragic, Grace would laugh. But the truth was that Elin could not have been more different from her own mother, Alys. 'They say the apple doesn't fall far from the tree,' Grace had despaired to John once, 'but in Elin's case, the apple has looked for the nearest wheelbarrow and begged the gardener to carry it as far from the tree as is humanly possible.'

When Greg had come along, Grace had rejoiced. The man had had a bit of *oomph* about him. He didn't let Elin take herself too seriously and they'd seemed genuinely besotted with each other in those early years. And how she'd bloomed! There was no doubting that Elin had inherited Alys's good looks, but she didn't seem to be aware of her own beauty. Not until she met Greg. And he brought out the absolute best in her: the sex probably helped, of course. It usually did. Grace knew as well as the next person that the honeymoon period in relationships wasn't infinite. But recently she'd noticed an unravelling, a disconnect between Elin and Greg. And she wasn't really sure how she could help. It was at times like this that she wondered what damage Alys's absence had inflicted on Elin's life. Which led her to think about the letter and whether Alys had received it yet. If she had, could a reconciliation really be on the cards, and if so, would this help poor Elin at all?

Grace realized she'd not been listening when Elin suddenly snapped, '. . . and please don't blame it on the menopause. Seems to me women aren't allowed to just have emotions – it's either got to be PMT or pregnancy hormones or the sodding Change of Life. Which incidentally is a stupid sodding expression.' At which point she started crying again. 'Sorry, Grama Grace.'

Truth was, the menopause probably *did* have something to do with it, Grace thought. And she tried to find some words of comfort for her unhappy granddaughter. 'I know it might feel a bit final,' she whispered. 'But when it happened to me, I was really rather relieved. Like I could reclaim my body after biology had taken it hostage for all those years.'

Between sobs, Elin went on to tell Grace that she'd been in denial about it for over a year now, somehow believing it wouldn't happen to her. That she would be the exception. But night sweats and flushes had been a regular occurrence, whilst periods had not. Elin knew the writing was on the wall, she just didn't want to read it.

'There, there, bach,' soothed Grace, taking Elin's hand. And with a heavy heart, Grace thought about Alys again, realizing this was another milestone conversation she'd never had with her own daughter.

Elin was cwtched up now on the patched-up sofa by the wood stove, which was covered in mismatched blankets and Welsh tapestry cushions. The familiarity of these surroundings seemed to be a comfort. She had always said how much she loved this kitchen: the Rayburn oven that had been there for ever and the cupboards that had never been changed or upgraded. She'd joke that Grace's middle name was 'make-do-and-mend'. Grace didn't mind. She'd never been one for being flash or fancy – functionality was all that counted as far as she was concerned.

'Thing about getting older, cariad, is you've just got to accept it face on. As R. S. Thomas says, we are all *"in servitude to time"*. No point thinking about what's gone, or what's coming over the hill at us. It's where we're at right now that counts.'

'We've not been getting on for a while,' whispered Elin, mindful that Beca could walk in at any time.

'You're changing the subject, bach,' Grace gently chided her.

'Not really – I think they're connected – me, the menopause, Greg . . .' Her voice faltered, but she cleared her throat and carried on. 'He says I'm moody all the time, fussy, impossible to please.'

'And *are* you?'

'I dunno. Yes, probably. Beca agrees with him most of the time, so I must be.'

'Poor lamb,' said Grace, and Elin turned to her grandmother, burying her head in her neck for comfort. 'That's it, better out than in.'

Her voice shaky and tired, Elin recounted what had happened

that morning. How they'd all been getting on fine; how Beca had been unusually buoyant – even singing around the house as they got ready to leave. 'And she *never* does that any more.' Greg had made them all breakfast, and he, too, had been very upbeat. 'Though his mood swings these days are so unpredictable,' she said. 'I mean, he goes on about *me* being difficult to read, but he's worse – I swear.'

Grace nodded, encouraging her to go on.

'So we'd packed up the car,' Elin said, 'and I was just doing my usual security check – which I *know* irritates Greg, but he'd be laughing on the other side of his face if the house got burgled when we were away.'

'Fair point. Why does it irritate him, then?'

'Because I check everything four times.'

Grace hid her smile.

'And no, I am not a compulsive obsessive.'

'Not obsessive, just obsessed, is it, bach?' Grace smiled. 'Go on.'

'I dunno, it just came from nowhere, Gram. I'd taken this phone call about . . . well, about something, and okay, so I *was* on the phone for a while, but it was important! And then when I finished, it was like he was *trying* to start a row, just so he could conclude it by saying he wasn't coming. As if he'd never intended joining us in the first place.'

Whilst Elin was explaining, Grace went to the dresser, opened a drawer and took out some Rescue Remedy. She proffered it to her granddaughter.

'No thanks, you know I don't believe in all that nonsense.'

'Yes, well, I do, so open wide.'

Not wanting to offend her grandmother, Elin indulged her and allowed Grace to administer the clear drops from the little brown bottle straight on to her tongue. 'There now, carry on.'

'Well, that was it really,' said Elin, her sobs beginning to fade. 'He announced it would be good for us to have a couple of days away from each other. Beca stomped off saying, "I'll wait in the car, you coming or what?", and I was just left staring daggers at Greg across the granite island.'

'The what?'

'The breakfast bar in the kitchen. Actually it's made of marble, not granite, but for some reason—'

'I get the picture.'

Grace watched as Elin's eyes began closing, trying to fight sleep and failing.

'So rude of me to just turn up then fall asleep within an hour of arriving,' she mumbled.

'Hush now, bach,' said Grace. 'You're exhausted. You've had that long drive, all that pent-up anger . . .'

'I feel such a failure, Grama Grace.' Her voice was barely audible now.

Gently Grace covered her granddaughter with a blanket, just as she had when she'd been a little girl. 'That's it, bach,' she whispered, 'have a little sleep now, is it?'

Elin tried to object, but she couldn't formulate the words and all that came out was a muffled groan.

'. . . And I'll walk down the seafront with Beca for an ice-cream. Neeta at the caff would love to see her. That's it, hush now.'

And Grace smoothed her granddaughter's forehead till she gave in, finally defeated by sleep.

12

elin

When Elin awoke an hour later, the house was silent. She sat up and stretched, inhaling the comforting aroma of a lamb casserole – 'cawl' as Grama Grace called it – slow-cooking in the oven. She knew that Grace would have made it from scratch. Local lamb from Carwyn the butcher, with leeks and carrots from her allotment and fresh thyme and bay leaves from the herb garden. There was a pan of new potatoes to accompany the cawl, scrubbed ready for boiling, perched on the stove. They'd have come from the allotment, too. Whenever Elin thought of her grandmother, the word that always came to mind was 'wholesome'. Grace made her feel safe, and wanted and loved. She'd been her rescuer, after all.

She ran herself a glass of water from the tap, and looked out at Grace's steep garden, boasting the famous ugly 'swimming pool' at the end. She smiled, remembering how Beca used to love jumping in it when she was little. Back then, Grace still had lodgers and the house was buzzing with friendly, welcoming chaos. All three of them – her, Greg and Beca – would cram themselves into Grace's bedroom, which she surrendered whenever they visited. Trips to see Grama Grace in the holidays were always a joy, and sorrow tugged at Elin's heart now as she mourned the loss of those happier days.

Running a boarding house had always seemed to be Grace's *raison d'être*, though she hadn't had lodgers there for several years. Elin knew it was for the best, but she did worry sometimes that her grandmother might be lonely. Especially since John had gone into Cadwallader House. Elin loved John. He was the grandfather she'd never had and a perfect match for Grace with his sharp wit and refusal to suffer fools. That his body struggled these days to keep up with his brain was one tragedy visited upon him by old age. But at least mentally he was still the John he'd always been – his mind not lost to the ravages of vascular dementia like his poor sister, Cissie.

It didn't matter to Elin any more that John and Grace had never married. Though there'd been a time when she'd been desperate for them to do so. For years when she was growing up she'd fantasized about their wedding day and the possibility of being a bridesmaid, holding the big frothy train of Grama Grace's bridal gown, like the one Princess Diana had worn. They'd humoured her then, with a *maybe* and *one day*. But when she was fifteen and old enough to understand, Grace had explained the situation: that John had been married in his twenties, to a woman called Doreen Cuttle. 'I never met her, bach, but according to your Aunty Cissie she was not the nicest of people. She left your Uncle John for another man – I think John was glad to see the back of her, to be honest. But because she was a Catholic, she refused to grant him a divorce. Even though Doreen had left *him*! So technically – legally – he's still got a wife. He wouldn't be allowed to get married.'

'Even if he wanted to?' Elin had asked mournfully, and Grace had answered with a sad smile, 'Even if he wanted to, bach.'

After that, the subject of Grace and John's wedding was never mentioned. And Elin stopped looking at bridesmaids' dresses in her grandmother's Grattan catalogue.

Wandering into the front room, she stood at the bay window and took in the view – the first quay in the distance was built, she believed, in the seventeenth century by philanthropist Lord Henry Dylan, after whom the town was named. The newer quay built two hundred years later echoed its predecessor, and the two unevenly lengthed arms stretched out into the sea, attempting to enclose the sweeping bay and port that had once been alive with merchant ships and traders. Now Dylan's Quay was a thriving holiday resort, teeming with ice-cream-licking, sunhat-wearing holidaymakers, who gave the place its zest and energy. Grama Grace's house on the much sought-after Sea Captain's Parade had been built by a nineteenth-century ship-owner, and Elin liked to imagine his wife looking out of one of these sea-facing windows, like she did now, watching her husband sail off into the distance. She wondered for a moment whether Greg was sailing away from her and thought about the last time they'd attempted to have sex.

It had been Valentine's Day. Five whole months ago! She'd instigated it. And it had been one of the most embarrassing nights of her marriage. Elin had never been one to give in to the pressures of commercial nonsense like Valentine's Day, but having read an article in *Woman and Home* about 'using it or losing it', she'd decided to take the plunge and make the effort. The feature writer had gone on about the importance of keeping romance alive in long-term relationships, advising that even the smallest of gestures could make the biggest of impacts and stop potential cracks from appearing. Elin hadn't been aware of cracks as such – tiny hairline fractures, perhaps, allowing Life and Work to hijack time that the two of them could have spent together; kisses that had lost their lustre and been replaced with polite pecks on the cheek; the failure of one to even look up when the other entered the room. Neither of them had mentioned this slow disintegration, but it was undoubtedly there. Then, having decided to sort out Greg's sportswear drawer one evening, she'd found an unwritten Valentine's card, still in its cellophane. She'd been more than surprised that Greg would indulge in a bit of mindless commercialism – his feelings were the same as hers when it came to Valentine's Day – but maybe he'd been aware that things between them needed spicing up of late. Fair play. If Greg was going to make the effort, then it was only fair that she did, too. Even though she found it difficult to dredge up any enthusiasm for the mission.

Nevertheless, she'd popped to Marks and Spencer's one evening after school to find something a little more glamorous than her day-to-day cotton briefs. Settling on a sage-green basque, she'd tried it on in the changing room and taken a selfie before WhatsApping it to Greg with the message *Hey Valentine! fillet steak for dinner, and this is what's for dessert.* Okay, so she was being very cheesy, but Elin had hoped he'd take it in the ironic spirit by which it was meant. And after all, there'd been a time when she and Greg did lots of silly things like that together. Her heart had been racing when she did it – this was just so out of her comfort zone these days. Still, she *did* look rather good in that basque. Even if she said so herself.

The meal hadn't quite been the romantic event she'd intended it to be. Beca, who rarely ate with them these days, decided that *she* fancied fillet steak actually, and of course, Elin wasn't about to exclude her. 'Unless you and Dad are doin' something romantic?' she'd laughed before miming being sick.

'Don't be silly, how old d'you think we are?' Elin had joined in with the joke, dying inside when she thought of her message to Greg and now regretting ever sending it. What had made things worse was that his only reply had been *Sounds good, see you after tennis.* Bloody tennis.

By eight o'clock, Beca had said she couldn't wait any longer and could she have hers now? So when Greg eventually did come home twenty minutes later, Elin was scraping Beca's leftovers into the bin and stacking the dishwasher. The table was still laid for two.

'I'm sorry, I didn't manage any flowers,' he said. 'They'd sold out everywhere.'

'Don't be daft,' she'd laughed, surprising herself at how disappointed she felt and wondering when he was planning on giving her the card. 'You hungry, then?'

'Can I be honest? No. I'm not. Maybe I'm going down with something? Still, steak'll keep till tomorrow, won't it?'

'Of course. I'll just cook mine, then.'

And there had been a moment – an excruciating moment – where, like absolute strangers, they just stared at each other – she with a couple of portobello mushrooms in her hand, and him fiddling with the toggle on his hoodie. The wiring of the basque beneath her dress had begun digging into her ribs and she wondered what on earth she'd been thinking. She prayed that Greg had forgotten about the photo – the moment had so well and truly passed. But embarrassingly he whispered, 'And, er . . . once you've eaten, we'll have that early night, shall we?'

He'd clearly been conscious that Beca might be within earshot. And Elin had wanted to die.

'Sure,' she'd said, turning away from him in an attempt to hide her mortification.

She'd eaten her steak alone in the kitchen, the other place setting untouched and the muffled sounds from the TV filtering through from the living room. The occasional laughter of a studio audience seemed to mock her solitude.

In the bedroom an hour later, they'd both stood facing each other, an overwhelming sense of obligation to this event burning between them.

'Haven't done this in a while,' Greg had joked. And she'd grinned back before attempting to undress seductively and reveal the new underwear beneath. 'Nice!' he'd said, looking genuinely impressed, and reached forward to start kissing her. His arms around her back, they fell into their twenty-year-old predictable routine – begin with the kiss, then a hand on the boob, before reaching down to squeeze her buttocks. It was how things between them had always begun, but Elin felt herself rise up and outside of what was happening. *God, I feel like a big sofa cushion,* she thought as Greg continued kissing her. She had tried to put the thought out of her mind and reach into the depths for some grain of desire. But there was none to be found. She'd felt entirely empty. Devoid of all sensuousness. If anything, she'd simply felt foolish. She could have faked enjoyment, made all the right noises of encouragement till they reached the other side, were it not for the fact that Greg's fitness watch got caught on the lacing of the basque. And then the whole process descended into farce. It wasn't even a comical sexy moment that led from laughter into lust. It was just awkward beyond belief and, what was worse, it was irritating. 'Oh for God's sake, Greg, I don't see why you have to wear that bloody thing *all* the time!'

'Because it's monitoring my heart-rate variability!'

'And does it monitor how annoying you are as well?'

'Oh shut up, Elin. Bloody hell. Look, have you got some scissors?'

'In my bedside drawer.'

They'd had to move together as if in a three-legged race, edging their way carefully towards the bedside, with Greg's hand still attached to the delicate lace. Reaching into the drawer, Elin saw with horror the tube of KY, another magazine suggestion that she'd bought into to 'help things along'. The article, no doubt written by someone half her age, had buoyantly announced that it was perfectly normal at Elin's age to require a little assistance. 'Let me get them,' Elin had snapped, attempting to hide the KY as she reached for a small pair of nail scissors and passed them to Greg. 'Try to minimize the damage,' she said, aware that now she was sounding like a head teacher. 'When you cut it, I mean! This thing wasn't cheap, y'know!'

She'd stood patiently as Greg snipped at the lace, freeing the links of his watch. She'd tried not to stare at his bald patch, which seemed to have grown infinitely bigger. Once they'd finally become disentangled, they both sat down on the bed in silence. Elin noticed that one of her suspenders had wriggled free, leaving the stocking on her right leg to sag forlornly. She thought about reattaching it, but wondered what the point would be.

'I guess we shouldn't force these things,' Greg had said, before sloping off to the bathroom. His pee seemed to go on interminably and Elin sighed to herself at the thought that this had become the soundtrack to their intimacy.

Their intimacy.

What intimacy?

Greg had referred to it as *these things*.

She struggled to get out of the basque before he returned to the bedroom. She didn't think she could take any more humiliation and yet was drawn to it like a masochistic moth to a candle. 'I take it you decided against the card?' she muttered.

'What card?'

'The card in your sports drawer. I saw it.'

'Jesus, Elin, you snooping on me now?'

'No, I was pairing your socks.'

There was a painful silence and then he said, 'I took it to work. I was going to post it, but I forgot.'

'Yeah, well, that just about says it all, doesn't it?' she sighed, desperate to hide the sob that had caught in her throat.

That night they slept with their backs towards each other, like they always did these days, and the following morning they got up and went about their day as if the events of the night before had never happened. *Happy sodding Valentine's Day.*

She checked her phone again for messages. Nothing. And her broken heart sank. Again.

Looking out of the bay window, she watched holidaymaking families and besotted couples enjoying the lazy summer's day and felt a sudden, profound loneliness. How she longed for Grace's return so that she could seek comfort again in her grandmother's love.

13

beca

Maybe it was just the mood she was in. Or maybe it was because the weather was so good. But this trip to Grama Grace's was sick. Dylan's Quay had never looked so good and Beca actually felt like she was on holiday – she was buzzing. Even though the day hadn't started off well, with her parents arguing.

The chocolate fountain had been to blame. Her mum had been harping on for days about getting one for Grama Grace's party and as they'd been loading up the car she'd got a call from the company that rented them out. 'I've got to take this,' she'd said, and ended up talking to them for a good twenty minutes, which left her dad to finish the packing. When Elin finally came off the phone she was all full of beans about the great deal on their top-of-the-range option called the Luxury Cocoa River. But after she told Greg how much it would cost, he said Elin was being ridiculous – started saying she was going *way* over the top, that she was encouraging diabetes in the elderly and that she ought to rein in 'this whole damn party fiasco'. Her mum had gone ballistic in response, shouting that Grama Grace was *everything* to her and she was going to give her the celebration of a lifetime, whether he liked it or not.

When her dad responded by refusing to come on the trip, her mum got upset again and had a total meltdown, saying he was being selfish and childish. And for once, Beca had seen her mother's side of things – what was wrong with Dad, just changing his mind like that? The end-of-term trip to Grama Grace's was something they *always* did, so he had absolutely no leg to stand on. But then again, Mum was hysterical – she'd never seen either of them like that before. They were both basically batz.

Still, that had been hours ago and now nothing was going to bring down her mood. Especially when she thought about last night's gig. Had it actually happened? Had she, Beca Matthews – a nothing of a sixteen-year-old from North Cardiff – actually played the keyboard live in front of an audience? Okay, so she was only in the background, only the accompanist – but as Soozi had said, without *her* there'd have been no show. 'No Punch without Judy, babes,' she'd said. Which was true. It was Soozi who'd had the real wow factor. That voice was something else. Truly. 'What you doin' working in a pizza joint when you sing like that?' Beca had asked her during their speedy makeshift rehearsal.

'All part of the big plan, bird,' she'd answered. 'Got to build up a following first. An' I can't starve in between gigs, can I? Anyways, I could ask you the same question – what you doin' washin' dishes in a Cardiff pub – you got talent, girl. You needs to get yourself out there.'

'Give me a chance, I only just left school,' Beca had answered.

'So? You're a player. Top notch.'

True, Beca knew she'd been impressive – picking up the sheet music like that and just playing what she saw. Easy-peasy, nothing complicated about it. But Soozi, who admitted she *couldn't read a damn note*, had thought Beca's playing was superb. And she'd taken up the offer to accompany her in a flash. 'Fuck Jezzer, the prick. You're ten times better than he is, anyways.' And Beca had felt herself purring inside.

Standing now with Grama Grace at the end of the quay, she inhaled the soft, salty sunshine and smiled to herself. 'You're so lucky,' she said. 'Dolphins on your doorstep.'

71

'That sounds like a song lyric,' Grace laughed.

'I love it here,' Beca said. 'It's sound.'

They both looked out to the glitterball-glinting sea, gulls and ravens swirling above them in boisterous, hungry chatter, always on the lookout for discarded chips or ice-cream cones. For a moment, Beca considered telling Grace about her stage debut. It certainly wasn't something she could share with her mum, but Grace was different. She didn't make a fuss about things, didn't get overexcited. How did her mum get to be so uptight and naggy when her great-grandmother was so cool, she wondered?

And as if reading Beca's mind, Grace turned to her and touched her on the arm. 'Listen, bach, I think your mum's going through a bit of a tough time at the moment.'

'She's *always* going through a tough time,' Beca grumbled, aware that she sounded like a five-year-old.

'Yes, well, just cut her a bit of slack for now, is it?'

On their way home, they popped in to see Neeta at her busy café. Whenever they called in, Beca allowed her great-grandmother's friend to *ooh* and *aah* at her as if she was a baby in a pram – *How much you've grown!* she'd say in her bustling, energetic Welsh accent.

Accepting the offer of a free ice-cream, Beca enjoyed the mini-celebrity status that her great-grandmother was afforded in this town, the limelight rubbing off on Beca herself. Grama Grace knew *everybody* in Dylan's Quay.

'We're all *so* excited about the party!' whispered Neeta when Grace was out of earshot, chatting to one of the staff.

'You haven't said nothing, have you?' Beca was alarmed. 'My mum'll lose it if Grama Grace finds out!'

'No chance,' said Neeta and, checking Grace was still busy chatting, she whispered conspiratorially, 'You know I'm doin' the cake, don't you? I've spent weeks designing it. Gonna make all these miniature Graces out of marzipan, doin' yoga and swimming and so forth. And I'm hopin' to put you and your mum and dad on there, and John of course, even Cissie if there's room.' Neeta hesitated for a moment and then grimaced. 'I *did* wonder whether I should make a marzipan Alys, but I thought it might be a bit insensitive, given the circumstances. Plus, I never knew her, to be fair, so I've got no idea what she looked like.'

Beca nodded, and realized she'd never actually seen a photo of her grandmother either. Bizarre, really. That a member of their family could be eradicated like that, never discussed, as if she'd never existed. When Grama Grace had mentioned Alys on Face-Time a few weeks back, it felt like it was the first time Beca had heard her say her name.

'What are you two in cahoots about?' said Grace, smiling as she approached.

'Ice-cream,' said Neeta, quick as a whippet. 'I'm givin' you some to take home for your tea.' And as she turned on her heel she sneaked a little wink at Beca.

After supper the three of them washed up together, chatting and laughing in a way that just didn't happen back home. Beca put it down to the sea air and the easy atmosphere in Grama Grace's house, but her mum was definitely more relaxed when she was here. Beca no longer thought it weird that Grace didn't own a dishwasher – she was actually enjoying doing the washing-up by hand, the three of them working like a little team to get the job done. And the frown that was usually settled on her mother's brow had disappeared tonight. Maybe Grama Grace had put some Valium in her rice pudding.

When they'd finished, Beca headed upstairs, leaving her mum and Grace to chat about the row with her dad. She lay on her bed and looked up at the ceiling. She was feeling full of butterflies – unsettled and nervous, but in a good way. Because there was something she'd been planning to do for the past couple of hours. Phone in hand, she tapped on the search engine and her breathing sped up. After typing in 'Bellamy's Italian Palace, Cardiff', she was instantly bombarded with dozens of names, promising customers a perfect pizza experience. Locating the right number, her finger hesitated, and then she tapped on the screen before she could change her mind. It rang. And it rang. And it rang.

She was about to hang up when a voice answered, shouting over the background noise of a busy takeaway business on a Saturday night. 'Bellamy's – delivery or pick up?'

She recognized Soozi's voice straight away, but couldn't bring herself to speak.

'Hello? Can you hear me?' Soozi demanded.

More silence from Beca.

'Look, stop dickin' around. I got a queue of customers here long as my arm! You gonna order or not?'

But Beca was too intimidated now by Soozi's short fuse and hung up, tossing the phone away from her. She lay there, breathless, feeling like she'd committed some heinous crime. Why didn't she speak? What was wrong with her? She was disturbed from her reverie by the ring of her phone, which made her jump out of her already shaky skin. *Number withheld*. She pressed Accept.

'Hello?'

'I'm givin' you the benefit of the doubt. Now what was it you wanted?' barked Soozi.

'It's Beca.'

There was a beat. She could hear people shouting orders in the background.

'Who?'

'Beca?' She knew she now sounded unsure of her own name. 'I played the keyboards last—'

But Soozi didn't let her finish. 'Oh, thank fuck for that! I been tryin' to get hold of you!'

'Have you?' This was the last thing Beca was expecting to hear.

'I asked in the pub, but they wouldn't give me your number.'

Beca realized she needed to explain herself or else risk

appearing to be some kind of stalker. 'Sorry about just now, I'm in West Wales and the signal's dodgy,' she lied.

'Bollocks to that,' said Soozi. 'ALL RIGHT, HOLD YOUR HORSES!' she shouted to what Beca presumed must be a queue of impatient customers.

'Listen, what you doin' Tuesday night, bird? 'Cos you an' me got another gig.'

14

elin

Elin struggled to locate and identify the voices in her sleepy head. Then she remembered. Opening one eye, she hoisted herself up slowly and looked out of the window to see Beca, tentatively dipping her toe in the 'swimming pool' at the end of the garden. Grama Grace was already in, up to her neck of course, and splashing her great-granddaughter.

'It's FREEZING!!!'

'Don't be such a baby, come on!'

Beca screeched delightedly before taking the plunge, applauded by Grace.

Smiling at the sight, Elin lay back on the single bed, stretching away the night's sleep and rubbing her eyes like a child. The alarm clock on the bedside table told her it was past ten. She hadn't slept so well in a very long time and she felt replenished.

The sense of contentment didn't last long, though. Reaching for her mobile, she saw there was nothing from Greg. No missed call. No text. No email. She'd been so tempted to contact him last night, but she'd decided – petulantly – to follow his suggestion of 'having some space'. Admittedly, she'd expected *him* to get in touch. And now that he hadn't, she felt an overwhelming lurch in the pit of her stomach. *What was happening to them?*

Talking it out with Grama Grace last night had really helped.

She'd been able to see things more objectively – yes, she probably had been a handful of late, and yes, she probably had been too caught up in work. But then that was always the case by the end of the school year – she was frazzled! And Greg knew that. Maybe, though, he was right. Maybe this weekend apart would give them the breathing space they both needed, give them a chance to reset.

She felt like a lovelorn teenager, sitting waiting by the phone for her boyfriend to deign to call. *I am not having this!* she thought. *I am a head teacher of a comprehensive school, for God's sake! I'm fifty-one years old!*

So she picked up her mobile and tapped on his number.

It rang.

And rang.

'Hi. You're through to Greg – can't speak right now, soz . . .'

'Soz!' she repeated, appalled.

'. . . but leave a message!'

She decided not to. And terminated the call. She was livid. Unjustifiably so, she knew that.

Feeling lost, she watched Beca and Grace splashing about in the pool on this glorious West Walian sunshiny Sunday morning, both of them happily unaware of the angst churning around inside Elin's mind.

Her phone buzzed and she jumped. A text. From Greg.

Soz missd call – tlk l8r? when u home?

No, Greg, she thought. *Since when are you in charge?* And she called him again. This time it went straight to voicemail. And this time she *did* leave a message. Which she would later regret.

'Greg? What the hell? You are actually IGNORING me! I'm your wife, for God's sake, your bloody wife!!! Ring me. I want to talk to you. NOW! And for the record, the word is SORRY, not SOZ. Grow up.' And she ended the call and sat staring at her mobile, willing it to ring. It didn't. She wanted to cry. She wouldn't. She mustn't.

'What's wrong?' Beca stood in the doorway, breathless, a towel wrapped round her, hair wet and clinging to her flushed face, her joyful energy out of place in the sadness of that little bedroom.

'Nothing!' said Elin, forcing a smile. 'Nice swim?'

'It was sick!'

'Beca, please don't use that word to describe something good, it's so misleading and so—'

'Mum,' Beca said, 'we're not in school now. You're off duty.'

Elin tried to laugh at herself, but the performance wasn't very convincing. 'I had *such* a good sleep, did you?'

'Yeah,' said Beca, rubbing her hair with the edge of the towel. 'Grama Grace is doing eggs in the coddler. Remember I used to call it a *cuddler*?' She laughed and Elin smiled back. Coddled eggs for breakfast were a mainstay of a visit to Dylan's Quay, and the little ceramic lidded pot – the coddler – was a stalwart piece of her grandmother's crockery. She hadn't heard of anywhere else in the world where eggs were cooked that way.

'Have you spoken to Dad?' Beca asked.

'Yes,' she said, attempting to sound believable. 'Just now – he's fine. Sends his love and says he'll see us later.'

'So you two are okay?'

'Of course we are! Come on, I'm desperate for a cuddled egg.'

After breakfast they walked to Cadwallader House to see John. Grama Grace suggested he show Elin and Beca the sweetpeas he was growing in the home's garden. All the time, the polite smile on Elin's face belied the turmoil in her head. She still hadn't heard back from Greg and now her whole weekend was being spoiled. *Selfish, selfish, selfish man.* In the flower garden she let John and Grace command the conversation with Beca as she sat apart, on the wooden bench, eyes closed, her face turned to the sky, hoping the combination of sleepy sunshine, bee buzz and birdsong would calm her frazzled nerves.

It would be nineteen years this autumn.

Nineteen years since they married and twenty-one since they met.

Elin had been thirty at the time and Head of Music at St Stephen's, with her eye on the deputy headship. Her career was going brilliantly. It was just the rest of her life that was lagging behind. By then, the few friends she had – most of whom she'd now lost touch with – were either married or cohabiting. They'd all passed the mortgage stage, and were either at the visiting-Homebase-every-weekend stage or the contemplating-getting-a-dog stage. A couple of them were pregnant. But Elin had remained steadfastly single. And not for want of trying, though admittedly she could have tried harder and not always put her career before everything else. Nonetheless, she was starting to worry she'd end up a lonely spinster (without the cats, though, she couldn't abide the smell of cats). She'd celebrated her thirtieth birthday with Grama Grace and John and Cissie at Swn-y-Môr and had vowed to make it a year of change and progress, sharing her ambition with them all. Grama Grace had looked delighted and relieved – Elin suspected that she was worried her granddaughter might end up alone and lonely. So in a rare act of spontaneity she booked herself on to an eight-day river cruise up the Danube that coming Easter, starting in Budapest and ending in Passau, flying home from Munich the night before term started. It was a big step for her and certainly out of character, throwing caution to the wind, but maybe it was time she started taking some risks.

The cruise itself was pleasant and exceeded her expectations, if she was honest. She'd worried that it might be staid or lacking in imagination, and had expected the focus to be on over-eating and cheesy night-time entertainment with dancers in sequinned leotards singing show tunes. But the itinerary was varied and if the daytrips didn't appeal then the classes and talks on board were fascinating.

She hardly spoke to anyone else, except at dinner, where she'd make polite conversation with fellow guests sitting on either side of her. She'd then excuse herself early and get some fresh air on deck before heading to her cabin, where she'd wrap herself up against the night-time cold, order hot chocolate with marshmallows and read a good thriller out on her little balcony.

On the fourth day of the cruise, the ship docked at Vienna, a place she had always longed to visit, with all its musical associations – to walk in the footsteps of Mahler and Schubert, of Brahms and Strauss, and of course Beethoven and Mozart. She attended a mid-morning concert that moved her to tears and asked a passing tourist to take a photograph of her outside St Stephen's Cathedral. There was something satisfying about visiting such a monumental building that bore her own school's name and she thought her pupils might be impressed.

'You're on the cruise, aren't you?' said the obliging tourist as he handed back the camera.

'That's right,' said Elin. And an awkward silence followed. When she looked back at that first meeting, she would honestly say she couldn't remember much about it – what he looked like or how he was dressed. It certainly wasn't a lightning-strike moment where she fell instantly in love. 'Are you enjoying it?' she asked, more out of politeness than anything else.

'Yes. A lot more than I'd expected and today has been spectacular.'

'Oh?'

'Yes. I've always wanted to come here. Bit of a Brahms addict,' he joked.

Elin wasn't really sure what to say next and was conscious that time was ticking on and she still had the Volksgarten and Palmenhaus to visit if she was going to cram everything in before getting back on the ship. 'Right,' she said. 'Better get on.'

'Yes, me too. Have fun!' he replied, and they went their separate ways.

Later they would laugh together at how useless they had both been, what cowards: how their actions embodied the exact opposite of 'seizing the moment'.

'We annihilated the moment really, didn't we?' he would say with a smile.

Elin's last planned Viennese 'must-see' of the day was the famous Ferris Wheel, or Wiener Riesenrad, as she never tired of saying. She relished the Austrian sounds, as delightful on her tongue as the Sachertorte she'd eaten for her dessert at a little coffee shop in the Stephansplatz. She was due back on the ship by 10 p.m. at the latest, so had pre-booked her ticket for an 8 p.m. slot, when the sun would just be setting and she could take in the beauty of Vienna bathed in golden light.

The tourists had dwindled by now and Elin thought it a shame that people would miss out on such a stunning panoramic view, but hey-ho, their loss.

Just as the gatekeeper was letting them on, there was a cry from behind her and a latecomer pleaded to be allowed aboard. It was the tourist from lunchtime, her fellow traveller, clutching his ticket. She didn't pay much attention till she was safely inside the car with the door locked and the four-minute journey had begun.

'I'm not following you,' he laughed as he stood next to her, gazing out through the window.

'Oh, hello again,' she said, looking at the view, not at him. 'Good day?'

'Amazing. Went to the Schönbrunn Zoo. Oldest in the world, y'know.'

Elin nodded, and then they were quiet again, savouring the spectacle of the panorama that unfolded before them. As they reached the top, she turned to him and said, 'I'm Elin, by the way.'

'Greg.'

A tight, shy smile was exchanged between them and the car began its descent.

They walked back to the ship together. It was a fine, clear evening and the air was potent, full of springtime mischief. They didn't say much on their way, just polite chat about where they'd been that day and what they had loved. And then it dawned on her. 'Why Brahms?'

'Sorry?'

'You said you were a Brahms fan. I mean, I love him too, but it's Mahler who really pulls the heartstrings, don't you think?'

And with that they were off, gorging on a classical music fest that took them down the gangplank and into the bar on board, where they ordered hot chocolate and Danish pastries, whilst those around them sipped cocktails. In between comparing Strauss and Schubert, they offered up some basic information about themselves. As ever, Elin gave the edited version of her life, in that she didn't mention her mother, but described Grace in her place. Greg told her that he and his previous girlfriend had split up over three years ago and he'd gone travelling to shake himself up a bit. He'd used his English Language teaching qualification all over the world and was now deciding where to settle. 'It's a bit like hairdressing, really,' he said. 'Teaching English as a foreign language. You can take it anywhere.'

'Take it to Cardiff, then,' she said, inwardly shocked at her own boldness.

'What?'

'Cardiff. It's a nice city. Birthplace of Roald Dahl and home to the oldest record shop in the world.'

'Seriously?' he laughed.

'Yes! Opened in 1894 – used to sell wax records.'

'Ha!'

'And I live there of course.'

He smiled awkwardly and she couldn't believe she'd said it. She wasn't even drunk. It was just that there was something so warm about him, so enthusiastic about life. And he had a dimple in his left cheek that partnered the twinkle in his crystal-blue eyes. *Oh God*, she thought. *I'm flirting.*

When they realized they were the only two left in the bar, they decided to call it a night. It was 2 a.m. by now. He walked her to her cabin. She didn't invite him in and he didn't kiss her goodnight. But they arranged to meet the following morning for breakfast.

After that, they spent every waking minute of the remainder of the cruise together. And yet they didn't so much as hold hands. They did, however, talk. And laugh. And argue (about music).

On the last day of the cruise, they'd docked at Passau and decided on a daytrip to Prague, where they attended two lunchtime concerts in succession, ate meatballs and drank a modest amount of local beer. They were both quiet, knowing that this unexpectedly joyful holiday was coming to an end.

When they returned to the ship, they opted to avoid the farewell dinner and spent the evening on Elin's balcony instead, drinking tea.

The inevitable moment arrived, of course. 'It's nearly midnight,' said Greg, testing the uncertain waters of this as-yet-undefined relationship.

'Will you turn into a pumpkin?'

'No, but I might turn into a fool.'

'How come?'

'If I try and kiss you and you push me away,' he said quietly.

'Well, you won't know if you don't try . . .' Elin replied, shaking. And not from the cold.

'Okay, well, here goes.' And he leaned in slowly, gently pushed away a strand of hair that had fallen across her cheek, curling it behind her ear . . . and finally kissed her.

It would have been the kiss to have topped all kisses ever kissed.

Had it not been for the fireworks.

Which went off at that precise moment, making the whole event so ridiculously unbelievable that they started laughing and couldn't stop. Could their first kiss have been more cheesy? Fireworks?! They realized that it was part of the last-night celebrations laid on by the cruise company. But still. Talk about perfect timing.

The laughter helped. It made the sex easy. Easy and utterly gorgeous.

Within a month, Greg had found a job in Cardiff and moved in with Elin.

And within twelve months they'd returned to Vienna to celebrate knowing each other a whole year. They bought tickets for the Ferris Wheel and when they reached the top, Greg got down on one knee and proposed. Elin didn't hesitate in saying yes, much to Greg's relief, seeing as there were eight other passengers in the car with them, who proceeded to applaud.

They were married in Cardiff's register office on 3 October 2003 and became parents to Beca two years later. It was a text-book romance. A fairy-tale love story.

'I think your phone's ringing,' said John, disturbing her reverie.

'Oh, thanks.' She looked at the screen – Greg. 'I'll just take this,' she smiled, trying to look nonchalant, her heart racing as she tapped Answer and moved away from John and Beca. 'So you finally deign to call me, do you?' she hissed, hoping she was out of earshot.

'Elin, can you just . . . not *start* . . .'

Elin took a deep breath. 'Go on, then. What d'you want to say?'

Greg sounded tearful as he said, 'We need to have a proper conversation, El. There are things I need to tell you.'

For a moment she was seized by fear and her voice softened. 'Oh my God, are you all right? Has something happened? Are you ill?'

'No, I'm not ill,' he said quietly. 'But something has happened, yes.'

15

beca

Beca woke up to the sound of a dull thud above her head, followed by a dragging noise and more thuds. It was Monday morning and she was back in her Cardiff bed.

Curiosity trumped sleep, so she climbed out and slumped over to the landing. The attic hatch was open and at the base of its ladder lay four large plastic crates, all empty. A fifth crate came hurtling down and crashed to the floor.

'God, Mum!' Beca shouted. 'They're gonna break, you carry on chuckin' 'em like that!'

The only response was the appearance of her mother's plim-solled feet purposefully descending the ladder. She looked fraught and a little unhinged, Beca thought, her hair uncharacteristically unkempt. 'You can help me carry them downstairs if you like,' said Elin.

But Beca wasn't getting involved. 'I'm going back to bed,' she mumbled.

Lying there with sunlight squeezing through the gaps in her blinds, Beca thought of the Larkin poem they'd studied in Year Ten. She could only remember the first two lines: *They fuck you up, your mum and dad. They may not mean to, but they do.* And she sighed, angry with both her parents for doing absolutely that.

She'd been having such a good time, for a change. For once, her life was feeling relatively normal. A job – even perhaps a fledgling music career. And then her dad had decided to be a complete twat and have an affair with some idiot woman called Fleur. *Fleur!* For fuck's sake, what sort of a name was that anyway?

Beca pulled the duvet over her head and tried to go back to sleep. But her mind was too busy to rest. She knew she should really go and help her mum, or at least talk to her. Let her rant some more.

Last night had been such a rage fest she'd thought her mother would lose her voice.

'The deceit! Beca, that's what I can't come to terms with!' This was one of Elin's most uttered lines, along with 'I feel such an incredible fool.' There was a *lot* of anger, and a *lot* of swearing. But strangely there'd been no tears. Nor had her mum tried to stop her dad from leaving. In fact, as shock marriage break-ups went, Beca decided her parents' one was actually quite straightforward. Her dad had calmly explained that he had met a woman at the Language School who'd shown him another dimension to his life, shown him who he really was. He felt he'd been living a lie until now, and that at last he'd discovered his 'true self'.

'What a load of absolute bullshit!' her mother had yelled. And silently Beca had agreed. Her dad never used to talk like a knob, but then, when she came to think of it, he'd started using a lot of wanky phrases over the past few months. That, along with other little things – like wearing Superdry T-shirts and downloading Miley Cyrus. Plus he'd started meditating before work in the morning – strange *Ommmmmm*ing sounds would emanate from the study at an hour too early to process. It should have been a warning sign. Why hadn't they realized? Presumably it was all Fleur's doing – new dad, new man, nama-fucking-ste.

'How old is she?' her mum had demanded.

'Age is an irrelevance, El,' he'd replied, a tad on the patronizing side, Beca thought.

'HOW BLOODY OLD IS SHE???'

'She's thirty-one, okay?'

'No, Greg. No, it is NOT okay. You're the biggest cliché in the book. Literally old enough to be her father.'

'A very young father,' he'd replied petulantly.

There'd been this awful silence then and Beca had tried to creep out of the room. But her mother had yelled at her, too. 'Don't you even THINK about leaving, Beca Matthews. You will stay here and listen to your father state his case for abandoning his wife and child.'

'I'm not really a child, Mum,' Beca had mumbled, only to be ignored.

Her dad had taken a piece of paper from his jeans pocket and placed it on the granite island. 'This is my new address,' he'd said.

Her mum snatched it up and pompously scoffed, 'Thirty-seven B, Greg? Christ, what's this? A return to your student days? Some grotty little flat in Grangetown?'

'It's not grotty, actually. Fleur's made—' And then he'd stopped himself, but too late.

'No, go on,' said her mum, her eyes wild with rage. 'Fleur's made what? Made it all pretty? Aw, *bless*.'

Her dad had stood up then, pulled on his jacket and made for the door. 'I'll call in a couple of days, yeah? Give everything a chance to settle down.'

'No point, Greg. You've made your decision, with no thought to prior discussion . . .' Beca had wondered if her mother ever spoke *without* sounding like a head teacher. 'I will contact a solicitor tomorrow and initiate divorce proceedings.'

Her dad hadn't been expecting that, by the look of things. 'Whoa, hang on, Elin, you're getting way ahead of yourself now!'

And this time, Beca inwardly agreed with *him*.

'Greg, you've met someone else. You've been unfaithful, therefore we have nothing more to say to one another. Please shut the door on your way out. Beca, say goodnight to your father.'

He'd lurched forward then and grabbed her in a soppy dad kind of way. 'Don't worry, baby girl, I'll be in touch, yeah? It's all going to be okay, yeah?'

Beca's face was squashed up against one of the zips on his jacket and she was finding it hard to breathe, the hug was so forceful. But thankfully, he'd eventually pulled away, wiped his eyes – oh God, he was crying! – and then left. *He's never called me 'baby girl' before*, she'd thought.

The whole thing had been completely surreal. Beca had stood still. So had her mum. The only sound in the room was her mother's fast and furious breathing, and the fading engine of her father's car as it sped away from the house. It was then that Beca realized she was still holding half a gingerbread man baked by Grama Grace which she'd started munching in the car. She wasn't sure what else to do, so she finished it off – only the top half was left – stuffing his head into her mouth more out of nervousness than anything else. She must have been in shock. Because why wasn't she crying? Her parents were splitting up!

'I'm making faggots for tea,' her mother had announced, before slamming cupboard doors and banging chopping boards and clanking pans with unnecessary force. It wasn't far off a percussion rehearsal at school orchestra.

'Mum! You *know* I hate faggots – they make me parp!' Beca'd moaned, instantly regretting it.

'Do you really think NOW is an appropriate time to discuss your digestive system?' Elin had demanded, and Beca had muttered a *Sorry*. But then her mother had stopped stock-still mid onion chop and turned to her. 'I'm so sorry, Bec,' she'd said.

Beca hadn't been sure where to look. 'It's not your fault.'

'It is. I should've seen it coming. I've let you down.'

Beca hardly ever saw her mother looking vulnerable, but in that moment she did. It had been made worse by the fact that she was wearing the 'fun' apron Dad had bought her for Christmas. It bore a picture of a koala and the phrase *I can't bear washing up*. So, in a rare act of tenderness, she had reached out to her mum for a hug. Elin had seemed as surprised by the gesture as Beca was, and failed to reciprocate properly. 'I'm fine, don't fuss,' she'd snapped, turning back to her onions. Which were probably the cause of the tears now running down her face.

Presumably the plastic crates were needed to pack the rest of Dad's stuff, a process her mum had begun the night before, after they'd finished eating. 'No point in hanging around!' she'd declared, heading out to the shed and the makeshift gym where her dad had stored his protein powders and multivitamins. Her mum was apparently so eager to dispose of any trace of her dad that Beca wondered if she was glad he'd gone.

16

alys

From the description Kirsty had given of her husband, Douglas, he sounded like he might be a bit of an arse. So for the first few days in her new home, Alys kept expecting him to knock on the cottage door, explaining that his wife's generosity had been misplaced. He would stand there full of apology, saying that sadly Alys needed to move on. But a week had passed and then another and there had been no knock at the door from Douglas. Alys had continued to see Kirsty regularly, both inside and outside of AA meetings, and things between them couldn't have been more genial. Kirsty would frequently call by for coffee and tears, and to work through the Twelve Steps with Alys, her stalwart and very wise sponsor. Alys enjoyed the process – it warmed her heart to feel she was giving something back, helping a fellow alcoholic to stay sober, which in turn helped to keep *her* sober. That was the theory, and one to which Alys could honestly say she adhered.

One principle of the recovery programme that Alys *hadn't* been able to master was that of never borrowing money from anyone. She hadn't yet paid back the cash that Kirsty had lent her and, contrary to what she'd intended, she had continued using the credit card beyond the purchase of a few essentials. Little things at first – a new electric toothbrush, some good-quality face products, a coat she'd seen in the sale of a high-end Brecon boutique, and the impetuous purchase of a brand-new bike. She wasn't sure how she was going to explain that one away, although she *could* say she needed it to cycle to meetings. If there was one thing Alys was good at, it was burying her head in the sand. And in fairness, Kirsty had reassured Alys on several occasions that she did not expect to be repaid.

The non-surgical facelift was probably a step too far. But on seeing herself in the mirror one morning, Alys had decided something had to be done, and that it would be worth the risk. She had two options. One was to use the credit card to buy a ticket to India and visit her surgeon 'friend' for a proper nip and tuck. But the problem with that was that it would mean disappearing abroad for at least three weeks and then she'd never be able to return. Plus, she was really rather enjoying her new home. The second and best option would be to make an appointment at the pricey clinic in Brecon. There, she could get her facial hair re-lasered, her eyebrows microbladed, and have a few new fillers thrown in for good measure. The nice girl on reception said if she paid up front they'd give her a ten per cent discount. What wasn't to love? She booked herself in, and two days later walked out with a new uplifted face and a dent in Kirsty's credit card to the tune of four hundred quid.

That night her conscience got the better of her. Which was a rare occurrence. She calculated that she must've run up a bill of about seventeen hundred pounds by now and surely it wouldn't be long before Kirsty would get her monthly statement. Of course, judging by the way Kirsty talked, she wasn't on the ball with financial matters and didn't concern herself much with credit card bills. But Alys couldn't take the risk. She had to make the effort to pay off *some* of the debt, at least. Especially if she wanted to carry on living in the cottage. And then came the brainwave.

Once a month, an antiques fair came to town, setting up in the comfortable function room of the Black Lion Hotel. When she'd lived in the flat, Alys often spent time wandering round the fair on a winter's afternoon. This was mainly to save on her heating bill, but she also liked admiring the antique jewellery, trying it on and pretending that she could afford it, but she just didn't know if it suited her.

Kirsty's cottage was not only tastefully decorated, it also boasted several classy antiques. Would Kirsty really miss that pair of 1940s onyx table lamps? Or the nineteenth-century porcelain dressing-table chest? A quick check online showed that collectively they could fetch at least a grand.

Luckily, the fair was due in town that very Thursday. Alys put on her smartest clothes, wrapped up the items in two clean towels and headed off to the Black Lion. She didn't rush, wandering round the various stalls, checking out the ones with the most expensive items – those who sold the larger pieces like Queen Anne chairs, rather than the cheaper end of the market selling royal wedding memorial cups, cigarette cards and Whimsies. There was a little coffee-shop area in one corner of the room where Alys sat herself down with a latte and a bun, and spent an hour people-watching. She felt like a cougar in the wild, waiting to pounce. Eventually she spotted her prey: a well-turned-out gentleman in his mid-sixties, wearing shirt, tie and blazer. She waited till he'd completed a sale on a silver cutlery canteen that left him smiling and counting his cash. 'Hello,' she purred. 'I'm Alys. I wonder if you could give me some advice . . .'

She didn't even have to negotiate. His eyes lit up when she revealed her wares and he dived straight in with an offer of eleven hundred pounds. She momentarily toyed with the idea of accepting it, but bravado got the better of her and she announced that she couldn't part with them for anything less than fifteen hundred. She held his gaze as he took a moment to decide, then exhaled and agreed the deal. The items were placed carefully in front of him, the cash put into her bag, and with a kiss on the cheek and a 'Nice doing business with you,' Alys went on her merry way.

*

She was stopped in her tracks ten yards or so outside the hotel when she bumped straight into Kirsty. *Who was en route to the antiques fair!* Alys had to think on her feet, and with some ingenuity managed to persuade Kirsty that she needed to talk, diverting her away from the fair. They settled upon a greasy-spoon café, where Alys came clean about the credit card and her spending spree.

'It's really important to be honest, Kirsty, and there's no point my banging on about that to you if all the time I'm lying myself! So' – she took out the wad of cash – 'I want you to have this. It's not all of the money, but it's a good wedge. And I'll pay back the rest as soon as I can, I promise.'

Kirsty looked at the cash and shook her head. For a moment, Alys thought she was going to say don't bother, but instead she scooped up the money and put it in her bag. 'I'm only taking it because I know it's what you want me to do,' she said.

With great effort, Alys managed to smile and look humble, muttering, 'That's right.' Then she took the biggest risk of all and produced the offending credit card. If she played it right, she might get the outcome she was hoping for. She sighed before diving in. '*This* has been a lifeline for me, Kirsty, but I feel I'm taking advantage.' Looking up into Kirsty's eyes, she attempted to affect solemnity and more humility and pushed the card away from her.

Kirsty looked back and shook her head again. *Oh bollocks*, thought Alys. But then Kirsty pushed the card back at her. 'No, Alys, I want you to keep this for now. You really do need it more than me.'

Bingo.

'Well, if you insist . . .'

They parted company outside the café, Alys watching Kirsty go before turning to unlock her bike.

'Yoo-hoo! ALYS?!' a woman's voice called out from behind her. It was Marcia from the art gallery. 'Well, at last – the Scarlet Pimpernel!' Marcia said, a little out of puff as she approached.

'Sorry?' said Alys, bemused.

'*They seek him here, they seek him there* . . . Oh, never mind. Listen, this came for you,' she said, passing Alys a handwritten envelope. 'A few weeks back now, but I didn't know where to send it, so I've been hoping to catch you on the off-chance—'

Alys had stopped listening.

Her heart was in her mouth.

Even though three decades had passed since seeing it, she recognized the handwriting instantly.

It belonged to her mother.

She grabbed the envelope from Marcia's hand and put it straight into her jacket pocket. 'Mystery lover, is it?' Marcia teased.

And Alys dug deep, put on a smile and said, 'Oh, I expect so, dear. I've got so many!' before rushing off.

When she got back to the cottage, she pulled out the envelope and placed it in the centre of the little pine table in the kitchen. As if it was contaminated. Then, drawing up a chair, she stared at it for what seemed like a decade. Her mother's distinctive looped letters had neatly and clearly marked out the address:

For the sole attention of:
Ms Alys Meredith (artist)
c/o The Arcadia Gallery
Barker Street
Brecon

She turned the envelope over and read the back. The sender's address was written in the top left-hand corner, followed underneath by a short, formal message:

The enclosed is intended for Alys Meredith of Dylan's Quay, formerly Neath. If this is not you, then please disregard and accept my apologies for any inconvenience caused.

Thirty years, she thought. *Thirty bloody years.*

Taking a deep breath, she picked up the envelope and with a small cheese knife carefully eased it open, her hands shaking as she removed the contents. A single page, bearing twenty-seven words in a simple message.

Dearest Alys
On September 2nd I shall turn ninety. More than anything in the world I long to see you again. Won't you come home? Please?
Mum x

She wanted a drink.

She wouldn't have one.

She picked up the note, hardly bearing to touch it, and tore it into four before throwing it in the bin. Then she strode out into the garden and stood there shaking, breathless, staring out at the majesty of the Brecon Beacons beyond and trying to calm herself down. Why was she reacting like this? Surely she should be over the moon to hear from the mother she'd not spoken to in three decades. But a line from a poem she'd learned in school flashed into her mind:

> *To be forgiven pains me more than when*
> *You did forsake and loathe my lonely soul.*

It was true. She deserved her mother's anger, not her love. Grace's anger she could handle; Grace's love she could not.

She stood there, uprooted. Blasted. This unexpected contact with her past, for which she was so unprepared, had knocked her beyond measure.

She marched back indoors and retrieved the note from the bin, carefully piecing it back together on the table. 'Oh Mum,' she whispered. Then she broke down. And wept.

grace and alys

1968–1971

17

grace

On the morning that it happened, she'd spilled his tea and he'd had to change his shirt. He told her not to worry. 'Not the end of the world,' he'd said, attempting a levity that clashed with his character. He was always light-hearted the morning after one of his *special* nights. And she longed for him to return to his usual sombre self. She knew where she was when he was sombre, when he donned the serious mantle of 'man of the house', the bread-winner, the professional. But when he tried to be a 'fun-time' husband, it made her very uncomfortable.

He came back downstairs newly changed and stood behind her at the sink. She stiffened as he pressed his body up against hers, the smell of tea and black pudding on his breath and his sharp little moustache digging into her earlobe like it had the night before. Forcing herself to imagine he was not there, she carried on washing the dishes.

Then he leaned in closer and whispered, 'I know you liked it last night, Gracie.'

She bit her lip, forcing herself to focus on the dishes in the bowl.

'A man can tell when a woman is enjoying herself,' he continued, cupping her right breast and squeezing it, clumsy, grasping. And with as much might as she could muster, she elbowed him in the ribs.

He let out an agonized groan and doubled over, coughing.

'What's going on?' Sixteen-year-old Alys was standing in the doorway, pulling on her school blazer.

Grace said nothing and returned to the washing-up whilst he attempted to turn the cough into a laugh that hid his discomfort. 'Just larking around with your mother, dear. Don't be late, now!' He smiled, playing as he always did the loving dad to his Daddy's girl, heading out into the hallway and surreptitiously rubbing his stomach. She could sense Alys staring at her, awaiting an explanation, as she always did. But none would be forthcoming. There would be no point.

It had been an accomplishment, over the years, to keep his 'pestering' down to a minimum. 'You've got your child, I've done my duty. Now leave me alone,' she'd told him just after Alys was born. She had never spoken back to him like that before, so he'd presumed it was just the 'baby blues' and that soon she'd be 'back in working order'. He did indeed leave her alone for a while, but then began pestering again. At first she'd use the predictable excuse of a headache or her 'monthly'. Then she'd simply say she didn't want to. He'd nod and attempt gentle persuasion, reaching for her hand and telling her she would enjoy it once she 'got going'. Still she'd refuse. He'd become impatient then, saying that it was their Christian duty to bear children, and that one was not enough.

'Oh, that's nice!' she'd retorted. 'Why don't you call Alys in here now and tell her that? *Sorry, bach, but you're not enough!*'

He'd tried to quieten her, reiterating that he was merely pointing out their obligation to prosper.

'To breed, you mean. What am I now, some Friesian cow getting ready to calf?'

Disgust flashed in his eyes when she said this and he stormed off, calling her 'an ungodly bitch'. He must've gone to his mother-in-law – his biggest fan and ally – to complain: she'd supplied him with faulty goods, after all. Because shortly afterwards Grace's mother took her to one side, telling her to 'Pull yourself together and fulfil your husband's needs.' When Grace had innocently asked, 'What about my needs, though?' her mother told her not to be vulgar. 'There's hundreds of women'd give their right arm for what you've got, my girl. A headmaster's wife? Lovely house? Healthy child? You owe that man everything. And don't you forget it.'

Soon after that, he began seeking her out again. Usually after a visit to his 'gentleman's club' in Swansea, a place he went to once a month with the local chief constable and a Justice of the Peace. She'd heard there were 'dancing girls' there, and she secretly hoped there were, and that they'd do more than just dance, alleviating the frustration he'd otherwise take out on her at home.

On the night of the Queen's Coronation, there'd been a party in the street and day-long celebrations that had gone on around the clock. Alys was still a toddler then and Grace had taken her home to bed, exhausted and exhilarated. It was past midnight when he climbed in next to Grace, his breath sour with whisky and tobacco, even though he claimed to neither drink nor smoke. He whispered her name. 'Grace. Gracie?' She lay there unmoving, hardly breathing, hoping her being out for the count would put him off. But then the pawing began, his hand sliding underconfidently between her legs as if searching for lost cash down the side of the couch. He pressed himself into her back and she could feel him, hard now and desperate.

'No,' she said quietly and pushed his hand away.

'Come on, eh? Do it for Her Majesty the Queen!'

She sat up, pushing him away in the process and reaching for the bedside lamp. 'I said no!' she repeated. And his face flushed with sudden anger.

'You took a vow on our wedding day to obey me,' he hissed, 'and obey me you *will*.' He tried to slap her, but the whisky had the better of him and he missed. She wanted to laugh then, to mock his feeble attempt at asserting his authority. But she knew that even the most docile of dogs had teeth. And she might not be so lucky next time. It was easier for her to agree to his demand, knowing that the whole thing would be over in minutes, his inexperience in bed a godsend.

She closed her eyes and her mind against his grunting, heaving body, which quickly reached its destination before rolling off to sleep.

He tried again the following week and she told him she would allow him his 'marital privileges' just once a month. He seemed content with that. And for her it meant a quieter life. *Grit your teeth, lie back and think of Wales.*

When PC Cogbill came to break the news, she fainted on the spot. *Understandable*, they'd say later – *the grief-stricken young woman, a widow at the tender age of thirty-five.*

But Grace knew that when she'd fainted, she'd fainted with relief.
Not grief.
And only Grace knew that at last she was free.

18

alys

If she hadn't made the effort, there'd have been no obituary in the *Western Mail*. Mrs Joyce from across the road told her she should get on and write one because 'Your mam isn't up to much at the moment, bach. She's in shock, see?' Well, they were all in shock, weren't they? But that was no excuse not to honour him. Not to do things properly. Like *he* would have done. Mrs Joyce had been a godsend, in all fairness. There wasn't a lot Alys could remember from the day itself, but she did remember Mrs Joyce bringing them cawl cennin and freshly baked bread. They'd sat in silence, she and her mother, whilst Mrs Joyce fussed and buttered around them.

'Right you are,' she'd chirped, drying her hands on a tea towel. 'I'll leave you in peace now then, is it? Let you gather your thoughts.'

Grace had remained silent, but Alys had managed a feeble thank-you and a smile, watching their helpful neighbour put on her coat and leave. She shut the front door respectfully behind her, having already closed the curtains for them in the parlour and the bedroom upstairs. All in the name of *parchus*, respect for the dead. *The Welsh are so good at death*, Alys thought. And then started crying again.

It had only been three days since it had happened: three days since her father had been up on the school stage, taking his weekly assembly, gripping the lectern so hard with both hands that his knuckles were white, reading a passage from the Bible in his fire-and-brimstone delivery, followed up by his *moral of the story*. Alys always dreaded the Headmaster's Assembly on Wednesday mornings. How painful she found it, listening to his overpronounced consonants and exaggerated pompous Welsh accent: a voice that he never used at home. She would squirm with embarrassment at the way he dressed, in his Headmaster's robe and mortar board. 'He looks like a giant bat!' Elisabeth Bullimore had said. And Alys had pretended to find this hysterical. Because to the other kids in school she always acted like she didn't care that she was the Headmaster's daughter. She'd laugh along with them, openly mocking his delivery and the way he would sway back and forth when he spoke. But she hated herself for doing it. Because he was her daddy. And she adored him.

He'd been reading a passage from St Matthew's Gospel. She only remembered that because there was a boy in the sixth form, Matthew Evans, who she fancied like mad. So she was always alert to the name *Matthew*. And then suddenly, for no apparent reason – no distraction in the hall, no fainting schoolgirl or misbehaving schoolboy – the Headmaster – Bat Man – her dad – just stopped speaking. He continued to sway for a second or two and then that stopped and time stood still.

Silence descended like a velvet gown over pupils and teachers alike. And then he dropped. Thud. Collapsed on the stage, the heavy black fabric of his robe billowing around him as he fell. For a moment, nobody moved. Then somebody started laughing – she thinks it was Elizabeth, who always made fun of everyone. A lone snigger that would in other circumstances have triggered a ripple of copycatting. But instead there was a rushing and screams and shouts to *Call an ambulance immediately!* and everybody, it seemed, turned to stare at her.

Alys Meredith, Headmaster's daughter.

Alys Meredith, daughter of a dead dad.

After that, it was all a bit hazy. She remembered being offered brandy, but that was back at home, sitting with the Reverend Jenkins and a policeman who she thought was called PC Cogbill. He was nice. And Mrs Joyce was there that day, too. Good old Mrs Joyce. It was she who had given her the brandy. Which was welcoming and warming and flowed down her throat and made her feel safe. She remembered going to bed without eating, sneaking another brandy to take with her, and crying herself to sleep. Her daddy. Her beloved, adored and cherished father. Gone. And she had seen him die – right there in front of her very eyes. The image would appear less frequently as time went on, but it would never leave her. That night, she'd let her mother sit on her bed for a while, attempting to comfort her, holding her hand. But it all felt so forced and disingenuous. Because they both knew, didn't they? The real reason he had died.

A heart attack, yes.

A heart attack brought on by stress.

And what had caused that stress? Not his job – he loved his job.

And not Alys – he adored his only child.

It was his wife. His heartless wife.

The woman who had never shown him any love: she'd killed him in the end. And Alys would never, ever forgive her for it.

'You're being a bit dramatic,' Jackie Protheroe had said the next day as they sat smoking a Regal Kingsize out of her bedroom window. 'Sorry, I know you're grievin' an' all that, but you can't go blaming your mother!'

Downstairs in the best room, Jackie's parents sat drinking tea with Grace and expressing their condolences.

'You didn't see them together,' Alys snapped. 'She was a bitch to him.'

'Don't call her that! It's not right.'

'I'll call her what I bloody well like,' said Alys, inhaling hard on the cigarette, fresh tears running down her already tear-stained cheeks. 'Didn't you see how happy she was when she came to the door? She's glad he's dead, I promise you!'

Jackie thought it best to stay quiet and took her turn on the fag. She didn't really know Alys Meredith that well. She was only there because her parents had made her go with them to pay their respects. *Probably a grief reaction*, she thought.

'I hate her,' Alys whispered, a sob of grief catching in her throat as she stared out of the window at the icy backyard below.

Funny how things fell into place now. How her eyes had finally opened to the tension that had always been there, yet which she had never been able to articulate. Growing up, her mother had never been cruel, never raised her voice or her hand. On that front, it was ironically her father who'd been the disciplinarian on the few occasions when she'd misbehaved. No, Alys's mother had been an exemplary parent in so many ways – encouraging her with her music and schoolwork, always ensuring she was fed and watered, dressed smartly, kept clean. And there had been physical affection, too – cwtches when she was smaller, tucking her in at night with a kiss and a lullaby. In fact, she'd be hard pressed to complain about Grace's performance as a mother: it was her performance as a *wife* that had been so upsetting.

When she was a small child she'd been unaware of a problem. To any outsider they'd have seemed the perfect family. It was only when Alys looked back that she realized that she'd never once witnessed her mother show her father any affection. Not a holding of a hand, not a peck on the cheek, rarely even a smile. Yes, her mother was a courteous and efficient home-maker, the evening meal was never missed, clothes were always laundered and pressed and the house was always clean. But in the middle of it all was this huge, gaping hole. Where *love* should have lived.

What made it more heartbreaking to Alys was that her father seemed to feel differently – she would often see him reach for her mother's hand, or look to her with affection; he'd call her 'cariad' and 'sweetheart' and desperately seek her approval. She remembered the day when he'd bought a new suit from Thomas and Moore. 'What d'you think, Gracie?' he'd asked eagerly – the label was still pinned to the cuff and the sleeves were a little on the long side. Her mother, barely glancing in his direction, had muttered, 'It's fine.' Alys, aged eight then, had been doing a jigsaw by the fireplace and watched as his shoulders slumped. And she realized this was another rejection. In that moment, she understood the meaning of the word 'unrequited'. Acutely aware of her father's hurt feelings, she'd jumped in to compensate with a compliment. 'I think you look really smart, Daddy! Like a posh prince or something.' And he'd kissed her on the top of her head and said, 'Well, thank you, kind lady!' He'd tickled her then and she'd laughed and the rebuff from her mother had been forgotten. Until the next time. And the next. A whole catalogue of minor diminishments that added up over the years. Sometimes she'd hear a muffled argument at night – never distinguishing any words, just processing the tones: his – pleading and needy, hers – cold and harsh.

*

On the morning it happened, she'd gone into the kitchen and seen more than she should. Her father, once again attempting affection, had been embracing her mother as she stood at the sink. Suddenly her mother had jabbed him hard in the ribs with her elbow. He bent over, groaning in pain and coughing. Alys had just watched from the doorway for a heart-stopping few moments. Afraid to admit what she'd seen, unable to bear his humiliation or the fact that she'd witnessed such physicality from her mother, such *abuse*, as she'd come to understand it with hindsight, she'd asked what was going on, trying to make it sound like an innocent question. He'd come up with some excuse – *larking around*, he'd called it – but her mother stayed turned away at the sink, showing nothing: no remorse. For all the world as if she wasn't there.

And within two hours he was dead. The heart that had yearned to be loved could take the rejection no more and had simply given up.

When composing the obituary, she'd wanted to write *devoted husband of Grace, who gave him nothing in return*, but of course she couldn't do that. It wouldn't be *proper*. And it wouldn't be fair on him. To tell the world of his loveless marriage.

The funeral was two days away now. How she was going to live without him, she really did not know.

19

grace

Why black? Grace had thought as she stood on the hard, unforgiving ground around his grave, watching as his coffin was lowered in with ropes held by burly men. *Why do we have to wear black?* The gathered mourners, like oversized crows, were poised awkwardly amongst the other graves, the older headstones covered in lichen and moss, the newer ones bright, even flamboyant in comparison.

She couldn't feel her toes, despite the sturdy boots she wore, and her fingertips, like tiny cubes of ice, could not be thawed by gloves. The February wind showed no mercy, echoing the grim intoning of Reverend Jenkins's voice as he told everyone that *I am the Resurrection and the Life.* She wanted it to be over so much. For the earth to cover him up in a final blanketing and to let him rest in peace. Yes, she *did* want him to rest in peace, this was not disputed. His dying had softened her heart towards him now. He had thought that in marrying her he would somehow find contentment, that he could make her love him back. And had he known what he was agreeing to, he perhaps would not have gone ahead. So with his death had come forgiveness. And understanding. It hadn't been his fault, after all. He wasn't a bad person, just naive. And in dying he had given her the best gift. The gift of liberty.

Alys was standing next to her now, shaking from the cold and the heartbreak, her sobs audible and unashamed. They threw soil on to the coffin lid, covering the brass plate on which his name was inscribed, along with the years he'd inhabited this world. Reverend Jenkins led an incantation of the Lord's Prayer, as the wind gently howled around them and the slate-grey clouds threatened a deluge.

> *'Our Father, who art in Heaven,*
> *Hallowed be thy name . . .'*

And that's when she saw him.

John.

Standing apart from the other mourners, in a dark, smart suit and black tie, an armband for respect, his face partially shaded by his trilby as he looked down at his Order of Service. It couldn't be, could it? Maybe her mind was playing tricks on her. She hadn't eaten much over the past few days, after all, nor slept. She blinked to clear her vision, but still he was standing there.

> *'Give us this day our daily bread . . .'*

'And forgive us our trespasses,' she said, along with everyone else, aware that those around her had their eyes closed in prayer. She kept hers firmly open, fixed upon him, until he looked up. She reddened, her face thrill-flushed. The gaze they shared lasted what felt like an age before he nodded. She wanted so desperately to smile back at him, her heart pounding so hard she thought it would propel her off the icy funereal ground and elevate her above them all as she flew into the granite sky. Fighting to keep her composure, she bowed her head and willed Reverend Jenkins to hurry up and bring things to a close.

There was tea and sandwiches served up in the chapel hall afterwards. Mrs Joyce and her helpers from Merched y Wawr were at the helm, refreshing cups and bustling about, a strangely calming force in an otherwise awkward atmosphere, full of solemnity and reverence. The mourners were mostly men, colleagues from school, fellow worshippers from chapel, a few distant cousins in attendance out of duty. Grace scoured the faces, looking for *his*, and panicked in case she saw him. What would she say? How could they speak openly? How could she do what she really wanted to do – hug him and look at him close up and ask him where he'd been all these years and other far more important, private questions. She would need to be prepared for a possible fleeting encounter. She would need to write him a note. And pray that the opportunity arose to pass it to him.

Excusing herself, she headed to the WC, swiping a pencil and hymn book from the Sunday School corner. Safely hidden away in the cubicle, she'd had to think fast: meeting in Neath itself was too risky. If she were seen, especially in mourning, all hell would be let loose. And even though she didn't care any more about living in hell, there was no reason to cause upset unnecessarily.

'Are you all right in there, Mrs Meredith?' It sounded like Mrs Edmunds, one of her neighbours, checking on her, expecting no doubt that she'd taken herself off for a private weep.

'Yes!' she shouted back, a little too enthusiastically. 'Just getting myself together.'

'Well, we're all here for you, dear, you know that.'

'Thank you.'

She waited for the door to shut and then began scribbling: *Aberavon Promenade, Thursday 2 p.m.*

Her pulse racing, she folded the note and placed it in the pocket of her skirt before heading back into the hall, heavy with propriety and solemn chat.

Twenty minutes later, she was stuck with Marjorie Bowers, Head of French at the school. Marjorie had been wittering on – 'Your husband was an inspiration to us all, Mrs Meredith' – and Grace was trying to look interested, all the time glancing over her shoulder for the only face she wanted to see. Had he left already? Surely not. Why would he turn up like that, after so much time, so much silence, and not say a word?

'Sorry to interrupt.'

Grace turned around and there he was. Inches away from her. And with all her might she forced herself to show nothing on her face other than mild, courteous appreciation of his condolences, in keeping with the behaviour of a young widow.

'John! How very kind of you to come,' she said. And shook his hand, pressing the note into his palm. Mild surprise registered in his eyes as he took it.

'I read the obituary in the *Western Mail*,' he said. 'I'm so very sorry for your loss.'

'Thank you,' she replied, and turned to Marjorie Bowers. 'This is John Jenkins, Marjorie. He's an old family friend. John, this is Marjorie, she was a colleague of Aneurin's.'

The conversation continued, though she knew nothing of what was actually said. All she could think about was the note, and whether he realized her intention and, more importantly, if he would turn up.

He didn't stay more than a few minutes before making his excuses to leave. They said a polite goodbye and she turned away to talk to someone else, terrified that she would melt into a puddle of emotion if she looked at him a moment longer. His presence signified more than anyone in that hall could ever have imagined.

'Who was that man?' asked Alys that evening when they were back at the house.

'Which one? There were a lot of men,' said Grace, knowing exactly who she meant.

'That chap with the hat – John somebody?'

'Oh, just a friend,' she said. 'From the past.'

And she left the room before any more questions came her way.

20

alys

The room was pretty. Alys couldn't deny that. Fresh and whole-some spring sunshine bounced off its walls, which were papered with a pattern of yellow roses. It was on the second floor at the front of the house, and the sash window looked out at the Irish Sea in the distance and the harbour and village below. Much as she wanted to hate it, she couldn't. Her new bedroom was a hundred times brighter and better than her old one in Neath, with its dingy, dark atmosphere that never seemed to brighten even on the sunniest of days.

They'd been in Dylan's Quay a week. But it was only today that she'd begun to unpack her possessions. Maybe because she hadn't wanted to 'move in', or to accept that this was now her home and there was no going back. And maybe because she didn't want to feel disloyal to her beloved father. Barely two months had passed and the pain was as raw as if he had died only yesterday.

She took from a large trunk the framed photograph of the two of them together. Father and daughter at the Coronation street party in 1953. She would've been almost two then, dressed in her Sunday best with ribbons in her long, ringletty hair, one hand held by her daddy, the other waving a Union Jack. It was a captured moment enshrined in glass and silver. A treasured memory.

Made all the more important now that she had lost him. Behind them in the photo was a long trestle table, covered in a smart cloth and laden with goodies. Sitting along the sides was a mixture of adults and children of all ages, wearing paper hats, merrily tucking into the home-made sandwiches and sausage rolls and iced buns. It was a joyous occasion and both she and her father were beaming. The print was in black and white but the ribbons, she was sure, had been a patriotic red, white and blue. She wasn't sure if she could actually remember the day itself or whether she'd looked at the photograph so often she'd created a memory. She'd never really given much thought as to why her mother wasn't in the shot. Maybe she'd taken the photo? Or was she busy filling people's cups with tea?

Always when she thought of her father she felt loved. *You can do anything, Alys, bach, if you just put your mind to it.* She could almost hear him saying it.

'Alys?'

She sighed and gave the photograph pride of place on her dressing table.

'Alys, may I come in?'

It was John, gatecrashing her nostalgia with a jolt. He tentatively opened the door, cumbersomely holding her easel and paints. 'Your mother thought you might like these in your room? Or if you'd prefer we can find a place—'

'Stick it in the corner,' she said, instantly regretting her tone and adding a softer, 'Thanks.'

John smiled at her. She knew he was wary and who could blame him? Alys had hardly treated him well so far. They looked at each other. And the silent awkwardness between them said a thousand words that neither of them could voice. She knew he wanted them to be friends; she also knew they never would be.

'Your mother said you've signed up for sixth form?'

She shrugged.

'I think with time you'll grow to like it here, you know. Dylan's Quay is a lovely place to—'

'Yes, so everyone keeps telling me,' she interrupted. 'Better get on.'

John took the hint and left.

Alys looked outside at the daffodils nodding in the planters at the front of the house. She watched as John's sister came out with a broom and began sweeping the path, smiling to herself as she did so. Christ, everyone in this house was so bloody *jolly* all the time, she thought. She knew they all wanted her to be, too. To join in. They walked on eggshells around her, especially her mother, who she knew was ridden with guilt for taking her away from Neath. How easy would it be for Alys to take that guilt away, to make it all right, to say, 'Well done, Mother, for not letting bereavement define us, for opening a new chapter in our lives!' But why should she? Why should she make things easier? The house might be nice, but she'd give all of it – *all* of it – to have her beloved daddy back. Tears crept into her eyes and she felt her throat tighten, but she wouldn't give in. There'd been enough crying.

Especially back in March, when Grace had broken the news that she was selling up. It had only been a week – a *week* – after the funeral when she had sat Alys down at the dining table and told her she had some news. Alys noticed her mother's hands shaking as she poured them both a cup of tea, spilling the contents of the pot a little as she did so.

'An opportunity has come our way, lovely girl,' said Grace.

Alys showed no curiosity and her mother gingerly continued. 'Some old friends of mine, John and his sister, Cissie—'

'Is John that bloke at the funeral?' Alys interrupted.

'Yes, dear,' Grace answered quickly, and Alys noticed her mother's skin flush at the base of her neck and the colour creep up to her cheeks. 'Anyway, guess what! They want us to move to West Wales and help them run a boarding house! It's called Sŵn-y-Môr. I've seen photographs – I have some here, in fact – and it looks perfect. Just the fresh start we need after—'

'I'm not going,' said Alys, spooning sugar into her cup.

She expected Grace to plead with her, to try to persuade her. But instead her mother stayed silent, sipping her tea, deep in thought. Eventually she said, 'The thing is, bach, you're only sixteen. And I have to make decisions for us both now. I have to decide what's best for us – as a family – and in my mind, moving to Dylan's Quay is the right thing to do.'

'So you're going to force me? Even though *this* is my home? This is the place where Dad is buried—' Her voice trembled when she mentioned his name – her poor father, not yet cold in his grave and already her mother was dancing on it.

'Until you're eighteen,' Grace said quietly, 'you're my legal responsibility.'

Tears started rolling down Alys's cheeks. It all felt so unfair. 'And what about my exams? They start in six weeks! Or did you forget that as well?'

'They have O levels in West Wales, y'know,' said Grace gently, attempting a little smile as she reached for her daughter's hand. Alys let her, and Grace looked into her sad eyes. 'Do you remember when you were little, whenever you didn't want to try something new, at school or whatever, your father used to quote Herbert Spencer?'

Alys nodded. He was always quoting things, her dad. *There is a principle which cannot fail to keep man in everlasting ignorance. This principle is contempt prior to investigation.* She smiled as she remembered him saying it. On so many occasions.

'Please, Alys,' said Grace, kissing her daughter's hand. 'Just give it a chance.'

There was no point in arguing. Though inside, Alys made herself a promise that she would leave for London as soon as she turned eighteen. She nodded, an unenthusiastic assent. And Grace, now encouraged, proceeded to tell her more about Swn-y-Môr, the house that was to be their new home. 'It's Georgian, double-fronted – with *eight* bedrooms, can you believe? You'll have a lovely room on the top floor, and we'll have paying guests, so it will involve a bit of housekeeping, changing beds and making breakfast and so forth—'

'So where will those two live, John and Cicely?'

'Cissie,' corrected Grace. 'Well, they'll be living there too, bach. It's Cissie's house, really. She's a widow, you see, like me. But John moved in to help her when Cissie's husband died . . .' Grace's voice faded away.

'John sounds like a complete hero,' Alys sneered. 'Is he widowed as well?' She watched her mother squirm with awkwardness and look down at the floor.

'Not exactly,' sighed Grace. 'He's . . . he's separated from his wife.'

'How convenient!' said Alys sarcastically, finishing her tea and scraping her chair defiantly as she left the table.

Grace called after her, 'I know it's all a bit quick, but we'll need to start packing up. The movers will be here a week tomorrow.'

And now here she was – in her new bedroom, her new home, and living with strangers. Because even her mother seemed like a stranger to her now. Her whole life had been turned upside down. She felt a shiver as she looked out at the sea beyond. *I'm on my own*, she thought. And turned back to the trunk to continue unpacking.

21

grace

It had felt strange having her name on the advert. Presumptuous, almost. But when the three of them – Grace, John and Cissie – had discussed how Operation Sŵn-y-Môr was going to work, it was decided that Grace would take on the business side of things, whilst John and Cissie stayed very much in the background. The responses had come in thick and fast. She'd expected *some* interest, but not *that* much.

'Everyone wants to live in Dylan's Quay, that's why!' John had told her as he chopped mushrooms for breakfast.

Grace had laughed and buttered herself another piece of toast, made from Cissie's home-made bread. 'I'm going to get so fat living here!' she moaned and John threw a mushroom at her.

'You, Gracie?' he teased. 'Fat? Never!'

Today they were getting ready to paint the attic room, which had finally been cleared out and replastered. It had been transformed from a dark and dusty storage space into a bright and airy bedroom, thanks to newly installed dormer windows and a widened staircase. This was to be the final room to let, and the new lodger, a gentleman called Mr Harman, was due to arrive at the weekend. Grace still could not believe she was here.

The whole process had been an act of pure serendipity: if John hadn't seen that obituary, and if he hadn't come to the funeral, or if she hadn't arranged to meet him – he might never have come up with his exciting proposal and shared it with her that cold afternoon on Aberavon Promenade.

'It's a risk, I know,' he'd said, clutching his cup of coffee brought in a flask by Grace to keep them warm. 'It's been eighteen years, after all, and I'm basing everything on how life *used* to be, and of course I'd understand if your feelings have changed—'

'My feelings have never changed, John,' she'd interrupted firmly.

'I'm so glad,' he'd said, turning to her and smiling the broad smile she'd always remembered.

'To old friends,' she'd replied, raising her coffee cup in a toast.

'And new beginnings,' John had added with a wink.

And sitting back, she'd thought that maybe after life's cruel twists, there was room for its kindnesses, too.

Grace fell in love with the big rambling house straight away. She learned that Cissie's husband had died four years previously, without ever fulfilling his dream of turning Swn-y-Môr into a thriving business, and although John had moved in to support his sister, he was out of his depth when it came to running a boarding house. But Grace's enthusiasm had energized them both. Together they made an impressive team and it wasn't long before the place was ready to receive its first guests.

Optimistically, Grace hoped that in time Alys might be tempted to take on a more formal role in the running of Sŵn-y-Môr, although so far she'd shown no interest in this whatsoever. In fact, Alys had shown no interest in doing *anything* much. Her O-level results had not been great and she'd only managed to scrape a handful of passes. This, predictably, had been *Grace's* fault. Alys had then changed her mind about sixth form and signed up for an art foundation course at the local tech, where she seemed to be very popular, even if she spent more time out socializing than going into college. And the boyfriends she had were numerous and often unsavoury. But if it kept Alys happy then let sleeping dogs lie, thought Grace.

The dogs unfortunately didn't stay sleeping for long. As the months went on, Alys became more and more unruly. Grace wondered how much of it was normal teenager behaviour and how much was the grief she still suffered at the loss of her father. Grace tried to be patient, tried to understand how her daughter might be feeling, but it was getting more and more challenging by the day. Cissie would often break down in tears at the way Alys spoke to her, but apologies were never forthcoming and Grace would watch helplessly as her daughter's heart seemed to close up, common sense and compassion becoming distant strangers.

On several occasions she'd been brought home drunk by men of dubious character, old enough to be her father, and once or twice by a sympathetic, kindly policeman. Grace got nowhere when she tried talking to Alys about her behaviour. And poor John was simply told to piss off and mind his own business. 'Who are you to nose around in my life?' She'd been drunk at the time.

Things became markedly worse after the 'Mr Andrews incident'.

It was the week before Alys's eighteenth birthday. John was away in Porthcawl on a golfing trip and Grace and Cissie decided to go shopping in Aberystwyth, leaving Mr Andrews to look after the house. One of the rooms which Grace rented out to tourists was currently vacant, and Mr Andrews had offered to be on duty should any potential guests come knocking at the door. Mr Andrews was a thirty-something committed bachelor who'd been with them from the start, a mild-mannered accountant from Anglesey, who worked for the local council and wouldn't say boo to a goose. He often offered to look after the house and so Grace thought nothing of it.

They found what they were looking for sooner than they'd expected – a special present for Alys's eighteenth. It had been Cissie's suggestion. 'She's got a lovely singing voice, Grace,' she said as they stood outside Bundock's Music on the high street. 'Might be just the ticket. Give her something to focus on – y'know, a bit of direction. I bet she'll pick it up in a jiffy!' Grace thought the gift idea was inspired. And half an hour later they came out of Bundock's carrying a Spanish guitar in a hard shell case.

They'd planned to hide it in the garden shed till the big day, but when they arrived home, there was music blaring from Alys's bedroom and they were distracted from their plan. 'What a ridiculous racket!' Grace had said and headed upstairs to tell her daughter to turn it down.

The door was unlocked.

Grace walked straight in.

Only to be met by two pairs of eyes: Mr Andrews' – startled; Alys's – unrepentant, as she sat astride the petrified lodger and made no moves to climb off him, just bellowing at her mother to get out.

It was as if she had *wanted* to be caught. Grace later discovered that Alys had also persuaded Mr Andrews to smoke some marijuana and that when they'd been interrupted they were at a crucial point in the whole experience, 'Which you completely ruined, thanks, Mother.'

At dawn the next day, Mr Andrews packed up his room and moved out of Swn-y-Môr. Alys showed no remorse for what she'd done, saying that she was proud of her sexual spirit and would continue to follow her primal instincts as and when they arose.

This for Grace was the final straw, and the patience she had tried so hard to cultivate dissolved in a heated row. 'What more can I do for you, Alys? You have a lovely home, in a lovely place, and I know . . . I know you still miss your father, but—'

'Well, somebody has to. 'Cos Christ knows YOU don't! He wasn't dead a week and you were already jumping into someone else's bed!'

The slap came seemingly from nowhere. Grace's hand stung and she stared at it as if it belonged to a stranger. 'I'm sorry,' she said, unable to look her daughter in the eye. 'I really shouldn't have done that.'

But Alys, infuriatingly, was smiling at her, her cheek red raw. 'It's all right, Mother. I'm surprised you've not done it sooner, to be honest.'

'It's not my fault,' Grace whispered.

'What?'

'It's not my fault your father died!' Her voice louder now. 'I'm sick and tired of you blaming me, Alys.'

'Of course it's your fault!!' Alys was crying now. 'He was desperate for you to love him and you pushed him away time and time again because you loved John!'

'Stop it now, you're getting hysterical,' Grace said, her voice filled with fear.

Alys stared at her mother. 'Don't you realize that I know, Mother? I *know*.'

'What on earth are you talking about?'

Alys marched over to her dressing table, pulled out a drawer and removed a book. Inside it was hidden a letter, which she held up triumphantly. 'I found it. The letter from your mother. The deal she made with Dad. Well, I say 'Dad', but—'

Grace reached out to grab the envelope from Alys's hand. She could see that the letter was indeed from her own mother, recognizing the handwriting instantly. 'Give me that!'

'Temper temper now, Mummy!' Alys sneered as she proceeded to read the contents of the letter, whilst keeping Grace at arm's length.

'*Dear Mr Meredith, blah blah blah – I cannot tell you how grateful I am, that you have come to my daughter's rescue like this. You have saved our family's reputation and your discretion in this matter is appreciated beyond measure. Your marriage to Grace will of course resolve so many of the difficulties she has recently had to endure and I know that her gratitude will know no bounds. She will prove to be a loyal and trusted wife in return for your kindness . . .*'

Grace was rooted to the spot. No longer attempting to grab the letter from Alys's hand. Her passivity in turn took the wind out of Alys's sails. 'It was in amongst his things,' she said sullenly, like a small child caught doing wrong. 'Says it all really, doesn't it? So don't try telling me you loved my father, because the evidence is here.'

'You had no right to read his personal letters.'

Alys ignored her and ploughed on. 'Tell me the truth.'

'Alys, you—'

'John's my real father, isn't he?'

The silence was so loud it filled every crack and crevice of the room.

'What?'

'John got you pregnant and, for whatever reason, abandoned you. And Dad—' She faltered at the mention of his name. 'Dad, I dunno, *defended your honour* – Christ, so archaic – by marrying you. It's so bloody obvious, Mum. Why don't you just admit it?'

'No, Alys—'

'Look, you were young, I get it, I really do! It can't have been easy back then.'

Suddenly Grace was filled with anger. How dare she? How dare this daughter of hers, barely an adult, ignorant of life and its harsh realities, sit in judgement like this? She grabbed Alys by the shoulders and faced her squarely. Unblinking, unflinching, she looked her straight in the eye. 'Your father was Aneurin Meredith, d'you hear me?'

'And you hated him.'

Grace remained silent. Alys remained determined, attempting bravado but not quite pulling it off.

'But *why* would you marry a man you hated?'

'Oh, just stop it, will you?' hissed Grace as she turned away. 'You have absolutely no idea. You *stupid, STUPID* child!'

It was all she could manage and she walked out of the room, leaving her daughter shocked and tearful.

Alys boarded a train for London the day before her birthday. The guitar purchased in Aberystwyth remained in its case, unopened and unplayed. And because it upset Grace to even look at it – the gift that had given her such joy, so full of optimism had she been when she bought it – she asked John to return the unwanted instrument to Bundock's and get a refund.

'But she might come home next week, bach,' said John gently, though he sounded unconvinced.

'No, I don't think we'll see her for a while, John.' And she swallowed down the sob that was catching in her throat.

22

grace

Grace had been in Dylan's Quay for over two years now. When she thought of all that time she would never get back, all those years of living in an unhappy marriage, it made her want to weep. But what would that achieve? *It's the here and now that matters, Gracie.* That's what John would say. And Grace would try to push regret to one side and concentrate on the good stuff. Like the fact that two years after Aneurin's death, the house in Neath had finally been sold.

Which meant she could buy her share of Sŵn-y-Môr and help fund a small extension. John told Grace privately that Cissie in particular would be very glad of the cash: Cissie's husband, Syd, had been a kind man, by all accounts, but where money was concerned he'd been impossible. And his death had left Cissie with several debts. Knowing that the solution to her friend's worries had lain in her hands made Grace feel so pleased. She just wished she could feel the same about Alys. But sadly her only child continued to be a source of worry. The scant correspondence she received – usually via a hastily written postcard – was an indication that Alys was still cross with her and did little more than let Grace know she was still alive. There'd been a few pieces of information – such as mention of the jobs she'd got. And lost. The one in Selfridges had seemed like a good bet, but once the

January sales were over, it was a case of last in, first out, and Alys had been 'let go'.

And then there was the never-ending possibility of a singing career. This last option had appeared promising when she'd auditioned as a backing singer for a band called Silver Edge. Alys had called her mother one day – a rare occurrence in itself.

'I got the gig!' she shouted down the line from London on a cold January morning.

'Sorry?' Grace was confused.

'The job with the band! I'm going on tour!!'

Grace sighed with relief. 'Congratulations, bach! And will you be playing anywhere near Dylan's Quay?'

There was a pause, and Grace, sensing Alys's irritation, immediately regretted the question.

'Are you crazy?' Alys laughed. 'Why would a band like Silver Edge even cross the Severn Bridge?'

That told you, thought Grace, and tried to hide her hurt feelings. 'Yes, of course,' she said. 'Just being daft.' The pips went and Grace hurriedly said, 'I'm really proud of you, Alys!' before realizing her daughter was no longer listening.

Over the next six months, Grace longed to hear news – more than anything, she just wanted reassurance that Alys was safe. There'd been one postcard in April from Germany – all it said was *'Tour going brilliantly, all good, love A.'* But that was it. And now it was June.

'I just wish I had some way of contacting her,' she'd complained to Cissie and John one evening as they sat eating dinner.

'Bit irresponsible of her,' said John. 'The odd phone call wouldn't hurt.'

Grace began clearing the table and noticed Cissie and John exchange a sympathetic look. What a dreadful mother they must think her to be.

*

Two days later, Grace had been returning from her early-morning swim in the sea – a habit she'd found to be both relaxing and invigorating, and which she indulged in all year round, despite the fact that other people thought she was a bit of a fruit cake.

'If it makes you happy,' said John, 'then sod what people think.'

'Gonna join me, then?' Grace had teased.

'What d'you think I am, a fruit cake?'

Grace smiled to herself now, heading up the path. It was promising to be a glorious summer's day and she felt positive and uplifted. So it was a shock to see what she saw: sitting on the front step, mug of tea in hand, in a maxi dress and flip-flops, was Alys.

'They told me you wouldn't be long,' she said with a smile, looking remarkably content.

'Oh my goodness!' exclaimed Grace, delighted. She dropped her things and ran to hug her daughter, who surprisingly hugged her back. 'What on earth are you doing here?'

'Well, that's a nice welcome!' Alys had laughed. 'Shall we go in? I have some beautiful news!'

Grace watched as Alys's face lit up with excitement and optimism and it made her want to cry. She tried smiling back, nodding, fearful of dislodging her daughter's enthusiasm, of saying the wrong thing. But she looked so naive, so young. Nearly nineteen years of age – the same age Grace herself had been. How could life be dealing her the same hand of cards? And before she could stop herself, the words were out of her mouth. 'I think you're making a mistake.'

'What?' Alys looked confused.

Grace sensed a storm brewing and attempted to head it off with gentle reasoning. 'You're too young. Still technically a teenager—'

'Same age as when you had me!'

'I know, but I was married. Will this man, this . . . what did you say his name was?'

'I didn't.'

'Well, will he—'

'What, *make an honest woman of me*? I'd have thought *you*'d understand, Mother. Of all people.'

'Oh, not this—'

'Just because *your* mother forced *you* to get married, you think I should follow suit, is it? In case the neighbours gossip, in case they talk in chapel!'

'I don't go to chapel. You know that,' said Grace. And a horribly uncomfortable silence descended. Grace spoke first.

'All right, so you won't get married, but is he going to support you?'

Alys said nothing, and stared at her ringed toes. The realization struck.

'Are you even . . . still with him, bach?' Grace ventured gently and Alys shook her head.

'He's . . . he's older, you see,' Alys said, still looking down. 'And it only happened the once. He thinks . . . well, he thinks I'm trying to trap him.' She looked so vulnerable in that moment, so defenceless. And Grace, like a lioness, was filled with rage, feeling instantly protective of her young cub. How dare he! How dare that faceless, nameless stranger have his kicks with her beautiful young daughter, then drop her like a hot stone the minute she was in trouble.

Before she could stop herself, the words were out of her mouth. 'I think you should consider your options. You do have options, y'know.'

'An abortion?'

'A termination, yes.' The word seemed kinder somehow.

Alys shook her head, angry tears brimming and threatening to tumble down her cheeks. 'I can't believe you're saying this.' She stood up and began gathering her things.

'Please, Alys, just think it through. How it will ruin—' She corrected herself. 'How it will *affect* your life!'

But it was too late. And Alys was already through the door. Grace followed, pleading with her not to leave.

'Alys, no, don't go like this. I'm sorry. You're right, I shouldn't—'

'Forget it.' Alys carried on walking.

'I want to help you, bach. Please – just let me help you.'

And Alys turned on the doorstep, the June sunshine behind her. 'I don't need your help, Mother. And I don't need you. I'm just sorry for ruining your fucking life.'

She slammed the door behind her, leaving Grace standing in the coolness of the hall. John came out from the kitchen. 'Oh Gracie,' he said. And Grace turned, sobbing, into his arms.

23

alys

January 21st, 1971
London

Mother
The baby you didn't want me to have was born on 5th of
this month, weighing 7lbs 6oz. I have called her Elin

Alys

2022

24

elin

'Come on up, sweetheart. First floor.'

Bad start, no manners these days. *Sweetheart?* And it wouldn't kill her to call her 'Mrs Matthews', would it? Although she was going to need to get used to changing her name. Back to Elin *Meredith*. Dear God! The kids would have to start calling her Miss Meredith. Or should she be a *Mizz* these days? She could feel the stress building up again. Just another obstacle put in her way by Greg's catastrophic behaviour. She swallowed the tears as she climbed the cold stairway.

At the top, she was greeted by a vision of flamboyance in a floaty, floral maxi dress and high-heeled boots. This was Maxine Letterman-Brace: early forties, curvaceous, heavily made-up and sporting a pair of those strange slug-like eyebrows that seemed to be all the rage these days. It was beyond Elin why any self-respecting woman would want to make themselves look like Groucho Marx, but hey-ho.

'Take a seat, my love!'

Elin took an instant dislike to the woman and immediately regretted her choice of legal adviser. But she could hardly turn back now.

She'd found Ms Letterman-Brace half an hour into a forensic internet search for local solicitors who specialized in divorce.

This one had jumped out at her from the screen, promising dedicated one-on-one counselling and personal attention, in addition to the requisite legal advice. *I've been there, so I know exactly what my clients are going through!* said the quote beneath a heavily filtered headshot of Ms Letterman-Brace. Elin suspected a lot of her fees went towards Botox and filler bills. But she'd been particularly drawn in by the fact that, unlike the other solicitors whose details came up in the same search, Maxine's USP was that she was a one-man band and as a result much cheaper than a big law firm. Elin had no idea how much a divorce was going to cost, but presumed choosing a cheaper solicitor would be a good precaution. And so she'd emailed and made the appointment.

'Coffee? Tea? Prosecco?' Maxine winked at her.

'No, I'm fine, thanks.' *Can we just get on with it?* she thought.

They sat opposite each other across a large white table, a blank notepad and pen with a fluffy pink top in Maxine's hand, ready to note down the details of Elin's marriage to date.

'Right, tell me all about it and don't hold back. 'Cos nothing you say will shock me.'

Elin's instincts were screaming at her to leave. This let's-all-be-friends-together approach was a complete anathema to all that Elin stood for – professionalism, respect and quiet discretion. And yet within seconds she found herself pouring out her heart to this total stranger whose confident cleavage rose and fell when she spoke. The tears were instantaneous, and Maxine pushed the box of tissues towards her, whispering, 'It's okay, babe, knock yourself out.'

The anger was the easy bit. Elin lashed out at Greg's selfish, home-wrecking actions, peppering every other sentence with a *How could he do this to me?* or *I had no idea he could be such a shit.*

Maxine interrupted her. 'Tell me,' she said, 'you an only child, babe?'

'Er, yes, but . . .'

'Single-parent upbringing?'

'Also true,' said Elin, irritated now.

'And what about your mum? D'you get on with her?'

'I'm sorry, but I fail to see what this has to do with anything. You're meant to be my solicitor, not my analyst.'

'I know, babe,' said Maxine, unbothered by Elin's tone. 'But I'm very holistic in my approach. Need to see the bigger picture, 'cos it all helps in the long run.'

Elin certainly had no desire to start talking about her mother – the parent that never was. If there'd been a diploma in parenting, or a grading system, Elin's mother would have failed with sinking colours. Still, she wasn't about to reveal this to Maxine Letterman-Brace.

'I see it time and time again, babe. Really strong, independent women, successful in their careers, who fall at the first hurdle when it comes to relationships. And it's all because they've got a crap relationship with their mums—'

'Now hang on a minute—'

'No, let me finish, don't jump straight to being mardy. I did a course, see, called "Accessing the Inner Feminine". It was fascinating stuff. Turns out, if you had a great relationship with your old man then it's likely your career will go well, but similarly if you don't hit it off with your mother then you're likely to suffer relationship breakdowns.'

'Well, first of all that simply isn't true, because I never even knew my father—'

'Oh babe, that's harsh.'

'And secondly, mine and Greg's marriage was hardly a disaster area. We were together for twenty-one years! I wouldn't exactly describe that as falling at the first hurdle.'

'What happened, then – with your dad?'

'Nothing. As I say, I never knew him. Not that this has . . . actually, this is a mistake. I shouldn't have come.'

Elin stood up and made to put her jacket on, but was stopped in her tracks.

'I'm sorry. Really,' said Maxine, holding up her hands in

conciliation. 'It's a default of mine – I take all my cases really seriously and treat all my clients as friends.'

'Well, I don't need any friends,' Elin snapped. 'Especially when I'm paying you by the hour. I just need you to get my divorce through as quickly as possible, with the best financial outcome so that my daughter and I can get on with the rest of our lives. Do you think you can do that?'

The meeting eventually produced a practical result, despite Elin having to hack through the pop-psychology nonsense. Maxine promised to start the ball rolling by sending Greg a letter of intent to seek divorce on the grounds of his infidelity. It was a huge shock for Elin to learn that infidelity was almost impossible to prove.

'Think about it, babe. Unless you're actually *in the room and in the bed* with them, then you can't actually say they've done the biz. But Greg's not disputing the infidelity, so it'll be an easy ride.'

An easy ride, Elin thought. What a joke.

Maxine also explained that financially she'd be okay until Beca turned eighteen, but that after that she may have to prepare herself for selling the house and sharing the profit. Furthermore, Greg might be entitled to a cut of her teaching pension and that spousal maintenance may not come her way, seeing as she was the main breadwinner.

Elin was incredulous. 'Are you seriously telling me that my husband can go and have an affair with a younger woman and I have to pay him for the privilege?'

'I know. It's shit. But the courts don't make a moral judgement on people's behaviour. They just look at the money, stick it all in one pot and split it down the middle.'

When Maxine tells her this, Elin feels a bit faint. The injustice of it all, the utter unfairness.

'You'll need to pay five hundred pounds in the first instance to register the divorce with the courts. But we'll try and get that reimbursed by Greg further down the road.'

'What's the point? He'd only be using my money to pay for it!'
God, how she hated him for doing this to them all.

Maxine arranged another appointment for the following week and engulfed Elin in a suffocating hug before looking her directly in the eye and saying, 'We are going to get you through this, yeah? Team Elin, yeah? This time next year you'll be a brand-new woman, yeah?'

Elin left the office eleven hundred pounds poorer, after paying her court costs and initial solicitor fees. She felt worse than she had done when she'd arrived and her head was pounding. She'd not had a migraine for almost six months and could tell she was in for a humdinger – she knew the pain, starting behind her right eye, boring into the back of her socket, would spread until she could no longer bear the light. She had to get home quickly.

The house was empty. There was no note from Beca – nothing new there, of course. And Greg's presence was very much notice-able by his absence. As she waited for the kettle to boil, she looked around at what had been until a few days ago a perfectly lovely home. She filled a hot-water bottle to put on the back of her neck, swallowed two Migraleve and headed upstairs to bed. Closing the curtains she shut out the light, before lying down and donning an eye mask. The pain in her head was unbearable and compounded by the pain in her soul. She had lost; she was lost. And she begged for sleep to take her prisoner and obliterate her awareness of everything.

25

alys

In an act of masochism, Alys pulled out the letter from Grace, now Sellotaped together and looking even more forlorn than she felt. She ran her thumb along the word *Mum*, a pathetic attempt to seek comfort. The timing of its arrival was nothing short of spooky. Why now? After all this time, and after all these years coping on her own – making it work, hopping from one domestic configuration to the next – why *now* had her mother stepped back into her life? She felt like she was being hypnotized, helpless to resist the pull. *Stop it*, she cajoled herself. It was time to take action.

At first she thought about simply writing back. Surely that was the answer? That way she could put all her feelings down on paper. Everything she'd thought and felt since that fateful day in 1992 when she'd taken it upon herself to single-handedly blow up their relationship. And so she sat down with an A4 notepad she'd found in Kirsty's desk, and began to write.

Except nothing came.

Not a single word.

She had plenty of feelings, yes, plenty of thoughts. But the problem was she couldn't actually articulate them. Thirty years was an embarrassingly long period of separation – where would she begin? Furthermore, did she even *want* to begin?

She put down the pen and made herself a peppermint tea, which she took outside to drink, sitting in the wrought-iron patio chair that overlooked the Beacons. Her life had not been filled with joy, that was true. And at times the gaping hole created by the absence of both her mother and her daughter felt bigger than at others. But essentially, Alys had tootled along fairly calmly, avoiding major dramas when she could, remaining cool and collected. Staying sober had been a must, of course, because staying sober had kept her grounded. And maybe that's what she didn't want to jeopardize.

Dismissing the letter idea, she thought about actually phoning Grace. Although her mother hadn't enclosed her number, a quick Google search of Sŵn-y-Môr gave her the information she needed. The Google search was a mistake, though. It meant seeing photos of Dylan's Quay and the house. And this upset her again. But she rose above it and pressed the number into her phone, careful to prefix the call with 141 so that she could remain anonymous. She thought she would hyperventilate as she waited for the call to connect. It rang once. Twice. And in a flash of fear she ended the call. No. She wasn't ready to speak to her mother. Wasn't even ready to hear her voice on some answer machine.

When in doubt, go to a meeting. That's what she always advised newcomers to AA. And so that's what she did. She cycled down to the town on her new bike, enjoying the balmy summer-evening air. She felt like she was taking control, after having been so spectacularly discombobulated. And as she locked her bike to the railing and said hello to two old-timers, she felt an overwhelming wave of gratitude for her sobriety.

The Thursday-night meeting was a Step meeting. Every week, the Step meeting focused on one of the Twelve Steps of Recovery. She knew them inside out, of course, and tonight was Step Nine:

**Made direct amends to such people wherever possible,
except when to do so would injure them or others.**

It couldn't have been more pertinent to her situation! And it was just what she needed to hear. As they sat around the room, sipping their instant coffees and weak teas, people shared what it was like to face the excruciating pain of saying sorry for something they'd done during their drinking days. Some members admitted that although they'd found it easy to make amends for certain things, for others they could just never see it happening. One man talked of how he'd stolen a thousand pounds from his father's account and had blamed it on his brother. He'd tried on three occasions to come clean and had failed every time. Until yesterday, seven years after the event, when circumstances had aligned to enable him to admit his misdemeanour. He said the relief had been overwhelming and he felt closer to his father now than he'd ever done before. And his brother too, for that matter.

But then there was a woman with ten years' sobriety behind her, who had made amends to virtually every person she felt she'd hurt in her life, except her best friend. During *her* drinking days, she'd slept with the best friend's husband. Twice. And just couldn't bring herself to tell her. 'Thing is, if you look at what Step Nine actually says,' the woman went on, 'you basically shouldn't make amends if you're gonna hurt the person by doing it – that's what it says, isn' it? So I'm just gonna have to live with the guilt, aren' I?' Murmurs of understanding rippled around the room, and before she knew it, Alys found herself speaking.

'My name's Alys and I'm an alcoholic,' she said.

'Hi, Alys,' came the collective reply.

'Erm . . .' She hesitated, unsure of how to start. 'I just want to make amends to you guys, really,' she continued, and a few people muttered in confusion. 'See, I sit here all full of humility, like I'm Mrs Sobriety embodied, like I've done it all, done the Steps, made peace with life. But I'm just a fraud. I've been lying to you all.' Her voice was suddenly hijacked by emotion and she had to fight hard to keep the tears at bay.

'My mother's not dead. She's very much alive and living in

West Wales. I just haven't spoken to her for thirty years, because I'm too ashamed of how I behaved the last time I saw her . . . or my daughter . . . the last time I . . . Sorry.' And she couldn't go on. She stumbled to her feet and made her way outside.

A woman from the meeting followed her out. 'You okay?' she asked.

'Yeah. Yeah – just needed to clear my head.'

'Why don't you come back in?' said the woman gently. 'It might help.'

'No, it's helped already,' said Alys with a sad smile. 'More than you can imagine.'

She clambered on to her bike and began the ride back to the cottage. She could see it all clearly now. And the decision was made. She would not contact Grace. It was for the best. Because returning into her mother's life would cause nothing but pain and chaos. *Except when to do so would injure them or others.* Yes, the best gift she could give her mother was to leave her in peace.

26

beca

They'd done another gig at a pub in Cathays that Tuesday night. And it had gone down a storm. As they waited for Beca's bus outside the castle, Soozi started talking about gigs further afield, even getting an agent, but Beca felt this might be going a bit fast. 'You do realize I'm not even seventeen for another two months,' she said, laughing.

'And?'

'I'm not technically an adult for over a year.'

'So? I'm eighteen. I'll be your chaperone, bird. Easy as.'

Beca smiled. She did love Soozi's optimism. Her determination. She just wasn't sure how realistic her attitude was to life. For now, though, she'd go along with it. They had another booking coming up at a trendy new bar in Pontcanna. 'The bloke says if we goes down well, he'll book us for another six nights straight off the back.'

'Bat.'

'Eh?'

'Straight off the bat. Like in cricket. Not back.'

'Oh, get a life, Mrs Tight-Arse!' Soozi laughed and out of the blue reached out and pinched Beca, then started tickling her.

Beca screeched hysterically, begging her to stop. Soozi *didn't* stop and they fell to the pavement in a heap. 'Get off, you nutter!'

Beca shouted out and a passer-by tutted disapprovingly at them. They stood up and dusted themselves down and Beca felt strangely elated. Soozi's carefree positivity was catching.

As the orange Cardiff bus approached the stop, Beca took a deep breath and said, 'Come to mine tomorrow, if you like. We can rehearse. Two o'clock? I'll text you my address.'

'Tidy!' said Soozi as she watched Beca climb aboard the number 54.

Beca sat in a window seat at the back, and as the bus pulled away Soozi stuck two fingers up at her, laughing. Beca laughed back and returned the gesture.

The next morning, Beca surreptitiously confirmed that her mum was indeed planning to be out all afternoon. She couldn't face the thought of practising with Soozi in her room when her mother was listening downstairs – she'd be bound to say something embarrassing and parentish.

'What time you back?' she'd asked Elin, trying to sound nonchalant.

'I don't know – five-ish? The solicitor's at two and then I've got an appointment with the bank. Oh, and the keepsake woman.'

'Who's the keepsake woman?'

'She's making some little love-spoons for people to take home, for Grama Grace's party.'

'Mum . . .' Beca ventured cautiously. 'Don't you think you ought to cancel the party? Seeing as you and Dad are—'

'Don't be ridiculous!' Elin snapped. 'It's the only thing that's keeping me going right now. And have you any idea how much work I've put into it? Not to mention the financial outlay. The love-spoons alone are costing an arm and a leg. *Plus* I've sent out all the invitations!'

'All right, calm down!' said Beca, completely regretting bringing up the subject.

Entering into any sort of discussion with her mother right now would be dangerous. Soozi was due in half an hour, and Beca didn't want to risk her meeting her mum on their garden path. 'Okay, well, good luck,' she muttered, and watched as Elin picked up her bag and car keys and left the house. She looked really sad. But Beca couldn't deal with that right now.

By two o'clock, she and Soozi were belting out 'I Will Always Love You' – at least, Soozi was belting it out as Beca accompanied her. It was strange hearing the keyboards echoing around the house for a change and not secretly hidden away inside her headphones.

'I still think Dolly's version tops Whitney's,' said Beca.

'Yeah, well, I just did Soozi's version, not Whitney's nor Dolly's, alrigh'?' And she took a big glug of iced water. 'Let's have a break now then, is it? Show me round the manor.'

'It's not a manor,' Beca squirmed.

'It is compared to *my* place. Come on.'

She insisted on a full guided tour, including a peek inside the parental bedroom.

'That's one fuck of a big bed,' Soozi declared, before promptly leaping on to the silk cover and spreading herself out.

'What you DOING?' yelled Beca.

'Just tryin' it for size. Your parents won't be none the wiser.'

'You don't know my mum. I'm goin' downstairs.'

And she left, hoping Soozi would follow her out to the back garden.

A few minutes later, she did. 'Your mother's clothes are all colour-coordinated! Man, that's sick!' Soozi laughed, obviously amused by the whole idea.

'Yeah, well, she likes to be organized.' Although Beca was embarrassed by her mother's obsessive tidiness, she found herself feeling a bit defensive of her.

'What about your old man? Couldn't see any of his clothes in there.'

'You in the habit of looking through wardrobes of people you don't know?'

'I didn't *nick* nothin', if that's what you're thinkin'. Not my style.' Soozi laughed, lighting up a cigarette as she lay on the grass.

Beca watched as Soozi swung her knees to and fro, languid and lazy in the sleepy sun. She was wearing shorts, utterly confident to be baring her legs to the world. Beca compared them with her own pale limbs, which rarely saw the light of day, and was once again consumed with envy and admiration, wishing she could look as good as Soozi.

'So where is he, then? Your dad?'

For a moment, Beca considered lying – *He's working abroad . . . he's in prison . . . he's dead*. But she couldn't find the energy to lie. 'He's left,' she said. 'They're getting divorced.'

Soozi didn't seem bothered. She inhaled deeply on her cigarette and blew smoke rings into the air. An emerald emperor dragonfly hovered above her feet, deciding whether to land. 'Man, look at them wings!' Soozi whispered, half in fear and half in awe. 'All see-through and cobwebby. Like something out of a Disney film, ain't it?'

They watched it in silence for a few seconds.

'I always think,' Beca whispered back, not wanting to disturb the beautiful insect, 'that dragonflies look like a cross between a fairy and a doll's helicopter.'

Suddenly the dragonfly decided to land on Soozi's leg, which made her scream and leap to her feet.

'It won't hurt, you donut!' shouted Beca, grinning. 'They don't *sting*!'

But Soozi wasn't convinced. 'Get it off me!' Beca watched, helplessly laughing as Soozi batted the air in a panic. 'Go on, PISS OFF!' she screeched, though by now the dragonfly was long gone. When she realized the coast was clear, Soozi sank back on to the grass, her fear receding as she caught her breath. Eventually she asked, 'He met someone else, then?'

'Who?'

'Your old man. Is he shaggin' some other bird?'

'She's called Fleur.'

'Ooh, la-di-fuckin'-da.'

'Exactly.'

Soozi laughed. 'Life's a bitch, mate, and then you die.'

'Thank you, O Wise One!' mumbled Beca sarcastically.

Then, without looking up, Soozi reached out, took Beca's hand and began stroking her palm with her thumb. '*My* dad left when I was ten.'

'Harsh,' said Beca, trying not to show her embarrassment at the physical contact between them.

'It was okay. He was a bit of a loser, truth be told, so I liked it bein' just me an' my mum. She was cool, y'know?'

There wasn't a single incident in Beca's life when she had thought of her own mother as *cool*.

'Then when I was fifteen she hooked up with this dude from Bristol. Wanted me to go with them. I did for a while, but I missed the Diff too much.'

'The Diff? Oh yeah, Cardiff, right.'

'Yeah, keep up.'

Beca smiled, realizing she didn't want Soozi to let go of her hand.

'They talks funny in Bristol, know what I'm sayin'? *Oo-ar, oo-ar* . . .'

Beca smiled again, mesmerized.

'So soon as I turned sixteen I came back. Moved into my little palace of a bedsit.'

'That's really young to be livin' on your own,' said Beca.

'Nah.' And as suddenly as she'd taken her hand, Soozi pushed it away, squeezing Beca's knee in an annoying, irritating, sisterly way. 'It's not what happens to you in life, bird. It's how you *reacts* to what happens. I done alrigh', haven' I?'

'Er, yeah,' muttered Beca.

'You'll get over it. Bit of time, that's all you needs. Get used to the new norm. Now' – she sprang to her feet again – 'how's about we try a bit of Gretchen Peters, yeah?'

27

elin

'These are absolutely incredible,' Elin said, as she stood in the local workshop, looking at sixty little love-spoons all individually hand-carved for Grama Grace's celebration. She held one of them in her hand and ran her finger around its edges, admiring the craftsmanship. The stem of each love-spoon comprised an intricately carved daffodil – Grace's favourite flower – intertwined with her name. Then embedded in the bowl of the spoon was *1932*, the year of Grace's birth, and at the spoon's tip, the number *ninety* to denote her age. What was spectacular about these creations was that each one had been carved from a single piece of wood, in keeping with the age-old tradition of love-spoon carving. *There are still beautiful things in the world,* Elin thought. And felt so moved by the work that had gone into them that she feared she might cry in front of the artist. But she dug deep and put on her best head-teacher smile before paying the bill and leaving.

Next was the bank. Her appointment there was slick and efficient – a far cry from Elin's meetings with Maxine Letterman-Brace. She opened a new account in her name only and arranged for her salary to go directly into it, bypassing the joint account she shared with Greg. Elin was damned if she was going to fund his new lifestyle or pay the bills in his Grangetown flat.

The bank manager was a kindly faced chap called Simon. He didn't ask any questions when Elin told him she was going through a 'domestic reconfiguration', but nodded sympathetically and told her he understood. Maybe he, too, was divorced. So many people *were* these days – it just appeared to be the norm to end a marriage after a couple of decades. Nobody seemed to stay together any more. Her own mother and father had only been together for a solitary, whisky-soaked evening in 1970. She'd been the product of a one-night stand. Not the product of a stable relationship, the cherished daughter of two loving parents. And all she knew about her father was that he'd been a married Norwegian who'd never wanted anything to do with her.

She'd been seven years of age when she found out: she'd come home from school one day in tears because Julie-May Codman had teased her for not having a daddy. And in a rare act of motherly protectiveness, Alys had marched round to Julie-May's house and demanded to speak to her mother. She insisted on an apology both from Elin's classmate and her classmate's mother, who Alys berated for not teaching her child the values of kindness and compassion. 'My daughter may be fatherless,' she shouted, 'but she's not a heartless bully like yours has turned out to be! You should be ashamed, bringing your child up like that.' It was one of the few times Elin remembered being proud of her mother and it somehow lessened the pain of the paternity revelation that followed.

Alys had taken her to Ferrari's on the way home from the confrontation for an iced bun and 'the talk'. First, she told her the Facts of Life, explaining where babies came from in a jolly tone that Elin had never heard her use before. She didn't really understand what her mother was saying other than it involved the daddy giving the mummy a seed which grew inside the mummy's tummy for nine months until a baby popped out. Looking back, she presumed that the euphemisms were Alys's attempt to sanitize the sad reality of her situation.

'Your daddy was a man called Kurt,' she said, smiling as if

delivering exciting news. 'And he was a bit older than Mummy. And Mummy met him when she was a singer, touring around Scandinavia.' The smiling continued during the killer blow. 'Sadly, Daddy already had a family so we couldn't go and live with him.' In her head, Elin equated Norwegians with Vikings and imagined her father wearing a brass hat with two big horns sticking out of the top as he handed Alys an apple pip to put in her tummy in order to grow a baby. It was a lot to take in over an iced bun.

Eventually she asked, 'Did he love me?'

And Alys replied brightly, 'Oh, I'm sure he did!'

Elin nodded and took another bite of her bun, and with her mouth full said, 'Will I ever see him?'

She distinctly remembered her mother pausing at that point, the smile wavering. 'I don't think so, darling. He lives very far away. And he's such a busy man. Eat your bun now, there's a good girl.' And that was that.

Years later, she'd managed to persuade Grama Grace to share the scant information *she*'d had from Alys back in the day. And it all amounted to the same thing – this stranger from a foreign land had wanted nothing to do with the daughter he'd never met or the woman he'd impregnated on a one-night stand.

And so all through school Elin just had to accept that she was different. That everyone else in her class had two parents and most of them would stay married till death did them part. Just not hers. And although she would wonder about her father from time to time – mainly whether he was still alive – her inherent sense of self-preservation taught her to just accept the status quo. Because if she didn't accept it, if she kept alive some sort of quest to find him, then it would be like continuously picking at a scab. And she'd never feel at peace. Her birth certificate stated 'father unknown', and strangely this definition was reassuring. The door was firmly closed.

Greg knew the score, of course. She'd always been up front with him about her family history. When they'd first met, he'd asked her about it more. But he, too, soon learned to accept things as they were. He couldn't help her find her father. Nobody could. So the best and only thing she could do was accept the situation. 'It's like kids who are the product of a sperm donor,' Greg had said gently. 'It's only in recent times they can find out who the donor was. You're in the same boat as them, I guess. And it doesn't make you *less than*. It makes you *more than*, if anything. You're a woman of mystery.' He was trying to be kind. She knew that. And that was enough for her.

Funny to think of Greg being kind, of a time when she was his whole world, and he was hers. But that was then. And this was now. She and Greg were no more.

And as if she needed reminding of this fact, the next port of call was the solicitor's. Already the bill was growing and Elin was beginning to feel out of control, which was not a place she enjoyed inhabiting. So she went there specifically intending to put boundaries in place with Maxine Letterman-Brace – to tell her that this divorce needed to be quick, clear and efficient; that she couldn't waste any more time faffing around with pop psychology or this holistic approach that Maxine kept banging on about – a privilege for which Elin was paying by the hour! And yet once again, she found herself giving airtime to Maxine's off-the-wall ideas.

'Trust me, you have *got* to meet Lolly,' Maxine said, her eyes lighting up.

'Trust me, I *don't*.'

She didn't know how Maxine did it – how she managed to charm Elin every time and make her come away having agreed to some silly plan that had nothing to do with legalities or the usual procedures associated with a divorce.

'I know I'm unorthodox,' Maxine said gently, 'but you have to believe I *will* get results.'

She'd gone on to tell Elin about this friend of hers called Lolly, who was, according to Maxine, *the embodiment of a powerful female*. 'She's been through it *all*, babe!'

'Please don't call me "babe",' Elin muttered, only to be ignored.

'I get her to talk to all my clients – the girls and the boys. She'll put some fire in your soul, find the warrior woman inside you.'

'Oh, will you *please* stop this nonsense or I swear I will go elsewhere.'

'Your call, Elin,' said Maxine. 'But it would be such a waste of money to have got this far just for you to go with a different brief. And think of all the recapping you'd have to do! Come on, we're nearly there.'

'Well, that's a lie, to begin with,' said Elin, though she realized that Maxine had a point – she'd come too far to start again.

'All I'm saying is just *meet* Lolly, just hear what she has to say, and I promise you, if you don't get anything from it, then fine. No obligations on either side. She can't see you for at least a fortnight anyway, hun, she's going on a Wild Woman retreat. Building campfires in the nude. That kind of thing.'

Elin thought the woman sounded dreadful but she agreed. Partly because she'd lost the energy to dig her heels in any more and partly because, despite her better judgement, she was actually intrigued by this Lolly woman. Elin said she would go for an alcohol-free cocktail with them both at a new bar in the trendy Cardiff suburb of Pontcanna in a couple of weeks' time. Maxine felt alcohol-free was the best way to start the evening. 'And then we can move on somewhere else if things go well!'

'You make it sound like a date,' Elin retorted.

'Well, it *is* a date of sorts,' Maxine beamed. 'A date with your new best friend! 'Cos everyone needs a friend like Lolly.'

Elin wanted to hit her. But she restrained herself and headed for the door.

On the way out, Maxine said, 'Oh, and I nearly forgot, we had an email from Greg. He wanted us to ask you something . . .'

She arrived home earlier than planned and clearly a lot earlier than Beca had expected, because as she walked through the front door, Elin was greeted by the sound of singing, accompanied by keyboards played at full pelt. It wasn't Beca's voice – her daughter could sing, yes, but not like that. The sound was astonishing – full and mellifluous, rich and mesmeric.

Elin made her way upstairs and the singing got louder – it was coming from Beca's room. She tentatively opened the door, and was taken aback by the sight before her: Beca at the keyboard, engrossed in the sheet music, whilst a tall, Black girl she didn't recognize was belting out Carole King's 'Natural Woman', eyes closed and lost in the song. Elin couldn't believe what she was seeing. Or hearing. She stood in the doorway, praying they wouldn't notice her and stop. They didn't, and when the song finished, Elin began clapping.

'Mum!' whined Beca, like a self-conscious five-year-old. 'How long have you been there?'

'That was superb!' said Elin, wiping away a couple of stray tears and continuing to applaud.

'Don't clap!' Beca gulped, blushing to her roots.

'So . . . how . . . I mean what . . . who . . .?' Elin stumbled over her words.

'Alrigh'?' said the stranger, reaching out to shake Elin's hand. 'I'm Suzanne, I am. But I prefer Soozi. Double oh zed i.'

'Lovely to meet you, Soozi – Elin Matthews, Beca's mum. I don't underst—'

'We does gigs together,' Soozi jumped in.

'Gigs?' Elin frowned.

'I was gonna tell you,' mumbled Beca. 'But you've been so caught up in the . . . y'know, all the Dad stuff an' that . . .'

'When you say "gigs",' interrupted Elin, her head-teacher tone slowly creeping into her voice, 'what exactly do you mean?'

'Listen, bird, I gotta go,' said Soozi, leaning in and kissing Beca on the cheek. 'I'll call you, yeah? Nice to meet you, Mrs M.'

And she was gone in a whirl.

'Are you cross?' asked Beca once they heard the front door slam.

'Of course not!' said Elin. 'I think it's wonderful.'

'Serious?'

'Yes, of course. Suzanne seems very nice and I'm thrilled you're using your musical skills . . .'

'What's the but?'

'There isn't a but!'

'Yes there is, I can hear it in your voice.'

Elin sighed. 'It's nothing to do with Suzanne—'

'*Soozi*,' Beca corrected.

'Nothing to do with Soozi or your gigs. It's your father. He wants to see you.'

'So?'

'He emailed my solicitor, can you believe? This is what we're reduced to now.' Elin cleared her throat and went on, 'Apparently he wants you to stay over.'

Beca paused. 'Will *she* be there? The woman?'

'I should imagine so, yes.'

'Are you all right with that?' asked Beca nervously.

Elin tried to hide the strain in her voice, attempting to sound unbothered. 'It's not up to me, Beca. It's entirely your decision. He's your father, after all.'

28

grace

Grace was making Welsh-cakes. She found the whole process comforting and therapeutic – the rolling of the dough to a half-inch thickness, the cutting of the rounds and the griddling of them on the baking stone, as her kitchen filled with the delightful aroma of warm butter, currants and spice. Certainly this morning Grace needed some Welsh-cake therapy as she mulled over Elin's situation.

Had she been surprised when she heard? Had she seen it coming? Certainly she knew things were a bit bumpy between Elin and Greg – probably had been for some time, although Grace had just put that down to the highs and lows of married life. Nobody's marriage was perfect, after all. But *divorce*? It just seemed so extreme. And an easy way out. Just like consumerism had become dependent on a throw-away culture, marriage seemed to be treated with the same cynicism these days. *It's stopped working, so chuck it away.* Rather than looking for a way to fix it. Surely, though, this was just a knee-jerk reaction on Elin's part?

And then she stopped herself in her tracks: what a hypocrite she was being. Hadn't her view on divorce been completely different where John's estranged wife was concerned? Doreen Cuttle – the woman she'd never met and yet had demonized, the woman who had caused her dear John such grief for decades – unwilling to give him the divorce he'd so desperately wanted, all in the name of a religion she'd followed as and when she felt like it. Divorce had been off limits, but infidelity and cruelty were fine, it seemed. When Doreen died at the age of seventy-two, Grace was not ashamed to admit that she'd received the news with glee. *Ding Dong! The witch is dead!* she'd said to herself. Fifty-one years Doreen had made John keep his life on hold. And it had taken her death to finally set him free.

It was different with Elin, of course it was. She and Greg had been married nearly twenty years. They'd been happy, for the most part, and they had Beca. Still, when Grace had tried talking to her, tried persuading Elin to slow down and not rush into anything, she'd been snapped at and told that she *didn't understand*.

'He's having an AFFAIR, Grama Grace!' Elin had barked at her down the phone. As if Grace had never heard of the word. 'D'you understand? He loves someone else!'

'I know, cariad, and I understand that that might feel like it's the end of the road, but these things have a way of working themselves out. Lots of marriages withstand adultery and are made all the better for it afterwards.'

'What would *you* know? You were only married for five minutes,' Elin snapped.

'Seventeen years, actually,' said Grace quietly, and Elin immediately apologized. Profusely.

'It's all right, lovely girl. I'd rather you snapped at me than kept it all to yourself.' She made Elin promise to call her every day, just so that she could keep a distant eye on her. Elin had agreed. 'And you know your bed is always made up for you, bach. You can come here any time you like.' She'd said it as a comfort, but it just made Elin start crying again, and she hurriedly ended the call.

Grace's heart ached at the absence of a mother in Elin's life. And no father either. The girl was basically an orphan. Who would look after her when she herself had shuffled off her mortal coil, especially now Greg had gone? Grace planned on being here for a while, but even wild swimming and yoga couldn't make her invincible. And as she turned over the Welsh-cakes on the bakestone, the thought of her little Elin facing the world alone was simply unbearable.

Elin had been nearly four years of age when Grace first met her. Alys, the queen of grudge-bearing, had refused any contact whatsoever and, having no address for her daughter or any means of contact, Grace had been left helpless to resolve the situation. Four whole years that Grace had missed from Elin's little life – all the baby stages, the walking, the talking – she missed out on all of it. It had hurt her hugely and she'd given up hope of ever meeting Elin or seeing Alys again.

But then one Christmas Eve, Alys had turned up on the doorstep of Swn-y-Môr, announcing they'd come for a holiday. And it was as if they had never been apart. Alys had the ability to do that, to sweep aside all the elephants in the room and act completely normally. When Grace had tried to discuss the four-year silence, Alys told her it was unhealthy to dwell on the past and with a smile dismissed the whole subject. 'We're here *now*, aren't we?'

That Christmas she'd stayed for three weeks, during which time Grace had doted on her newly found granddaughter. John had commented privately to Grace that Alys seemed to be drinking a lot, but Grace had put it down to the 'Christmas spirit'. She knew deep down that John was right – she just couldn't face confronting Alys about it and risking another rift, another silence lasting years.

After the Christmas visit, things seemed to be on a better footing. There wasn't a lot of contact, but there was more than there ever had been and Grace treasured every phone call, every postcard and certainly every visit, one of the most memorable being in 1977, when Alys brought Elin to Dylan's Quay for the Silver Jubilee celebrations. That had been a happy time. But had Grace known then what was around the corner in little Elin's life, she'd have held on to her and not let her out of her sight . . . *Oh Alys*, she thought, stifling a sob and trying not to worry about the as-yet-unanswered note she'd sent to the Brecon gallery and whether it had even reached her elusive daughter.

The two dozen freshly made Welsh-cakes were cooling now on the wire rack and Grace prepared to head up to Cadwallader House to see John, and to take Cissie some home-brewed tonic. A week previously, Cissie had taken to her bed. 'They think it's a mild virus of some kind,' the manager had said when Grace arrived the next morning, 'but it seems to have knocked her for six. And don't worry, it's not Covid!' Despite warnings that Grace herself might be in danger of catching it, she'd taken up her post next to Cissie's bed for three or four hours a day, reading to her, singing, even pointlessly calling out crossword clues. Anything to keep her spirits up. And that's where she would go this afternoon.

Grace always wanted to find the positive and as she and John strolled around the Cadwallader House gardens together, she shared with him that she thought Cissie seemed a little better today.

'I told you,' said John. 'We've got good genes in our family, see?'

Grace smiled, holding his hand tighter. He stopped to check his roses, inhaling their sweet scent, and without looking at her said, 'So, any news?'

'No. Nothing.' Grace didn't need to ask him what he was referring to. When she'd confessed a few weeks previously that she'd ignored his advice and sent Alys's letter anyway, he'd just shrugged and said he always knew she would. 'Still think it's a bad idea, Gracie.'

And she was beginning to realize he was right. Every morning since posting it, her heart had been in her mouth as she went to

*

check the mail. But as the weeks had drawn on, her anticipation had turned slowly into despondency and she'd begun to accept that *that* particular Alys Meredith in Brecon was not *her* Alys Meredith, or that it *was,* and Alys simply wanted nothing to do with her. Grace had toyed with the idea of going to Brecon herself, in case the latter was true. Maybe she could track her down somehow – Brecon wasn't such a big place, after all, and a face-to-face encounter would be far more productive than a letter. But John had persuaded her against that idea. Secretly, she wished she'd never told him about sending it: she couldn't bear the pity in his eyes every time he asked her, 'Any news, bach?' And she'd begun berating herself for being a silly old woman with daft ideas. 'Just accept it, Grace,' she'd mutter to herself. 'You've lost her. And that's that.'

'They're going to do blood tests, by the way,' John said casually as they continued their stroll. 'On Cissie. They just want to rule a few things out, y'know.'

'Like what?'

'Don't ask me, I'm not a doctor!' he said, smiling, though she recognized an edge of worry in his voice. 'The usual stuff, I suppose,' he added. 'It's what they always do, isn't it?'

Grace sensed there was no point in asking him any more questions. One thing she'd learned over the years was not to pursue things when he seemed anxious. In all the time she'd known him, they'd never had a cross word. But when he was worried about something, she knew it was best to leave him in peace with his thoughts whilst he worked things out for himself. Grace also knew that worrying about the unknown was utterly pointless.

'Cup of tea and a Welsh-cake, then?' she asked, taking his arm as they headed back indoors.

29

beca

There was something disarming about Fleur. And not in a good way. It was Fleur who'd opened the door to the second-floor two-bedroom flat in Grangetown that was now Beca's dad's home.

'Oh,' said Beca, thinking for a moment that she might have rung the wrong bell.

'Rebecca?' whispered Fleur nervously.

'Beca, actually.' Not a great start.

'Oh my God, it's so good to finally meet you!' And she leaned forward, enveloping Beca in a cloud of lavender oil and a hug that was too tight and definitely premature. She looked older than her thirty-one years, Beca thought. But then maybe that was just the clothes she was wearing – a sort of hippy kaftan floaty top over leggings and espadrilles. She was quite pretty, no make-up, with a mass of black corkscrew curls and a nose piercing. When she smiled, Beca noticed that her teeth were quite gappy, which reminded her of Mrs Ellis, her Geography teacher.

Disengaging from the hug, Fleur grabbed Beca's hands and stared at her, eyes brimming with tears. 'I can't believe you came,' she said, shaking her curls to emphasize the point.

The silence and the staring were too much and Beca pulled away. 'Where's my dad?'

'You're angry. That's understandable.'

'Er, no,' replied Beca, confused. 'I just wanna see my dad.'

'Baby girl!' Greg's voice from the stairwell beneath came right on cue.

Despite feeling instantly irritated by this infuriating new moniker, Beca managed a smile and let him lunge forward for a hug. He dropped the shopping in the process and, just like Fleur, held her too tight. Though at least he had licence to – being her dad an' all that. Fleur's hug had been bad enough, but when she reached out and encircled Beca and Greg's embrace, mumbling 'Group hug, *family* hug!' Beca completely regretted coming. They stayed like that for what seemed an eternity, until Beca finally found the courage to break free, using the excuse that she needed the loo.

The flat was tired and shabby, infused with a staleness that someone – Fleur, she presumed – had tried to disguise with the infernal lavender oil, burning away in a little china dish on a bookshelf. There was a definite attempt at 'homely' – Indian throws over the sofa and cheery cushions on the two dining chairs. Had her father really changed that much? The place really wasn't him. She noticed the fridge was decorated with magnets bearing epigrams and natty sayings such as *To Love Yourself is to Love the World*. In the living room, apart from the sofa there was a bean bag, into which Beca sank, glad of the separation it afforded.

They sat for a while in excruciating silence, Fleur desperately smiling – as if by doing so she could enforce a happy ambience. Beca willed her father's girlfriend to leave her and her dad in peace, and as if reading her mind Greg hinted, 'D'you want me to check on the supper, Fleur, or . . . ?'

'No, no, I'll see to everything. You two will want to catch up.' And thankfully, at last, she headed to the tiny kitchenette only a couple of metres away, making her presence felt as she clanked around.

*

Left to themselves, the silence became even more palpable. Until eventually Greg gave a little cough and said, 'Thank you so much for coming, baby girl.'

'Dad,' she snapped, 'please stop calling me that.'

'Sorry.'

More silence.

'So how was your day?'

'Good, thanks.'

'How's your job?'

'Oh look, Dad, everything's fine, okay? So stop asking me. I only came here today because you wanted me to. The whole thing is nuts. I mean, what are you *doing*? Have you lost it or something, 'cos this – *this*' – she gestured around the sad and soulless room – 'this is mental. And who is *she*? Where did you meet *her*?'

'I know it must be really difficult for you to get your head round, but sometimes grown-ups stop loving each other like they did and—'

'*Grown-ups*? Dad, I'm not eight! Why you talkin' to me like that?!'

Just then, Fleur popped her head round the doorway. 'It's a vegan bake, by the way. I hope you're okay with that?'

'That'll be lovely, angel.' Greg answered for them both and he signalled to Fleur to leave them alone for a bit longer. She disappeared back into the kitchenette. 'We're saving money with the vegan thing,' he apologized.

Beca rolled her eyes and more awkward silence ensued.

'We need to talk about your mum, Bec. She won't speak to me and—'

'Do you blame her?' snapped Beca.

'Of course not, but this divorce lawyer she's using, the demands she's making are crazy, and all I'm asking is—'

'Sorry, I can't do this,' said Beca quietly. She tried pulling herself up from the bean bag, but it was easier said than done and she ended up having to roll on to her knees before clambering to her feet, which just made her look a bit silly, especially when she had to brush herself down afterwards.

'You can't go!' said Greg desperately.

'I should never have come in the first place.'

Once again, Fleur came bustling out of the kitchenette holding a grater and a packet of vegan cheese. 'What's going on?' she mewled, though the answer was obvious.

Beca picked up her bag and jacket and headed for the door. 'You're obviously having some sort of breakdown, Dad.'

'Hey now, come on!'

'He's never been happier!' interrupted Fleur, and Beca noticed that a piece of spinach had become wedged between her front teeth.

'Just come home, for God's sake,' Beca sighed. And she left without waiting for a response, running down the two flights of stairs and out on to the street before her father had the chance to catch up with her.

She walked along the Taff Embankment towards the city centre. It was a warm evening with a cloudless sky, and music drifted out of open windows, mingling with the aroma of yeast and hops from the Brains Brewery nearby. People were sitting on doorsteps and front walls, drinking, chatting, smoking, enjoying the ease of the city summertime. Home was a half-hour bus ride away. But she wasn't ready to go there yet. The thought of her mother waiting with bated breath to hear every shred of news about her dad and Fleur – *What is she like? What's the flat like? What are THEY like together?* – was unbearable, but she could at least put the interrogation off for a couple of hours.

She headed over the bridge and into Steeple Street, in the direction of the bus station. Soozi's bedsit was number ninety-nine. The address had stuck in Beca's mind because it had led on to a silly conversation about ice-cream and why shoving a chocolate flake into a scoop of vanilla transformed it into a 'ninety-nine'.

At the turning into Sophia Close and the bus station, Beca

hesitated, her stomach turning cartwheels for some unknown reason. She carried on walking, past the Victorian terraces that once comprised entire homes, mostly now sectioned off and split up into flats and bedsits or dental practices and doctors' surgeries. Ninety-nine was on the other side of the road. A Transit was parked just in front of her, offering a hiding place from which to get a better view. She peered round the rear of the van and looked up to the first floor.

She heard Soozi before she saw her: the richness of that voice she knew so well now floated out on to the air. Beca froze and dared herself to look closer. Soozi was sitting in the bay window, lost in her own musical world, singing 'Can't Help Lovin' Dat Man of Mine' and infusing every note with her soul.

When the song finished, she heard a male voice shout 'Bravo' and someone started clapping. Was that coming from Soozi's flat? Beca couldn't pull herself away. She watched, mesmerized, as Soozi reached for a bottle of water and drank it down steadily before picking up her mobile. A smile danced on her lips.

The vibrate alert on Beca's phone came as such a shock it made her physically jump. The sound was barely perceptible, but to Beca it was as loud as a foghorn. She grabbed her phone from her back pocket, expecting a message from her dad. But there in bold letters was *her* name: Soozi. Beca was terrified that somehow Soozi knew she was there and was laughing at her. Hands shaking, she opened the text:

What was she like then, bird? The step mum?

Beca felt her pulse race as she dared to reply and watch the message land.

Annoying. Weird. I left after half an hour. What you doin?

She pressed Send, and peered round the van again, watching to see Soozi respond. Her heart was in her mouth – the thrill of watching Soozi from afar, unaware she was being watched as she quickly typed her reply.

On L8 shift @ 7. Just fuckin around till then. U?

'Not planning to steal it, I hope?' A man's voice, gruff but friendly, came hurtling into Beca's world.

'Eh?' Then realizing she was still leaning against the back of the van, she pulled away, mortified. 'Sorry, I was just—'

'Watch yer back,' the van-owner chirped, before yanking open the door and jumping in. Within seconds he'd driven off, leaving Beca exposed. She'd waited too long to reply and Soozi texted again.

Where 2 R U?

Beca stared at the text. *It's one of those moments*, she thought. *Walk away, or take the risk.*

I'm standing across the road from your flat . . .

She watched as Soozi looked up from her phone, scanning the pavement outside. Beca stood stock-still, waiting for Soozi's eyes to find her. They did. A beat. Then –

'BIRD!! YOU SNEAKY FUCKER!' she shouted. And Beca laughed. She'd never known anyone swear as much as Soozi, but somehow it didn't sound offensive. It was always done with such affection. 'COME ON, THEN! WHAT YOU WAITIN' FOR!'

Soozi opened the communal front door and engulfed Beca in a warm hug. 'Well, this *is* a fuckin' treat!' she said. 'Hey, you can meet Parker!'

'Who's Parker?' Beca ventured.

'He's my boy. He's a peach.' And she bounded up the stairs at a lick.

Beca followed, confused. Surely Soozi didn't mean 'boy' as in 'child', did she? So was Parker her boyfriend, then? Is that who she'd heard applauding earlier? God, she'd never even thought! *Soozi could have a boyfriend.*

'Parks? You decent?' Soozi asked as they hovered outside number four.

'When am I anything but?' came the well-spoken reply, and Parker swiftly opened the door. He was in his late seventies, not as old as Grama Grace but certainly much older than Beca's mum. He was carrying a couple of new shirts on hangers, their labels hanging down.

'Christ, you made me jump, you numpty!' laughed Soozi. 'Been on a shopping spree, haven't you, babes?'

'Hi,' said Beca, suddenly shy.

'Parker – Bec; Beca – Park,' Soozi waved the introductions.

'Ah, so this is the great musical genius!' he said as they loitered in the doorway. He held out his hand to Beca.

Beca shook Parker's hand as a burning blush spread into her neck and cheeks.

'Come and meet Bettina sometime.'

He shuffled past them, Soozi depositing a smacker of a kiss on his cheek as he went. 'Toodle-pip! And definitely keep the blue short sleeves.'

'Yeah, bye,' muttered Beca as she watched Parker make his way down the stairs.

'He lives in number one,' explained Soozi.

'Oh! And who's Bettina, then? His wife?'

'No! Bettina is his grand piano. You are gonna love her. Just got no time tonight, but be patient, my friend. Now . . .' Soozi led her into her home.

The room took Beca's breath away. It was so *Soozi*. Two of the walls were fuchsia pink, with a massive painting of a roaring lion taking up the whole of the third.

'Oh my God,' Beca said.

'It's good, innit? All my own work.'

'Seriously?'

But Soozi had disappeared into the bathroom. 'Stick the telly on if you like!' she shouted. 'I'm gonna have a quick shower before work. My pits stink.' And with that Beca heard the hum of the electric shower and Soozi's dulcet tones belting out 'The First Time Ever I Saw Your Face'. Beca smiled – did that girl *ever* stop singing?

Left alone, Beca took in the rest of Soozi's home. She wasn't sure what she'd expected – probably something more chaotic. Certainly not this: a large room with a vast bay window that let the summer evening light flood in. Above a two-seater sofa bedecked with cushions was a bookshelf boasting a selection of novels – mainly crime thrillers. There was a big wicker rocking chair and a small table opposite a kitchenette that contained two old-fashioned but clean units, one bearing a fruit bowl bulging with lemons and peaches and avocado pears. No wonder Soozi's skin was so good, she thought. There was a hob and microwave and a stainless-steel sink, also clean, and pans hanging above it from a ceiling rack. Every inch of useable space was utilized. How different it was from Fleur's sad flat.

She took in the rest of the room. The double bed was perfectly made, covered by a white cotton duvet, hotel-room smooth, boasting four plump pillows that stood impressively to attention. She wondered how Soozi managed to get her sheets so crisp – surely she didn't iron them herself? On top of the bed was a faux-zebra-skin throw that gave the Soozi game away. There was no wardrobe, just two metal clothes rails up against one of the walls, bursting with clothes on hangers – the only hint of chaos in an otherwise tidy and organized room. It may have been compact, but this home was loved and cared for and spoke volumes about its inhabitant. In fact, Beca thought, there was something confidence-instilling about Soozi's nest-making. And once again she wished she could be more like her exquisite friend.

The singing had stopped now and Soozi came back in, wrapped

166

in a big purple towel, dripping water as she walked and clutching a bottle of Nivea. 'I been thinkin',' she said, nonchalantly dropping the towel and beginning the process of moisturizing her skin. Beca turned away, embarrassed. 'Next gig, I reckon we should end with the Bette Midler – more upbeat than the Roberta Flack – don't you?'

'Er, yeah,' said Beca.

'What's up, bird? Never seen naked beauty before?' She laughed, and carried on rubbing the cream into her skin. 'Not that I don't prefer Roberta, if I'm honest. But let's try 'em both next practice sesh, yeah?'

'Sure,' mumbled Beca, her gaze remaining firmly on the traffic outside. She wished that Soozi would just get dressed.

'I was talkin' with Parker just now about us usin' his place. So how you fixed tomorrow after your shift?'

'Er, yeah, sounds cool.'

Silence.

'It's okay, you can look now,' said Soozi, her voice quieter, different.

Beca turned around. Soozi was still naked and standing stock-still.

At first Beca thought she was joking, and, blushing, she made to turn around again. 'Oh, for f—'

'No,' Soozi urged her, clearly *not* joking. 'Look at me.'

Beca couldn't. Her breathing was going at such speed now she thought she might pass out.

'Beca . . .' Soozi rarely used her name and it made the atmosphere more potent.

Finally finding the courage to look up, she gasped at what she saw. And the moment between them was so charged she felt if anyone touched her right now they'd be electrocuted.

Soozi's black skin glistened from the moisturizer, defining the subtle muscle tone of her upper arms and thighs. Her stomach was flat, her belly button pierced – *of course*, thought Beca – and there was definitely a hint of a six-pack. Soozi's breasts were smaller than her own, and the neat line of hair between her legs was immaculately trimmed. Her body was perfect. Perfect. And yet the most striking part of Soozi's attractiveness was the confidence with which she held herself, standing proud and totally at ease in her body.

'See? Wasn't difficult, was it?' she asked Beca gently, before taking steps towards her, holding her gaze the whole time.

Beca was gripped by a mixture of excruciating self-consciousness and overwhelming desire. She wanted to step out of her own clumsy body and be somewhere else, simultaneously wanting to be *nowhere* else on earth.

'Shall we get this bit out of the way, then?' whispered Soozi, reaching out with one hand and touching Beca's cheek, searching her eyes for permission.

'I haven't . . . y'know . . . nothing like this, ever.' Beca could barely get her words out.

'It's okay,' Soozi said. And she put her other hand out and cupped Beca's face, before pressing her lips into Beca's.

At first she didn't know what to do. She shut her eyes, it felt easier that way, and she just followed Soozi's lead. Her mouth, that mouth. The deliciousness of her full and sensuous lips. And she felt sensations she'd never known existed coursing through every capillary, the heat between her legs crying out for something undefinable. She knew nothing except that she was kissing this most wonderful, beautiful creature, and in that tiny microcosm of life, in that infinitesimally small moment, it all made sense: she loved Soozi Cole.

The kiss seemed to last an eternity. And when Soozi elegantly brought it to an end, Beca carried on standing there, eyes closed, mouth still open. She felt like she would never move again.

Soozi rested her forehead on Beca's and sighed. They stood like that for a few seconds before Soozi gently broke the spell, whispering, 'To be continued, yeah?'

Beca nodded and Soozi pulled away from her, shifting gear and returning to practicality mode. Pulling some clean underwear from a drawer, she hurriedly dressed, taking her freshly pressed Bellamy's overall off its hanger and preparing herself for work.

'Okay, so tomorrow at three, yeah? And we'll look through them songs down in Parker's gaff.'

Beca nodded.

'Exciting, isn' it, bird?'

'Yeah,' she managed to say, still in shock from what had just happened.

Now fully dressed, Soozi announced, 'Right. Let's get on. I'll catch the bus with you.'

'Okay.'

At the door, as she locked up, Soozi turned to Beca and said, 'And don't be goin' all weird on me now, bird, okay? Promise?'

'Yeah,' she replied, with a smile so wide she thought her face would crack.

30

elin

Elin was home alone. Again. She'd begun to receive replies to Grace's invitations and was once again looking at her table plan. Her heart sank when she realized there'd be one less on the top table, seeing as Greg had been most definitely *un*invited. But then she wondered whether he could be replaced by Beca's new friend, Soozi. Hmm. Maybe she was rushing ahead of herself. She'd have to sleep on that one. Also, according to her list there were still twenty-five invitees unaccounted for. Honestly, where were people's manners these days? She really shouldn't be kept waiting for a response.

She was just contemplating sending out reminders to people when her phone rang. Grama Grace. Elin felt herself blush, as if Grace had somehow sensed that Elin's illicit party organization was underway. But she'd just called to see how the latest solicitor trip had gone.

'So you're still going ahead with it, then?' she asked.

'Of course,' said Elin. 'I don't understand why you think I shouldn't?'

'I know Greg's behaved badly, bach, I'm not disputing that. I just think you both need to talk. You're throwing the baby out with the bathwater – twenty years of marriage has to count for something.'

'There's no going back,' Elin said firmly before steering the conversation in a different direction. 'Beca's been invited round there for supper. Did I tell you this woman's called Fleur?'

'Several times,' said Grace. 'Oh, bach, I do worry about you . . .'

'How's Cissie?' said Elin, desperate to change the subject. 'Blood results back yet?'

'God, no, they'll be a couple of weeks with the backlog. She's okay, bach. Still frail, but still smiling,' Grace enthused. 'I got her singing today!'

'Must be in the air – your great-granddaughter seems to have turned into something of a performer. She's accompanying a young singer called Soozi. They're ever so good. They've got themselves a few gigs.' Elin shocked herself at how old she sounded when she said the word.

After the call, Elin made a fresh ginger infusion and wandered out into the garden. It was six o'clock and the sun was still belting out its rays. She could hear the soothing sound of a water sprinkler in next door's garden and could just discern the movements of another human being. She called out over the wall, 'Mr Chakrabarti, is that you?'

There was a rustling in the foliage, but she could barely make out a face. 'No, it's me. We met the other week.' It must be the guy charged with tidying up Mrs Latham's old garden. He pulled off one of his gardening gloves and shoved a hand out towards her over the wall. 'I'm Rory,' he said, and she detected an accent.

'Ooh, Australian?' she said.

He gently corrected her, 'No, I'm Kiwi, actually.' He laughed. 'Fush and chups.'

'Sorry?'

'Fush and chups? Fish and chips. It's supposed to be the giveaway phrase. Y'know, the difference between us and the Aussies?'

'Oh. Right.' An awkwardness descended, compounded by the fact that they could barely see each other through the foliage.

'How's it going over there?' she ventured, unexpectedly enjoying a little human contact with someone other than family members or divorce lawyers.

'Truthfully?' he said. 'I'm not enjoying it. Mr C wants everything cut down and cut back. He plans to pave over. It's a crying shame, really, I wish I'd not taken the job.'

'Oh no, that's really sad,' said Elin, beginning to feel daft that she was essentially talking to a human camouflaged in green leaves, bushes and branches. 'Mrs Latham loved that garden.'

'Yeah, you can tell. I guess he just wants an easy life. He seems like a busy guy.'

'Well, good luck,' she said, turning to go. 'Ooh,' a thought struck her. 'Are you thirsty? D'you want a cold drink?'

'Ah yeah, that'd be immense.'

She returned two minutes later with a pint glass full of ice-cold pink lemonade. Unsure as to where she was aiming, she called out to him and thrust it through the hole in the greenery.

His large garden-gloved hand grasped at it. 'Cheers. Mrs Matthews, is it?'

'Er, yes . . . No . . .' she floundered, unsure of what to call herself any more. 'Elin is fine.'

She waited as he downed the lemonade in five big glugs, crushed ice included. When he'd finished, he sighed, replenished, and she could just make out the action of him drying his mouth on the back of his hand before handing the glass back. 'Really kind, thanks, Ellie.'

She was too embarrassed to correct him. 'I'll leave you to it,' she said, taking the glass back.

As she headed inside, she smiled to herself, realizing that she'd never be able to recognize him in the street, or in a line-up, or even if he was staring her right in the face. She'd know that voice, though. And then another thought struck her: she was actually smiling.

When Beca arrived home shortly after, she too was smiling and looking a little bit dazed. Elin launched straight in wanting the

172

low-down on Greg's new place and, more importantly, Fleur. But Beca was in such a daze that it took a few seconds to register what her mother was talking about.

'Who?' she asked.

'Your father's new girlfriend, Beca! What is *wrong* with you? Have you been drinking or something?'

'Oh, *her*!' said Beca. 'Oh, you got nothing to worry about there, Mum. She's a right donut. She's making Dad go vegan, for starters. Well, that's *never* gonna last. Plus she reeks of lavender oil. It's mingin'.'

'Don't say "minging", please, Beca, it's common.' Elin tried to sound annoyed. But it was no good. *Greg? A vegan?* The smug smirk grew into a victorious smile. *How hilarious,* she thought.

31

beca

She woke up smiling, at first not knowing why. And then she remembered. *This is what in love feels like*, she thought.

She wanted to open the windows to her mother's Juliet balcony and tell the world. Instead she had to settle for a stomach full of butterflies and a worry that she would not survive the wait until she could see Soozi again that afternoon. How would she get through the next few hours?

She decided to pack a little rucksack and a change of clothes to take with her to work. It felt like a very 'sensible' thing to be doing and not very spontaneous. But she was hoping Soozi would ask her to stay the night after their rehearsal and she wanted to feel prepared.

Looking through her wardrobe, she found a floaty blue dress she'd hardly ever worn and a pair of diamanté flip-flops. She knew she looked good in the dress, but she'd never really had a reason to impress anyone before. Sticking it all in her rucksack to change into at the pub, she took a deep breath and headed downstairs to face the music. Something inside was telling her to nip things in the bud and tell her mother straight away. About Soozi. She just felt it would save a lot of faffing around and that waiting for the 'right moment' could take an age. She'd already anticipated the dramatics: questions like *Are you sure you're not confused? How long have you thought you were gay? Have you had feelings for any other girls in school?* Blah blah blah. But surely once she'd got through the Spanish Inquisition, things would get easier. Much better than dragging it out.

Her mother was in the garden. 'Mum?' she called out, then realized her mother was talking to someone out on the lawn. Some old surfer-type dude in shorts, wellies and gardening gloves, who was drinking a mug of tea with Elin.

'Bec? Come and meet Rory,' her mum replied.

Bad timing, Beca thought, worried that any delay would cost her her resolve.

'Alrigh'?' she said. 'Mum, can I—'

But Elin was on a roll. 'Rory's going to sort that pear tree out for us,' she said. Beca was hoping her mother would pick up on the fact that she needed to talk, but she was obviously too deep in conversation with Gardener Man. 'It's sadly died and needs chopping down,' Elin said.

'Yeah, your mum said you had a load of pears last year, like more than ever?'

'Dunno, did we?' said Beca, losing the will to live.

'Oh Beca, you *know* we did!' Her mother rolled her eyes at Rory and laughed slightly weirdly, in a way Beca had not seen her laugh before. Except when Alun Wyn Jones, the Welsh rugby captain, had come to the school to give out prizes and she'd gone all coy and giggly on meeting him. That had been *very* disturbing.

'Anyways, that's what happens,' said Rory. 'One final mega harvest, then zap. Dead.'

'Okay, well, I gotta go to work,' said Beca, realizing there was no chance of chatting to her mother that morning.

'What's with the rucksack?' Elin said, just as she was turning to go.

'Oh, I'm staying at Soozi's tonight, okay?'

'Er, yes. I suppose so. Text me her address.'

'Why?'

'So I know where you are!' She did the weird smile again.

'Okay. See you tomorrow. Good luck with the apple tree.'

'Pear!' laughed Elin and turned back to Rory, shaking her head in an affectionate *What's she like?* way.

Oh well. Telling her mother that she was about to pass the momentous milestone of losing her virginity would just have to wait. Probably a good thing. She didn't want to jinx it, after all.

When her shift finished, she asked Jonty if she could use the staff shower room so that she could wash off the kitchen and shampoo her hair. She applied some tinted moisturizer, a clear mascara and a very pale lipgloss – her only concession to wearing make-up – and emerged half an hour later in her blue dress, a large pair of sunnies and her flip-flops. She looked pretty damn good, even if she did say so herself. Jonty did an archaic wolf whistle at her, which had she been in a different frame of mind would've given offence. But she decided that life was too short for getting offended. Especially today.

'Who's the lucky fella?' Jonty asked. And Beca smiled back in what she thought was an enigmatic way.

She caught the bus and got off at the stop on Steeple Street, nearest to number ninety-nine. It was a gorgeous day. Not too hot, and with a refreshing breeze.

When Soozi opened the door, she was full of beans. 'Alrigh', bird?' she yelled, giving her a friendly hug. She was just like the Soozi she'd first met. The pre-kiss, pre-naked Soozi. In fact, she was so like the old Soozi that Beca wondered for a moment whether she'd imagined the night before. But it wasn't long before her mind was put at rest. 'You look fuckin' stunnin', babe,' Soozi said, looking her up and down approvingly. Then snapping out of it, she announced, 'Come on. First work, then we can play.' Beca's stomach did a somersault.

Soozi led her this time not up the stairs but along the dark corridor to number one, where she took a key from under a plastic plant pot that held a dusty fake geranium. She turned the lock and went inside, Beca dutifully following.

The first thing that hit her was the smell – a mixture of warm cake and tobacco. Not the acrid chemical smell of cigarettes – this was honeyed, rich. Pipe tobacco! A doorway in the lobby led through to the living room, the walls of which were a deep red, the ceiling and picture rails cream gloss. There was a large chesterfield sofa along one wall, next to a walnut coffee table and a welcoming armchair that was covered and made cosy by a Welsh blanket. A drinks cabinet on the other side of the room proffered a silver tray of crystal decanters, all containing liquids of varying golden hues. The bay window was lined with sheets of sheer white voile that diffused the sunlight from outside. Emerald-green velvet drapes hung at either end of the bay, framing a stage for the room's star act – a Steinway grand piano, lid open and begging to be played.

'Oh my God, that's lush,' whispered Beca.

'Meet Bettina!' Soozi laughed. 'Knock yerself out.' And she disappeared into the kitchen. 'I'll get us some squash.'

Beca sat herself down on the silk-covered piano stool that had seen better days. Several pieces of sheet music, yellowing and curling at the edges, lay across the top, and in the stand, flimsily held up by two clips – Debussy and Chopin jumped out at her, and she couldn't resist. When Soozi came back in, carrying two glasses of orange cordial, she found Beca lost in playing *Prélude à l'après-midi d'un faune*.

'God, you're immense, you are!' she declared, and put the glasses down on the coffee table.

Beca stopped playing and beamed. 'This is gorgeous. A world away from my crappy keyboard.' And it was. The texture of the ivory and ebony felt exquisite beneath her fingertips as they danced along the keys – as if they were alive, made of living matter, which, Beca realized guiltily, they once had been.

177

'Turns me on, hearing you play like that, B,' said Soozi. 'It's talent, see. Exquisite talent. So fuckin' erotic.' She held Beca's hands as she said it, turning them over in her own and marvelling at the music they could create. Kissing first the right palm, then the left, she looked at Beca directly and without dropping her gaze put Beca's right hand between her legs. The softness and heat Beca felt there were incredible. Soozi closed her eyes for a moment, before moving Beca's hand away. 'Later,' she whispered and began warming up her voice, humming and buzzing, running scales and singing vowel sounds. 'Right, let's have a bash at the show tunes.'

'I'm surprised, to be honest,' said Beca, having regained her composure. 'Never had you down as a West End Wendy.'

'Oi, less of the lip. A lot of them songs are dodgy as. But there's a few winners.' And she handed Beca a copy of *South Pacific*.

They practised for over an hour, losing themselves in the music, the repetition, the working and reworking of different parts until they were satisfied their performances were sharp and gig-ready.

'Hello?' A male voice interrupted them. Parker had returned, and Beca felt a little sinking of her heart at the prospect of not being alone with Soozi any more.

'IN HERE, BABE!'

'Wanna hear what we just done?' Soozi asked him, throwing her arms around his waist and nearly toppling him over.

'I'd be delighted.'

They launched into 'I'm Gonna Wash That Man Right Outa My Hair' and Parker applauded. 'Bravo! Bravo!!'

They performed a few more songs from their set before Soozi announced they should leave Parker in peace and give her voice a rest. She grabbed Beca by the hand and led her out of the door.

On the stairs, Beca asked, 'How comes we didn't practise there before? You never needed to come to mine. That grand piano is amazing.'

'Yeah, well, I wanted to check out your crib, didn't I?'

'You mean you were being nosey.'

'Somethin' like that.' Soozi grinned and winked at her. It was an extraordinary thing to do. Winking didn't seem to be quite Soozi's style. And Beca felt her stomach do another somersault.

As soon as they were through the door, Soozi shut it, locked it and pushed Beca up against the wall. She kissed her with a deeper intensity than the night before and with far more urgency. Breaking away, she said breathlessly, 'Been needing that all fuckin' day.' And with a confidence Beca did not know any earthly being could possess, Soozi raised an ironic eyebrow, whispered, 'So let the games commence!' and promptly dropped to her knees. It took about five seconds for Beca to process what was happening. But only two before she began to feel blissed out. And then she thought she would die from ecstasy.

Beca spent the next three nights at Soozi's, going to work at lunchtimes, rehearsing at Parker's, waiting for Soozi to come home, and spending hour upon glorious hour having sex. Years later, she would look back at that rite-of-passage week as one of the happiest of her entire life.

On the fourth day, she thought she should go home. Partly because she felt guilty for abandoning her mother, and partly out of necessity as she needed some more clothes. She'd called her mother every day during her time away as well as texting regularly. This was more out of selfishness than consideration – she knew that if she didn't stay in regular contact, Elin would flip. It just wasn't worth the hassle.

When she got home, she thought her mum seemed a little brighter than she had been, which lessened Beca's guilt, and when she finally found the right time to sit down with her and tell her about Soozi, the whole event was pretty much a *non-event* and did not provoke the dramatic reaction she'd envisaged.

'I'm thrilled for you, Bec,' Elin said, holding Beca's hand across the table.

'Serious?'

'Of course I am. You seem really happy and that's all I care about.'

In that moment, Beca felt a huge rush of love for her mum, and she even thought she might cry.

'Please do feel that you can stay here though as well. Don't feel you can only stay over at Soozi's. It'd be nice to get to know her a bit.'

'Yeah, okay,' said Beca, though she wasn't entirely sure she was ready to have her girlfriend stay the night. It was difficult to stay quiet when things got going between them, and the thought of her mother being in the next room was just a bit too much.

32

alys

The warning bell came in the form of a text. From Kirsty.

We need to talk.

Alys knew straight away that the lack of kisses or emojis spelled Trouble with a capital T.

You know where I am! Xx

Waiting for Kirsty to arrive, Alys did a few calculations on the back of a free newspaper to see how she might make enough to repay her debt. For some time now she'd wondered about offering to walk people's dogs or babysit elderly relatives. And, of course, she still did Tarot readings at the market on a Saturday, charging thirty quid a pop. Would people pay more? Doubtful in Brecon, but let's be hopeful. If she could do eight sessions on a Saturday and maybe start doing readings at home, surely that would bring in a few hundred. She could always bite the bullet and get down the benefits office – that option was always there. But even the thought of this made her go cold. In all her adult life, Alys had never signed on or claimed any help from the state.

Simply because she couldn't bear being part of any system. The old hippy spirit was a hard one to quash.

She was stopped in her thoughts by the front door opening. No standing on ceremony, things must be bad for Kirsty to just walk in like this. She was normally so polite.

'ALYS? WHERE THE HELL ARE YOU?'

God, she sounded angry. But within seconds of seeing Kirsty, Alys realized that her friend wasn't just angry: she was crying.

She was also very, very drunk.

Coffee. Water. More coffee. And a ham omelette. Alys inwardly begrudged using up her last two eggs, but she could hardly say no to her benefactor – Kirsty actually owned the eggs, in effect. The younger woman sat there in front of her, red-faced and utterly distraught. It took a good half-hour before she managed to stop crying long enough to speak. And explain that Douglas had left her. For his personal trainer. Trevor.

Kirsty went on to explain that she'd known that Trevor the trainer was gay. She'd just had no inkling whatsoever that Douglas was as well.

'Really?' Alys asked.

'We had sex in the steam room last Tuesday! Of course I didn't know!'

Alys thought sex in the steam room sounded *really* uncomfortable and would most likely induce a panic attack if she ever tried it. God, she felt old.

'They've moved in together. The little shit. THE LITTLE SHIT! I need a drink, Al. Get me a drink – please. Please! I'll stop again tomorrow, I promise, I just need it to get through—'

Alys shook her by the shoulders, feeling a little foolish doing so, as if she was just copying what they did in *EastEnders*. 'Now look,' she said sternly, as Kirsty collapsed back into an armchair. 'You've had a shock. But you're still alive.'

'Hardly,' sobbed Kirsty.

'Oh, cut the dramatics, you're going to get through this. But not if you turn to the bottle. Now, I am going to run you a hot bath and then you are going to have a sleep whilst I pop to the shops and get us something more substantial for supper.'

This was a major setback. Admittedly, it wasn't as bad a situation as Kirsty getting heavy about the growing debt, but it was bad nonetheless. Alys enjoyed her own company. Thrived on it, in fact. The last thing she wanted was a roomie, or, worse still, a roomie who was off her face on booze. So hopefully, once Kirsty had sobered up, Alys could get her to an AA meeting and back on track. Alys found drunks annoying at the best of times. She certainly didn't want to be sharing her home with one. Even if the home belonged to the actual drunk.

But if Alys had had hopes for how the evening would pan out, they were dashed as soon as she came home from her trip to Londis with a Fray Bentos steak & kidney, some Aunt Bessie's mash and a tin of baked beans – sometimes processed food was the only solution. She found Kirsty in her bathrobe, smoking a More Menthol and screaming down the phone. Presumably at Douglas or Trevor. And by her side sat a brand-new bottle of gin. Alys took in the scene, noting that Kirsty was unaware she'd come home, so lost was she in the phone call. So, seizing the moment, Alys swiped the gin and swiftly poured it down the sink, at which point Kirsty turned and saw her, screamed and lunged at her like an angry cat.

33

elin

Elin had wanted to tell Greg about Beca's new relationship, but they didn't talk about things like that any more. They didn't talk, full stop. Beca said she'd tell him when she felt ready and shut the subject down. According to Greg's whining emails, Beca had refused to see him or speak to him since meeting Fleur. Elin knew she shouldn't gloat, but she couldn't help feeling smug that Beca was very much on her side. And she relished the fact that *she* knew so much more about Beca's life than Greg did: he wouldn't know about the singing and he wouldn't know about Soozi. *Oh well, Greg*, she said to herself, *you made your adulterous bed, my dear!* And then she felt a bit silly for using such an alien expression, even in her head. Maybe spending time with Beca and Soozi was starting to loosen her up a bit.

She'd really warmed to Soozi. She'd been round for supper a couple of times and had even stayed over, despite a reluctance on Beca's part for that to happen. Despite that, it had all gone surprisingly well – Soozi was quite remarkable. Her outwardly bolshy, brash demeanour completely belied the reality: she was incredibly helpful around the house, clearing the table, washing up, even offering to do some ironing. 'I loves ironing, Mrs M,' she'd said. 'Sorts my head out.'

'Oh, please call me Elin, Soozi. It sounds so formal calling me "Mrs". Plus I'm not technically sure I *am* one any more.'

'You can be called whatever you wants to, mate,' said Soozi. 'Always telling *you* that, aren' I, angel?' And without the slightest hint of self-consciousness she put her hand through Beca's hair and kissed the top of her head. Elin thought that such a public display of affection might have unnerved her, offended her even. Actually she quite liked it. It made her smile to watch Beca blush when Soozi did it. The love between them was so sweet and real, it cancelled out any awkwardness or embarrassment. Yes, Soozi was *definitely* a godsend. Even if her swearing and lack of appropriacy were at times a bit much.

'Why *do* you swear, d'you think?' Elin asked her one evening.

'No idea, mate. I think it's just I'm impatient with life. Can't be arsed working out the dos and don'ts of *nice society*.'

At which point Beca shrugged her shoulders at Elin as if to say, *What can you do?*

A text came through from her solicitor:

Hey sweetie.

(*Eugh!*)

Don't forget we're meeting Lolly this eve – 6pm at Salomé's.

Oh God, Maxine's 'guru' friend. She'd forgotten all about it – so caught up she'd been with Beca's love-life news and sorting out the house. The garden had taken up a lot of her attention, too. Rory had worked his magic on the pear tree, planting a sapling in its place, and had even built in some new raised beds. He'd finished the project the day before and Elin had paid him in cash, adding a tip for doing such a good job.

'Well, you got my number, Ellie,' he'd said. 'If that bindweed shows its ugly head again, give me a shout.'

It had been nice having him around for the week. Although he was a good ten years younger than her, he was very mature and obsessed with gardening. His company had made a refreshing change and she was a little sorry to see him go.

Elin told Beca about the Lolly meeting. 'I think I'll cancel,' she said.

'Salomé's? In Pontcanna? That's where me and Soozi are giggin' tonight! You've got to come, Mum. It'll be cool you seein' us play.'

'Won't you be nervous with me there?'

'Nah, I'd like it,' Beca said. And Elin marvelled at how their relationship had become so much calmer since Beca had fallen in love.

'Okay, then,' she said. 'I'll try not to wear anything embarrassing.'

A few hours later, she found herself sipping a Virgin Mojito at Salomé's Bar with Maxine Letterman-Brace and this awful woman Lolly, who was a size six if she was a day, poured inside skin-tight leather jeggings, wearing impossible heels and sporting ice-blue hair. Her insanely thick lash extensions gave the appearance that a pair of tarantulas had landed on her eyelids.

The 'look' Elin could handle. It was being barked at that she found most annoying: Lolly was currently lecturing her on the importance of 'keeping your man happy in the sack', claiming to be able to take bets on which couples in the bar were enjoying a rewarding sex life.

'See him over there?' Lolly nodded towards a swarthy chap with a head of thick blond hair a few tables over, who was deep in conversation with his girlfriend. 'He's not a happy bunny. 'Cos he's not getting it. Or if he is, what he's getting is boring as. I guarantee you, Elin, I could have him' – Lolly clicked her fingers – 'just like that.'

Elin wanted to laugh – partly because she thought Lolly was a huge joke and partly because she'd just been reminded of Tommy Cooper and his catchphrase. Elin doubted Lolly would have even heard of Tommy Cooper. And she suddenly felt very old. 'Sorry, what's this got to do with anything?' she sighed.

Maxine gave Elin a gentle chastisement. 'Let her finish, El.'

El. Only Greg called her El.

What on earth was she doing here? She could've just cancelled meeting Lolly and come to watch Beca instead. She sipped her drink, relishing the sharp tang of lime and fresh mint, and tried to switch off from Lolly's babbling. She was saying something about embracing her fire. Which was a ludicrous notion, because even if one *could* embrace fire, surely all it would do would be to inflict first-degree burns. Lolly continued on about the import-ance of self-confidence and how self-belief was 'sexier than all the silk underwear in an Ann Summers outlet'. Elin nodded in agreement and scanned the bar. It was filling up now, clearly a popular place with all ages, couples, singletons, groups . . .

And then she saw him.

And she choked on her drink.

Unaware of what Elin had seen, Maxine thumped her on the back a few times as Elin tried to explain that Greg was standing at the other end of the bar. She managed to splutter his name and point in his direction. Then, in a panic, she climbed down indec-orously from the bar stool and stumbled towards the ladies' loo, signalling to Maxine with a forced coughing smile that she would be fine. Just needed two minutes. She was in such a rush to get away that she didn't witness Lolly set her sights most firmly on Greg and make her way over to where he stood.

34

alys

The bruises and the cut on her face would heal, she knew that. God knows she'd had enough experience – albeit not for many years – of recovering from physical abuse, boyfriends who'd been a bit handy with their fists. But the whole event had taken it out of her. With her entire body aching from shock, all she wanted to do was sleep. Now she found herself in a taxi heading for Merthyr and a cheap hotel where she could stay for the night. It wouldn't be long before Kirsty caught on and blocked the credit card – if she hadn't done so already – and Alys, once again, would be out on her ageing arse.

She'd had to marvel at Kirsty's ingenuity – though most alcoholics were manipulative and exceptionally clever when it came to getting a drink. Turned out the minute Alys had left the cottage to get the food supplies, Kirsty had leapt up from her fake sleep on her sofa and called the local off-licence, who she persuaded to deliver two bottles of gin pronto via a local cab. Oh, the power and lure of ready cash. It had taken less than fifteen minutes, so that by the time Alys returned, Kirsty had already written her name into the best part of a bottle of Bombay Sapphire and was several sheets to the wind. Again.

Alys had had no option other than to chuck the gin away.

When Kirsty got violent (*that* was a turn-up for the books!), Alys had had to think on her feet and bundle her into the pantry, grabbing the key in an instant and locking her in. 'It's for your own safety,' she kept shouting, with Kirsty screaming blue murder back at her.

Remaining remarkably calm, Alys had packed together as many of her things as she could in such a short space of time and called a taxi. Turned out it was the same taxi driver who'd delivered the gin. Life was so full of ironies. When he dropped her off in Merthyr, she gave him an extra tenner on top of the fare to return to the house and let Kirsty out of the pantry. The driver seemed to find it all very amusing, thank goodness. Someone of a different disposition might be tempted to report her to the police for false imprisonment.

A shower and two hours later, Alys was sitting on her hotel bed in a 'Lo-Price' hotel on the outskirts of Merthyr Tydfil, a place used mainly by contractors and lorry drivers and people passing through. That was her life now really, wasn't it? Continually passing through. Had she been rash leaving the cottage? Should she have stayed? Maybe called someone else from AA to come and help? Too late now, anyway. She'd never be able to go back to Brecon. Especially as she'd absconded with Kirsty's credit card and left a hefty debt behind her. Of course it was wrong. Of course it was criminal. But needs must. She was her own protector and defender, for God's sake. Nobody else would save her now and although at her age that was rather sad, it was nonetheless true.

Alys counted the cash she had to her name: forty-one pounds and thirty-seven pence. She fought the urge to cry. Self-pity would get her nowhere. And so what if she didn't yet know where to go next. Wasn't that what made life exciting? The unpredictability? The not-knowing? She tried to relish the excitement. But was too consumed by tiredness to feel any sort of thrill. She lay back on the bed, her feet still on the floor, and within two minutes she was asleep.

35

elin

Thankfully the Ladies' was empty. Elin locked herself into the furthest cubicle and sat for a moment with her head in her hands, gathering her thoughts. The remnants of her choking cough subsided and she managed to catch her breath. *Had* it been Greg? His hair was different – she'd only had a passing glimpse, but she had a feeling he might have had highlights. Dear Lord! And the clothes he was wearing – a very tight T-shirt and, what were they called, *cargo pants*? Something like that? Either way, it wasn't the Greg she knew. No. Maybe it wasn't him, after all.

She heard someone come in and lock the cubicle next door. Her cue to leave. She stood up, brushed herself down and headed out to the sink to wash her hands. Suddenly a voice – 'Hey there – you couldn't pass me some loo roll, could you? This one's run out.'

'Er, yes, hang on,' Elin said, returning to her cubicle and pulling a wad of tissue from the dispenser. She passed it through the gap under the cubicle door, to be gratefully grabbed by a hand covered in henna tattoos, with silver rings on every finger. Including the thumb.

'Thanks!'

Elin looked in the mirror and washed her hands. She ought to top up her make-up. A little more lipstick. A touch more eyeliner. *Just in case*. Just in case it *was* Greg. And her stomach did a flip.

The henna-handed woman came out from the loo and made for the sink. They shared a smile, then both returned to their own reflections. Elin side-eyed her companion and noticed she wore a nose ring and barely any make-up other than a pale gloss on her full lips and an astonishing electric-blue mascara. There were no lines on her suntanned forehead and the faint aroma of lavender oil emanated from her plaited hair. *Oh, to be young again*, Elin thought.

'Have you heard her before?' asked the woman.

'Sorry?'

'The live music tonight. She's meant to be amazing.'

'Oh. Right,' said Elin, feeling too awkward to start a conversation and explain that the singer was her daughter's girlfriend. 'I'm not staying that long,' she lied.

'Well, you're going to miss a treat!' said the woman, before proceeding to take out a tatty make-up bag and reapply her blue mascara. Elin smiled feebly before mumbling a goodbye and heading back to the bar.

Maxine and Lolly were no longer in their seats and for a fleeting moment Elin wondered if they'd simply abandoned her and moved on somewhere else. Although she couldn't quite believe that to be true, part of her hoped it was, because it would mean she could sneak out of Salomé's and make her way back home, avoiding the possibility of bumping into Greg. Beca would be disappointed, but she'd think of some excuse. Thankfully the bar was getting full now and she politely made her way towards the door.

Suddenly somebody grabbed her arm. It was Maxine. 'You're coming with me, young lady,' she said, her voice brimming with excitement. To Elin's utter horror, Maxine was leading her in the direction of – yes, it *was* Greg, who was standing looking aghast near the stage, backed into a corner by Lolly. She was reading

191

him the riot act – asking him when he was going to grow up. Was he a narcissist? Did he care a single toss about destroying the lives of his wife and child? When he saw Elin, he looked positively relieved.

'Greg,' she stuttered.

'I've just been introduced to your *friend*,' he said. And she thought she saw desperation in his eyes, pleading with her to get this Rottweiler of a woman away from him.

Up on the small cabaret stage a few metres away, an MC was checking the microphone and introducing tonight's live music act.

'I was just going home, actually,' said Elin, suddenly very tired. Greg looked twitchy.

'You're not going anywhere yet,' said Lolly firmly. 'Not till you two have had a proper talk. I can see from the energy between you that there's still some very unfinished business needs addressing . . .'

Maxine nodded enthusiastically, as if watching a highly skilled dancer. 'Isn't she just brilliant?' she asked, more to herself than anyone else.

Elin was about to say, *Er, no, actually, she's a fraud and a fool, and if I have to stay in her company a moment longer I might inflict harm*. But she was distracted by seeing Greg. She just wanted to reach out to him and ask him to come home, to apologize for being rash about the divorce, and to ask if they couldn't just go somewhere and talk.

Up on the stage, the music began – loud, edgy chords and an upbeat intro on the keyboards heralded the sublime voice of Soozi Cole as she started singing 'I'm Gonna Wash That Man Right Outa My Hair'. For a moment, Elin was distracted.

There were so many people in the bar now, everyone was jostling for space and the heat was rising.

'Is that . . . *Beca*?' asked Greg, incredulous, staring at the stage.

'Yes,' Elin said proudly.

'What? But since when . . .? I didn't know she—'

'Yes, well, there's a lot you don't know about Beca, Greg,' she replied. *Slam. Dunk.*

Beca caught Elin's eye first and smiled. But when she saw Greg, her look turned to horror. She momentarily stumbled and played a bum note. Greg and Elin watched as their daughter corrected herself, turning her attention back to the music and seeming to ignore the fact that her newly separated parents were within spitting distance and watching her play!

For a moment, Elin forgot it all, transported back ten years to a primary-school concert at which Beca was playing, she and Greg looking on, the epitome of proud parents.

Her nostalgia was interrupted by a familiar voice announcing over the singing, 'Oh, you stayed! Well done!'

It was the woman from the Ladies', who was now standing next to a horror-stricken Greg, curling her hennaed, silver-ringed fingers around his neck proprietorially and snuggling in close. To *Elin's* husband.

It happened in seconds.

Greg gulped and said, 'Elin, this is Fleur.'

Fleur smiled and said, 'Oh, we just met!'

Lolly sneered and said, 'Is that it? Is *she* what you left your incredible wife for?'

Maxine retreated and said, 'Come on, ladies, let's go.'

Despite the overwhelming evidence, Fleur seemed unable to read the room. 'It's so good to meet you, Elin. I really hope we can be friends.'

And Elin just stared. Whilst her keyboard-playing daughter accompanied Soozi Cole and her smooth, honeyed tones as she sang:

'*Cancel him and let him go! Yea, sister!*'

And suddenly Elin launched into a deep, primal roar that boiled up from inside her and blasted out of her mouth. Years of pent-up frustration, years of playing by the rules, of obediently walking down the middle of the road, of staying small and quiet – years of it came tumbling out of her now. And the last thing she heard as she launched herself at Fleur was Beca shouting from the stage, 'MUM! NOOOOOOOOOOOOOO!'

36

alys

''Scuse me, you can't sleep here, I'm afraid.'

'What? Sorry, I was just—'

Sleeping. Sandwiched between several carrier bags that contained her entire worldly possessions. Her first instinct was to check the cash was still there, and her hand leapt to the left cup of her bra. Yes, all safe. She felt the hard edges of the credit card, too. So far, so good – it hadn't been cancelled yet. She knew this because she'd bought herself a hot meal with it a few hours ago. The place had been busier then. Tourists en route to some pretty Welsh destination, lorry drivers taking a break from a long haul. She must have dropped off shortly after the cheesecake and cream. Served her right for gorging on processed carbs – an indulgence she couldn't afford, but which gave her some momentary comfort.

Today had been so long. At the Merthyr hotel she'd woken with a start, showered and made the most of the inclusive buffet breakfast. Aware that eyes might be upon her, she'd tried to subtly secrete some extra slices of bread, margarine and packets of honey from the self-service station. It wasn't the sort of hotel that offered croissants and pastries otherwise she'd have stuffed her pockets full of those. She *did*, however, manage to wrap a few sausages in a napkin – they might come in handy over the next few days.

Back in her room, Alys lay on her bed and distracted herself by reading. Bizarrely, one of the things she'd grabbed during the hasty pack-up and departure was her trashy crime novel, *He Kills in Blue*. She was grateful it was such a thick tome – a six-hundred-pager. So far, Detective Inspector Parrish had bumped off a visiting Russian oligarch as well as his bodyguard and she'd been strangely gripped by the tale. When she was in the world of the novel she didn't have to think about the mess her own life had become. *Thank God for books*, she thought.

She'd stayed until well past checking-out time, until the cleaners knocked on her door and politely told her to sling her hook. Carrier bags once again packed, she headed over to the truckers' caff, where she asked for a free mug of hot water, much to the disdain of the woman behind the counter. Taking it over to a corner, she surreptitiously made herself a coffee from a sachet and milk portion stolen from her room, before scanning the tables for a friendly-looking lorry driver.

He'd been a nice enough chap – Derrick or Darren or something beginning with D. And he'd offered her a lift as far as Pont Abraham. She'd expected he might be tricky. In the past, she'd discovered there was rarely any such thing as a free lunch, or a free lift. But she'd been younger then, and, harsh but true, she'd been a damn sight more attractive. Alys sometimes had to remind herself that she was no longer the willowy femme fatale she'd once been. Yes, she looked good for her age, but gone were the days when she could ensnare a man with little more than a smile. The driver wasn't much younger than her and not far off retiring. He would have given up work sooner, he'd said, but with the crisis in long-haul lorry drivers kicking in after Brexit, it had seemed foolish not to make the most of the earning potential. He liked to talk, did Dwayne or Desmond or whatever he was called. And most of it had been excruciatingly dull. The good thing about his holding forth on the subject of his own life was that he didn't ask Alys anything about hers, so she could happily switch off as he wittered on in the background. The only time Alys *did* get genuinely interested was when he mentioned Spain. 'Me and the missus go there every year. Costa Dorada. Hoping to move out for good next couple of years, though of course it won't be as easy as it was pre-Brexit.'

'Tell me what you like about Spain,' she said quickly, hoping to stave off another launch into his deathly-dull take on socio-politics.

'Well, the obvious one is the weather,' he said and began waxing lyrical about paella and siestas, sangria and the sound of night-time crickets. Alys gazed out of the truck window at the motorway and the August-afternoon traffic. Her head was pounding. And she fought an overwhelming urge to cry. Gone was the warrior woman she'd always purported to be, the eternal optimist, the woman who embraced an uncertain future as an opportunity, not an obstacle. She thought about another hitch-hike over thirty years ago on a Spanish freeway that snaked along the coastal road towards Marbella . . .

'Fancy a mini pork pie?' Darren had asked, handing her the packet without taking his eyes off the road.

'Not right now,' she said. 'But can I keep one for later?'

He'd dropped her off about six p.m., where much to her surprise, the travellers' lodge had been full. At least, that's what the man on reception had said. He probably just didn't like the look of this bedraggled septuagenarian carrying her life in plastic bags and smelling of day-old sausages. She didn't blame him. But it meant her only option had been to catch a few hours' kip at one of the restaurant tables and try cadging a lift later on. She'd looked for somewhere far enough away from the counter to hopefully be left in peace.

She must have dropped off for a couple of hours, at least. The man who'd woken her and politely asked her to move on had a kind face and an accent she thought was Eastern European, maybe. Looking around her, she saw that the place was virtually empty – just a loved-up couple at one table, annoyingly laughing too loud as if to announce to the world that *they* were happy, even if nobody else was. And in the opposite corner to Alys, a teenage girl who looked lost and alone with the weight of the world on her young shoulders. She reminded Alys of herself at that age.

'Fancy a refill?' Alys asked as she headed to the counter. 'I'm just getting one for myself.'

The girl didn't respond at first, seemingly unaware of her surroundings and deep in thought. Then she looked up and shook her head. 'No, thanks.'

Alys stood there for a moment too long, before realizing she was staring and must be coming across as a bit of a weirdo, especially with her scratch-marked face and earnest smile. She moved away and headed to the counter, where she ordered herself a hot chocolate. But when she attempted to pay, the machine told her the card had been declined.

'Try sticking it in,' said a cheery Brummie voice behind her. She turned to see a burly driver with an all-day breakfast on his tray, accompanied by a side order of chips. 'You've probably overused the contactless,' he explained. Alys did as she was advised, her heart in her mouth, simply going through the motions. Because she knew the truth. And sure enough, after tapping in the PIN she got the same response. Declined. She'd been found out. Kirsty had cancelled the card.

'You got cash?' asked the assistant. And Alys was aware that Burly Brum was getting a little impatient. She hesitated. She'd have to go without now, especially as she only had that forty quid left to her name. She was about to walk away when the burly Brummie said, 'Stick it on my bill, bub.'

'No, no, I couldn't,' Alys protested.

'Don't be daft. It's only a cocoa. And I wanna get this down me, 'fore I get on the road.'

Alys thanked him profusely, then seized the moment. 'Don't suppose I could scrounge a lift, could I?'

'Where you headin', bub?'

'Anywhere,' she said. 'I'll go anywhere.'

37

grace

'You're like some geriatric superhero,' John had teased Grace when she told him her plans.

'I feel guilty abandoning you,' she said.

'Don't be daft. We'll survive twenty-four hours without you. Just don't be getting swept off your feet by some Cardiffian Lothario with evil intentions.'

She laughed. 'I'll take the mobile so you can call if there's any problem. Or if you hear back about the tests.'

'Of course.'

'Oh, I don't know,' she hesitated. 'Are you sure Cissie will be okay? She's been used to me going there every day.'

'If she's up to it, and if it stays sunny, I'll take her out in the garden.'

'Well, make sure she's wrapped up, won't you, and don't—'

'Grace,' John admonished gently. 'We can manage. Just make sure you sort that girl of yours out.'

It had all been arranged so quickly. Beca's phone call on Monday night had been bordering on hysterical when she'd told her great-grandmother all about the fight. So first thing on Tuesday morning, Grace rang Dolly Hughes from yoga, who she'd remembered was planning a trip to Cardiff with her daughter the next day. 'Can I join you?' she'd said. 'Just to have company on the train. I'll be fine once I get there. Beca will meet me at the station.' The journey to Cardiff would take three hours all told, so the plan was to leave early, arrive by eleven and catch the five o'clock train back that afternoon. She was going to be exhausted. But she knew she must go. *It has to be done*, she said to herself. *They need you!*

Beca had been so upset on the phone. 'A fight! My mother was in an actual *fight*. And now it's all over the internet.'

It was astonishing how quickly people had heard about what happened. Even Dolly's daughter had questioned her about it on the train. Testament to the terrifying power of social media and its potential to do harm or good, depending on which way the wind was blowing. Unfortunately for Beca – *and* Elin – the wind that night had been blowing in the direction of Pippa Bowen. Forty-five-year-old Pippa came from a family of professional and vicious gossips, who seldom had a good word to say about anyone. That evening, she had been out with 'the girls': a lethal combination of heightened bitchiness and toxicity which, when faced with seeing Elin Matthews, the 'stuck-up' Head Teacher of St Stephen's, getting into a fight with her husband's new lover – well, the situation was too delicious for words. And out came Pippa's phone, recording the whole incident and posting it on Instagram within seconds of the bouncers pulling the two women apart. Elin had a bloody nose. Fleur had a three-line scratch across her cheek. Both women were thrown out on to Pontcanna Street, much to the surprise of the customers enjoying their rosé al fresco.

'And what made the whole situation worse was that we were only at the start of our set, so I couldn't let Soozi down by abandoning the keyboard,' Beca had cried, barely pausing for breath. If only she hadn't made the fatal mistake of shouting *MUM!!!*, thus identifying herself as the daughter of this embarrassing middle-aged woman who was brawling like a Millwall supporter on match day. She'd just sat there, playing jolly chords, whilst Soozi belted out the lyrics, confusion on her face, her voice faltering momentarily. One of the bouncers had hissed at them as he manhandled Elin outside, 'Carry on playing, for Christ's sake!' Beca had played as if in a trance. She'd watched as her father looked mournfully in her direction, palms up in contrition, mouthing the words *I'm so sorry* before heading outside himself. She'd noticed Pippa Bowen filming the entire debacle. When the grinning Pippa turned the camera towards Beca for a final beat to the drama, she wasn't disappointed: Beca had taken her hand away from the keyboard long enough to flip the finger, accompanied very clearly with a silent *Fuck off*. If the owner of the bar hadn't seen that happening, she might have got away with it, she said. But when they finished their set – to muted applause on this rare occasion – they were paid in cash and told they wouldn't be invited back. 'Can't have the entertainment swearing at the fucking customers! I won't have any left!'

'It's been a nightmare, Grama Grace.'

On several occasions during their call, Grace had had to ask Beca to slow down and explain. 'What do you mean, you were *at the start of your set*? And who is this Soozi?'

Beca had paused then.

'She's a singer,' she said. 'I accompany her on the keyboards an' that.'

'Oh yes, of course! Your mum did mention your gigging.'

'What else did she say?' asked Beca suspiciously. 'About Soozi, I mean?'

Grace detected that Beca was holding something back. 'Nothing much, just that—'

'Aw, look,' Beca interrupted. 'She's also my girlfriend, okay? But don't go all judgey on me, that's just the way it—'

'Whoa, hang on now, who's being judgey?' Grace said, trying not to show her surprise. 'It's just a lot to take in, that's all. Now let's prioritize. How is your mother? And more importantly, where is she?'

201

This had been the main reason for Beca's call. It turned out she'd been so mortified by Elin's behaviour that she'd shouted at her. 'In front of everyone, Grama Grace. I feel so bad. And she just sort of stumbled off into the night. I tried calling her when I'd calmed down, but it went to voicemail. And then she just texted me and told me not to come home. Because she's so ashamed. Oh God, what am I gonna do? This is all Dad's bloody fault.'

Grace suggested they ring the bell first. 'Why?' Beca complained. 'It's my house too!'

They were standing on the doorstep, deciding what to do. It was almost midday and the curtains were still closed. 'Out of respect, bach,' Grace said. 'Just to give your mum a bit of warning that we're here.'

'She've got a point, B,' said Soozi. 'Now stop bein' a bitch to your great-gran an' ring the bell.'

Grace suppressed a smile. She *liked* this Soozi!

As expected, Elin didn't answer the door, even after they'd tried a couple of times, so Grace gave Beca the go-ahead to use her key.

Elin hadn't been in bed, as they'd expected. She was just sitting by the French doors, her coffee gone cold, still bearing the remnants of last night's make-up and wearing a dressing gown.

'Mum?' Beca called out from the hallway.

And without turning round, Elin replied, barely audible, 'I thought I said not to come home.'

'Well, that's a nice welcome to give your old gran!' said Grace as she walked into the kitchen.

Elin stood up, shocked. 'Grama Grace!'

'*Duw Duw*, I've seen you look better, my girl.'

Grace held out her arms. Elin needed no encouragement to fall into them. 'I'm such a disaster,' she sobbed, too upset to even question Grace's presence.

'That's it, bach, get it all out of your system.' Grace smoothed

Elin's back, encouraging the tears, and when there were none left she stood back, held her granddaughter by the shoulders and looked at her.

'What am I gonna do, Grama Grace?'

'Well, that's why I'm here. First thing, Beca's going to run you a bath . . .'

'I'll put some of that rose oil in,' said Beca, springing into action.

'. . . and you are going to get out your cleansers and creams and what-have-you and give that face a good going-over. I've seen pandas with less black under their eyes than you right now.'

'I just can't bring myself—'

'Ey, ey,' Grace interrupted. 'It's not up for discussion. We four are going out for lunch!'

'No!'

'Oh yes.'

'But how can I ever go out in public again? It was even on Wales Online this morning – *Head teacher headbutts and heads for disaster!*'

'That's a lie, for starters,' Soozi chipped in, picking an apple up from the fruit bowl and sinking her teeth into it. 'She never head-butted no one, Grama Grace. It was just a girlie scrap, that was all. Pathetic! Didn't even throw a punch.'

'Hardly the point, Suzanne!' snapped Elin. And Grace gently signalled to her that maybe it was best not to say anything right now. Soozi held up her hands in a placatory gesture and carried on munching her apple.

Grace took Elin's hands. 'Now, I'm no stranger to being gossiped about,' she said.

'Really?' Elin was thrown.

'Let's just say I've set a few tongues wagging in my time. I lived with a married man for years, did I not?'

'Oh that was hardly the same th—'

'You old slapper, Grama Grace!' interrupted Soozi, shrieking with glee.

This time *Beca* glared at her, but Grace seemed unbothered and carried on.

'The one thing I know to be true is that if you hide away, the tongues will wag faster and louder. You've got to nip it in the bud. Go out there and face off the enemy. Stand proud, don't shrink small.'

'She's right, El,' said Soozi. 'I mean, all you did was fight for your fella. What's the big deal? Most folks in the Diff would call you a hero for doin' that. All about perspective, innit, Grama Grace?'

It was odd that Soozi had taken to calling her 'Grama Grace'. But she really rather liked it. 'Absolutely, bach. So go on. Get in that bath, and me and the girls will find somewhere for lunch. Preferably somewhere you'll be recognized.'

'Oh, God,' said Elin as she sloped off upstairs.

'And wash your hair, El!' shouted Soozi. 'I'll do you a nice up-do.'

Grace wasn't sure what that was, but assumed it was a hairstyle.

They went to Romano's for lunch, smack bang in the middle of town. As expected and dreaded by Elin, a few people *had* recognized her. But whether it was just that people weren't very bothered, or whether – as Soozi had said – they thought Elin's actions had been justified, even cool, nobody gave her a hard time. In fact, she seemed to have garnered a certain level of kudos and a couple of people even asked for a selfie. Grace could see Elin squirm at the thought, but headed off her refusal by saying, 'Oh, there's posh, Elin! You're famous!'

It ended up being a warm and happy occasion, with Soozi and Grace getting on like old friends. Being one who didn't suffer fools herself, Grace had warmed to this no-nonsense girlfriend of Beca's. When they were tucking into their coffees, the atmosphere relaxed and relieved, Soozi launched in with one of her direct questions.

'So, Grama Grace, I gotta ask . . .'

Grace noticed Beca glare and mumble, 'Aw, what now?' under her breath. Soozi ignored her.

'. . . what d'you reckon to the fact your great-granddaughter is into girls? Bit of a shocker or what?'

Grace stirred her coffee and Elin stepped into the silence. 'Oh, let's not get into all that now, Soozi. Grama Grace is a different generation and—'

'Excuse me,' interrupted Grace with a faux-offended look, 'I *can* speak for myself, y'know.'

'Exactly,' said Soozi. 'Go on, mate.'

'I think it's . . . rather lovely,' she said, her voice breaking a little. 'You seem to belong together. So here's to you.'

She raised her coffee cup and Soozi joined in. 'Nice one.'

Beca threw her arms around her. 'Aw thanks, Grama Grace.'

'Hey,' Grace joked. 'What am I? some sort of Mafia Mama who's given her seal of approval?'

'The Godfather!' joked Elin.

'No, the Godmother!' laughed Soozi.

'Oh my God – GIGI!' blurted out Soozi as if she'd just realized something. 'That's what I'm gonna call you, get it? Grama Grace. GG. Gigi!'

'Shut up, you donut!' Beca mock-hit her and they launched into a play fight. They made so much noise that the waiter had to ask them to quieten down. Which made the four of them get the giggles.

When Grace caught the train back that evening, she slept almost the entire journey, worn out in the best possible way and feeling grateful to have had such a heart-warming day.

38

elin

Grace's visit had also done Elin the world of good. Put a bit of *oomph* back into her soul. As she sat by the open French doors sipping a camomile tea, she looked out at the fading light of the day gently lulling the garden to sleep. Yes. She'd learned a lot in the past couple of days. For one thing, she'd realized she needed to be a bit more thick-skinned. She *had* been thinking about apologizing to Greg, but then she thought, sod it, why should she? No. If he was embarrassed, if she'd humiliated him, then good. It was no more than he deserved. She was sick of apologizing for herself. 'Warrior woman, that's who I am!' she whispered.

Enjoying this new-found confidence, she decided to do something she probably should have done a couple of weeks ago: it was time to fire her solicitor. She composed an email explaining that she just wasn't happy with how things were proceeding and had decided to go down the DIY divorce route online. She'd researched the whole thing, and provided that Greg was amenable, they should be able to complete the whole process relatively pain-free. Huh, *pain-free* – that was a joke. But at least it would cost her a fraction of the price that Maxine Letterman-Brace was charging. *How wrong it is*, Elin thought, *that when people are at their most vulnerable and reeling from the heartache of a break-up, some divorce lawyers capitalize on their pain*. She wished Maxine all the very best, but didn't thank her for the privilege of paying her ridiculous fees. Feeling proud of herself, she pressed Send.

Suddenly, *thwack!* She couldn't locate where the noise had come from at first. Sitting still, she waited for it to happen again. And it did. *Thwack, thwack.* Followed by the mumbling voice of a man. 'Bloody messy things . . .' It was coming from next door. Could it be Rory, back to do more work? But why would he be gardening so late? It was dusk now, after all. It must be Mr Chakrabarti. She was about to call out to him when – *thwack*. It happened again, and if she hadn't seen it with her own eyes, she wouldn't have believed it. But bold as brass, whoever was there was flagrantly tossing apples on to Elin's lawn! She crouched down and tiptoed over to where the flying fruit was coming from, and as soon as the fifth apple shot through the air she stood up sharply and put on her most formidable head-teacher voice. 'Excuse me, what d'you think you're doing?'

Silence.

Then a rustling of leaves and a head popped through the foliage. It was indeed Mr Chakrabarti.

'They're dropping all over my garden,' he said. 'You need to sort them out.'

Not the most neighbourly of exchanges, thought Elin. True, her beautiful apple tree, which took pride of place near the left-hand wall, generously stretched its boughs into next door's garden, too. But Mrs Latham Deceased had always loved that. Every autumn she'd make delicious apple crumbles and tarts and bring them over from next door. Suddenly Elin was hit by a pang of sorrow at the thought of no more apple desserts from her lovely old neighbour.

'Please do *not* throw the apples on to my lawn, Mr Chakrabarti. If you do not wish to eat them, then collect them up and give them to me. Or put them in the bin. And if you don't like the branches hanging over your wall, then cut them off. Though if you damage the branches on *my* side, you'll be hearing from my solicitor!' *Who I've just fired*, she realized.

She was shaking when she went back inside. The house felt so terribly empty with the lack of Greg and the lack of Beca now too, who spent most of her time at Soozi's. Elin thought she'd got used to it, but evidently she hadn't. And the hostility from her new neighbour served to show her how dreadfully alone she was, how lacking in support. In the old days, Greg would have dealt with Mr Grumpy next door with charm and humour. He'd have had him eating out of his hand by now, pouring him a drink and inviting him round for a barbecue.

Momentarily Elin was distracted by the thought that there'd be no more barbecues for Greg, now that he was a vegan. Of course, he could always barbecue a few vegetable skewers, but they wouldn't touch the sides. If there was one thing her soon-to-be-ex-husband loved, it was a big juicy ribeye.

She shook her head. What was she doing, thinking about Greg? Her mind had to be a Greg-free zone from now on. A taste of things to come. She thought about distracting herself with admin for Grace's party, but just couldn't face it. How she wished she hadn't had that run-in just now with Mr Chakrabarti. It would no doubt keep her awake tonight, and she had a big day ahead of her tomorrow. One of the biggest in the school calendar: A-level results day. Next week, of course, would be the GCSEs.

She ought to remind Greg, really. *Oh, and here you are*, she thought, *back inside my head again!* Deep down, she knew the reminder was a pretext to contact him, but she pushed the thought aside and composed a message.

Beca's results next week – don't forget.

Almost instantly a reply:

U seriously think I cd 4get?

Before she could think about it, she quickly typed back:

Can we talk?

Three moving dots appeared, indicating he'd read the message and was composing a response. She stared at the screen, holding her breath in anticipation. But then the three dots disappeared and the message turned green and she realized Greg was no longer online. Instantly she felt stupid, and all the hurt she'd experienced when he'd first left came hurtling back. She switched off her mobile – a futile attempt to protect her dignity, figuring that if her phone was off then she wouldn't know if he was messaging her or not. She locked the French doors and headed upstairs for another early night. Alone.

Of course, in the staff room the next day there were plenty of comments about 'fight night', as it had become known. She was at least prepared and just hoped that the subject would eventually tire itself out. Generally people were sympathetic. 'Yesterday's news, Boss!' Kimberley James, the Art teacher, had said. 'Tomorrow's chip paper!'

Elin appreciated the good intentions and smiled a thank-you.

'Ah, but chips don't get wrapped in newspaper any more!' Ted Rowett, the resident pessimist and Head of Science, interrupted. 'It's all polystyrene boxes these days. And polystyrene takes centuries to disappear.'

Kimberley James rolled her eyes and shook her head, as Ted dug himself an even bigger hole. 'And no one even *reads* newspapers!' he said gleefully. 'It's all digital, isn't it! Oh.'

An awkward silence descended and Elin rapidly changed the

subject, remembering with horror the 'headbutting head-teacher' story in Wales Online. Still, if that was the worst it was going to get, she needn't worry. The truth was, nobody was interested in Elin Matthews today: all they were interested in was grades, and university offers, and celebrating or commiserating. It was, after all, a milestone day in the lives of all those young people and their families.

Everything wrapped up at the school around four. Some of the staff invited her to come for a drink, but she politely declined. Having spent the day surrounded by colleagues and pupils and parents and buzz, she wanted nothing more than to get home for some peace.

As she was getting in her car, a text came through. It was from Rory the gardener.

**Are you home this evening? I've been asked to
pass something on to you.**

Intrigue got the better of her and she decided she'd forego her solitude for the sake of satisfying her curiosity.

'Don't shoot the messenger,' he said as he stood on her doorstep with an armful of branches and a boxful of windfall apples.

It took a moment for her to work out what had happened. 'Oh my God, did he make you chop down my apple tree?'

'Just on his side,' he said. 'I'm afraid he's legally allowed to.'

'I know,' she said forlornly. 'Blimey, I didn't think he'd actually do it!'

She stared at the load in Rory's arms and an awkwardness descended.

'Er . . . shall I just leave these here, or . . .'

'Dear God, what's the matter with me? I'm so sorry – d'you mind taking it all round the back?'

'Sure.'

*

'It felt sacrilegious doing it,' said Rory as Elin handed him a cold beer. They were sitting on the decking looking out at the garden, the lopsided apple tree now impossible to ignore.

The late afternoon was warm and surprisingly quiet for Cardiff. No distant sirens or summer parties going on in the park. The air felt strangely potent.

'How can anyone *not* like a tree?' Elin said for the second time in half an hour. 'I mean, look at it! It's mutilated!'

'I know. I'm so sorry,' said Rory, and he sounded as if he might cry. 'I thought at least if *I* did it I could control how much was lost. Someone else might have just hacked away at it or, God forbid, cut all *your* branches and said it was a mistake.'

Elin sighed. It had made her feel quite weepy too.

'I'll never work for him again,' said Rory.

'D'you know what? I don't think I can sit here and look at it any longer.'

'Yeah, can't say I blame you.' He downed the rest of his beer, taking the hint, and stood up. 'I can see myself out.'

He picked up his phone and keys and headed for the front door.

Elin suddenly felt gripped by loneliness. 'Rory, d'you fancy staying for supper? If you've got nothing else to do?'

'What did you have in mind?' he asked.

'Fush and chups?' she ventured with a smile.

In the end, they'd had a Niçoise salad followed by a coconut sorbet that Greg had made a few months back.

'Ah, that was immense, Ellie.'

She still couldn't bring herself to correct him. They'd shared a bottle of Pinot Grigio and Elin's head was a bit woozy. It was most unlike her to drink more than a glass, but results day always made her feel like celebrating. She just hoped she'd feel the same in a week's time when Beca's GCSE results were out.

It had made a welcome change spending a couple of hours with Rory. A much better option than drinks with the teachers at the Fox and Hounds. He was an absolutely fascinating person – a fact well hidden beneath his sometimes serious demeanour. He had two degrees – a Bachelor's in Chemical Engineering and a Masters in Maths. 'Oh, and I'm also a fully qualified plumber,' he laughed.

'As well as a gardener?' Elin smiled. 'Gosh, a man of many talents. I'm surprised nobody's snapped you up.'

'Haven't met the right woman, I guess. I mean, I thought I had, but . . . Anyway . . .' He didn't look at her when he said it, lost in thought as he swirled the wine round in his glass. Originally from Tauranga on the east coast of New Zealand, he'd left five years earlier when his marriage broke down.

'No kids?'

'Nah,' he said, and she could hear the regret in his voice. 'Still, I couldn't have travelled to the other side of the world if I had.'

'Some people would, you know.'

'Yeah, well, I'm not *some people*.' Their eyes met briefly when he said it and Elin recognized a familiar flicker she'd not felt in a long time.

She'd been right about his age. He was approaching his fortieth in a few weeks.

'October the what?' she asked.

'Fifteenth.'

'Ha, same as my daughter. She'll be seventeen.'

Which opened up the subject of *Elin*'s family status. Surprisingly, she didn't feel embarrassed at all about telling him everything – Greg's affair, the divorce proceedings, the solicitor. Even the horror of Salomé's Bar. Which thankfully he found hilarious. He tossed his head back and laughed the most richsounding, throaty and genuine laugh, and Elin felt good to be entertaining for once.

She made them coffee as he stacked the dishwasher and wiped down the table. 'Thanks for the meal,' he said as she handed him his mug.

'It's been nice,' she said and they sipped in silence for a moment, their backs against the granite island, not facing each other but looking straight ahead. Which made the conversation surprisingly intimate.

'D'you know one thing I've learned since I've been over here is that Brits can be too polite.'

'Tell me who they are, I'd love to meet them!' she joked.

But Rory was pensive, serious. 'What I'm saying is, I've met a lot of people here who ignore their real feelings and end up with a load of missed opportunities.'

'Regrets, you mean?'

'Yes.'

Elin nodded. 'Hmm.'

A comfortable silence ensued as they sipped their coffee, both deep in thought.

'I'm going home in two months,' he said.

'Well, I can't blame you. New Zealand must be spectacular.'

'Yep . . . Though so is Wales.'

'Yep.'

More silence. She could feel the warmth of his bare arm next to hers, even though they weren't touching.

'So . . . will you be taking any regrets with you?' she asked.

'I don't know yet,' he said. 'That depends.'

'On what?'

'On what happens in the next thirty seconds.'

They stood there, their breathing becoming shallower, still both looking straight ahead.

Then, before the thirty seconds were up, she had put down her mug, taken his out of his hand and reached up to kiss him. It was the most daring thing Elin Matthews had ever done in her life and it felt fucking wonderful.

Rory was a good ten centimetres taller than her and she had to stand on her tiptoes. But having made the first move, she let Rory take over, luxuriating in the strength of his arms as he lifted her up on to the granite island with complete ease. 'God, you're beautiful,' he whispered as he reached inside her dress, confidently removing her cotton briefs single-handedly. The thrill was delectable. And as she lay back on the smooth granite surface, two things came to mind: one – *Please God don't let Beca walk in right now,* and two – *Lady Chatterley, eat your heart out.*

39

grace

John was in the day room when Grace arrived at Cadwallader House. One of the carers directed her to the little alcove in the corner. It was a peaceful nook away from the bustle of organized activity and interaction with others, or the blare of daytime television. John often went there to read, but today he was sitting alone in one of its two comfy armchairs, looking out at the gardens beyond.

'This is all very mysterious,' she said, attempting levity, though she knew he was going to tell her something she didn't want to hear. She took off her jacket and sat down next to him. He held her hand, but he couldn't look at her straight away.

'Cissie's blood tests,' he said. And Grace's heart sank. He didn't need to say any more.

She took a deep breath. 'Okay,' she nodded.

Cissie had had three cancer scares in the past, but had always gone into remission. Each time it happened, Grace would wonder if their luck had finally run out. 'Well, we know the routine,' she said to John, trying to sound upbeat. 'When do they start the chemo?'

But John remained still, his eyes focused firmly on a starling outside as it took a sprightly wash in the bird bath. He shook his head. 'This time,' he said, 'they don't think . . . They're saying it would be better just to make her comfortable.'

Grace was not by nature a crier. But hearing him say that brought instant tears to her eyes and a hard lump to her throat. She didn't dare speak for fear of losing control and just sat there, holding his hand even tighter, willing this debilitating emotion to go away. Eventually she channelled her sadness into indignation. 'And who's decided that, then, eh?'

'I spoke with Dr Choudhary—'

'And what did he decide? That spending money on drugs for an eighty-nine-year-old with dementia was a waste of resources? Did he? Is that what he—'

'Grace!' John held her gaze. 'You *know* that's not how it is.'

'No I don't, John. I don't know that at all.'

And she stood up and left, making her way upstairs to see Cissie, who lay there in her bed, eyes closed but not really appearing to sleep. Her limbs were restless and she was humming and occasionally emitting small indecipherable chatter. Her eyes remained shut when Grace reached out and held her friend's hand.

What a lottery life was, Grace thought, as she did so often. Why was it that she, Grace, still lived such a full and active life, hardly changed since she was younger, give or take a few aches and pains? But poor darling Cissie had endured such health challenges and overcome them with such tenacity, only to face new ones further down the road.

'Ciss?' she whispered, and for a moment Cissie's busyness settled and she opened her eyes. Seeing Grace, she smiled, a rare moment of connection between two people who'd known each other all their adult lives. And just as quickly, the moment was gone; Cissie closed her eyes again and returned to her chatter.

John was still sitting there when Grace came back downstairs.

'I'm sorry, cariad,' she said, wrapping her arms around him and kissing the top of his head.

He put his hand on hers. 'Never apologize to me, Gracie,' he said with a smile. But his voice was laden with sorrow.

By the time Grace got home it was gone nine. She'd stayed at Cadwallader House longer than usual, comforting John and adjusting them both to the news. The manager had offered her a bed for the night, but John had insisted she go home and get some proper rest. She agreed but promised to go back there tomorrow.

Despite her exhaustion, she headed for the kitchen to make her nightly Ovaltine. Funny how old habits die hard. Ovaltine was hardly a trendy drink to take to bed these days – she was meant to have camomile tea or even a little whisky. But Ovaltine was a night-time comfort from her early years that had stayed with her for decades.

The milk was just starting to bubble and a memory of her own mother came to mind: *Never let it boil, Grace. Boiled milk will burn your tongue.* Nearly seventy years now since her own mother had died. They'd not had an easy relationship and a sob caught in her throat when she realized she'd been bookended by rejection: her own mother had cared more for appearances than for Grace's happiness, and her own daughter had absented herself from Grace's life long ago. The generations on both sides of her had withdrawn their love, hadn't they? But she had her granddaughter. And her great-granddaughter. *So it's not all bad, Grace Meredith*, she chided herself. It was just overtiredness and sorrow about Cissie that had brought on the self-pity. She carried her Ovaltine to the cosy kitchen sofa. Putting on her specs, she picked up her book. She would read a chapter before bed. It was a police thriller called *He Kills in Blue,* lent to her by Neeta. Load of nonsense, really.

When she awoke four hours later, her half-drunk Ovaltine was cold by her side; the book had fallen into her lap, her place in it lost. She stood up and stretched, finished the cold Ovaltine and switched off the side lamp. Feeling stiff and still half-asleep, she shuffled in the semi-darkness out to the hallway, reaching for the newel post at the foot of the stairs, light from the street streaming in through the frosted window of the front door.

And just as she was about to turn and climb the stairs, she saw it: the silhouetted figure on the other side of the glass. She didn't dare move, and watched in horror as the cast-iron handle slowly moved down, then up, then down again. Thank God she'd remembered to lock up. Would they smash the glass next? Try to break in that way?

Suddenly she felt her age. Whoosh – the adrenalin was sprinting through her veins at a rate of knots. *Fight or flight, fight or flight . . .* Her heart raced, her breathing struggled to keep apace. She gripped the newel post for support. Should she shout out? Cry for help? But who would hear her? It was two in the morning, and the walls were thick. The chances of alerting Julie and Jeff next door were non-existent. No. There was only one thing for it: she'd have to take on the intruder herself.

Looking around for something with which to defend herself, she grabbed a golf club languishing in the umbrella barrel next to the front door. She didn't even know whose it was – she certainly didn't play golf. Was it John's, maybe? And why was she even thinking about golf right now?

'THE POLICE ARE ON THEIR WAY!' she lied, shouting with as much force as she could muster. 'AND I'LL HAVE YOU KNOW I AM ARMED!' She gripped the nine iron and pressed herself up against the architrave. *You lived through the War*, she told herself. *And a pandemic. You can do this.*

'Don't be scared, Mrs Meredith!' a voice called from the other side of the door, sounding far more fearful than Grace. 'Everything's okay.'

She didn't recognize the voice, but its tone triggered relief, which flooded her system, and she unlocked the door. Throwing it wide open, she stared in disbelief at the two people standing on her doorstep. One of them was a male police officer; the other was a rough-looking woman who seemed weak and beaten up by life, not fists. It took a few seconds for Grace to process what she saw.

'Alys!'

'I had nowhere else to go.'
    Grace stared back at her only child. Mouth open, megalith-still.

40

alys

Admittedly she hadn't had much choice. When the police had found her, she was huddled up next to an industrial bin at the back of an all-night garage somewhere outside Llanarth. It hadn't been that cold, but age was against her and her body was just not as robust as it had once been. Plus she'd hardly eaten over the past few days, desperate to keep hold of the only money she had, which was dwindling fast. It wasn't the first time in her life that she'd slept rough, but let's face it, she was very out of practice. The Brummie driver had dropped her off at Fishguard. He was heading to Ireland and she'd toyed with the idea of going with him, but even Alys's innate sense of adventure wouldn't stretch that far. How would she survive when she was over there? Age and tiredness were beginning to kick in and she seemed to be losing her grip on reality.

She'd hung around the ferry port for a day and a night, using the shower facilities and sleeping in the waiting room, pretending she was early for her ferry, until it became apparent that this was just a ruse and the ferry staff politely asked her to move on. *Move on!* If she knew where to move on *to*, that would help. But she was in such a state of vagueness, compounded by hunger and cold, she just couldn't focus on what she should do. *Come on, Alys!* she said to herself. What about heading north? Was there anyone up there she could turn to? She scoured her memory for names of old friends, alliances she may have made during her nomadic years. Nobody sprang to her now hazy mind. She'd just have to start walking.

Leaving Fishguard, carrying her bags, she stuck her thumb out and tried to hitchhike. The truck driver who eventually picked her up spent the entire journey berating her for travelling on her own. 'There's all sorts of nutters out there! Christ, if *my* mother even *thought* about hitchin', I'd have her guts for bloody garters, I tell you now!' Her wandering mind was beginning to play games and she tried to shake off the horrendous image of garters made from guts.

The driver had dropped her off at another service station, where he was stopping for the night. It was more of a lorry park than a fully fledged Services and certainly a step down from where she'd stayed a few nights before. She recognized the 'nutters' the driver had warned her about. Though when she passed the full-length mirror in the Ladies' and caught sight of her own reflection, she realized she was one of them – rootless, disenfranchised, unloved and, let's face it, unwashed. A seventy-year-old woman with her whole life wrapped up in four carrier bags.

From there she'd cadged a lift with some Germans in a campervan. They were heading for Aberaeron. She'd lied to them and said that would be perfect – she had friends at a farm just outside the town. They dropped her off at the end of a track. 'I'll be fine from here,' she said with as much enthusiasm as she could muster. 'It'll do me good to stretch my legs and walk the last bit to the farm.' She waved them off before turning round to head in the opposite direction. By then she'd lost all sense of what to do with herself. She was literally waiting for someone to sweep in and sort out her life. What a mess. She couldn't remember arriving at the closed garage. Or setting up camp round the back. Sleeping next to some bins was probably the lowest point she'd ever reached, but by then she was so exhausted by the whole trip she no longer cared.

*

The policeman who'd found her had been kind. At first she'd tried resisting him, frightened that he was about to arrest her for the Kirsty fiasco and misuse of her credit card. But when she mentioned it he appeared none the wiser, concerned only with getting her somewhere safe for the night. He'd asked her where she lived, she'd said she didn't know. He'd asked her if she'd been drinking. When she said she'd not had a drink for thirty years, she could tell he thought she was deluded. *How unfair*, she thought, *that people presume if you're down-and-out you must be a drinker*. Assumption was a terrible thing, really. Next he'd asked gently if he could check in her purse. She didn't have the stamina to refuse. And suddenly he was looking at the letter she'd received from Grace, nodding as he took down the address from the back of the envelope. 'Come on, then, Miss Meredith,' he said, helping her up. 'Let's get you home to your mam's, is it?' By then Alys had been devoid of any energy and hadn't had the wherewithal to protest.

They'd arrived in Dylan's Quay around 2 a.m. As they stood on the doorstep of Sŵn-y-Môr, Alys felt more than ever that she was in some sort of dream. The place looked distorted and strange in the lamp-post light and yet more familiar than ever. She persuaded the policeman not to ring the bell at such a late hour and suggested looking for a key under the boot brush, remembering that's where it used to be kept. But there was nothing there any more, so he gently tried the door handle. Suddenly a voice rang out. Her mother's. Strong and brave.

When Grace opened the door, she was holding a golf club and had a look on her face that could have slayed dragons. Alys didn't know whether to laugh, cry or run away. Nor did the policeman, for that matter.

It felt as if they stared at each other for an hour. But it could have only been a matter of seconds. A matter of seconds before Grace threw down her weapon, opened her arms and engulfed her prodigal daughter in a massive hug. Pulling back, Grace cupped Alys's cheeks in her hands and looked at her intently, as if checking every pore of her face, confirming that this was indeed her long-lost child.

The policeman was understandably confused. Not realizing that the two women hadn't seen each other for three decades, he simply presumed Grace must be a passionate and melodramatic Welsh-mam type. He left them to it, with Grace shouting her thanks to him as he retreated down the path.

'You can sleep in your old room if you like,' said Grace. As if the past thirty years had been a mere blip. Ten minutes later, Alys climbed into bed and was snoring deeply within seconds.

When she woke up, it took a while for her to process where she was. The clock on the bedside table said it was ten past ten – Christ, she'd slept for hours. She tried moving and every muscle, every joint ached in protest. Attempting to recall her journey to Dylan's Quay, the memory of Grace's response to her arrival was hazy. But she felt confident that her mother had been pleased to see her. Still, she'd need to get out of there as fast as possible. It was too embarrassing for words – turning up like that in the middle of the night, looking such a mess and barely uttering two words. Oh God, and that copper – what on earth must Grace have thought? *Nothing changes then, Alys – still being brought home by the police even at the age of seventy.* No. She'd have to go. Though to where, she did not know.

A gentle knocking on the door made her freeze. 'There's fresh towels in the bathroom, beaut, and breakfast downstairs when you're ready.'

She managed to mutter a feeble 'Thanks' and waited for her mother's footsteps to fade on the stairs. Then, finding something vaguely clean amongst her things, she headed to the bathroom to shower.

The sight in the mirror was mournful. She barely recognized herself. The scratches inflicted by Kirsty were still visible, though a little less raw, and her hair was matted with something indescribable. There was a slight bruise on her forehead and the remnants of her last meal stuck steadfastly to her chin. 'Jesus, Alys,' she whispered. 'What have you become?'

Turning on the shower, she stepped in carefully and luxuriated in the comforting warmth of the water and the nostalgic fresh smell of Grace's Imperial Leather soap. *Slowly, slowly*, she thought. *Just take it slowly.*

41

grace

Grace had made porridge, coddled eggs and a large pot of tea. It felt like the most natural thing in the world to fuss around the kitchen like a big Welsh mother hen, buttering fresh bread and overdoing the supplies. *When in doubt, get the food out*, she thought with a smile. A solid Welsh philosophy. This mother hen had a little chick to look after again. Though she was aware that Alys's visit was unlikely to be straightforward. The night before, they'd only said a few words to each other. She'd managed to garner from the policeman that Alys had been found sleeping rough, but that was all she knew. She'd have to tread softly, for sure.

Alys came into the kitchen carefully and sheepishly, attempting a polite smile.

'Morning,' she muttered awkwardly.

She looked a lot better than she had done the night before, but she still seemed very fragile, the good looks she'd once possessed a distant memory right now. But Grace remained positive and bright. 'Now then, sit yourself down and let's get you something to eat, is it?'

The coddled eggs were clearly very tempting and Alys dived in ravenously. *God knows when she last ate*, thought Grace.

*

The ritual of breakfast masked the stark reality of their situation: a mother and daughter reunited after decades apart, with a world of hurt and misunderstanding, retribution and pain all simmering under the surface just waiting to escape.

Eventually Alys said, 'Look, I'm sorry about turning up like this.'

'But I invited you!' replied Grace with a smile.

'I know, but to be honest, I never meant to come here,' Alys said, and Grace's smile was replaced with an expression of hurt.

'Oh, I see.'

'What I mean is, I wouldn't have come if the police hadn't picked me up. And they found your address and put two and two together. And I was too tired last night to argue, so I just let them bring me here, but once I've eaten this – which is fantastic, by the way, thank you – I'll get out of your hair.'

Grace hid her disappointment well and poured them both more tea. 'So where will you go? Back to Brecon?'

'Er, no. Can't go there. Long story.'

Grace nodded. 'Are you in trouble, bach?'

Alys looked away. 'Just waiting for the other shoe to drop, y'know?'

'Such a strange expression.'

'Yes.'

There was silence for a moment. 'You need money, I take it?'

'Ha, I always need money.'

'Then let me give you some.'

This seemed to distress Alys. 'What? No! Sorry. Look, I'm fine! I shouldn't have mentioned it. We've only just met and already I'm fucking things up—'

'Watch your language, Alys Meredith,' said Grace, pretending to admonish.

Alys smiled back nervously.

'Tell you what,' ventured Grace. 'How about you stay just a couple of days, is it? Get yourself back on your feet, at least. 'Cos

you don't look to me like you're in much of a state to go anywhere right now.'

Grace could have been mistaken, but the suggestion appeared
to make Alys tearful. The poor girl was exhausted obviously, not
just physically but emotionally, too.

All she could manage to do was nod and mumble, 'Okay,
thanks,' before swallowing mouthfuls of tea.

They discussed shallow, safe topics such as what Brecon was
like to live in, whether Alys still painted, whether Grace still
swam, and all the while they skirted around the subject of the
Past.

More obviously, they avoided the subject of Elin.

But after her third cup of tea, Alys seemed a little more relaxed.

'What's happened to John? . . . Oh God, did he die?'

'No, love,' said Grace, smiling. 'He's still very much alive. But
he has his health challenges, bless him. And Cissie. They've both
been in a home the past few years. Cadwallader House? Up on
Bryn Gwyl? She went first, he followed a while later.'

'That wife of his ever give him a divorce?' Alys asked with a
wry smile.

'No,' Grace smiled back. 'But she popped her clogs twenty-
odd years ago, so in effect—'

'Oh.' Alys looked surprised. 'Well, let's hope I inherit *your*
genes. Look at you, still going strong at ninety!'

'It's definitely the swimming,' smiled Grace.

More awkward silence, till eventually Alys said, 'I want to say
sorry to you, Mum. For all of it. What I did – not just the last
time I saw you, but with everything that went on before . . .'

'You were just unhappy, bach. After your dad, I think you
just—'

'No, that's no excuse for how I behaved. I don't . . . I never
deserved you. And saying sorry just feels so inadequate, you
know? It's such a piddling, ineffectual fucking word.'

'Language!'

'Sorry,' she said with a smile. 'But I mean it. I don't trust myself

227

not to mess things up again. I'm the proverbial bad penny and you don't need me turning up in your purse.'

'Ooh, full of the metaphors today, aren't we, my girl? Come here.' Grace reached out and pulled Alys to her, wrapping her arms around her shoulders and kissing the top of her freshly shampooed hair, which smelled of lemons.

'Cariadus,' Grace whispered.

'You used to call me that when I was little,' said Alys, teetering on the verge of tears again. 'And now I can't remember what it means.'

'*Beloved*,' said Grace. 'You were always my beloved, bach. You still are.'

Alys let herself be hugged by her old mum. And in that hug, a whole lifetime of unbelonging seemed to melt away.

The phone interrupted this tenderest of moments.

Grace ignored it.

But when the answerphone kicked in, the mother–daughter reunion was brought abruptly to an end. '*Hiya, Grace, it's Betty from Cadwallader House, love. Now don't panic, but we've had to get the doctor out for Cissie. She's not in a good way.*'

42

beca

There'd been two occasions that week when Soozi had rejected a phone call.

'Who's that?' Beca asked innocently the first time, out of idle curiosity, nothing more.

'My cousin. He's goin' through some shit and I can't be arsed to talk to him right now.'

So when the second call came, Beca presumed it was Soozi's cousin again.

When the third call came, they'd been discussing how they were going to mark Beca's results – now ominously only a day away.

'We won't be celebrating, we'll be drownin' our sorrows,' Beca said. 'But I wanna do *something*.'

'You don't need any poxy GCSEs, beautiful,' said Soozi, kissing her neck. 'You're a fuckin' musical genius. Bet Mozart never took any exams.'

Beca laughed, partly because the neck nuzzling was tickling her. 'Stop it!'

'Tell you what,' said Soozi, her face full of excitement. 'We'll wear red if you passes and blue if you fails. Knickers, that is.'

And that's when Soozi's phone rang.

When she looked at the screen, her face dropped. 'I gotta take this,' she said.

'Alrigh', how's it goin'?' she mumbled into the phone, and as she left the room, she mouthed to Beca *Won't be long* before shutting the door behind her.

Beca presumed it was an ex. It must be. Soozi had been quite open with her about her previous girlfriends, one of whom, Dani, had been something of a handful, apparently. Maybe she was back on the scene, or at least trying to get back on the scene. Beca had never seen any photos and was glad. Because although her self-confidence had rocketed since she and Soozi had got together, she didn't know if it was strong enough to withstand competition or comparison. These old girlfriends would probably be much more beautiful than she was. 'I wish you knew how fuckin' gorgeous you are,' Soozi had said time and again. 'I told you before, I don't date munters.'

'Hate that word.'

'Whatevs. I got taste, is all I'm sayin'. Mind you, so have you.' They'd ended the conversation with a long, slow kiss. And Beca had decided there and then to take Soozi at her word and believe what she said.

Trust had never raised its head as an issue. Maybe because this was Beca's first relationship and she was too naive to know any differently. Or maybe it was because Soozi was so completely believable. Beca didn't think for one moment that Soozi would ever lie – it just wasn't in her nature. She could be abrupt, yes, even offensive at times. But she wasn't two-faced and she always said it as it was. Which was why discovering her dishonesty came as such a massive blow.

The phone call lasted a good ten minutes and when Soozi came back in she looked as if she'd been hit by a bus.

'Heyyyy,' said Beca, going to her and wrapping her arms around her. 'What's happened? You okay?'

But Soozi stayed silent.

'What?'

She'd never seen Soozi cry. Never seen her vulnerable. But now she was shaking and could barely make eye contact.

Pulling herself out of the hug, Soozi held up her hand to stop Beca coming closer, visibly gathering the strength to say something important.

'I got a recording contract.'

'What?'

'And a manager.'

'Fuck.'

'Yes. Fuck.'

Beca could tell Soozi was waiting for *her* reaction, before deciding what she herself should say and do next. It was too much to take in for a few seconds. But then from somewhere tears came. Happy, proud tears.

Encouraged by this, Soozi said more. 'And there's a tour!'

'A *tour*?'

'Yeah. Belgium, Germany, possibly Sweden. Supporting this guy called Seb Lowe. I've heard his stuff actually, it's cool and—'

'THIS IS AMAZING!' Beca screeched, laughing and then crying.

'Aw, man, don't go all soft on me now,' said Soozi as Beca hugged her tightly.

'Sorry. Just a bit of a shock, that's all – I mean, it's a brilliant shock, but still . . .'

'Yeah.'

But then . . . Then, as if in slow motion, the pieces began to fit together.

'So is that who's been ringing you?'

'What d'you mean?'

'The calls, your cousin . . . I take it there *isn't* a cousin who's going through shit.'

Soozi looked in the mirror, fiddling with her hair. 'Er yeah, well, I didn't want to say nothin' till it was all confirmed.'

And that's when Beca knew. That *she* wasn't part of this amazing news. That it had been kept back from her because she didn't belong in that world. Soozi's new world.

Was it an act of self-sabotage? Some masochistic drive that made her ask the question? Because she didn't need to. She could have just assumed the answer – but somehow she had to hear Soozi actually say it.

'So am I coming too?'

Soozi kept looking at her own reflection.

'No, bird. You ain't.'

Beca nodded. Understood.

'They've got a band for me. Fuller sound, y'know? Needs more than just a keyboard, plus you're—'

'I'm only sixteen.'

'Yeah.'

There was a beat. And in that beat, Beca made a decision, of which Soozi was completely unaware.

'So glad you're happy for me, B,' Soozi said, looping her arms around Beca's waist.

''Course I am. It's immense!' said Beca, forcing herself to sound happy, elated. 'We'll have to celebrate. I'll bring us, like, about ten desserts back from work tonight, yeah?'

'Sounds lush,' said Soozi. Then, lifting her chin and looking right into Beca's eyes, she said, 'You *are* all right with this, aren't you? You'd say if you wasn't, wouldn't you?'

''Course!' she said. And hugged Soozi quickly so that she could hide her face from scrutiny. 'Right! I gotta get changed.'

'Me too.'

Beca surprised herself at how organized she was. Especially considering the rage and sense of betrayal that were coursing around her body, her stomach in a permanent state of butterflies. Not happy butterflies. Terrified, angry butterflies.

How could she?

It wasn't the news itself or even the fact that Soozi had agreed to this tour without even discussing it with Beca first. No – it was the deceit, the hiding, the lying. The fact that she'd had these meetings, these conversations, made deals, arrangements . . . and Beca had known nothing about it. Soozi had just presented it to her as a fait accompli. How could Beca ever trust her again? The strength of feeling was overwhelming. Anger didn't even come close.

She hated, hated, *hated* Soozi for trampling all over what they had in the name of ambition, without even *thinking* about Beca in all this.

She knew exactly what she was going to do.

She phoned the pub and told them she wasn't well. Considering she'd never taken a sickie, they were completely sympathetic. Next she called Grama Grace. Her house was the only place she wanted to be right now. She couldn't face going home – with the results out tomorrow it would be bad enough spending a fraught evening with her mother. But throw into the mix the questions that would inevitably come her way about Soozi and why she wasn't with her – no. It was too much.

There was no answer at Grama Grace's, so she left a message on the answerphone, telling her she'd like to stay for a few days. 'Hope that's okay. Just need to get away for a bit.' She knew her great-grandmother would understand. She just had to trust she'd be at home when she arrived, although the way she was feeling right now, she'd sleep in the garden if she had to.

The train to Carmarthen pulled into platform two at Cardiff station and Beca climbed aboard.

Half a mile away in Bellamy's Italian Palace, Soozi was buzzing with excitement at her news, singing as she served customers, dancing as she made pizza, completely unaware that Beca had just ended their relationship.

233

43

elin

In less than fifteen hours Elin would know Beca's results. She couldn't stop thinking about it and wished Beca would come home so that they could at least chat things through, work out some next steps, depending on her grades. Beca's shift was due to finish at nine tonight. Should she offer to pick her up from work? Or was she being an overbearing control freak again?

In an attempt to distract herself, she went out into the garden to collect some windfall apples. From *her* half of the apple tree. The apple tree that would always remind her in a bitter-sweet way of the night she'd been *outrageous*. What a lovely man Rory was. What a deliciously unexpected and erotic night they'd spent together. And how refreshing and out of character it was that she didn't feel one iota of guilt about what she'd done. Her one concession in that direction had been to sleep with him in the guest bedroom, but still. As soon as she'd confirmed that Beca would be staying at Soozi's that night, Elin had bolted the front door and enjoyed hours of pure, unadulterated adultery. She was technically still married, after all.

The next morning had been lovely, too. She'd made them breakfast, the sun had been shining and they had parted company on the best of terms.

'I'll be perfectly upfront with you, Rory,' she'd said. 'I'm going to delete your number when you've gone. And I'd appreciate it if you did the same.'

'Sure,' he'd agreed.

Did she feel a tweak of disappointment that he didn't offer a tiny bit of protest? Maybe, but still, it was for the best. There was absolutely no future for them, they had been a pair of passionate ships passing in the night, somewhere between Wales and New Zealand.

'You'll never know how much it's done for me,' she'd said. 'Having sex on the granite island and carrying on till dawn.'

'Me too.' He'd smiled, standing up and collecting his things. 'I hope everything works out for you, Ellie,' he'd said before opening the door. 'You deserve to be happy.'

She'd wanted to wish him the same. But she'd been so choked up by his kind words that all she could manage was a wobbly smile.

She'd waved him off, shut the door and leaned against it for a minute, eyes shut tight against the tears. 'Right,' she'd said firmly to herself. 'You've had your fun. Now get back to the real world.'

With all that had been going on over the past few days, Elin had been neglecting Grama Grace's party and a pile of responses had built up, stacked neatly on the dining table, unopened. Admittedly her enthusiasm had waned a bit of late and she'd been understandably distracted. But that wasn't Grama Grace's fault. And why should her grandmother suffer just because Elin's mind had been elsewhere? She began opening the replies, writing down in her notebook those who'd be attending. She was pleased that most replies were positive, but there *were* a couple of declines and she wondered for a moment whether she should create a B-list of lesser-known guests to bolster the numbers. Just as she was mulling this over, her phone buzzed with a text from Beca.

On train. Staying at Grama Grace's tonight. Felt like a change. Speak tomorrow.

Grama Grace's? What on earth . . . ?

She instantly rang Beca's number, but it went straight to voice-mail. So she tried Grace's landline. Another answerphone.

'Hiya, Grama Grace, I take it you know Beca is on her way to you? I hope that's okay. She didn't mention it to me till now. Call me when you can to let me know she's arrived. Sorry about this.'

Of course, she knew why Beca was doing it. She thought she could run away from tomorrow's results. In all honesty, Elin totally understood – she, too, was immensely worried about how many passes Beca had managed. Maybe it was good that she'd gone to Dylan's Quay. But then again . . . Oh, and what about Soozi? Was Soozi with her? She presumed so. On the other hand, she didn't say *we* in her text . . .

Elin took a deep breath to calm herself down and returned to opening the party replies. 'Concentrate on what you *can* con-trol,' she said aloud to herself. There was nothing she could do about Beca's results. But organizing the party was completely in her hands. And it was going to be spectacular.

44

grace

John had fallen asleep in the worn-out hospital chair and Grace sat at Cissie's bedside, occasionally smoothing her hand and talking to her as if they were merely having a natter over coffee and buns.

'I can't say it wasn't a shock, mind, Ciss. I mean, especially seeing the policeman standing there as well. Went all dizzy, I did!' Grace laughed, but it was tinged with hysteria. 'That would have been a palaver, wouldn't it? If I'd collapsed and banged my head – we could've ended up in here together, beaut!'

There was no response from Cissie, of course, who seemed remark-ably peaceful despite the oxygen mask and syringe driver attached to her frail body. It was a relief that she was not distressed.

'And don't get me wrong, at first we didn't have anything to say to each other. Well, you can imagine that, can't you? I mean, where do you start? Especially as I don't think she really wanted to be there. Just didn't have any choice, it seems – and you should have seen the state on her, Ciss, oh my God. Like she'd been dragged through a hedge backwards, what a sight. Still, a good night's sleep and a few cups of tea have done her the world of good. I can't believe it! You wait till you see her, beaut, I know she's looking forward to it . . .'

Her voice faded then. Her energy was dwindling. She'd been there since midday and now it was pushing eight o'clock.

*

When she'd arrived at the hospital, John had been waiting with one of the carers from the home. He looked drawn and exhausted and so, so sad.

'They think it'll just be days,' he said.

At first, Grace reacted angrily. As if she'd been short-changed, cheated. 'Don't be ridiculous. How can that possibly be right?'

But she knew even as she said it that it was pointless putting up a fight. There was nothing to be done. And Grace had always known this day would come, she'd just thought she'd be better at accepting it when it did.

She found denial the best place to hide, and continued with her enforced bright chatter.

'Tell you what, Ciss, I've been thinking about my birthday. A while ago, Beca mentioned us going for lunch somewhere to celebrate and I wasn't sure back then, but maybe it'd be nice. So I want you getting ship-shape again and we'll both buy new frocks, eh? Maybe go to Alfredo's in Aber? Push the boat out, what d'you think?'

The steady breathing continued, Cissie in repose remaining dignified and calm as a chaos of emotions swirled around Grace in the room.

The nurse came in and John awoke from his sleep. 'I really think you two should go home now,' she said gently. 'Cissie will be moved to St Luke's tomorrow. They'll make it nice for her there, don't worry.'

'I want her to come back with me.'

Grace had demanded to see the oncologist, who was doing her best to keep the atmosphere calm. 'I do understand, Mrs Meredith,' said the doctor, 'but, with respect, at your age and in your circumstances, I don't think that's a very good idea. There's your own health to consider, of course . . .'

John looked at Grace and squeezed her hand, then turned towards the medic. 'Well, *with respect* to you, Doctor Kearns,' he said, 'I don't think you realize what a capable woman Mrs Meredith actually is. She still swims in the sea, you know. Twice a week. You're probably half her age, and yet I bet you couldn't match that stamina!'

Doctor Kearns smiled. Grace could tell she was beginning to thaw.

John continued, 'There really is no better place for my sister to live out her final days than in her old home. And in the care of her dear friend Grace, who—' But his voice broke at this point and he couldn't say more. Everyone in the room knew that Cissie's end-of-life journey had well and truly begun, but admitting it out loud was still incredibly difficult.

'Please say yes,' said Grace, despising the desperation in her voice.

Doctor Kearns thought for a moment and then gave in, with the proviso that there would be a nurse on call and that if it all became too much for Grace, she must be completely honest and say so. Grace agreed, and permission for Cissie to be moved back to Sŵn-y-Môr was granted.

It seemed odd, smiling at this minor victory. Especially as John wouldn't be coming with them. He would return to Cadwallader House and visit Cissie every day at Sŵn-y-Môr. 'You don't need me adding to your nursing duties,' he smiled, winking at her.

With Cissie drifting in and out of consciousness now, they were able to explain to her as best they could that Grace was going home to get things ready, and that the ambulance would be bringing its precious cargo over by two o'clock the following afternoon.

Grace and John shared a taxi from the hospital, holding hands the whole way, and dropping him off at Cadwallader House first. 'I'll call you when she's in and settled,' she said, and kissed him before he got out of the cab.

He turned to her, his face exhausted by sadness. 'We have to be ready, cariad. You know that, don't you?'

And all she managed to do was nod.

45

alys

It had been the strangest sensation: sitting alone in Sŵn-y-Môr whilst Grace was at the hospital. The phone had rung twice and the answerphone had kicked in. She'd heard first the voice of Beca, followed shortly afterwards by Elin's. Who'd have thought it? The voices of her own granddaughter and daughter in such quick succession. One she'd not heard since 1992 and the other she'd never heard at all. It was thrilling. Especially to think that Beca was on her way there right now. Nearly seventeen years old and this was the first time Alys would meet her.

When she'd heard Elin's voice, she'd stood right next to the answerphone, desperate to pick up the receiver and say *Hello, dear, it's your mother here*. But she'd quickly discussed the subject with Grace before she left that morning, and they'd decided to wait a while before breaking the news to Elin of her mother's return. As Grace quite rightly said, 'You've waited thirty years, bach, a couple more days won't make any difference.' Plus, Grace knew Elin better than Alys did, after all – sad, but true – she'd know how best to handle her. And judging by the slightly arch tone of her message, Elin was not one to be messed with. Thinking about it now, Alys decided she'd prefer a few more days of relative peace before landing the bombshell on Elin. She was getting a little old for all this drama. Of course, there was still Beca's reaction to deal with, when she arrived. If she was anything like Elin, she might respond very badly. Especially as the story she'd been accustomed to hearing was that Alys had died years ago.

'Oh. Hello,' said Beca when Alys answered the door.

'You must be Beca,' Alys replied, her voice shaking. 'Your great-grandmother is at the hospital.'

'Oh my God, what's happened?'

'Sorry, no! Nothing! It's all good! Well, not for Cissie – she's the one who's in hospital, and Grace has gone to visit her, and – oh God, I'm such an idiot. Look, come in, come in.'

They walked through the hallway into the kitchen and Beca put down her rucksack.

'Can I make you some tea? A sandwich? I think there's bread and—'

'Er . . . not bein' funny,' said Beca, 'but who *are* you?'

Alys dug deep and tried her brightest, jolliest smile. 'Well, the thing is, I'm . . .'

Beca looked back at her quizzically.

'Okay, so there's no easy way to say this,' Alys blurted out. 'I'm your grandmother!'

Silence. And then confusion on Beca's face. 'I thought you was dead?'

Oh, shit.

At first, Alys kept apologizing for being there, even offering to leave. 'It's all a bit complicated to explain,' she said. 'Why things are as they are with me and your mum. It's probably best if you ask her what—'

But Beca interrupted. 'Whatever's gone on with you and her, it'll be cool. Mum loves a drama, but she always calms down in the end.'

Alys thought her granddaughter was being a tad optimistic, but she didn't want to dampen the young girl's positivity. And she really liked the stoical attitude Beca seemed to possess. Was it just a feature of this young generation that they felt some things were worth raging about, protesting against and refusing to accept, whilst others – like the small issue of a dead grandmother coming back to life – could be seen as *just one of those things*? There was also the possibility, of course, that Beca was simply not interested in old family fallouts from long before she was even born. Or maybe she just had more pressing things on her sixteen-year-old mind. After all, in Beca's answerphone message she'd said she 'needed to get away for a bit'. But it certainly wasn't Alys's place to pry.

Instead, she concentrated on making friends with her newly acquainted granddaughter, sitting in the kitchen she'd once known so well and regaling her with the happier tales from her past. Stories from her time in Spain, where she said she'd worked as a tour guide for two years around the historical sights of Madrid.

'Wow, you must know a lot about them places, then?'

'Not really, love, I used to make it all up.'

'Seriously?' Beca's eyes were wide.

'No one was any the wiser – you'd be surprised what you can get away with when you act with a little confidence.'

Warming to the reception Beca was giving her, Alys went on to list her job history. 'I was a hairdresser in Portugal for a while. Didn't last long, though.'

''Cos you couldn't cut hair?' asked Beca.

'No, darling, because I slept with the boss's husband.'

'Oh!' Beca laughed, seemingly shocked but hugely entertained.

'And then I lived in Italy for a couple of years. Florence. Beautiful city. So romantic.'

'Were you a tour guide there as well?'

'Some of the time – but that didn't work out either.'

'Because you slept with the boss's husband?' Beca laughed, anticipating the punchline.

'Good God, no,' said Alys, wrongfooting her. 'On that occasion, I slept with the boss's *wife*!'

At which Beca laughed so much she started choking on her toast and Alys had to thump her hard a couple of times on the back.

When Grace arrived home from the hospital, she discovered her great-granddaughter and her daughter enjoying each other's company at the kitchen table. She looked confused and distracted. Alys rushed to explain that all was well, that she'd told Beca she wasn't a ghost, just the family's black sheep, and now they were getting to know each other a bit.

'Let me run you a bath, Mum,' said Alys, keen to help in some way.

'No, love, I'm going straight to my bed. I'll be back up at the hospital first thing, so I'd better get some sleep.'

'How's Cissie, Grama Grace?' asked Beca.

'She's not good, bach, not good at all. They wanted to move her to a hospice.'

'A hospice?' said Alys. 'Jesus, Mum, I hadn't realized.'

'Yes. But I've persuaded them to let her come here instead.'

'Really? Is that—'

Grace put a hand up to interrupt her, not in the mood to be contradicted. Especially by a daughter who'd been out of her life for thirty years and held no rights concerning her mother's welfare. 'Get Beca her breakfast tomorrow, will you, bach?'

'I can get myself a bowl of cornflakes,' said Beca softly.

'Cornflakes? Pah, we can do a damn sight better than *cornflakes*,' said Alys.

Grace managed a sad smile. 'Make the most of this, Bec. She's got a lot of making-up to do.'

Alys and Beca smiled back and watched as Grace headed for the stairs.

She stopped at the doorway. 'And what you doin' here anyway, Beca Matthews? Everything okay at home?'

'Er, long story,' said Beca, her eyes flitting briefly to Alys. 'I'll tell you tomorrow.'

Grace nodded, and seemed relieved not to have to talk any more.

As she climbed the stairs she called down, 'Lovely to see you two in the same room, it is. Who'd have thought it? *Nos da.*'

After she'd gone, Beca and Alys remained silent for a moment.

'Get my exam results tomorrow,' said Beca eventually.

'Ah. Is that why you're here?'

'Kind of. One of the reasons, anyway.'

Alys paused. 'I take it you don't think you've done very well.'

'Got it in one,' said Beca. 'My mum's gonna go ballistic. Couldn't handle being at home when she does.'

'Well, I tell you what, I always find the *anticipation* of a dreaded event to be much worse than the event itself. So how about I make you another hot chocolate and send you up the wooden hill to Bedfordshire for a good night's sleep?'

'The what?' Beca laughed.

'Haven't you heard that expression before? The wooden hill is the stairs and Bedfordshire is your— Christ, I feel old.'

When she'd handed Beca the hot chocolate, there was an awkward moment where Alys didn't quite know how to part company.

'I'll just wash up the pan and things,' she said. 'See you tomorrow.'

'Yeah. Really lush to meet you, Nana Alys.'

And Beca gave her a shy, awkward hug before making her way upstairs.

Alys was speechless. *Nana Alys,* she beamed. *I'm Nana Alys.*

46

beca

Beca was downstairs the next morning by eight. She'd set up her laptop, making sure it was charged, and checked into the results page, refreshing it every few minutes. Pointless really as they weren't due out until ten. She had to focus on it, though. It was a good distraction from Soozi.

At first she'd thought about not telling her where she was. Just disappearing out of her life. Just like Soozi was about to do to her. But the train journey to Carmarthen had given her plenty of thinking time and as she watched the Welsh countryside and coastline fly past, she was able to calm down and get some perspective. Not telling Soozi where she was would just be cruel. And she didn't want to hurt her that much, just make her realize how much she herself had been hurt. So she'd composed a text.

Gone to see my Grama Grace. Need some time away from you. Sorry but your news has done my head in. Thought I could handle it but I can't.

She'd pressed Send and waited for the reaction. Which came almost instantly.

WTF?????

Then her phone had started ringing. She pressed Reject Call. Then it rang again. Once more, she rejected it. Then another text.

WHAT THE ACTUAL FUCK, B????

And this time she had turned her phone off.

When she'd switched it back on at Grama Grace's there'd been thirty-seven messages and fourteen missed calls from Soozi. She had felt vindicated, switching her phone off again before she went to bed and slept the sleep of the dead.

But now it was morning again and she'd have not only more Soozi texts to deal with, but also her results *and* her mother. And her dad would probably be on her case, too – if he remembered what day it was, of course. One thing she knew for certain: she would not answer Soozi today. Give her something to think about. *You can't just take my heart and chuck it away when something more exciting comes along,* she said to herself, realizing she was still pretty angry. But more than anything, she felt unbelievably sad.

She refreshed the page on her laptop again as Nana Alys came in.

'Don't know why I'm doing this,' she said as Alys filled the kettle. 'They're not due out for at least another hour.'

'Well, let's hope everyone checks in at the same time and the system crashes,' said Alys, not really understanding how the whole thing worked. 'French toast?'

'Never heard of it, but yes please.'

Alys got on with making what she described as her signature breakfast dish, admitting to Beca that it was all a bit emotional. 'I've not done this since the early eighties,' she said. 'Y'know, *looked after* someone. My parenting skills left a lot to be desired, shall we say. Maybe life does hand out second chances, after all. Although in my case this is probably more like a *twenty*-second chance . . .'

Beca smiled. She liked listening to Alys. She was what her dad might describe as 'dotty'. And she was distracting. And one thing Beca needed right now was distraction.

'Tell me more about when you were in Italy,' said Beca, interrupting Alys's trip down not-so-happy memory lane.

'Ah yes, Italy. Well, I used to drink back then, of course.'

Beca said nothing.

'I expect you heard.'

'To be honest, Mum never speaks about you. The only scraps of info I have are what I've learned from Grama Grace, and she doesn't say much either.'

'Oh,' said Alys, and Beca felt a bit harsh.

'Sorry. I didn't mean—'

'God, don't apologize, darling. Who could blame them for deleting me from their lives? I was a fucking nightmare! Probably still am, to be fair. Although at least now I'm a *sober* fucking nightmare.'

A text came through from Soozi. The tenth that morning.

Bird, plz call me. I'm dying here without you. X

Beca inwardly gloated. She couldn't help feeling powerful, despite the hurt. Then she chose to ignore it, turning back to Nana Alys.

'So what made you give up, then? In the end?'

Beca watched as Alys took a big mouthful of coffee, delicately dabbing the corners of her mouth with a napkin, thoughtfully working out her reply.

'Oh, it's a very long story, but suffice to say I went on a humungous bender – in Birmingham, of all places. Lasted a couple of weeks, I think. Slept in shop doorways, got beaten up one night—'

'Oh my God, no!' Beca was horrified.

'—and found myself in A&E. Where this lovely woman, this *angel* she was, just took me under her wing, excuse the pun, gave me a bed for the night, clean clothes, oxtail soup! – I'll never forget that soup – and asked me to come to a meeting.'

'A meeting?'

'Alcoholics Anonymous,' she smiled. 'Best thing I've ever done. It was my second attempt, but I got it right this time. Been going ever since. I've just turned thirty years sober.'

'*What?*' Beca was stunned. 'You haven't had a drink for thirty years?!'

'Nope!'

Beca's phone buzzed again. Another text from Soozi. This time a solitary question mark. She turned back to Alys, who was putting the final touches to her French toast.

'Not even, like, a sip, a mouthful of champagne or something?'

'Not so much as a chocolate liqueur or a slice of tiramisu. I don't even use mouthwash, to be fair.'

'What's wrong with mouthwash?' asked Beca.

'You'd be amazed how many things have got alcohol in them.'

'Yeah, but no one's gonna drink mouthwash, are they?'

Alys raised her eyebrows and smiled.

Beca was lost for words. All the thoughts she'd had about her hitherto dead grandmother, all the gaps she'd filled in with her own narrative all these years, all the opinions she'd formed, based loosely on what her mother never told her but hinted at – all of these and more were hurtling round her head now, everything being rearranged. She was so confused.

Alys placed the French toast in front of Beca, garnished with a sprig of basil.

'Thanks. You're like . . . I dunno, everything you just told me, you're *immense*, Nana Al.'

'Heyyyy, just because I don't drink doesn't make me a saint. In fact, I'm far from it,' Alys said, a small frown forming on her brow. 'My sobriety is the one thing that's a constant in my life. If I lose that, then I really am fucked. Pardon the French. Talking of which, how's the French toast?'

'Immense.' Beca smiled at her. 'I wish you'd come back sooner, y'know.'

'Give me forty-eight hours, you'll be glad to see the back of me, I swear.'

Beca laughed.

'So come on, then,' Alys said. 'What about you?'

'Eh?'

'Tell me about *you*. Boyfriends? Girlfriends?'

'No!' Beca retorted a little too quickly, reddening to her roots.

'Okay! No need to bite my head off.'

'Sorry,' she said with a shy smile. 'There was someone . . . but it hasn't worked out.'

'Is that what all those texts are about?'

'Er, yeah. Kind of.'

'I notice you haven't been replying.'

'No. Not ready to do that yet.'

They shared a smile. And Beca felt relieved that her nana didn't pursue it any further.

'Well, if you ask me, relationships are a bloody nightmare. I reckon we should all become sologomists. Isn't that what you youngsters are into these days?'

'You what?' said Beca, out of her depth.

'Sologomy. When you marry yourself. I quite fancy the idea – reckon I'd make myself a rather lovely wife!'

Beca burst out laughing. And Alys joined in. The two of them looked like a pair of silly, giggly schoolgirls sharing a joke.

Then a notification pinged on Beca's laptop and her face changed in an instant.

The results were out.

'Oh fuck,' she said, looking at the screen. 'Right, here goes.'

She typed in her password and waited to see her name on-screen. Alys remained silent, putting a tentative hand on her granddaughter's shoulder.

And then she saw them: lots of letter Fs.

Capital Fs.

And two Unclassifieds for Maths and Science . . . as expected. No surprise there.

But what *was* a surprise were the 2 Cs!

Boldly curling around in a sideways smile of positivity.

'I got Music and Art!' she whispered. Then turned round to Alys and virtually shouted it. 'I got Music and Art!! 2 Cs.'

'Bravo!' said Alys. And even though they'd only just met, she hugged her. A congratulations hug from Beca's new grandmother.

Instantly her mobile started ringing. She looked at the screen. 'It's Mum.'

'Don't you think you ought to talk to her?' said Alys, though Beca could tell she wasn't sure this was any of her business.

'Not yet,' she said. She couldn't bear to talk to Elin right now. She knew the time would come when she'd have to face her, but for now she just wanted to enjoy this little moment of celebration. 'I got Music and Art,' she repeated quietly. As if saying it out loud confirmed it as fact.

Her mobile stopped ringing. Then five seconds later, the landline sprang into life.

Alys looked at Beca, waiting to take her cue. But she didn't move. And the answerphone's invitation to 'leave a message' boomed out.

'Beca, it's Mum. Why aren't you picking up? Listen, I've seen the results and I just don't want you to panic. We can sort this, okay? As soon as I've shown my face at the school I'll be getting in the car and coming down there, okay?' And she rang off. No congratulations, just sympathy for the disastrous situation.

Beca put her head in her hands.

'She doesn't sound too cross,' consoled Alys.

'I know. She's just *disappointed*. It's worse when she's disappointed, believe me.'

Beca's phone flashed a message again. Soozi:

U gonna tell me how you did? U gonna call me???
FFS CALL ME!!! (I misses you xxx)

'Oh, leave me alone!!' Beca whined, switching her phone off and tossing it aside. 'I'm going back to bed.'

'Right,' said Alys. 'And I'd better make myself scarce. Not sure your mum would be too pleased to have me answer the door.'

'Thanks. For, y'know, chattin' an' that. You're immense.'

Alys smiled back, and as Beca made her way upstairs she heard her grandmother call out, 'Think I'll go for a walk. Give you both a bit of space.'

Beca didn't answer, and heard her add a feeble 'Good luck!'

She was certainly going to need it.

47

grace

Grace had spent the morning shuttling between the hospital and Cadwallader House, making preparations for Cissie's arrival. She was exhausted – so much was racing around her head, but she had to keep it together. Cissie needed her to be strong, and so, God bless him, did darling John. She was just gathering her wits as she approached Sŵn-y-Môr, only to be surprised by the sight of Elin's car parked outside.

Elin.

Her heart sank as she realized the implications of this: by now Elin would probably have stumbled upon Alys and, not having been warned, the shock would be even greater. And then there were the GCSE results. If Beca had done badly, Elin was going to be heartbroken. Grace didn't really have the emotional where-withal to deal with this right now. The timing couldn't be worse.

As she put her key in the door and went inside, it sounded as if Alys was not around. Judging by what Elin was saying, her granddaughter was only focused on unleashing her disappoint-ment on young Beca.

'It's so embarrassing! For God's sake, Beca, have you forgotten you are the daughter of a head teacher?'

'Oh yeah, like you're ever gonna let me forget THAT!' Beca

shouted back. 'And as usual, you make it all about YOU! Doesn't matter about me, what I'M going through, just how bad it's gonna look for you. That's all you care—'

'Of course it matters what you're going through,' Elin said, softening.

Grace stood in the doorway and coughed politely. 'Something wrong, bach?'

'Yes, something is very wrong,' said Elin, without taking her eyes off Beca, who was curled up in Grace's big armchair, biting her already bitten cuticles. 'Your great-granddaughter has thrown away five years of secondary education and managed to spectacularly fail all her exams!'

'I didn't fail *all* of them!' Beca wailed, turning to Grace for support. 'I passed Art and Music!'

'She got two Cs,' wailed Elin even louder. '2 *Cs!*'

'Well, congratulations,' Grace said quietly, winking at Beca. 'That's two more than I ever got.'

Beca managed a little smile, which broke Grace's heart. She went over to her and sat on the arm of the chair, pulling the forlorn sixteen-year-old into a comforting cwtch.

Elin rolled her eyes. 'There's no point in mollycoddling her, Grama Grace. That will achieve absolutely nothing.'

'Oh, Elin, *Iesu Mawr*! Why does *everything* have to be about achievements with you?'

'I'm just saying—'

'I know what you're saying, Elin. But I think you're wrong. This girl needs a bit of support from you right now, not a telling-off.'

Under the crook of her arm, she felt Beca wriggle awkwardly and mumble, 'Yeah, exactly.'

Which sent Elin into a rage. 'What is *so wrong* with wanting the best for your child? Eh? Why am I the bad guy here, when all I ever wanted . . .' – and here the tears began tumbling down Elin's cheeks, her hitherto composed, cold cheeks – 'all I *ever* wanted, was for you to have the best in life, Beca. A good education and stability! A good home! That's all I *ever* wanted for you to have . . .'

Beca seemed fearful now and Grace doubted she'd ever have seen her mother like this before. Sadly Grace was all too familiar with Elin's propensity for a meltdown. She just hadn't witnessed it for years. She stood up, gently extricating herself from Beca's embrace, and reached out instead to Elin. Who almost collapsed into her grandmother's arms.

'Hey, careful,' Grace said gently. 'You'll topple me over!'

'Sorry,' said Elin, burying her face in Grace's neck and sobbing. They stood like that for a couple of minutes, Grace smoothing Elin's hair and soothing her with gentle coos and '*There, there*'s.

Having finally pulled herself together, Elin broke out of the hug and shook herself down, wiping her cheeks and attempting to regain some authority.

When am I going to do it? thought Grace. *When on earth am I going to find the right moment to tell her that Alys has come back?*

Elin was like a dog with a bone right now, and so fragile. To break the news that the mother who'd abandoned her had returned after decades away might just push her over the edge . . .

'What we need to do now,' said Elin calmly, 'is think about next steps, that's all. And that's what we were discussing, isn't it, Beca?'

'I'm *not* resitting and I'm *not* going to sixthform, so forget it.'

'Oh yes you are, young lady!' And Elin was back on the attack, her emotional outburst forgotten, her head-teacher mantle restored.

But Beca was in fighting mood. 'I'm staying here. I want to live here with Grama Grace.'

'Well, we'd need to talk about—' said Grace, but her voice was drowned out.

'DON'T BE RIDICULOUS! WHAT ARE YOU GOING TO LIVE ON? AIR??'

'I'LL GET A JOB, AT NEETA'S CAFÉ OR SOMETHING!' shouted Beca triumphantly.

'What about Soozi?' asked Grace, but again she was drowned out by Elin.

'Oh well, that's just marvellous, you're going to wait tables and scoop ice-cream into cones for the rest of your life, are you?'

'At least I'd be HAPPY doing that! You're ALWAYS complaining about your job. D'you know what they call you in school? THE MISERY MAGNET! – YEAH! 'Cos you're always so FUCKING MISERABLE!'

'THAT'S ENOUGH!' shouted Grace at the top of her voice. 'JUST STOP IT! BOTH OF YOU!'

Beca and Elin immediately shut up. If they'd been dogs, they'd have whined self-pityingly, their tails pointing firmly between their legs.

Grace shut her eyes and put her hands to her face, gathering her thoughts, mustering her strength. She turned to them both. 'A couple of hours from now, the ambulance will be bringing Cissie here to stay—'

'Cissie?' asked Elin, confused.

'She's coming home to . . . well, y'know.' Still Grace couldn't say the words.

'Why didn't you tell me? When did this—'

'Grama Grace, I'm so sorry,' whispered Beca.

Grace nodded, taking a deep breath and trying to fast-track recovery from the turmoil of the row – turmoil that her home hadn't seen in a very long time.

'Well, if you really mean that, then you'll put all this nonsense behind you, because quite honestly life is too precious to be arguing over a few silly exams. Don't you think?'

Beca readily agreed, but Grace could tell that Elin was just going along with her. They hadn't heard the end of this row, that was for certain.

The doorbell rang, breaking the tension.

'I'll go!' said Elin, understandably glad to leave the room.

Grace and Beca stood in silence for a moment. The storm that was about to break was unavoidable.

'I take it you haven't told her?' whispered Grace, surrendering to the inevitable. And Beca shook her head. Walking out into the hallway, they both waited for the fallout.

They watched as Elin opened the door.

And listened to the silence that followed.

Alys.

Smiling nervously at the daughter she hadn't seen for three decades, and struggling to find the right words. All she could manage to say was . . .

'Hello, Elin.'

alys and elin

1982–1992

48

elin

aged eleven

She's walking down Newport Road, the city-centre traffic performing its traffic-light dance alongside her – *stop, wait, slow, slow slide then move; fast, slow, stop.* Vehicles, open-windowed and dusty, let in the hot smog and let out a mish-mash of notes, tumbling from competing radio stations and cassette players. The sloppy musical chaos combines with horn toots and engine thrums, and mechanical clanking from a nearby building site. Summer in the city.

Elin recognizes one tune that everyone in her class loves singing – the Steve Miller Band repeating the phrase 'Abra-abra-cadabra, I wanna reach out and grab ya'.

Not music that Elin likes.

Though she knows she should like it. To be the same as the rest of them.

But she's not. Not when it comes to music. Not when it comes to anything.

Today was her last day of primary school. Mrs Rogers cried when she said goodbye to them all in their final assembly and gave everyone in the leavers' class an individually wrapped present – a key ring in the shape of a four-leaf clover made from shiny green enamel. Some of the boys chucked theirs away as soon as they'd run out of the school gate, in an act of bravado, chanting Pink Floyd's 'Another Brick in the Wall' at the tops of their voices – *We don't need no education*. But she's held on tight to hers. Because she loves her good-luck clover. She will always treasure it. She's already attached it to her front-door key – forcing it between the double metal rings until it's safely affixed.

She opens the dirty, cracked glass door at the side of Mac's – a run-down greasy-spoon café, the smells of which fill their home daily. She likes Mac. He's kind. And so is his wife. She has given Elin many a free breakfast. Not that she's ever asked for one.

She hears shouting. Fearfully, she treads the stained purple carpet that leads up the stairs to her home. The door is ajar and she steps inside. There's a man she doesn't recognize standing with two others, arms folded and scary. Her mother is crying – nothing new there.

The men don't see Elin straight away but her mother does and she changes gear, screaming now at the men. 'And this is my child! You're just going to throw her out as well, are you? Like a piece of unwanted rubbish?'

'You are squatting, Miss Meredith. You have no right to be here.'

Her mother grabs Elin's arm and pulls her daughter to her. Not out of love, Elin suspects, but to use her as a pawn in some domestic negotiation. 'Look, just let me stay here another week. Give me time to—'

'You said that last time. And the time before. You have one hour to gather your things and leave, otherwise my friends here will do it for you. Your choice.'

Her mother sinks to her knees and wails, 'I can't cope, I cannot deal with this. Please! Please, help me.' This isn't a shock for Elin. This is a regular occurrence and she has long become used to seeing her mother like this.

The men also stand unmoved. One of the arms-folded fellows attempts a kind little smile at her, but she scowls back. It's not a happy situation. It doesn't warrant a smile.

'We can call Social Services – get the child removed, if you like. Do better than she is at the moment—'

Her mother catches her breath and gasps, 'Don't you dare!'

'Come back in an hour, we'll be gone by then,' Elin says, helping her mother to her feet.

The men look unsure, floored by the maturity of this schoolgirl. When the bailiffs leave, the room is silent.

'I'm sorry, baby,' weeps her mother, wiping her eyes.

'You'll need to pull the suitcase down from the wardrobe,' Elin says, as she begins to extricate her key from its enamel clover.

49

alys

aged thirty

'It's just until I get myself sorted,' she says, red-eyed and shaking. She needs a drink. But she daren't ask, daren't push her luck.

'Just tonight,' he says. 'And the kid sleeps in the kitchen. Can't have her in the same room, wouldn't be right.'

To call it a studio flat is a tall order. In reality it's no more than a bedroom with three doors leading to a landing, a bathroom and a tiny kitchen. There's a tired two-seater sofa in the corner, a couple of hard-backed chairs and a yellow Formica table adorned with several empty beer cans and an overflowing ashtray. It's the last resort. The only place Alys could think of; the only person she could ask for help. She can hardly call him a boyfriend – more of a pub acquaintance whose bed she's shared a few times. And the bed was on the more glamorous occasions: a deserted beer-garden table and a damp alley also spring to mind. She flinches at the thought.

Looking down at Elin, Alys forces a smile.

'That'll be fun, won't it? Sleeping in a kitchen, of all places!'

Her child stares back. Boring into her with that guilt-inducing look that Alys has come to know so well. The look that tells her she's failed her. Failed them both. Again.

'Are *you* sleeping in the kitchen as well?'

Alys hesitates.

And before she can answer, he jumps in, 'No, your mummy's sleeping with Uncle Jack. Keep his feet warm at night.' And he laughs and slaps Alys's backside before heading to the bathroom.

The close proximity of the WC affords no privacy and the sound of him peeing for an interminably long time fills the room. Alys watches a flicker of light go out in her daughter's eyes.

Replaced by comprehension.

Disappointment.

Shame.

'Let's make a little den, shall we?' she says, trying to muster enthusiasm, and she takes the cushions from the sofa, placing them on the kitchen floor to fashion a makeshift bed. From the hastily packed suitcase she pulls out a couple of pullovers to act as a cover, rolling her coat up as a pillow. 'It won't be for long, I promise,' she whispers as she tucks Elin into the pathetic excuse for a bed. Next door, the two-gallon lavatory flushes.

50

grace

aged forty-nine

'There, there, bach,' she whispers. 'All will be well, you watch.' She holds the child tight, kisses the top of her head. They are sitting in the visitors' room of Cardiff Royal Infirmary, the August sun powering through the window, turning the fixed orange seats plasticine-soft. How familiar it feels to wrap her arms around her charge: familiar yet novel. Because she's only met this grandchild, her only one, a handful of times. *Such a quiet soul*, she thinks. Not like her own daughter was at this age.

A doctor comes along the corridor towards them, smiling, and sits down on the plastic chair next to them.

'Where's my mother?' asks Elin.

'She's having a little rest at the moment,' he says. 'She's very tired and needs us to keep an eye on her.' The doctor gives Grace a meaningful not-in-front-of-the-child look.

Grace takes her purse out and finds a few coins. 'Tell you what, bach. Go and fetch Grama Grace a cup of coffee, is it? And a hot chocolate for yourself.'

Elin looks back at her and sighs. She knows this is her grandmother's distraction technique, but accepts the mission without complaint.

Maybe the poor girl's tired of being kept in the picture, Grace thinks. *She's seen too much already.*

They watch Elin take herself off towards the vending machines and the doctor launches in.

'Alys is doing well,' he says.

'Can I see her?'

'Not yet. She's heavily sedated and will need to be transferred to Whitchurch Hospital. For psychiatric care.'

The words jar. They shout failure and weakness and Grace wishes she could just tell her daughter off, chastise her for being such a drama queen. It need not have come to this, after all. If Alys had just not been so stubborn. If she'd just let herself be helped.

'I've let her down.'

'No. That is absolutely not true.'

They sit there in silence for a moment, watching Elin in the distance navigating the instructions of the vending machine.

'We need to focus on the positives for now,' says the doctor.

'What's positive about an overdose?'

'The fact that it wasn't an intentional one. That makes a huge difference. It was a cry for help, for sure – but Alys cried for help and we heard her.'

Grace feels enraged at this and cannot bite her tongue. 'No, *we* didn't hear her – that eleven-year-old child over there *found* her. It'll scar the poor mite for life.'

The doctor nods. He's not disputing this. Grace tries to banish the image from her head, but it stubbornly remains: Elin in some godforsaken bedsit trying to rouse her comatose mother and failing; finding the pill bottle, running on to the street and stopping a stranger for help because there was no phone to call an ambulance. Taken by Social Services whilst her mother had her stomach pumped, being asked who else they could call. Elin knowing of nobody, no friend of the family, only some man in a café called Mac, who thank God had stepped in and taken control. Grace dreaded to think what would have happened had Elin not remembered visiting her – five years earlier, for the Silver Jubilee – not remembered this dim and distant grandmother whom Alys had since cut out of their lives. Her selfish, selfish daughter. Who had now left her eleven-year-old child stranded, almost orphaned, and terrified.

'Mrs Meredith?'

Grace realizes she's not been listening. 'Sorry, what?' She watches Elin approach, precariously holding two hot drinks in beige plastic cups, concentrating hard on not spilling them.

'I was saying that if you're not able to look after Elin, then Social Services will need to find temporary foster care until Alys is well enough to—'

'Oh, Elin will be staying with me,' she interrupts. 'There's no question of that, Doctor.'

51

elin

aged eleven

Elin's not sure if she prefers making Welsh-cakes or pikelets the most. Welsh-cake mixture tastes nicest, of course, and she loves cutting out the rounds with Grama Grace's pastry cutter before placing them on the heavy black bakestone so that they can brown slowly. But then pouring the pikelet batter is fun, too – she has to judge just the right amount to make the correct size, and meet the challenge of producing a perfect circle.

Aunty Cissie says Elin's pikelets are even better than Grama Grace's. And that's saying something. Because Grama Grace's cooking is amazing. Elin likes Aunty Cissie. She gets the giggles sometimes over the silliest of things and it's infectious. And once she starts, she takes ages to stop. Grama Grace calls her a flibbertigibbet. But she says it with a smile.

Aunty Cissie lives in Grama Grace's boarding house. She's Elin's favourite of all the residents. Mr Hughes is very polite, but keeps himself to himself. Grama Grace says it's because he's a very sad man whose wife died and they had no children. He moved into Grama Grace's because otherwise he might die of loneliness. There are three other people living there – Uncle John, who's Grama Grace's boyfriend, and Miss Jones, who teaches

Welsh and Music in a private school. She's tiny and mouse-like and always speaks in Welsh with Grama Grace. And then there's Mr Harman, who likes wearing dresses. He showed Elin his wardrobe once and let her try on his shoes. They were too big – he has to get them sent in the post from a special mail-order catalogue. He let Elin do his make-up last week when he was going out for the evening. She didn't do a very good job, but he obviously didn't want to hurt her feelings and told her she was a natural artist. She's not. Art is not her thing. *Music* is her thing. Miss Jones has been teaching her to play the cello. She says Elin should definitely continue. One evening, Miss Jones accompanied her on Grama Grace's upright piano and they did a mini-concert for the residents. Aunty Cissie cried when Elin played. She said it was one of the most beautiful things she'd ever heard.

Elin presses down lightly on the Welsh-cakes with the spatula. There's a plate already piled high with the ones she's finished. This is the final batch. She inhales the sweet baked smell – a comforting combination of butter and currants and spice; an aroma that she will always associate with this house, with comfort and with safety.

'That's a shopful you've made there!' says Grama Grace. 'We should have set up a stall in Dylan's Quay market and sold them.' Grama Grace gives her a big cwtch, forcing herself to sound happy. Even though Elin knows she's not. And nor is Elin. Because today her mother is coming to collect her.

'Mummy's all better and brand-new now, sweetheart!' Alys had said on the end of the phone last week. 'Isn't that fabulous?'

'Yes,' Elin had said quietly.

She wants her mother to be better – of course she does. But she doesn't understand why they can't all live together at Grama Grace's. Why do they have to go back to Cardiff?

'But we're not going to live in Cardiff, sweetpea!' Alys had said down the crackling phone line. 'We're going to live somewhere much more exciting than Cardiff!'

Elin finishes the final batch and stands back to admire her

work. She closes her eyes, committing this feeling to memory, the warm, invisible blanket of love and homeliness. She stores it up. Because she's not sure how long it will be until she feels like this again.

The soft *bing-bong* of the doorbell disturbs her trance and she opens her eyes. Grama Grace is smiling at her and whispers, 'Do you want to answer it or shall I?'

52

alys

aged thirty-one

The shoulder stand is much easier now. And so it should be after over three months of daily yoga practice. Alys breathes out and lowers herself back into lotus, under the shade of the Spanish palms, the grass fresh beneath her feet. She still cannot believe that they are living here – the excitement and beauty of Madrid, free accommodation and an education for Elin at the local Catholic school. All thanks to Eduardo.

She'd met him at group therapy in Whitchurch Hospital, three weeks into her stay there. Who would have thought that that day would have heralded such a monumental change in her life? A forty-nine-year-old Spanish psychiatrist on sabbatical from Madrid University, Eduardo had been observing the group, under the supervision of Dr Powell. At first Alys had barely noticed him. In all honesty, she hadn't had time to notice anyone else at that stage. All she'd cared about was convincing the powers-that-be that she was better now and should be allowed to go home. Wherever 'home' would be.

On the occasion when she did notice Eduardo, she found him to be very aloof and decided he was one of those arrogant intellectuals who thought himself a bit above everyone else. But later – much later – he'd confessed he'd fallen for her the moment he'd set eyes upon 'that glorious visage' and had been terrified by the strength of his feelings. He'd also known it was highly unprofessional for him to strike up any sort of relationship with a patient. For that's essentially what Alys was. Even though Eduardo was just an observer.

Six weeks after she'd been admitted, Dr Powell had felt that Alys had indeed made enough progress to be discharged. And as long as Social Services were satisfied that suitable accommodation could be found, then it looked likely that she could be reunited with Elin and make a fresh start.

Alys had been delighted and had gladly accepted Eduardo's offer to be her advocate and accompany her to the meeting with Mrs Ramsay, the social worker. During the meeting, Eduardo sat silently. Ever the observer, ever the Spanish gentleman. But once the meeting was over and the practicalities agreed, he'd accompanied Alys back to the day room. He'd asked her if she would like to take a small detour through the hospital grounds, seeing as the September sun was warming the day so delectably. Alys had been taken with Eduardo's flamboyant use of English and was feeling celebratory, so she'd agreed.

They'd sat on a bench under a large oak, and with little ceremony or warning, Eduardo had declared his all-consuming love.

'You are a remarkable woman. A feat of godly ingenuity. Come with me, please, to Spain.'

At first, Alys had wondered if her medication was playing havoc with her head, so unexpected was this outburst from a man with whom she'd barely exchanged more than a handful of words until now. But it didn't take long for her to realize that he was deadly serious. And when she weighed up the prospect of living in a hostel with her eleven-year-old daughter, scraping together some sort of existence in the dreary world of Cardiff city centre, against flying two thousand miles into the Spanish sunshine and living with a man who appeared to be the real deal, there wasn't much of a choice to make. The only fly in the ointment was Elin. Would he pay for her to come, too? And if he would – how would Elin feel about living in Spain?

Eduardo didn't hesitate. Of course he knew about Alys's daughter – she'd spoken about her often enough in group sessions – and it would be an honour to bring her, too.

So with that in mind, Alys had set off for Dylan's Quay to collect the daughter she'd not seen all summer, and to whisk her away to a better life amongst kinder people with a fascinating culture.

When she arrived at her mother's house, she'd felt the familiar lurch of sorrow. The cloud of negative energy and unhappiness from her youth that had shrouded the two years she'd spent living there felt as strong as ever. The place had too many bad memories for her. So much so that she'd only been back a handful of times, out of a sense of duty – once was for the Silver Jubilee, when she'd got very drunk on cheap champagne and ended up sleeping with the postman.

But whatever she might have felt about her mother in the past, despite the behemoth of resentment that was lodged inside her, she couldn't deny that Grace had come to her rescue two months previously when Alys had suffered her 'little incident'. And God only knows what would have become of Elin if Grace hadn't offered to take her in whilst Alys was recovering in hospital.

She'd spoken to her mother on the phone first – told her of the plan to move to Spain. Once the words were out, Alys awaited the disapproval. And as expected, she could practically hear Grace bite her tongue, could feel the judgement oozing out in waves – *What's silly old Alys gone and done now?* she'd imagined her mother thinking. *Away with the fairies, that girl. Spain? Ye gods.* But Grace had merely acknowledged the news politely, telling Alys that she hoped she knew what she was doing, and that if she preferred, she could leave Elin to stay in Dylan's Quay. The local comprehensive school nearby was really very good and

Elin had already been going there for a couple of weeks, of course.

'Why?'

'Well, because term has started, bach. She needs routine.' Grace's voice seemed to fade as the confidence drained from it. 'And I just thought if you're not feeling ready . . . to take her back—'

'You think I'm such a loser, don't you, Mother?'

'A what?'

'You don't think I can handle it. Just because I fucked up once—'

'Alys, please don't swear, it's so unnecessary.'

But Alys ignored her and the burgeoning resentment inside her came tumbling out. 'You can't get rid of me that easily, y'know.'

Grace had sighed on the end of the phone. 'Alys, cariad—'

'Don't call me that!' *Cariad* had been her father's name for her; it didn't belong to her mother.

Silence. Then Grace had tried again.

'I know how unhappy you've been, how difficult things were—'

'Elin's been moaning about me, I suppose?' Alys snapped. 'Been having cosy little chats together, have you?'

'Sweetheart, I only want to help, that's all.'

'By keeping me and my daughter away from each other?' she'd cried.

'Stop it now,' Grace had said. 'Please don't upset yourself. I really don't want you to be upset.'

Alys had tried to calm herself. She'd thought about the breathing exercises they'd been shown at Whitchurch and she'd closed her eyes and inhaled.

'Look, I'm sorry, Mum, okay? It's just I think this could be really exciting for me and Elin. And I'm doing my best to make up for everything.'

'I know, bach,' Grace had said gently. 'I'll fetch her for you now. Let you tell her the good news!'

*

Elin's response had been as muted as it was to anything her mother ever suggested. Alys had tried to engender excitement at the prospect of their new life in Spain, but Elin couldn't have been less interested. And then she'd delivered the killer blow.

'I want to stay here with Grama Grace,' she'd mumbled.

Alys had wanted to cry. To scream. To hit out at the unfairness of it all. She was trying, wasn't she? To make it all better. To make up for letting her daughter down so massively. She took a deep breath and said, 'Well, I can understand that, Elin, of course. But I'm afraid that's not possible. You're my daughter, and you're coming with me, okay?' It was an almost direct repeat of the conversation Grace had had with Alys about moving to Dylan's Quay years earlier. The irony.

That was almost four months ago now. And if Elin is still missing life in Wales, then she's doing a good job of hiding the fact. The Catholic school she attends is connected to an orphanage where Alys helps out, in exchange for board and lodging. Eduardo organized it all – being friends with the superintendent there has proved to be a godsend.

They've had to lie to Elin, of course. About Eduardo's wife. Alys is cool with the fact that he's married – marriage means nothing to her anyway, but she doesn't want to upset any cultural apple carts either in Spain or Wales. So if anyone asks, she tells them that Eduardo's mother is very strict. 'Soon she will pass on to the next world,' she says, attempting to look holy and pious.

She looks far from holy and pious lying naked in Eduardo's arms once a week when he whisks her off to a local hotel to drink sangria and have sex. *Life could be a lot worse*, she thinks.

'Mum?'

Alys opens her eyes and smiles at Elin, serious-faced as ever and wearing her school uniform.

'You're going to be late!'

Alys gathers her things. It's the Nine Lessons and Carols this afternoon at the little school chapel. Seems odd to be celebrating Christmas in the Spanish sun. But at least they're not stuck in some damp house-share in Cardiff, scrabbling around for 50p to put in the electric meter. 'Coming!' she says, jumping up.

53

elin

aged twelve

Dear Grama Grace,
Sorry this is so short but I'm in a bit of a hurry to get it in the post box before we catch the train. Mum doesn't want me to tell you, but I thought you ought to know that we are moving to Barcelona.

Things went a bit wrong with Eduardo.

Turns out he didn't have a mother.

But he did have a wife.

Who wasn't very pleased when she found out about Mum, as you can imagine. So now we're having to do a runner. Mum says it's exciting and that I should treat it like one big adventure, but it doesn't feel very exciting to me. I will write again when we are settled and send you our new address.

love you to bits,

Elin xx

PS I wish we could come and live with you instead.

54

grace

aged fifty

Easter 1983

Grace checks her purse again to reassure herself she has the cash – two hundred pounds' worth of pesetas in crisp new notes, collected from NatWest in Dylan's Quay only yesterday; how lucky they had some in stock.

Paulo the taxi driver is friendly and his English is good. At least they don't have to rely on Grace's very limited Spanish, which just about covers 'please', 'thank you' and 'where is the station?' She has been travelling now for almost a day and is desperate for a shower and a sleep. Paulo tells her there is a very good, cheap hotel near where she is going and common sense gets the better of her: she really should rest before she does what she's come here to do. In all honesty, another hour probably won't make that much difference, so she tells Paulo that yes, please, she would very much like to check in to the hotel first. She should've planned better, but the decision to come here was made hastily and without much forethought. *Just get there. Get to Elin, bach.*

John had driven her to Heathrow, which was enormously generous of him – especially as he didn't tend to venture further afield than Swansea these days. Cissie came to keep him company. She'd offered to come to Spain, too, but someone had to keep an eye on things back home. Plus Grace had no idea what she was going to find when she got there, and she felt that Cissie's presence might just add fuel to the fire, God bless her lovely, innocent soul. She didn't deserve that, of all people.

They pull up outside a smart but simple hotel boasting two stars from the Spanish Tourist Board. Paulo fetches her case from the boot and gallantly holds out his arm to assist her to the door. She politely refuses – a default of Grace's when it comes to old-fashioned courtesies like that, though she knows he means well and doesn't wish to offend. She follows him inside to a tiny reception desk, where he swiftly organizes her a room. He seems to know the receptionist, a kindly woman with sharp brown eyes and snowy white hair whisked into a loose bun like an unruly meringue. She's dressed in black and exudes the sombre bearing of a widow. *Just like me*, Grace thinks to herself, and remembers when she last wore mourners' black. But then the widow laughs and her face lights up with a broad smile – she's apparently fond of Paulo.

Grace offers him a tip, which he graciously accepts, smiling at her before he leaves. 'You sleep now. You very tired, I am thinking. Very tired and perhaps a little sad.' His gaze lingers, as if he's trying to read her mind. A combination of his kindness and her fatigue overwhelms her so much that she finds herself fighting tears. 'Good luck!' he calls as he walks out through the hotel's double doors.

She sleeps longer than she'd planned to, and when she wakes she rushes to shower, letting the water briefly refresh her whole body. It's dark outside now and as she dries herself she is gripped with nerves at what might lie ahead. But she has no option.

It was Elin's most recent letter that made her decide. It's only three days since she received it, yet it feels much longer. They've been writing to each other for several weeks now care of a P.O. box address, and Grace senses that the contact between them has been some sort of lifeline for little Elin.

There's been nothing from Alys, of course. Not since the phone call. 'You may as well know, it didn't work out in Madrid,' she'd gabbled on a line beset with crackles and beeps. 'And before you say *I told you so*, it wasn't my fault, okay?' Grace realized in that moment that Alys knew nothing of the correspondence between them, or that Elin had actually told her grandmother about having to move to Barcelona. She'd waited with bated breath to see whether Alys would tell the truth now or not. She didn't. 'Basically, the visa people said we hadn't filled out all the proper forms, so we've had to move on. We're in Germany now.'

Grace had swallowed, in pain from Alys's lie.

'Anyway, my money's running out. I'll call again sometime. Elin sends her love.' And the line had gone dead. She could only presume that Alys once again felt she'd failed and didn't want to be reminded of this by further connection with her own mother.

'You've got me so wrong, bach,' Grace had whispered pointlessly into the phone, which purred back at her, as if confirming that nobody was listening.

That had been nearly three months ago.

Through mimed actions and broken English, the lady at reception, whose name is Maria, directs Grace to the apartment block she's looking for. She tries to convey to Grace that it's not a nice area – she must let her nephew accompany her for protection.

Grace's first reaction is to refuse, but then she wonders why she's being so stubborn – how many times has John laughed at her and said, 'Let yourself be helped, you silly mule!' It turns out that the nephew in question is Paulo, the kind taxi driver. He is in the hotel reception within minutes. And this time Grace *does* take his arm.

As they walk purposefully along the main street, they are surrounded by the party atmosphere of night-time Barcelona – the colourful lights, the guitars and maracas, a flamenco display in the nearby square, the mouth-watering smells emanating from tapas bars, friendly cheers and laughter. But then they turn down a side street and the atmosphere changes in an instant. It doesn't feel dangerous as such, but it does feel a million miles away from the city centre, not just a few yards.

Their conversation is understandably sparse. Grace tries to explain what she is about to do. That she has come to find her twelve-year-old granddaughter and take her home to Wales. Because her granddaughter's mother is no longer capable of looking after her. She doesn't explain that she doubts Alys ever *was* capable. But she does say that she thinks Alys is in trouble.

'And your daughter, Alys – will she come home with you, too?'

Grace sighs. 'I hope so,' she says.

They reach the address that Grace has written down, copied diligently from Elin's recent letter. The letter that it still pains Grace to remember. *I don't like it here, Grama Grace. Sometimes Mum doesn't wake up for days and the other people are always shouting or drunk . . .*

Grace rings the intercom doorbell. There is no corresponding sound, nothing to indicate that anyone knows they are there. She tries again. Nothing.

Paulo shakes his head.

Then, with some force and ferocity, a laughing couple come tumbling out of the entrance, drunk with love or lust or sangria, unaware of the two strangers waiting outside. Paulo catches the door before it closes and the two of them step inside.

They climb three sets of steps, the cold stone stairwell echoing with hostility. They reach number four. At first the door looks closed and they go to knock, but it gives way, opening up into a dark hallway. The silence is unnerving. In some ways it might have been better to hear voices shouting, an argument even – at least that would indicate life was going on, albeit angrily. But there is nothing.

Paulo calls out, 'Hola?' Nobody replies.

They continue along the hallway. The place smells stale.

Cigarettes and damp, mixed with old onions. *No place for a child to live*, Grace thinks.

Paulo slowly opens the door to a small kitchen and is met by a voice Grace recognizes instantly, despite its fearfulness: 'If you come near me, I'll hit you with this!' It's Elin.

Grace pushes past Paulo and into the room. 'It's all right, bach, it's all right!'

'GRAMA GRACE!' Elin screams and runs to her, dropping the large, rusty pan she'd been holding in defence. They hold each other for what feels like a year, Grace attempting to infuse her granddaughter with love and reassurance just through the power of a cwtch.

'Where's your mam, bach?' she whispers.

'In there,' Elin sobs, pointing to the other room.

Paulo goes in first, holding his hand out in an attempt to stop Grace from following, clearly worried at what he may find.

Difficult at first to adjust to the darkness and the shadows of this sad space, a pitiful excuse for a bedroom. There's a mattress on the floor, covered in two blankets and a coat. Next to it three empty wine bottles and an overflowing ashtray. An abandoned china cup on its side contains the remnants of some black coffee. The windows have no curtains, no shutters, and night-time Barcelona carries on regardless beyond them. A form in the makeshift bed lies there, stone-still.

It's Alys.

Her back to them, turned away from questions, from recrimination and responsibility. Turned away from life.

Paulo kneels and gently shakes her arm. 'Excuse? Miss?' There is no response and Grace gasps involuntarily, fearing the worst.

Paulo takes hold of Alys's shoulder more robustly now and pulls her round on to her back.

Still nothing, and then a low moan. 'Errrrghh . . .'

'Señora?'

Alys recoils, suddenly finding the energy to be scared. 'Who the fuck are you?'

Paulo backs off and Grace, losing all sense of patience and compassion, filled with anger once again at the selfishness of her daughter, shouts out, 'We'll have less of that foul language, Alys Meredith, thank you very much! Now sit up and tell me exactly what's been going on.'

55

alys

aged thirty-one

It's been such a long time since she's experienced comfort like this. Even though her surroundings are nothing special, to Alys they are luxurious. Because this clean, sparse, budget hotel room is a world away from where she's been. She stares out of the window at the sunny day lolloping about its business on the street below. People with lives to live, routines to follow – happy chat with passers-by, exchanges of niceties, jokes, commiserations, gossip. All the stuff of human interaction. Something which Alys has long since foregone. She thinks this might be the second day she's been here, or is it the third? All so hazy. Her head still hurts, although she's been obediently drinking the copious jugs of water that keep being brought to her room. Along with trays bearing little dishes of food. She tries her best to eat. She's definitely getting better at it.

Over and over in her mind she replays what has happened, how she has ended up here. The man woke her up and her mother was there. *Her mother!* She still cannot believe it. She'd thought it was some sort of nightmare at first – Elin standing next to her, looking terrified. And there was shouting, and then tears, and suddenly she was being held – her mother was holding her, telling her it would all be all right. The next bit is missing from the narrative in her head. She knows she slept. She remembers a bath, her mother there – kind, quiet, bathing her like she did when she was a child, lovingly washing her hair with shampoo and rinsing it away with warm, clean water. Rinsing away the pain. Cooing soft encouragement all the while. 'Nearly done and then we'll get you into bed, is it, bach?'

Madrid seems like another lifetime now. Eduardo's face as he stood helplessly behind the woman who had ranted at her, screamed at her. His wife. Not being able to make sense of what she was hearing, of what she was seeing – Elin's clothes, her possessions, all of her things, being thrown out. Exiled. Again. Eduardo returning when his wife had gone, apologizing, begging her forgiveness, whilst simultaneously packing her things into his car so that he could get them both to the train station. Get them out of his life. Hastily arranging the journey to Barcelona, and foisting the name and address of a stranger on to her who would help her when she got there.

But on arrival the stranger was nowhere to be found and once again she was left to carve out some sort of existence for the two of them, trying all the while to convince Elin that this was part of their great adventure together. Her only means of income once her cash ran out was to sing on the street with a mortified Elin. It was slapdash and desperate – they were begging, in truth, though Alys tried to disguise the fact. 'It's called *busking*, darling! It'll be fun! Mummy used to be a singer, don't forget. In a band!' She saw the disillusionment on Elin's face, watched as her daughter once again had to endure her mother's failure to parent her properly. At least that was one thing in which Alys showed consistency: her failure as a mother.

A gentle knocking at the door. Alys doesn't move. She doesn't feel she has any rights in any of this – it's as if she's a guest in her own space.

'How are you feeling today?' Grace comes in with Elin in tow. Elin looks scared, as usual. How dreadful it is to know that her own daughter is scared of her.

Grace sits on the bed. Elin stands by the door. Awkward. She's at that age now – having to navigate her way through the mine-field of puberty, with no control over what her young body is deciding to do, not knowing how to stand, arms crossed uncom-fortably across her chest to shield herself from being looked at. Alys tries to remember if she's explained to Elin about becoming a woman – how to deal with the monthly upheavals, how to buy bras. But, like everything else, it's a blur.

'Better,' she lies.

'Well, you've certainly got more colour in those cheeks, hasn't she, Elin?'

Elin nods, looking desperate to be anywhere but in that room.

'So you think you can manage some fresh air?'

They walk to the beach. The magnificence of Barcelona – a city by the sea. Tourists abound. It's Easter time now, so Grace tells her. Alys can hear bells – it's comforting in a funny way, even though she's never been religious.

'That'll be Santa Maria del Pi!' Grace announces with forced jollity. 'It's a stunning church. We went there yesterday, didn't we?' she asks Elin, who nods. She's barely said a word all morning.

The three of them sit looking out to sea, sipping cans of lemon Fanta, the refreshing coldness and bitter-sweetness zinging in Alys's mouth. She wishes it was wine. She wishes she could numb this too, too real feeling of failure. Of crippling sorrow.

And then it comes.

The ultimatum.

'Now then,' says Grace, clearing her throat with a little cough. 'We need to make plans.' She waits for Alys to answer, and when she doesn't she carries on. 'Obviously things can't go on like this.

And I've talked to Elin a lot, haven't I, bach? And we've decided that the best thing is for her to come and live with me.'

Grace pauses for a moment, making space for a reaction, but again, none is forthcoming. Because Alys has been somehow expecting this, and doesn't have the energy to protest. Nor the desire.

'She can go back to the school in Dylan's Quay – it's a lovely school, it really is. D'you remember it from sixth form? I know you weren't fussed, but I think Elin liked it those few weeks she was there, didn't you, bach?' Grace is wittering now. Fearful, no doubt, that Alys is about to explode in rage.

She puts her mother out of her misery. 'I think that's a really good idea,' she says quietly.

Grace is thrown by this, knocked off her stride. 'Well, hang on, I haven't finished yet. We haven't talked about you. Obviously you'll come too – I want you both to live with me. Now, you'll have to share a room to begin with, until I—'

Alys interrupts. 'I'm not coming.'

'What?'

'I'll stay here. Get myself together. I'm going to do it this time, I know I am.'

She sees Grace and Elin exchange a look – disbelief, distrust, pity. But above all, disconcertedness that Alys is planning to stay.

'Yes,' Grace says. 'You're right, you *will* get yourself together. But you'll do it at home. In Wales.'

Alys looks at her mother. She knows it is pointless trying to argue. She manages a smile. 'Okay.'

Relieved, Grace smiles back, and for the first time today there's a glimmer of relief on Elin's face too, a softening of the ubiquitous frown. 'Well, that's wonderful,' exclaims Grace. 'I'm so proud of you, cariad.'

'And me,' says Elin shyly. And Alys feels her heart break.

Grace puts her arms around her daughter and her granddaughter. 'The flight leaves at seven, so we'll have an early start, but that's all right. And Paulo the nice taxi driver is booked to take us to the airport. Oh, this is exciting! A fresh start, isn't it? The three amigos!'

And Alys allows herself to be hugged. Because it's easier this way.

56

elin

aged twelve

They knock on Alys's door and wait for a reply. None comes and so they knock again. Thinking she may have overslept, they persuade Maria the manager to let them into the room. It's empty. A note on the bed reads, *You are better off without me for now. I will come back soon, when I've sorted myself out.*

Elin bursts into tears. So convinced had she been that things were going to be okay, that they were going to be some sort of family at last, and that they could live happily ever after back in Wales. She watches Grama Grace dig deep, finding the emotional strength to disguise her true feelings and reassure her twelve-year-old granddaughter that it isn't the end of the world. She explains that it was always a long shot that Alys would want to come back to Wales with them right now. As gently as she can, she tries to tell Elin that her mum is a law unto herself, that she hates to be pinned down, that she has a thirst for adventure which means she can't stick to a conventional life. 'And you need some stability, bach. I think your mam knows this in her heart, and that's why she's—'

'—abandoned me.'

'*No!*' Grace says, a little too defensively. 'You must never think like that. Your mother wants you very, very much, she just can't cope with the responsibility right now.'

To Elin, this just sounds like an excuse. But she says nothing, not wanting to upset Grama Grace. She can see she is trying her best to be strong for them both.

'So what we're going to do is to get on with things, start you back in that school, get you settled in, is it? And before you know it, your mam will be turning up on our doorstep asking for a bowl of hot cawl.'

57

grace

aged fifty

John picks them up from the airport, fearing the worst when he sees Alys is not with them.

'Oh no, Grace! She's not—'

Grace interrupts, 'Alys has decided not to come back yet,' she says, and with a firm glance communicates to him that she will explain all later, when they are alone.

Elin cries for almost the entire journey home, wishing things were different, wishing her mother was different. As they drive back to West Wales, Grace lets her nestle into her, kissing the top of her head, and John tries to distract her with his cheery stories, telling her that he and Cissie have redecorated the attic bedroom in readiness. 'Now that Mr Harman's moved out, it's perfect timing!' he says.

And Grace explains, 'He's found love, Elin, bach. A lovely man called Murray.' She can see a weak smile form on her granddaughter's face, but that's the best she can do.

It's still light when they arrive home and Grace takes her granddaughter to her new room. When Elin sees that there are two beds in there, she begins crying afresh.

This will take time, Grace thinks.

58

alys

aged forty

nine years later

Aberystwyth is buzzing today. The July sunshine lifts the already high spirits of residents and holidaymakers and students alike. Students in black robes and mortar boards – this is graduation week, after all. Alys, now forty, sits on the seafront wall, clutching a takeaway coffee and breathing in the sea-salty, happy atmosphere, serenaded by oystercatchers on the lookout for lunch. She is feeling good. So good. Sober now for three months, she can feel the positive effect on her whole being – physically she feels healthier than she has in years, and emotionally she is feeling content and optimistic.

They call it the Pink Cloud. The feeling of euphoria that accompanies early sobriety. Several people in the AA meetings she's been attending have warned her about it. 'Be careful you don't start thinking the world's suddenly become perfect, 'cos it ain't,' said one of the old-timers at a newcomers' meeting in Newport. She'd dismissed him as being a grumpy old sod and resolved not to let him – or anyone, for that matter – dampen her new-found enthusiasm for life.

On her return to Wales after years wandering around Europe, Alys's drinking had gone into overdrive. Maybe it was the ghosts of her past coming back to haunt and taunt her. She'd known they would, and if she'd had a choice she'd have stayed in Portugal for good, where the outdoorsy life had kept her boozing 'civilized', at least. But a Welsh guy she'd hooked up with over there had had to do a runner and, thinking she was in love with him, that he was *the One*, she'd played the loyal girlfriend and stuck to him like glue. Big mistake, as it turned out. They'd found a place in Cardiff, which soon became the hub for all and sundry wanting to party twenty-four-seven. And not just with booze. Drugs were a-plenty, too. Alys could just about have handled that, but when she found *the One* in a threesome on her living-room floor, she decided to pack her bags once again and leave, heading down the road to Newport, where she had a few vague acquaintances.

She'd sofa-surfed for a couple of months, getting turfed out whenever her drinking became too much. In the end, she'd had no other option than to drag herself – unwillingly at first – to Alcoholics Anonymous. At her first meeting, she'd still been drunk and was told to come back the next day. She did so, having managed to abstain for twenty-four hours. She'd spent the entire meeting crying her eyes out. An older lady took pity on her and gave her a bed for the night – or longer if she could manage to stay sober. 'But you're out on your arse the second you reach for that drink,' she'd said. 'Can't risk my own sobriety.'

Alys hadn't understood what she meant at the time, but looking back now, she does. She'd managed a second day without drinking, and then a third, until she'd reached the milestone of a whole month. At the lunchtime meeting in Newport, they'd given her a shiny one-month 'chip' to mark her achievement. Her first thought, out of habit, had been to have a drink to celebrate. But then she'd remembered she'd stopped. Doh!

She'd taken to AA like a duck to crispy pancakes, going every day to a meeting, sometimes two. She'd lived and breathed it. And had tangibly felt herself getting better. Getting herself a sponsor – a woman about her age with five years' sobriety behind her – Alys had embarked on the Twelve Steps of Recovery. This was seen by some in the meetings as rushing into things – they thought she ought to wait till she'd got more time under her belt. But Alys was keen as mustard and had wanted everything AA had to offer. Having completed Step Eight, where she'd *made a list of all persons harmed and became willing to make amends to them all*, Alys realized she would have to take the bull of humility by its very long horns and go back to Dylan's Quay so that she could apologize to her mother for her past misdemeanours. She'd have to do the same to Elin, of course, but all in good time.

And so it is that she now finds herself in Aberystwyth, having taken the train from Newport that morning. She'd stopped off for a coffee and a gathering of courage before boarding a bus to Dylan's Quay, making the half-hour journey to Sŵn-y-Môr.

John is in the front garden when she arrives. She stands at the gate unseen for a moment and watches him weeding the flower beds. He looks exactly the same, maybe a little greyer, and Alys feels a sudden wave of affection for him. *Better late than never*, she thinks. God, she'd been positively vile to the poor man back then, when his only crime had been to give her mother a better life. To give Alys a better life, for that matter.

'John!' she calls out tentatively. He straightens up, shielding his eyes from the sun and trying to make out who it is.

Confusion turns to recognition. 'Well good God, Alys? Is that you?' She beams at him and does a little bow as he walks towards her, arms outstretched and shouting over his shoulder in the direction of the house, 'Grace! GRACE! COME AND SEE!'

He hugs her without reservation and she detects tears in his eyes.

Behind him comes the sound of urgent bustling. 'What's wrong? What's—' And then Grace sees her daughter. 'No! Oh my goodness, my lovely girl!'

It is the sweetest of reunions, with all of them falling over each other in an attempt to fill in events from the past nine years. They sit in the kitchen drinking tea and Alys makes a big show of turning down a celebratory sherry offered her by Cissie, who's equally pleased to see her.

'Don't drink any more!' she says proudly. 'Nearly three months now. And that's kind of why I'm here.'

Half an hour later, John and Cissie have made themselves scarce, whilst Alys sits in the front room with Grace, who's willingly agreed to let her daughter 'make amends'.

'If it helps you to do it, then that's fine, but you really don't have anything to say sorry for, bach. You were younger, and troubled. And life was just a bit much for you, that's all. But—'

'Anyway, I'd like to do it, please, Mum,' says Alys, a tad irritated that Grace is raining on her parade.

Digging deep and silently asking her Higher Power for patience, Alys begins with what she feels is a grand gesture: returning the hundred pounds she'd stolen from Grace's purse when they'd been in Barcelona. Grace looks at it and seems to be weighing up whether she should take it or not. 'This is very kind of you, Alys,' she says sternly. 'But I don't want it. I haven't seen you for nine years. A hundred pounds is a drop in the ocean of what I would have spent on you in that time, so please. Keep it.'

Alys knows this comes from a good place in her mother's heart, but she can't help feeling resentful that Grace hasn't taken the money or shown a huge amount of thanks. It's a big deal, after all. 'No, Mum,' she says, pushing the money back at her. 'It's important that I don't have any debts. Don't spoil this for me.'

Sensing Alys's irritation, Grace takes the money without further comment.

Next, Alys takes out a large notebook and proceeds to recount all the injustices and instances of bad behaviour she's inflicted on Grace over the years, apologizing for each one with consummate remorse.

Grace listens quietly whilst Alys reads out her list. When it's finished, true to her name, she graciously thanks her and says she hopes they can now move on.

Alys should leave it there, of course. But she just can't let it go. Overwhelmed with resentment that her mother will not say sorry for *her* part in the breakdown of their relationship, she demands a reciprocal apology.

'What have *I* got to apologize for?' asks Grace, confused.

'Well, if you can't answer that, then what's the fucking point?' Alys replies angrily. And what had started out so positively, with such good intentions and a jolly atmosphere of reconciliation, turns into an awkward silence. Alys sits there like a sulky child, and Grace doesn't appear to know what to do with herself.

Things aren't helped by Grace surreptitiously looking at her watch.

'What's the matter, Mum? Got somewhere else you'd rather be?'

'It's not that!' says Grace. 'If I'd known you were coming I'd have cancelled, of course. But I'm getting my hair done at three. We've got . . . well, we've got an important event tomorrow.'

'More important than spending time with the daughter you haven't seen for nine years?' Alys pouts.

And Grace sighs. 'Look, there's no easy way to tell you this,' she says. 'Tomorrow is Elin's graduation. In Aberystwyth. And the three of us are going. She got a First-Class Honours. In Music.'

Alys feels as if her insides are being sucked out of her – instantly both proud and rejected. Proud that her daughter has gained a degree, and rejected that she hasn't been part of this monumental achievement. 'That's . . . amazing,' she stammers.

'Yes,' says Grace gently. 'We're all very proud.'

And there it is again. The rejection. Grace is talking about *her* daughter – *Alys*'s daughter. Who she can't help feeling has been taken from her. Even though she knows rationally that this is not true. Elin has been *saved*, not taken.

'What time is the ceremony?' asks Alys, and she sees a look of concern flash across Grace's face.

'Why?'

Alys laughs. 'Well, because I'd like to go, of course!'

Grace shakes her head. 'You can't do that, bach. You have to have a ticket, for a start.'

'I'll have Cissie's, then. Or John's. It's not like they're *related* to her. I'm her mother, for God's sake.'

'Alys – you haven't been part of Elin's life for nearly a decade. And even before that, you were—'

'I was *what*, Mum? A crap parent? Go on, say it!'

Grace sighs and rubs her temples, before reaching out and taking Alys's hand.

'Cariad, I'm over the moon to see you again, I really am. And I hope that you'll be back in our lives for good. But Elin is only twenty-one. She's been through a lot—'

'That's right, rub it in!' snaps Alys, pulling her hand away.

And at this point Grace's patience runs out.

'You abandoned her, Alys! She's not heard a single word from you since she was twelve years of age. You can't expect to come waltzing back into her life as if all's well and dandy, because it's not. It will take time.'

'Well, thanks a lot, Mum,' says Alys, her voice choked with tears as she stands up, grabs her things and heads for the door. 'I'm trying, y'know? I really am.'

As she storms out of the house, Grace shouts after her, 'Alys, please don't leave like this! Not again!'

But Alys is marching down the path, passing John and his secateurs on her way. 'You not staying for supper, bach?' he says as she passes him.

'Oh piss off, John,' she hisses. And as she slams the gate behind her, she knows exactly where she's going next.

59

elin

aged twenty-one

'On the count of three – *un, dau, tri*!'

All twenty-eight of them cheer and throw their mortar boards into the air, looking skywards with beaming smiles, the whole of their lives stretching tantalizingly ahead of them. It's a memorable moment and a beautiful photograph, captured on John's Olympus Trip. Behind them on the beach, the crashing waves applaud the achievements of these young people on this cloudless July day. Elin loves to say the words over and over: *Elin Meredith, Bachelor of Music* – with a First-Class Honours degree from Aberystwyth University, soon to begin the PGCE training that will qualify her to teach at secondary school. The world is her big shiny oyster. And she is very, very loved.

Aberystwyth was always going to be her first choice of uni. Other kids in school longed to go far and wide, to put as much distance between themselves and their parents as possible. But not Elin. She'd already done the far and the wide. She'd tasted first-hand what others would perceive as the 'thrill' of living abroad, of living on the edge. Only to Elin it hadn't been a thrill. To her it had been an at-times-terrifying ordeal and one which she'd rather forget. Which was why, in her final year at school, she had put Aberystwyth as first choice on her UCCA form – just a half-hour's drive from Dylan's Quay and her beloved Grama Grace, who had rescued her nine years previously.

'Let's get one of you two and Ciss,' says John. And the three of them bunch up together, Elin in the middle, proudly wearing her gown, the mortar board now restored to her head, flanked on either side by Grama Grace and Aunty Cissie. 'And cheese!' shouts John as he clicks away.

'Right, and one of the four of us now,' says Elin, and she asks another graduate to do the honours. This will be the photo that she frames and gives pride of place in any future home. Because this is a photo of her family. Her only family.

John has booked lunch for the four of them at Alfredo's, the best and poshest restaurant in town. There are other proud parents there too, packed to the rafters at tables of three in this thriving, lively establishment, celebrating the academic achievements of their sons and daughters. And granddaughters.

After the tiramisu, John makes a short speech – 'You make us so proud, Elin, bach, so, so proud' – and they raise their glasses and cry with joy.

They are still buoyant when they leave the restaurant, linking arms and heading to the station.

'Elin! Wait!'

The voice is timid and uncertain.

But undeniably hers.

They all turn around in unison, floored by what, by who, they see.

She is drunk.

Of course she is.

And she is unsteady on her feet.

'Can we talk?' she slurs. 'I just want to give you this . . .'

Elin's mother, who she has not seen for nine years, is standing there, proffering a cuddly toy – some sort of fox or bear dressed in a graduation gown and mortar board and holding a scroll that says *Congratulations!* It is garish and crass. Alys's hands, like her voice, are shaking as she holds out the gift.

Elin looks at it but doesn't move to take it, still processing what's going on.

John speaks first. 'Alys! There's a surprise.' He doesn't sound convincing.

Alys ignores him, focused hard on Elin, willing her to take the gift.

'I don't understand,' Elin says, and looks at Grama Grace for help.

'Tell you what,' says Cissie, taking John's arm. 'Me and John will go ahead and let you three have a catch-up, is it?'

But John isn't going anywhere. He puts a protective arm around Grace.

'I wanted to see you,' says Alys nervously. 'It's a special day, isn't it? And I wanted to tell you how proud I am of—'

'How did you know I'd be here?' Elin asks, still trying to make sense of it all.

There's a pause, and Alys looks to Grace. Who sighs, and closes her eyes.

'I told her,' she says firmly. 'She came to the house yesterday and—'

'I wanted it to be a surprise!' Alys interrupts.

Elin wants to laugh now. It's like one of those programmes with the hidden camera. The whole thing feels like a massive practical joke.

Alys launches in to explain, stumbling over her words, desperate to get them out, to be heard. 'I've moved back, you see, to Wales! Staying with someone in Newport, Ellie—'

'DON'T. Call. Me. That,' says Elin, anger now rising up in her.

'I'm sorry, it's just—' And Alys starts to cry. 'It's just so good to see you. All these years. All this time, I've wanted to—' She steps forward to hug her and Elin recoils.

'What are you DOING?'

'Sorry. I'm sorry.'

Elin looks at her grandmother, the sense of betrayal even greater than the anger at seeing her mother again. 'How could you?' she hisses, and turns to go.

'Please, at least take this?' says Alys, and once again tries to give Elin the cuddly toy.

Without even looking at her, Elin knocks it out of her mother's hand. It flies into the air and lands indecorously on the pavement.

'I've stopped drinking, baby! For three months.'

There's a pause whilst Elin processes this contradiction, before she sneers, 'Are you for real? You can barely stand!'

'Just needed a bit of Dutch courage before I found you, that's all.'

Elin looks at her mother. The pathetic, needy mess of a woman who she cannot believe she's related to. 'Go away, Alys,' she says quietly. 'You're not wanted. You never will be. You're an EMBARRASSMENT!' The last word she shouts, and people in the street turn to look. Elin wants to be gone from there and she begins to walk away.

But then comes the roar. The retaliation of the wounded. And suddenly Alys is upon her, hitting out wildly and drunkenly screeching, 'I'm doing my best, you ungrateful little cow! I'm doing my fucking best!'

Elin tries to push her away, but Alys keeps coming at her. And Elin is scared. Not because the feeble punches have any power or even land very well. She is scared of the madness in her mother's eyes and the pain she feels at seeing it again.

Grace is now pulling Alys off Elin, and John is trying to get between them all. 'Leave it, Alys! LEAVE IT!'

But before anyone can stop her, Alys has turned on Grace, and WHACK – the smack comes from nowhere, right across her mother's cheek. Grace cries out in pain, clutching her face, and Elin screams in her grandmother's defence.

Alys collapses to the ground and now a policeman is there, pushing back the gathering crowd who've been drawn to the spectacle on this sunny Aberystwyth afternoon. He sends them on their way, 'Nothing to see here, off you go.'

The five of them catch their breath, checking they are still in one piece. Alys is crying, and continuously apologizing, and the policeman is asking Grace if she wants to press charges. Grace shakes her head, and Cissie, tissue in hand, dabs at the blood now trickling down her friend's cheek.

'Come on,' says John quietly. And he shepherds Elin and Cissie and Grace away from the scene. 'You've gone too far this time, Alys,' he says as they turn to go. Leaving Alys weeping drunkenly on the ground, resisting the arm of the policeman who tries to help her stand.

2022

60

elin

She didn't recognize her immediately. Her own mother, standing there at the door. And she didn't know who she was.

Ageing had played a part, of course, but really it was the unexpectedness of the sight, the out-of-the-blueness of the moment. That's what had caused most confusion, until her brain recalibrated and processed what and who she was looking at. Even then, all she could manage to say was, 'No.'

She turned back to Beca and Grace, in the hallway behind her, like a lioness protecting her young and said, 'Don't worry, I'll deal with this.'

But Grace was already walking towards her, and placed a hand gently on her arm. 'It's all right, love, she's been staying here a couple of days already.'

Elin frowned, looked back at Alys, who attempted a conciliatory smile, and then at Beca.

'We were going to tell you, there just hasn't been the chance—'

But Elin was already shaking off her grandmother and walking away, heading outside to the garden and beyond, anywhere to put distance between herself and the betrayal that was unfolding before her. As she opened the back door she heard Beca call after her and Grace gently shush her. 'She'll be all right, bach, just give her a bit of time, is it?'

She climbed the steps to the pool at the end of the garden and sat on a small stone wall, facing away from the house. How she wished Greg was here now. How utterly alone she felt.

There had been times in the early years when Grama Grace would bring up the subject of Alys in conversation. But Elin would just go silent until her grandmother started talking about something else and eventually Grace stopped asking. Then when Elin met Greg and he had first set them up online at home, she'd got in touch with some old university acquaintances via Friends Reunited. It had been exciting at the time to make contact with people from her past and it did make her realize that perhaps her mother could be found by the same means. She remembered one evening typing Alys's name into the search engine, her finger tentatively hovering over the keyboard as she decided whether or not to dive in. *Fast-forward the tape*, she'd said to herself. *What happens if you DO find her? What happens if she comes back into your life, messing everything up again?* And of course the age-old question, *What will people think?* The truth was, her connection with her mother had long since been eradicated. The hurt Alys had inflicted with her drinking and her disloyalty had rampaged through Elin's tender years, and they were years she would never get back. Some relationships were just not meant to be, she'd decided. Her relationship with her mother was one of them. And she'd stopped thinking about searching after that.

'Come inside, cariad,' said Grace, climbing the steps towards her.

Suddenly Elin felt about five years old and Grace put her arm round her shoulders, kissing the top of her head.

'It wasn't meant to happen this way. I promise I wanted to warn you, to talk it through with you first.'

'It's up to you what you do, Grama Grace – it's your house—'

'And she's my daughter,' Grace interrupted, firmly but gently.

Elin shrugged, attempting nonchalance.

'I want you to do me a favour, bach.'

'Don't ask me to talk to her, because—'

Grace interrupted. 'I want you to help me get things ready for Cissie.'

It was a sea-facing room, the aspect of which would let in sunlight for the best part of the day. The white gauze hanging at the half-opened window shuffled sleepily in the breeze. Infused with a beatific calm, the place felt sacred, *like Heaven's waiting room,* Elin thought, still numb from seeing Alys again. She watched her grandmother deftly adjusting the bed height and pillows, her face weary with sorrow. She didn't want to think about her mother. She forced herself to think about something else.

'You've made it really special for her, Grama Grace,' she said.

'I hope so, bach.'

Grace smiled back sadly, and plumped the pillows. Looking round the room, she seemed pleased with the results. 'Right, just need to move the armchair in from my room. Give me a hand, is it?'

'You're surely not planning to *sleep* in here? In a chair?'

'I'm not going to leave her on her own, am I?'

There was no point in arguing. As they manhandled the cumbersome armchair along the landing into Cissie's room, Elin couldn't hold it in any longer, exploding in a tirade of complaint.

'I'm sorry, but how can you even bear to have her in the house? I just can't get my head round it. You said she just turned up in the middle of the night, for God's sake!'

'You get to an age in life, bach, where nothing surprises you any more.'

'But why's she here? No doubt on the scrounge. 'Cos let's face it a leopard doesn't change his spots, and Alys certainly won't have changed hers. I just hope you—'

'Don't call her Alys, cariad. She's your mother.'

'In name only,' Elin retorted. 'I'm frightened she'll take advantage of you, that's all. Especially now – with Cissie and everything.

307

At the end of the day, she's a selfish, alcoholic narcissist who is more concerned with looking after number one than looking after her own child.'

'She's here because I invited her. I wrote to her.'

'What?'

Grace explained about the note and the gallery. 'Look, if it was Beca, if you'd not seen Beca for a lifetime and you had the chance to be reunited – well, you'd do it, wouldn't you?'

'I'd never have allowed things to get so bad between us in the first place!' Elin snapped.

'No, of course you wouldn't,' sighed Grace with an edge to her voice.

In silence, they turned the chair the right way and pushed it at an angle next to the bed. Downstairs the doorbell rang. 'That'll be them,' said Grace.

Elin stepped forward and hugged her grandmother. 'I'm so sorry all this is happening at once. But don't worry, I'm here, okay? And I'm gonna stay a couple of days. Keep an eye on things.'

'Thank you,' said Grace. 'You are always welcome here, Elin, bach, you know that. But I really don't need looking after. And you really need to stop trying to make the world behave properly. It must be exhausting for you and you'll never succeed.'

And with that, Grace headed downstairs to answer the door, leaving Elin standing there like an admonished child.

'It's just not fair, Greg,' she sobbed at the screen, seeking solace once more at the end of the garden. She didn't care what she looked like or that she was divorcing him and had foregone all husband–wife consoling privileges: he was the only person she could talk to right now. Beca had disappeared, and Grama Grace was understandably otherwise occupied with the arrival of poor Cissie. 'I mean, this is meant to be *my* sanctuary, *my* safe place, and now *she*'s turned up and ruined everything. I don't even want to *be* in the house when she's here—'

'Come on, now,' said Greg, his digitized face still managing to show sympathy. 'Take some deep breaths – you're not doing yourself any favours getting this upset.'

'And today was meant to be about Beca! Her results! I haven't had a chance to talk to her properly—'

'Me neither. D'you think she's okay? Her phone keeps going straight to voicemail when I try.'

Elin blew her nose hard, attempting to pull herself together. 'I've no idea, Greg, to be honest. I thought she'd be upset, but she actually seemed impressed with herself for getting Art and Music!'

'Well, she's got a point there, El.'

Elin gasped. When he called her that, she wanted to crumple into him and be gathered up in his arms. And before she could help herself, the words were out of her mouth. 'Wish you were here.'

'You sound like a picture postcard!' he said with a small laugh, embarrassed by her openness. She was sitting on the other side of the ugly swimming pool. In the distance she could hear the sounds of summertime play rising up from the beach and the seafront – daytrippers and holidaymakers living carefree lives, with nothing on the agenda other than indulgence and relaxation. And what was on Elin's agenda? An estranged mother, a distant daughter and a grandmother who seemed to be losing patience with her. All gathered under one roof.

'How can I go back in there, Greg?' she asked. 'How can I sleep in the same house as that woman? And how long is she planning to stay?'

'You could always come back to Cardiff.'

'No, Grama Grace needs me. And Beca needs me. I can't.'

There was a pause, a gap filled with the cry of chatty seagulls overhead, and then he said, 'What if I said *I* need you?'

Elin sniffed and stared at the screen, processing what she was hearing and seeing. And then it clicked.

'Greg . . .? Where are you?'

309

He sighed. 'Don't get cross, okay?'

'Oh my God, you're at the house!' She could feel indignation and helplessness rising up inside her. 'How dare you!' She wanted to tell him he'd be hearing from her solicitor forthwith, but then remembered she no longer had one. 'You have no right to be in that property any more, Greg.'

'I know, I know, just . . . just hear me out.'

'All your stuff is in the garage, to which you have the key. There is absolutely no reason for you to be in the house!' She was getting hysterical now.

'Elin, LISTEN!'

But before she could respond, she was caught off-guard. So lost had she been in her conversation with Greg that she'd failed to hear Alys approach.

'Elin?' said her mother. 'Can we talk?'

61

beca

The town was almost empty of tourists, the shutters from the gift shops rattling down. A few people queued outside the chippie, lured by the tantalizing aroma of deep-fried haddock for their supper, and above their heads the hopeful seagulls circled. Beca had been to see Neeta, to ask her for a job.

'Sorry, love, but chances are there'll be less hours now as the season slows down.'

'Thought you'd say that.'

She didn't really want to go back to Grama Grace's. The atmosphere was so crap – her new-found Nana Alys was staying out of the way in her room, avoiding running into Elin; Beca was avoiding her mum because she knew she would either be interrogated about Alys or her exam results, and Grama Grace was by the bedside of her dying friend. It was hardly a house of fun.

Suddenly she could hear music. Really loud music, and it was getting closer. She recognized the voice of Aretha Franklin singing 'R.E.S.P.E.C.T.' She looked behind her to see the car approach, its windows wide open, filling the Welsh seaside street with American soul. She carried on walking and the car pulled up next to her, braking hard. A red Ford Ka, circa 2010. Behind the wheel was Soozi. Shrouded in a cloud of vape, looking startlingly beautiful.

'Seriously . . . ?' Beca stammered, disbelieving her eyes, her stomach lurching.

'If my hammer won't go to yer mountain . . .' shouted Soozi over the music.

'It's Muhammed.'

'Eh?'

'Not *my hammer*.'

'Whatevs. You wasn't answerin' my messages, you wouldn't call me back, so I didn't have no choice.'

'But how d'you know I'd be here?' asked Beca, confused.

'I didn't. Just drove around seekin' you out.'

Fighting to stay cool and control the breathlessness that belied her excitement, Beca stepped back and looked at the car.

'Don't worry, I haven't nicked it,' Soozi smiled. 'It's my man Parker's. But he wants it back by ten, so I ain't got long.'

Beca started laughing.

'Oi! What's so funny?'

'Nothing,' Beca giggled. 'I just didn't know you could drive!'

'There's a lot you don' know about me, bird. Now get in and stick your seatbelt on. It's the law!'

Ten minutes later, they'd parked up on the headland, facing the setting sun. Several people had gathered on the grass with cameras to capture the sight and beers to drink a toast. It had become something of a Dylan's Quay tradition – Beca had heard about it from Grama Grace. 'When it goes down they'll all start clapping,' she told Soozi, who in turn pretended to be sick.

'Cheesy.'

'God, you're hard,' Beca laughed. 'I bet you never clapped the NHS during Lockdown, neither?'

''Course I did – but that's different. That's people helpin' folk. Not a fuckin' planet goin' round another fuckin' planet every day, sure as eggs is eggs.'

'Fair point.'

They sat in silence for a moment.

'How's your Gigi doin'? She's sound, that woman.'

'Not at the moment, she ain't. Her mate's gonna die any day,' said Beca, surprised at her own nonchalance.

'Ah, man, that sucks.'

'Yeah. And Grama Grace didn't want her dyin' in the hospital, so she got them to bring her over the house. Creeps me out a bit to think she's gonna cark it next room to mine, though.'

'Sweet,' said Soozi sarcastically.

'Just scared, I am,' replied Beca. Because she was. And she only realized it in that moment. *Too many endings*, she thought. She tried to lighten the mood. 'So, I failed my exams bar two—'

'Tidy.'

'—and my actual grandmother has turned up after being dead for thirty years.'

'Whoa! Serious?'

'Yep. My mother's furious. She hasn't said a word to her.'

'Not surprised.'

The setting sun glared back at them like a giant orange octopus collapsing into the sea, its rays like tentacles reaching out in a vain attempt to cling on to the dying day. Soozi reached across to the glove compartment and took out two small bottles of ginger beer, her arm touching Beca's thigh in the process. 'Here y'go,' she said, handing Beca one of the bottles. 'I wanna drink a toast.'

Beca's heart sank. She sensed another ending was on its way.

'So. I leave tomorrow!' Soozi blurted out, turning away from the performing sunset and looking at Beca directly.

Beca didn't return the look and kept her eyes firmly on the sun, its audience now in silhouette against the dying of the light. 'Exciting.'

They clinked bottles and sipped in silence. Try as she might to sound enthusiastic, Beca just couldn't do it.

'It's down to you, y'know, bird. The agent saw us play – that night at Salomé's.'

'Don't be a twat, 'course it's not down to me – it's you that's the singer—'

'Yeah, but you saved my ass, remember. Wouldn't've had any of the gigs if you hadn't come along.'

Soozi's voice was quieter now, devoid of its characteristic boldness and verve. She took Beca's hand in hers. 'Could you really imagine me turning it down, though? This chance? Is that really what you'd want for me?'

Beca shrugged.

'No you wouldn't, don't be a tit. You wouldn't want me carryin' on at Bellamy's for the rest of my days and never bein' more than a pub singer.'

'I know,' whispered Beca. And she knew she was going to cry. 'But I can't pretend, can I? That I'm not going to miss you. I fuckin' loves you—' She hated herself for saying it. Felt like she'd dug a hole a thousand feet deep and thrown herself right into it.

'An' I fuckin' love you, B,' Soozi whispered back, stroking the back of Beca's hair. 'Never in doubt.'

But there was doubt. There would always be doubt. Because there was no one else like Soozi Cole on the face of the Earth. And Beca couldn't keep hold of her. She remembered the dragonfly in the garden that day; the day Soozi had first held her hand. It had flown away, impossible to catch. And she wanted to weep now at the thought.

Outside, the light had changed; the octopus had finally slunk away and the gathered crowd clapped, as Beca had predicted they would.

'I'll be home in a month, y'know.'

'Yeah, with some new German girlfriend in tow, called Helga or Heidi or something, and then you'll be back on the road again. Stop making out like we'll just carry on as normal, 'cos we both know that won't happen. It's a year's contract! You're bound to meet someone.' Beca knew she sounded like a petulant child.

'Oi! Numbnuts!' Soozi yelled. 'I'm not going on some European shag fest! I'm gonna be workin' my ass off. Plus – I'm not gonna shag someone whose language I don' speak.'

'Racist,' said Beca, a tiny smile flickering on her lips, and Soozi mock-punched her on the arm.

Finding the courage to turn to her, Beca held Soozi's gaze, praying she'd never let go of her hand. They leaned in and kissed. The most tender, bitter-sweet kiss that spoke volumes of sorrow. *My love, my love, my love . . .*

Beca couldn't bear the pain or the approaching inevitable separation any longer. Lifting the bottle of ginger beer again, she forced levity into her voice. 'Here's to you, then. *Bird.*' And they clinked bottles one more time before gulping the fiery liquid.

'So will you start answering my calls again?' asked Soozi.

'Might do.'

'You are such a fucking drama queen,' said Soozi and turned the key in the ignition.

When they arrived back at Grama Grace's, the lights were on and Alys was sat out front, clutching a mug of tea. She waved and Beca nodded back. 'That's my new grandmother,' she said.

'Hippy chick! Bit different to your old girl, ain't she?'

'Tell me about it.' Beca tried to sound together and to hide the faltering in her voice.

She glanced over to the doorstep and was relieved to see Alys go back inside.

'Right,' she said, climbing out of the car, 'off you fuck. And text me when you get to Germany.' She shut the door and waited with folded arms, watching Soozi drive away.

As soon as the Ka had disappeared round the corner, Beca crumpled and silently wept.

62

alys

She lay restless on the bed. How strange to be in her 'old room' –
a term that suggested nostalgic affection, when in reality it had
just been a stopgap, a place where she'd slept nightly for two
years in the late sixties, before she'd found the wherewithal to
leave for London and never looked back. Sŵn-y-Môr was her
mother's home. Her daughter's home. Even her granddaughter's
home now. But it wasn't Alys's home. Then again, the notion of
'home' had never really existed in Alys's life. Not since her father
had died. Was she still holding on to that resentment all these
years later? What was it, fifty-five years since he'd gone?

She got up and went to the window, which was slightly ajar,
beckoning in the salty air. It was cooler now that September was
nearly upon them. In the near distance she could hear the rhythmic lapping of waves in the bay and, a few rooms away, the
sound of her mother's gentle movements as she watched over her
dying friend.

The house was becalmed after the drama of the day. Admittedly, her meeting with Elin could have gone worse: she *could*
have been thrown out – not been allowed over the threshold.
Yet Elin had just walked away. What *had* Alys been expecting?
Some Hollywood reunion with a daughter she'd divorced herself from for the past three decades? An emotional, tear-stained

reconciliation? Flags and bunting and a celebration cake? *Get real, Alys Meredith*. But the rejection in the garden – wow. That was something else.

She'd heard Elin talking heatedly on her mobile. The name 'Greg' was used a lot – presumably Elin's boyfriend? Husband? Boss? Whoever he was, he was making her very cross. Yes, she should have left them to it, and no, it hadn't been the best timing, but Alys had felt if she didn't strike now whilst the iron of reconciliation was hot, then the chance may never again arise. Bad move, though. Bad, bad move.

Elin was already in a rage when Alys approached her. Why hadn't she just turned around and gone back into the house? Was she on some sort of self-destruct mission, perhaps? The invitation to talk – *Can we talk?* That's all she'd asked! – was immediately and oh-so-aggressively thrown back in her face. Elin made it very clear that she wanted absolutely nothing to do with her 'shameful, embarrassing, immoral and horrific excuse of a mother'.

'Bit harsh!' Alys had said with a little smile she'd thought might soften things, but no. Elin pulled not a single punch. 'If I had my way, I'd have you removed from the premises, but this is Grama Grace's house and I will respect her wish to let you stay. Even if I think it's a huge mistake. But look out if you come anywhere near me whilst you're here. And don't even THINK about speaking to Beca again.'

And with that she'd stormed off, back into the house, where she would dedicate the next twenty-four hours to avoiding her 'horrific excuse of a mother'.

That'll learn you, Alys Meredith, she'd thought as she'd stood stock-still in the Sŵn-y-Môr garden, trying to laugh off the rejection and affect an outer indifference to what had just happened. Her shaking hands and dizzy head told a different story though, and for support she reached out to grab the railing that surrounded Grace's eccentric swimming pool. The hurt she'd felt was devastating, as was the belief that it was no more than she deserved.

She'd spent the rest of the evening either sat in her room or wandering like a lost soul around the house. From time to time she'd hear voices – muted conversations from which she was excluded. Elin or Beca on the phone maybe, or the Macmillan nurse talking with Grace in Cissie's room. When she was sure there'd be no one in the kitchen, she'd crept downstairs to search for something to eat. Opening Grace's pantry was like stepping back in time: shelves stacked with condiments, packets and cans, Ideal milk and Oxo cubes, Cadbury's drinking chocolate and Ovaltine. Ovaltine! What a blast from her past. She smiled when she looked at the sell-by dates – a bottle of tomato sauce from 2009. She'd even wondered if some of the corned-beef tins were left over from her childhood. Her mother had always abhorred waste, after all. She found herself smiling at the thought – an alien sensation, considering sentimental nostalgia had no part in her mother–daughter memories.

Alys had buttered two slices of home-made bread – incredible! Her mother still made her own bread at nearly ninety – chopped some fresh tomato and basil – from Grace's own garden, by the looks – and cut a chunk of Cheddar from the fridge. She'd forgotten how wholesome Grace's home-making was, and once again was overwhelmed by the urge to cry. She felt as if she was fifteen, not seventy.

When she'd finished, she rinsed her plate and made a cup of Ovaltine – the nostalgia was flowing thick and fast by now. She sat outside to drink it and saw a car pull up. It was Beca with a friend. Alys waved and received a nod in return. *Don't push it*, she thought. And took her cue to head back inside.

Creeping past Cissie's room, she heard Grace's voice, soothing and gentle, singing 'Suo Gân', a Welsh lullaby – the same one Grace had sung to Alys when she was small.

'Ai angylion fry sy'n gwenu
Arnat ti yn gwenu'n llon?'
(Are there angels in the heavens
Smiling as you smile at them?)

She hesitated outside the door. Drawn to the comforting tones, she considered going in – but it felt wrong to intrude. So she tip-toed softly back to her room, trying as best she could to blend in with the respectful hush afforded to the dying.

63

beca

'You're up early,' said Elin, coming into the kitchen with a dirty mug and plate. She'd obviously eaten in her room the night before and probably hadn't slept, judging by the dark rings under her eyes.

'Mornin',' Beca grunted through a mouthful of cornflakes.

'Lost the use of the letter G today, have we?'

Here we go, thought Beca. The head-teacher voice. All forced jollity with an edge of steel.

'What?'

'It's morn*ing*, not morn*in*' – you sound like that dreadful woman on TV,' said Elin. 'The one who refuses to say her I.N.G.s.'

'Oh Mum, give it a rest, will you?' Beca said, and instantly regretted it. Her mum was obviously in one of her niggled, irritated moods and looking for a fight.

'No need to be rude, Beca.'

'You're the one who's being rude!'

'I'm sorry,' Elin softened. 'I've just got a lot going on at the moment.'

'Yeah, well, you're not the only one.' She wondered where Soozi was right now. The airport? The train? The whole thing had been such a shock. She hadn't asked her any of the travel details. If she went back to Cardiff, maybe she could get to see her again before she left. But then what would be the point? It would only make the ache grow stronger. *Out of sight, out of mind*, wasn't that the saying? She sighed into the silence that had descended, watching as her mother filled the kettle and warmed the teapot under the hot tap.

'Has she said anything to you yet?' Elin whispered, looking into the hallway to check the coast was clear.

'Who?' said Beca, knowing full well who she meant.

'Your grandmother. Alys. Has she approached you?'

'Does waving count?' she asked sarcastically. ''Cos she waved at me last night when I come home.'

'*Came* ho— Sorry,' Elin quickly corrected herself. She spooned the loose-leaf tea into the pot, then stopped in her tracks.

'What's up?' asked Beca, frowning.

'Er . . . nothing. The tea – it reminded me of something, that's all.'

'What's the big deal with you an' her, anyway? Shouldn't you be glad to see her after all this time?'

'It's complicated.'

'You always say that about stuff you can't face.'

Elin sighed. 'I don't want to talk about it, Beca. What I *do* want to talk about is you. And your next steps.'

'Aw, Mum—'

'I'm not going to get cross, I promise. But we do need to have a plan. It's very tricky here with – well, with everything that's going on. I'm loath to leave Grama Grace, but I think it's best if you and I go back to Cardiff tonight.'

'No.'

'What d'you mean, *no*?'

Beca finished off her cereal and rinsed the bowl under the tap. 'Look, I'm sorry,' she said gently, tired of arguing, but absolute in her decision. 'I'm not going to sixth form and I'm not coming back to Cardiff.'

'Beca—'

'No, Mum. I know you think I was just kicking off yesterday but I meant what I said, so stop trying to persuade me.'

'You're making a very big mistake, Bec. Education will give you so much freedom—'

'There's more to life than school, y'know – you just won't see it, 'cos it's not how you did things. But I'm not you, Mum. I don't want the same things as you, okay?'

'BRAVO!' Unseen by Beca and Elin, Alys had come into the kitchen. 'I completely agree, m'dear.'

'Excuse me!' said Elin, turning round, horrified by the interruption. 'This is a private family matter, and seeing as you are not part of this family, I'd ask you please to butt out.'

'Fair enough. Cuppa tea, anyone?'

'Mum's just made a pot,' said Beca, keen to move the attention away from her.

'For *myself*!' said Elin, and Beca wanted to laugh at how childish her mother sounded. She couldn't help being quietly impressed by Alys, who ignored Elin's petulance and took a mug from the rack. 'I'll just stick another spoonful in and then we can have tea for two.'

Elin rolled her eyes.

'Oh Elin, d'you remember—' said Alys.

'Don't,' said Elin.

'What?' asked Beca.

'Aw, when we lived in Spain—'

'*You* lived in Spain?' Beca said to her mother. 'Why did you never tell me?'

'It's not something I like to remember,' mumbled Elin.

'I knew Nana Alys lived there, but—'

'*Nana Alys?*' repeated Elin, shocked at the sound.

'Anyway,' continued Alys, leaving the tea to steep, 'my boyfriend at the time, Eduardo—'

'Huh, what a joke he was,' said Elin, but Alys ploughed on.

'Eduardo took us on a little holiday to Portugal, didn't he? And we went one day to this island, to this tea plantation – oh, what was it called? San something.'

'São Miguel,' said Elin reluctantly.

'São Miguel! That's it! And we went to the tea factory and watched how they processed the tea – the leaves start off green, y'see, Beca, and then they dry them and that's when they go black, and – oh, and d'you remember Eduardo's car kept conking out on the way back and he'd have to fill a jug with water from the stream so that—'

'Oh, just SHUT UP, FOR FUCK'S SAKE!'

Alys looked as if she'd been hit.

Beca wanted to laugh – a knee-jerk reaction to hearing her mother swear, which was a rarity. Even on the night of the bar brawl – even then she hadn't sworn.

'Stop pretending!' hissed Elin. 'Stop acting like everything's okay, like we're playing happy families all of a sudden, just because you've deigned to come back and visit your mother. Your soon-to-be-ninety-year-old mother, who incidentally has managed perfectly well without you for the past thirty years. As have I. So why don't you just piss off back to whatever stone you crawled from under, Alys, and leave us all alone, because guess what, NOBODY WANTS YOU HERE!'

The silence was solid. As if the room had been filled with fast-drying cement.

Alys stared at Elin. Her mouth opened to speak, but no words came out. In turn, Elin stared back – defiant. Unrepentant.

'*I* do,' said Beca quietly.

The two women turned to look at her.

'I've never had a nan, have I?'

She saw Alys soften and swallow. 'Bless you,' she whispered, barely audibly.

And then came Elin's scream. Utter frustration and helplessness overcame her, and she picked up the milk jug and smashed it on to the floor.

Beca was terrified. 'MUM, STOP IT! WHAT ARE YOU DOING?' she yelled.

Alys started towards her daughter, wanting to help, frightened of making things worse. She reached out her hand, only to be pushed away. Beca wondered if her mother might even bite, her anger was so out of control.

'WHOA, OKAY, OKAY, JUST CALM DOWN!' Alys shouted.

Elin sobbed and sobbed until a voice interrupted the whole sorry spectacle.

'What on earth is going on?'

Grama Grace had come in, holding a hot-water bottle and an ice bucket. She looked exhausted. Elin seemed instantly to come to her senses, getting to her feet, wiping her face and smoothing down her hair, mumbling 'Sorry, sorry' like an embarrassed child.

Grama Grace was white with shock. 'There's a person dying upstairs,' she said quietly. 'Dying.'

'Sorry, this is all my fault,' said Alys, but Grama Grace ignored her.

'And you think it's acceptable, in *my* house, *my* home, to scream like banshees?'

They all looked at each other sheepishly, waiting for someone, anyone, to take the lead and get them out of this pitiful place.

'Shame on you all.'

'I'm sorry, I'm sorry,' repeated Elin, rushing out of the room.

'I'm goin' out,' said Beca. And she took her jacket from the back of the chair, leaving her Grama Grace and Nana Alys to pick up the pieces. *And I always thought my family was boring!* she thought to herself as she walked out and headed into the late-August morning.

64

grace

Grace emptied the hot-water bottle and left it to drain. As she stood at the sink, she worried she might fall asleep on her feet, the tiredness had taken such a hold.

'Can I do anything to help?' said Alys. She sounded like a polite stranger. Which in effect she was.

Grace's default was to say no. Ever the independent woman. But she was so exhausted and, although she'd not told her properly, so delightedly shocked that Alys was there. She wanted an exchange with her daughter, however small. 'Get me some cubes out of the ice tray, bach? And put them in this.' She handed Alys the ice bucket and watched her. She was clearly glad to be of help.

'Silly question, I know, but how's she doing?'

'Not silly at all. She's peaceful, put it that way. Can't ask for any more.'

'No,' said Alys as she bent the plastic ice tray back and forth, releasing the frozen cubes.

'They're all she can manage now,' said Grace. 'I just run one of them along her lips, keeps her sort of hydrated . . .' Her voice faded with the futility of it all.

'Why don't you sit down for five minutes?'

'John will be here soon and he can take over then.'

'It will be good to see him again,' said Alys, subtly communicating her remorse for how she'd treated such an innocent bystander in her mother's life.

Grace smiled at her sadly. 'Come and see Cissie,' she said.

It didn't sound like breathing. More of a wheeze. Crossed with a snore. Steady, rhythmic and double-noted, like a friendly foghorn reminding the world of her continued existence. Not for the first time, Grace wondered what places Cissie went to in her comatose head.

Alys approached the bed tentatively.

'Don't be shy,' whispered Grace, looking at her daughter properly for the first time since she'd arrived. What a beautiful woman she was. Seventy and still a stunner. Such remarkable features – her father's strong jaw, and his grey eyes. Good gifts to have bestowed upon her.

'Hello, Cissie,' said Alys, coming closer. 'Long time, eh?'

Grace squeezed a fresh cold flannel in the bowl, and gently wiped Cissie's forehead. Only small acts of care were left to her now, as Cissie's world diminished by the second.

'I came home,' said Alys, clearing her throat of nerves. 'Better late than never, eh, Ciss?'

Alys and Grace exchanged another polite smile as the noisy regularity of Cissie's breathing filled the room, leaving them to sit silently. Spotting Grace's copy of *He Kills in Blue* on the side table, Alys said, 'Funny, I read that not so long ago.'

'Well, I started it and left it. Picked it up again yesterday, and I've been reading it to Cissie, haven't I, Ciss? All a bit far-fetched, it is.'

Alys smiled and then the awkward silence fell again.

'How long have you two known each other, Mum? You and Cissie? I don't think you ever actually told me.'

Grace brightened at the chance to relive such a happy memory. 'A lifetime!' she said. 'Wasn't it, Ciss? We were sixteen. Living in Neath then, of course. And I'd started work at Protheroe's General Store. Do you remember old Mr Protheroe?'

'Jackie Protheroe's granddad! Yes, of course!'

'Well, he had a shop back in the day, sold all sorts – fruit and veg, corned beef – there was still a lot of rationing going on then. I tell you, people don't know they're born today!'

'Oh, listen to her, Cissie,' joked Alys. 'She sounds like a proper grumpy old lady now, doesn't she?'

'Watch it, you!' Grace smiled back. 'Anyway, it wasn't just food. We sold household goods – cleaning products, oil cans, tins of paint and so forth, and one morning this young woman comes running in, saying, *Oh Lord, you've got to help me, Mrs Crocombe has sent me out for something, but I don't know where to get it—*'

'Fantastic name, *Mrs Crocombe,*' said Alys. 'Who was she? Cissie's boss or something?'

'Yes – up at the Council Chambers,' said Grace. 'Poor thing, Cissie was only sixteen, like me, and she'd been working there for a few weeks, cleaning, making tea and what have you. We were all scared of the older generation back then. And if they asked you to do something, you'd never dream of answering back. That's something that's changed for the best . . .'

'So go on,' said Alys. 'Cissie comes running in—'

'Yes, and so she needs my help. I said, *Well, what is it?* And she says it's paint. *For the skirting boards.* And I say, well, that's no problem, we had a small selection, so not to worry. But Cissie is adamant it has to be a certain colour – *Tartan!* she says. Mrs Crocombe was very clear it had to be tartan paint. And I look at the cans on the shelf and there's green and brown and white, of course, but nothing anywhere near tartan. *Maybe it's a specialist paint or something?* I say. And Cissie is getting upset by now, she's worried she's going to get sacked. And I feel so sorry for her. And I tell her, I say, *Don't be daft, she can't sack you for that! Mr Protheroe will try and order you some in, don't worry.*

'And just then Mr Protheroe comes back in the shop – ever such a nice man he was. Very kind. And we tell him the dilemma. I said, *Mrs Crocombe's told this young lady –* 'cos don't forget I

327

didn't know her name then or anything, did I, Ciss? – I said, *She's been told she needs to buy a tin of tartan paint. But we haven't got any. Can you order some in?* And Mr Protheroe looks at me wide-eyed, as if he hasn't heard me properly. *Say again?* he says. *Tartan paint,* I repeat. And he starts – well, chortling is the only way I can describe it. Like a turkey, and he gets louder and louder – he's laughing at us! And me and Cissie, we look at each other – *What's so funny?* we think. And Mr Protheroe can't speak for laughing, and so we just stand there watching him, tears running down his cheeks. And then he gathers himself and he says, *Tartan paint? How can you have tartan paint?* And then he points at the calendar behind the till. *Have you seen what date it is?* he says. And we both look, don't we, Ciss? And it's April the first. And Mr Protheroe says, *You've been tricked, miss. You're an April Fool!*'

'Oh, that is priceless,' smiled Alys. 'Absolutely hysterical.'

'Well, we started laughing then, and we couldn't stop,' she said. 'And we've laughed a lot more ever since. Haven't we, cariad?' Cissie's eyelids flickered and Grace told herself she'd heard every word.

The jolly trill of the doorbell downstairs elbowed its way into the warmth of the room. 'I'll answer it,' Alys said, and she left Grace and Cissie to bask in their happy memories.

328

65

alys

The man at the door looked wrong-footed. 'Oh, sorry . . . I was looking for Elin?'

'Yes?'

'I'm Greg,' he explained. 'Elin's husband.'

'And I'm Elin's mother,' said Alys, slightly relishing his shock.

'Christ!' he said.

Behind her came footsteps on the stairs. 'What's going on?'

'I've just met my son-in-law,' Alys said to Elin.

'He's not your son-in-law actually, because *you* are no longer my mother and *he* is no longer my husband. We're getting divorced.'

'Jesus, and I thought *my* life was complicated. Nice to meet you, Gregory.'

And she left them to stand there in silence until she was out of earshot.

She didn't know where to go. The thought of returning to Cissie's room felt intrusive. And John would be arriving soon. But where else could she go? She couldn't really leave the house – she had barely a fiver to her name. The devil in her grinned at the reaction she'd get from Elin if she tried to scrounge from her. No, that was a definite no-no. An AA meeting would be the best idea, of course. At least that would keep her feet on the ground, and she could have a chat with a fellow alkie plus a cup of coffee – no doubt instant, but still free. Gift horses and all that. Yes. A meeting. That's what she would do. Her phone was now completely out of credit, she'd need to look elsewhere for some internet so she could google the local AA. Did Grace still have a study on the top floor? she wondered and made her way upstairs to find out.

Yes, still there. The dusty room with its crammed bookshelves and stee-grey filing cabinet in the corner looked pretty much the same as it had back in the day. Just like the pantry. The only major difference was Grace's home computer perched proudly on the desk.

Taking a deep breath, Alys sat herself down at the desk and moved the mouse, chivvying the computer to life. She was both relieved and dismayed to find there was no password protection – Grace was leaving herself open to all sorts of ne'er-do-wells getting a look at all her personal stuff. And then she felt immediately guilty. Wasn't that what *she* was? A ne'er-do-well?

The Google box came up on the screen and Alys typed in *AA Meetings, Dylan's Quay*. As she waited for the search to load, she wondered about her next steps. Much as she hated the idea, she was going to have to borrow money from her mother. It was just a case of finding the right time to bring up the subject. And Grace had offered, after all – the morning after she'd arrived. Alys kicked herself for not accepting the gesture at the time. Was it too late to ask? How much should she ask for? How much did she need? And for what?

She clicked on the *Find a Meeting* option and saw that there was one scheduled for midday at the Quaker House. She looked around for a scrap of paper and a pen to jot down the address, opening one drawer after another in her search. In the second drawer was a cash box, the key sticking out of its keyhole offering no security whatsoever. The temptation was too great. She turned the lock and opened it up. Inside lay a neat pile of banknotes, mainly fifties, some tens. Force of habit found her counting out the cash – nearly three grand. Two thoughts came hurtling into her mind: firstly, what on earth was her elderly mother doing with that amount of cash in her house, in an *open* cash box at that? Surely she was just asking for trouble. And secondly – how easy it would be just to take it.

She closed her eyes and tried to think practically.

Three grand. Her breathing quickened as she envisaged a way out of her current pickle.

In all fairness, it wouldn't go that far. She still owed Kirsty seventeen, eighteen hundred, in lieu of the items she'd stolen and sold. Ye gods, what *had* she been thinking? But at least if she paid that back pronto it might keep the police from her door – jump-before-she's-pushed type of thing. It might even earn her a few brownie points for her honesty and win an invitation to stay in the Brecon cottage again? Or was that pushing her luck? Okay, so pay Kirsty back, and then with the rest would she have enough for a deposit on a bedsit somewhere? Nothing fancy, just a place where she could sleep and eat and somehow start again. Yes, the money in her hand would give her a clean slate. And once she had an address, she'd have to finally swallow her pride and sign up for benefits. *Stay out of trouble this time, Alys!* . . . Christ, she was too old for all this, but yes, it could solve so much, this money. And okay, so she'd burn her bridges once and for all if she did it – wouldn't be able to come back here again, she'd have to disappear for good. But then, she'd managed for thirty years without a family. Would it really be the end of the world?

'Alys?' Grace's voice on the landing made her jump.

'In the study!' she shouted back, before quickly stuffing the cash in her pocket, closing the drawer and returning to look at the computer. Shutting down the AA page on the screen, she quickly googled *places to eat in Dylan's Quay*.

Grace appeared in the doorway. 'I'm just giving John some time alone with Cissie.'

Alys nodded sympathetically, hoping her mother didn't notice the guilt now reddening her face. 'Well, I'll get from under your feet, Mum. Thought I might buy myself a spot of lunch.'

Grace pointed at the screen. 'That's my friend Neeta's place,' she said. 'You should pop in and say hello, bach.'

'Won't she get a shock to learn I'm still alive?'

'Ha! That's true,' said Grace.

From downstairs, John called out, 'Gracie? You up there?'

'Coming, love!' Grace called back, and she headed out of the room.

Alone again, in a puddle of mulling, Alys took the cash from her pocket, stared at it and sighed.

66

elin

'Don't you think I should say hello to Grace?' said Greg. 'Feels a bit rude not to.'

'John is here! And I think you'll find she's otherwise occupied,' Elin snapped back. 'Her friend is about to—'

'Oh Elin, give me a break.'

She bit her tongue. He was right. She was relentless. Nag, snipe, argue, snap. It seemed to be her default with *everyone*. And in all fairness, he was trying his best, wasn't he? He'd made the trip to see her, after all. She sighed. 'I hate myself sometimes.'

'I wish you didn't, El.' And he looked back at her in that moment with such tenderness it made her angry again.

'Stop being nice to me,' she said. 'It just messes with my head.'

They were sitting in Grama Grace's front room, usually a place of such calm and tranquillity, with the stunning Irish Sea not far beyond its bay window.

'I just don't know where we're meant to go from here, Greg. Too much has happened.'

'That's why I'm suggesting the counselling.'

'Are you serious? Can you imagine what people would say if they found out? People already think I'm deranged after my appalling bar brawl.'

'But they *won't* find out. That's the point of counselling, it's *confidential*.'

Greg had always been bothered by her what-will-people-think obsession. Her 'appearances issue', as he called it. Which in itself sounded like something out of a pop-psychology self-help book. He was right, though. For as long as she could remember, she'd worried about being the subject of people's gossip, being talked about, mocked, humiliated. And Greg could never understand it – 'You can't stop people talking about you, Elin. But you can bloody well stop wasting your life worrying about it!' Pretty much what Grama Grace had said to her less than a month ago.

She'd refused to let him in at first. Tried to send him packing. But he wouldn't budge until they'd had a proper conversation. Knowing that Alys was within earshot and that John was about to arrive, she thought if they were going to have a scene then they should at least have it in private. As well as that, her meltdown that morning had left her completely drained and she wasn't sure how much energy she had left to stay standing.

They'd sat in silence at first, Greg making the occasional comment.

'Blimey, novel way to meet my mother-in-law!'

'Yes.'

There was a long and awkward pause.

'Have you had *any* sort of conversation yet?'

'No. And I wish she'd just leave, to be honest. There's enough going on without her adding to the stress.'

'Yeah, sure, but still. Thirty years. You must be a *little* bit curious, aren't you? Where's she been living? She might have had other kids, for all you know.'

'Don't be ridiculous, Greg. She was forty-odd when I last saw her. She was drunk and broke. She couldn't look after *me* – why would she have another child?' The thought, of course, was ludicrous, but in her paranoid state it did start her wondering. She knew nothing about Alys. The Olympian flame of anger she felt towards her mother had never been extinguished, so there had simply been no room for curiosity.

'I wish I could divorce *her*,' she'd mumbled, thinking aloud.

'Elin, you can't just divorce everyone in your life the minute they piss you off!' She'd started to respond, but Greg interrupted, 'And talking of divorce, that's why I'm here.'

Her heart had sunk. She'd been so gung-ho about firing her solicitor – after paying a hefty eight-grand bill that had incidentally got her nowhere. She was adamant that the online process would be simple, efficient and oh-so-much cheaper. But in fact she couldn't face going through the whole thing. She'd had so much else to worry about – mainly Beca, and Grama Grace's party, of course – that she'd just wanted to bury her head in the sand and hope it would all go away. That wasn't going to happen, of course. Because here was Greg, having driven all the way to Dylan's Quay to see how things were progressing.

'What were you doing back at the house?' she'd asked. 'You know you can't just take stuff without my agreement.'

'I made a mistake, Elin,' said Greg.

She couldn't help the involuntary laugh. Was it from hysteria? Surprise? Relief?

'It's over. With her, I mean.'

And that's when it had all come out. About Fleur. He wanted Elin to know everything, he said. She was a teacher at the language school. He'd given her a lift home after the Christmas bash.

'At Barry Latimer's?' said Elin. 'You said that night was really boring!'

'Well, I was hardly going to tell you I'd got chatted up by a thirty-one-year-old, was I?'

'God, you are such a cliché, Greg,' she'd muttered.

'I know.'

There was silence between them, but then with a masochistic need to know more, she urged him to continue.

'I dunno,' he said, irritated, embarrassed. 'You didn't seem to notice me much, and I suppose she did.'

'Oh well, that really *is* scraping the bottom of the barrel now. You're actually blaming *me* for your affair?'

Greg didn't answer the question. 'She was *different*. She seemed . . . enlightened? Maybe because of the profound effect she'd experienced when her father passed and—'

'Her father *what*?' Elin interrupted, and Greg closed his eyes, regretting his words. 'For God's sake, when did we start saying *passed* instead of *died*? Passed what, pray tell? A driving test? An A level? *Wind*?'

He tried stifling a smile then. Banged to rights. Elin noticed and a glimmer of joy flickered in her heart, a tiny moment of connection. 'Go on,' she said. It was painful, to hear a full-blown confession which she presumed was doing him more good than her, but something kept her listening.

'After Christmas, you'll remember I took up running.'

'Oh Lord—'

'That's when we used to—'

'What a *joke*!'

'Look, do you want full disclosure or not?'

'Two questions, Greg. What was the sex like and why have you really split up?'

He'd sighed then and put his head in his hands. 'Okay, it was *my* decision to leave . . .'

'Oh well, that's nice of you. First you break my heart and then you break hers!'

He ignored her and carried on. 'We just, I dunno, we were on different planets. She kept saying really cringey things. And as for the sex . . .'

'Yes?' she asked, suddenly vulnerable. But he just looked more embarrassed.

'I couldn't really keep up with her.'

Elin stared at him for a moment, taking in what she'd just heard. And then began laughing. She tried stopping, but to no avail.

'It's not funny!' said Greg, quite cross.

'That is *priceless*!'

'It became apparent quite soon that we'd be better off just as friends.'

'Oh great, so you come crawling back to second best. To your clapped-out old wife.'

'Nooooo.'

'It's hilarious when you think about it, Greg. You take the plunge to have an affair, thinking you're gonna get your end away with some younger model, and it turns out you're not up to the job!' Her laughter was infectious, and despite himself, Greg soon found himself laughing, too. But then Elin's tears turned into weeping and the mood changed back again.

'Thank you for being honest with me, Greg.'

'It's such a relief,' he sighed, smiling. 'Makes me feel there might be a bit of hope? For us?'

He looked at her and she wanted to melt.

She looked away. 'No, Greg. There's no hope.'

The hurt on his face was palpable. 'Jesus, you really know how to stick the knife in, don't you?'

'Well, surely you didn't come here expecting *sympathy* from me?' she said.

He frowned. Confused, quiet. Then he reached out for her hand. She let him take it, fighting hard not to fall. 'I made a mistake,' he said gently. 'I am a cliché. And all the accusations you want to hurl at me, yes, I am all those things. But you cannot – you *will* not – take away my love for you.' Elin's entire body tensed, and yet still she let him hold her hand. 'I just don't want to end our marriage without at least trying, and all I'm asking you to do is to *think* about us getting some help.' He looked at her, expectant, desperate. 'Elin . . .'

'No,' she said, staring out of the window, willing herself not to collapse. 'There is no hope for us, Greg, because I, too, have had an affair.'

It was nerves, she knew that. But still, his laughter didn't help the situation. 'You what?' he spluttered, incredulous.

'What's the matter, Greg? Can't believe that boring old Elin has it in her to have sex with another man? Well, I *did*! And it was stupendous. And, unlike you, he *was* up to the job!'

'You're lying,' said Greg softly.

'Believe me or don't believe me – up to you. But for the record, his name was Rory, he's only thirty-nine and a gardener from New Zealand. Yes, I'm lying about it being an affair, it was only a one-night stand. But still, what a night!' And then, childishly, she added, 'We did it on the granite island.'

'It's marble, not granite,' said Greg, who was now in shock.

'So you see, Greg, things can't go back to how they were, because we've *both* fucked up.' She coughed away the break in her voice. 'Because we've both been unfaithful.'

She knew how much she was hurting him, but she couldn't stop. It was totally uncalled for, and shamefully cruel.

'Oh Elin,' he whispered, 'this is so, so sad.'

'Isn't it just?' Her voice was hard. 'Shut the door quietly on your way out,' she said.

He did as he was bid, leaving Elin sitting up straight and taut and motionless. Until she heard his car pull away and she knew it was safe to cry.

67

alys

The midday meeting at the Quaker House had done her the power of good. She'd arrived half an hour before it began and been offered a cup of coffee and a rich tea biscuit by a friendly woman called Sheila. She'd found a seat near the back and waited for people to arrive. The room was pleasant – clean chairs, a well-swept floor and windows that let in soft, comforting sunlight. Certainly a cut above some of the dingier places she'd attended over the years.

The meeting had been surprisingly busy – amazing how many alcoholics there were on holiday in Dylan's Quay, she'd thought. When the chairperson had asked if any visitors would like to identify themselves, about a dozen hands shot up.

'I'm Barbara, alcoholic, on holiday here from Yorkshire.'

'I'm Steve, alcoholic, visiting from Glasgow.'

'I'm Alys, alcoholic,' she said, 'and I'm just . . . passing through.'

She'd decided that today she wouldn't say anything else, just keep schtum and listen to other people's shares. Sometimes there were people who loved the sound of their own voice a little bit too much. Alys hated the thought of being one of those. But then as she listened to the main sharer, she found herself overwhelmed with emotion. His name was Charles – a young guy, well, young*er*, forties maybe? And Alys had absolutely nothing in common with him. He was English, married with two children, a holiday home here in West Wales and loaded, she surmised. But when he shared his journey with the room, he talked about how he'd recently reconnected with his father after a five-year gap, apologizing to him for how he'd behaved in his drinking days and making amends, grateful to his sobriety for giving him the opportunity to do it. 'When I was drinking, I was so full of anger towards him, y'know? So resentful of how he'd been, when I was growing up, the way he'd treated my mother, his distance from us kids.' When he'd finished and the chairperson opened up the meeting again, Alys found herself desperate to share back. His story had chimed unexpectedly with her. She told the room that she, too, had been estranged from her family, but that things might finally be resolving with her mother. 'It's only taken me thirty years to get there!' Everyone laughed. 'Not sure about my daughter, mind, but then you can't have everything, can you? Where would you put it?!'

She'd left the meeting feeling uplifted and positive. Putting back that three grand earlier in the day had been a step in the right direction. It just meant that now she'd have to find a different solution – an honest solution – to her current problem of no money and nowhere to live. She had four pound coins and some coppers in her pocket, along with the now defunct credit card. Heading into the post office, she bought a blank greetings card and a first-class stamp. She addressed the envelope to Kirsty, care of the cottage in Brecon, and wrote inside the card:

I am forever indebted to you for helping me when you did and I am shocked at myself for how I've repaid your kindness. Please find enclosed your credit card, which I shamefully abused. I promise you that as soon as I am able, I will pay back what I owe you. I am so, so sorry.
Love Alys.

Once she'd posted it, she felt the curious sensation of being rootless and penniless yet somehow content, and she headed back to Sŵn-y-Môr buoyed up and optimistic. As she passed Neeta's café, she was thrilled to see her lovely young granddaughter sitting alone, looking at a menu. She couldn't afford to join her for lunch. But she couldn't ignore her either.

'Boo!' she said.

'Oh, hello,' replied Beca.

'What are you going for?'

'Dunno,' said Beca in a monotone. 'Panini?'

'Careful you don't explode with enthusiasm now!' And Beca beamed involuntarily. 'What an incredible smile you have,' said Alys. 'You should do it more often.'

'Shut up, don't be weird!' Beca laughed. 'Is my mum all right? She was a bit mental this morning, wasn't she?'

'Yesss – though that's probably my fault. I think I wind her up, just being in the same room as her. Your dad came.'

'God, he didn't have Fuckety Fleur with him, did he?'

'I presume Fuckety Fleur is the cause of your parents' divorce?'

'I guess so. Though nobody tells me anything.'

Neeta came out with her order pad. 'I'm bein' nosey, I am,' she said cheekily. 'But you two seem to know each other?'

Beca blushed again and mumbled, 'Er yeah, this is my nan. My Nana Alys.'

'Good God!' exclaimed Neeta. 'I thought you were meant to be dead!'

'Long story,' said Alys, with a wry smile at Beca.

Neeta was in her element. 'Well, I can see the likeness. You're the spit of your mam!'

'Thank you,' said Alys. 'Judging by my mother's longevity, I'll take that as a compliment.'

'Why don't you two have a bite together?'

Alys began her polite and penniless decline. But then Neeta

341

said the magic words 'It's on the house.' And who was she to turn down someone's generosity?

'The paninis are nice,' encouraged Neeta.

'So I've heard,' said Alys, winking at Beca.

'And d'you want a beer with that or something, Nana Alys? A cheeky rosé, maybe?'

'Not for me, thanks. Tap water is fine.'

As Neeta laid out the cutlery she said, 'Hey, Bec! I got no excuse now, have I? I'll *have* to make a marzipan Alys.'

This time it was Alys's turn to look confused and Beca explained about the forthcoming surprise party for Grama Grace. 'Neeta's doing the cake – she's putting marzipan versions of all the family on there, but she couldn't do one of you—'

'Because I was dead?' asked Alys, smiling.

'Exactly!' said Neeta. 'But you're gonna be a doddle to make. Ooh, I'm excited!' And she headed back into the kitchen.

Things were so relaxed between them. Was it the generation gap that did it? She'd heard people say grandchildren were so much *easier* than one's own children, and in truth she'd thought that was a myth. But maybe there was some truth in it.

'So you like art, then?' Alys ventured.

'Yeah, batik's my favourite. And silk-screen printing.'

'Wow, now that's something I've never tried. I'd love you to show me.'

'Sure,' said Beca.

'I'm just into boring old watercolours.'

'Nothing boring about watercolours,' said Beca. 'There's some gorgeous views up on the hill there.'

'Come with me one day,' said Alys.

'Yeah, I'd like that.'

And Alys felt a surge of warmth for this special young spirit with whom she'd so instantly bonded. Dare she imagine that Beca represented some sort of a second chance – not at motherhood, but at *mothering*. She could never put right what she'd

342

done in the past. But could she build something? Inspire? Encourage?

'D'you think you'll come to Grama Grace's party?'

'If I'm invited,' said Alys.

'Hmm. Mum may need some persuading on that one. But whatever you do, *don't* mention it to Grama Grace. If you think Mum's cross with you now, she'll internally combust if you go spoiling her party plans.'

They laughed and Beca's phone rang. It was Elin. 'Talk of the devil.' She rejected the call.

'Beca,' said Alys, taking her hand. 'I know it's pretty normal not to get on with our mothers sometimes – God knows I'm no advert! I was angry with *mine* for decades. But your mum is doing her best, y'know? And she's a good soul.'

'Why are you sticking up for her?' said Beca. 'After the way she had a go at you. If she was more like you, more laid-back and stuff, she'd be a ton happier.'

'Elin is a wonderful mother. And she didn't learn that from me.'

Beca sighed. And this time a text came through – Elin again.

Call me. Now. It's Cissie.

'Oh my God,' whispered Beca, as she looked up at Alys.

68

grace

Paddle-boarding. Now there's something she rather fancied. Like walking on water – hah, she could be a modern-day Jesus on one of those. They seemed to be enjoying it – the middle-aged couple nearby – concentrating on their balance as they scooped back the water with their oars in a slow, even pace. Right and left and right . . . Grace raised her hand at them in greeting as she swam and the man waved back. 'Perfect day for it, isn't it?'

'Rather!' she replied. And carried on. Yes, a perfect day. The sea was pancake-flat and lazy, its gentle waves barely breaking on the shore. A lot of people were in today, making the most of the calm water. The temperature wasn't so cold towards the end of August, when the seabed had had a chance to warm up.

In the distance, Grace could see two small sailing boats, slowly meandering past each other in an elegant criss-crossing dance. Such ancient skill. To navigate with wind and sail alone. In harmony with the elements. Peaceful. Benign. Unlike the angry buzz of the nearby jet-ski, ploughing its way to nowhere in particular but creating an impression of urgency and self-importance. *Out of my way, out of my way!* it seemed to shout. *Give me a sailing boat any day of the week*, she thought. And on she swam – bold, strong strokes, towards infinity.

*

She'd only been out of the room for five minutes. Downstairs the front door had closed as Greg had left, and she'd heard Elin run up to her room like a stroppy teenager. 'I'd better go and check she's all right,' she'd said to John. 'Be back in a minute, Ciss.'

As expected, Elin had been crying on her bed. She told her grandmother all about Greg's visit and what he'd said. 'I don't know what to do, Grama Grace,' she'd wept.

Grace had smoothed Elin's forehead as she lay on the bed, like she'd done when Elin was little. 'Well, you know what they say? *When you don't know what to do, do nothing.* I doubt Greg's going anywhere in a hurry. Why don't you stay here another night and think it all through? You could even ask your mother for advice!' she said, knowing she was pushing her luck.

'I think I'll pass on that one,' Elin had snapped. And Grace had shut her eyes in frustration.

By the time she came back to Cissie's room, John was standing on the landing, looking lost. A small, scared little boy.

'She's gone,' he said, barely audible. 'My little sister, Gracie. She's gone.'

She'd always thought she'd be there for the final moment. That it would somehow be like in all the films. What was the last thing she'd said to her? She couldn't even remember properly – *See you in a minute, Ciss? Be back in a mo?* Something pedestrian and unremarkable, that was for sure.

John had started crying, cumbersome and awkward as he tried to walk unaided, nearly falling on his way towards her. They held each other in their ageing arms and Grace consoled him with soft, comforting kisses, stroking his back and telling him it would all be all right. Then she gently broke away.

'Elin!' she called, aware that although her body was tense, her voice was relaxed and practical. She could for all the world have been calling to see if her granddaughter wanted a cup of tea. 'ELIN!' she shouted, a little louder.

A short scuttling and then Elin appeared.

'Phone the doctor, will you, love?'

She couldn't bear to see Cissie again. She didn't want that to be her final memory. John and Elin bustled around her, someone mentioned calling Beca. It was all a blur.

'I'm going for a swim,' she said. But nobody seemed to hear her. Maybe she hadn't said it out loud. Maybe she'd only said it inside her head. Calmly, as if her very being had been put into slow-motion mode, she made her way to her bedroom and took off all her clothes. Her arms felt like lead as she pulled on her Speedo bathing costume and re-dressed herself. She took a towel from the rack over the radiator, headed down the stairs and out of the front door.

By the time she'd reached the steps to the beach, the doctor's car was making its way along the promenade towards Sŵn-y-Môr. It would soon be followed by the undertaker, coming to take Cissie away. To carry Death out of the house.

She swallowed hard and made her way down on to the sand.

She must have swum a good half-mile by now. There was no one ahead of her any more. The sailing boats had passed and the paddle-boarders were way behind her. From the shoreline she could hear the indiscernible playful shouts and yelps of seaside joy, a soundscape of holiday happiness. She turned to float on her back, gazing up at the china-blue sky, a faint wisp of cloud lazily slinking by. *Funny how I can't see the stars*, she thought. *And yet I know they're still up there.* Her face was wet with tears now and her eyes shut tight against the pain in her heart.

69

alys

When they arrived back at Swn-y-Môr, the hearse was just pulling away. Alys stood with Beca and watched it go.

'Poor Cissie,' whispered Beca.

'Yes,' Alys sighed.

They turned and slowly made their way into the house, where John and Elin were sitting at the kitchen table. Alys rushed forward and hugged John. 'I am so, so sorry. Cissie was a lovely woman. Very kind to me for the short time I knew her.'

'Thank you, Alys,' he said and patted the back of her hand.

Beca stood in the doorway, blushing, awkward in her teenage naivety, inexperienced with death and its conventions of condolence. 'Yeah, sorry,' she mumbled and John smiled gently back.

'D'you want some tea?' Elin asked Beca quietly.

Beca and Alys replied in unison, 'Yes, please.'

Elin hesitated and Alys presumed she was about to turn on her and say, *I wasn't asking you!* but then realized how childish it would sound. In the circumstances. Instead, she got up to put the kettle on.

'So where's Mum?' asked Alys, presuming she was upstairs.

'We don't exactly know,' said Elin.

'What d'you mean, you *don't know*?' said Alys, irritated by her daughter's response.

'She went out,' said John. 'Everything was a bit of a muddle. I think she went for some fresh air after . . . y'know, after it happened.'

'But how long ago was that?' Alys was trying to contain her frustration.

'Stop fussing,' said Elin. 'She'll be fine.'

'You don't know that!'

'I do, actually,' snapped Elin, her voice breaking. 'Because, unlike you, I happen to know *your* mother better than you do! And for your information, she's an incredibly independent and competent woman who sometimes needs her own space.'

'Mum!' Beca turned to Elin. 'Don't be such a cow!'

'Excuse me! How *dare* you speak to me like that, Beca Matthews—'

'Oh, for God's sake, give the sanctimoniousness a rest, Elin—' said Alys.

'PLEASE!' said John, silencing all three. 'This isn't helping.'

Nobody spoke. Then Elin cleared her throat.

'Sorry,' she muttered, stirring the fresh pot of tea. 'Do you still take it black?' she asked Alys begrudgingly, avoiding eye contact.

'Yes. Thank you,' Alys replied, equally as begrudgingly, and thought she saw Beca rolling her eyes at their childishness.

'Elin is right, though,' said John. 'Grace likes her own space, especially when things get a bit much. There's really no need to worry.'

Well, that's me told, Alys thought.

Alys wasn't sure she could handle Elin's bossiness for much longer. Ever the Head Teacher, ever the organizer, she had opened up her laptop and begun helping John make arrangements for Cissie's funeral, searching for the best local undertaker and offering to phone around friends and relatives to tell them the news. Alys knew it came from a kind place. She just *personally* thought John might need a bit more time to absorb it all, rather than having to rush straight in and make plans. But then she didn't know John as well as Elin did, so who was she to judge what was best?

'There isn't anyone really,' he'd said sadly. 'We should tell them up at Cadwallader House, of course, but apart from that there's no one. *We* were her family. Me and Grace.'

'And us!' Elin had said brightly. 'Cissie was like an aunty to me, after all!'

At that point Alys had discreetly left the room, feeling very much excluded from this private 'family' time.

Lying on her bed, she thought back over the strangeness of the day. A day that had brought such big ups and such low downs. Even though it had been expected, even though she didn't really know her, Cissie's death had still been a wrench for Alys. And truthfully – *or rather, selfishly,* she thought – it had put a spanner in the works. Because now it would be even more difficult to talk to Grace about her own situation or to ask for the help she herself needed. Maybe there'd be an opportunity this evening, when Grace came home. Alys just needed to find time on her own with her, away from Elin's nagging and overprotectiveness. *Christ, she's like the woman's bodyguard,* Alys thought and smiled at the image of Elin all in black, wearing wrap-around shades and a headset.

The shelf unit in her room was crammed with bric-a-brac and board games, a layer of dust covering the parts that weren't filled. Alys reached over and ran her finger across one of the shelves. *That* was something she could help her mother with, she thought. Giving the place a good spring-clean. Evidently she and Grace were at opposite ends of the spectrum when it came to possessions. Alys had an almost Buddhist approach to 'stuff' – her belongings were transportable in a couple of carrier bags these days. Admittedly that hadn't been out of choice, but because she'd frequently had to make a sharp exit from places, but still. She'd learned to live with very little. Whereas Grace seemed to have clung on to possessions from decades ago.

Alys pulled out a jigsaw puzzle from under a Monopoly set – the Houses of Parliament stared back at her from the box and she remembered it from her childhood in Neath. 'Good God!' she muttered to herself. And then her eye was caught by a small collection of books, all stacked together. 'Milly-Molly-Mandy!' she declared, and felt a lump in her throat as she ran her finger along their spines, remembering clear as day how Grace would read the stories to her at bedtime when she was small.

On the top shelf was a photograph album, its brown hessian jacket faded after years of exposure to sunlight. Sitting on the bed, she opened it up, its distinctive smell transporting her once again to her younger days. On the first page were two wedding photographs. The faces of her mother and father stared back at her. Behind them a chapel door. He was smiling. She was not. Her ill-fitting two-piece suit seemed infused with gloom on what should have been a happy day. *Was* it covering a pregnancy bump? Alys had chosen to believe Grace all those years ago when she'd said John wasn't her father. For one thing, the dates didn't add up – Grace and Aneurin were married almost two years before Alys was born. So if Grace was pregnant on her wedding day, then she wasn't pregnant with Alys. Could there have been another baby then – before her? Was *that* why Grace had to get wed? And if so, then why didn't *John* marry her? He obviously loved her. Why abandon her and leave her to marry Aneurin? It didn't make sense. The contents of her grand-mother's letter to her father were hazy now – there'd been some mention of saving Grace's reputation. But why?

In the second photograph, they stood again looking out at the camera, flanked by a dumpy little woman who was smiling proudly – Alys's own grandmother, no doubt, who'd died when Alys was a baby. Next to her grandmother stood a man who looked vaguely familiar. Reverend something. Reverend Jenkins! A younger version. But yes, he'd been the one who'd led her father's funeral service.

She felt an overwhelming sorrow, looking at the photographs. Knowing what Grace had done, that she was not marrying the man she loved. Forced by social mores and protocol to abandon her heart and obey society's rules. Guilt raged through her as she thought once again of how unforgiving she'd been towards her mother. How she'd seen her as the villain of the piece in refusing to love Alys's poor father. And equally, she felt such sorrow for *him*. And anger, that the demands of society back then constricted people's lives to such a suffocating degree. In time she would broach the subject with Grace again, but not today.

She turned the pages – there were only a dozen or so. How precious were photographs in those days. She remembered her dad's Brownie camera! It would offer up just eight opportunities per film to capture a special memory. Photographs had been so cherished, so special. What a difference, compared to today's digital world of click, delete and retake. There'd been a flurry of snaps of her as a baby, in frilly white dresses and bonnets, being held alternately first by Grace and then by her father. There was just one photo of the three of them together, one 'official' shot, which she thought should really be in a frame: a vase of flowers stood on a tall stand next to a velvet chaise longue, upon which Grace sat, along with baby Alys, who was waving what looked like a Union Jack, her father standing proudly behind. Underneath was printed the date – *1953* – and the photographer's name – *Evan David and Son, Dylan's Quay*. It had been the Coronation year. She'd had a similar photograph once – her and her dad, in a silver frame. What had happened to it, she wondered?

The photographs seemed to stop then. Evidently Grace had given up. Or maybe it had been Alys's father who'd terminated his short-lived family-photography hobby. The other pages were blank.

Except one: a solitary print, older than the rest, which took pride of place in the centre of the final page. Three young people, standing on a railway platform in front of a train called *The Golden Arrow*. Their arms were linked and they were laughing.

Alys reached for her reading glasses and took a closer look. In the middle stood her mother! A beaming smile lit up her face.

Next to her was a young man, grinning cheekily at the camera. And yes – it was John, dashing in a 1940s suit and trilby, matinée-idol style. And finally, Cissie? It must be! Her blonde curls and bright eyes exuding excitement and anticipation.

Alys edged the photograph out from its corner holdings and read the back:

LONDON, MAY 1950 – CYNTHIA, ME AND JOHN.
BON VOYAGE!

Well, well, she thought. And smiling to herself, she took the photograph downstairs to show John.

They were sitting in the front room now. John was looking out of the bay window and Elin was on her mobile.

'Look what I've just found!' Alys said, holding out the photo to John, who was understandably distracted.

'Getting a bit worried about Grace, we are, bach. Beca's gone down the seafront, see if she's there.'

'Oh.' Alys felt a pang of guilt. So caught up had she been in her trip down memory lane, she'd stopped thinking about where Grace might be. 'I thought you said it wasn't unusual for her to go off?'

'I know, but it's been a while now. Elin's just checking with Cadwallader House, see if they've seen her.'

Elin looked over at him and shook her head, finishing the call. 'No joy, I'm afraid. I think I'll just give Neeta a ring. And I might try Dolly Hughes from yoga.' She began looking through her contacts. 'They were so sad about the news, by the way. I said I'd give you a lift back soon as Grama Grace gets home – Oh, Neeta? It's Elin . . .' And she headed out into the kitchen to carry on the call.

'What did you want to show me?' asked John.

'Eh? Oh yes. This. I found it upstairs.' She handed John the photograph.

He took his glasses out of his top pocket and put them on, gasping with delight in recognition. 'Well, *Duw Duw*!' he said, happy tears accompanying the memory. 'Where did you get this?'

'It was in an album upstairs.'

He turned it over. 'Nineteen fifty! Yes, that's right. War had been over five years, but we were all still exhilarated.'

'I bet,' said Alys, glad to see him smile. 'So what were you doing in London? What was with the train?'

'*The Golden Arrow*. Fantastic piece of kit. It was your 1940s equivalent of the Eurostar, in effect.'

'Really?' said Alys, surprised.

'London Victoria to Dover on *The Golden Arrow*, then a ferry from Dover to Calais, where you'd catch *La Flèche d'Or*—'

'*The Golden Arrow* in French!' Alys interrupted, smiling.

'—that's right, all the way to Paris!'

'Wow. What an amazing trip. And you were all so young – Mum would've only been, what, seventeen? Eighteen? What about you and Ciss?'

'Cissie would've been seventeen, yes, and I was—' He stopped. 'I was nearly nineteen.'

'God – so brave, the three of you.'

He looked at her for a moment, taking off his glasses. 'Oh, but I didn't go with them, bach. It was just Grace and Cissie.'

'But you're—'

'I drove them up to London and saw them safe on to the train.'

'Oh, right.'

He hesitated and started to say something, then stopped himself.

'What?' said Alys, curious.

'It was just the two of them went to France, beaut. Picking grapes, they were. Down in the south.'

And he handed back the photo. 'Imagine that! A whole summer they—'

But Alys had stopped listening, distracted by a police car pulling up outside the house. Her first thought was *Kirsty*. She must have finally reported her and now Alys had been tracked down. No doubt she'd been put on police records after being picked up last week and that's how they'd found her. There was no point in running away any more. The game was up.

'Hang on a minute, John,' she said and went out into the hallway. She opened the door just as the PC was about to ring the bell.

'Hello,' she said. 'You're probably looking for me. I'm Alys Meredith.'

'Er, yes, that's right.'

'How does this work? Do you arrest me or do I—'

'Arrest you? Are you a relative of Grace Meredith?'

Behind her, Elin came striding into the hallway, taking over with her usual head-teacher style. 'Officer. I'm Elin Matthews. What's the problem here?'

'It's Mrs Meredith. Grace Meredith.'

'Oh my God.'

'I'm afraid there's been an accident.'

354

70

elin

Greg had only just arrived back in Cardiff when he'd had to turn around again for West Wales. But Elin was so glad that he had.

'So who called the Coastguard?' he asked, when he found them in the waiting room.

'A couple of paddle-boarders. They'd seen her swimming out earlier and then realized they hadn't seen her swim back.'

'The lifeboat got there in under three minutes,' said Beca. 'D'you think it'll be on that programme *Saving Lives at Sea?*'

Her dad smiled.

'Inappropriate timing, Beca,' said Elin. Though she didn't have the energy to get cross. They'd told her that Grace had suffered a very mild heart attack in the water and had 'got herself into trouble'. The euphemism was glaring.

'You mean she nearly drowned?' Alys had asked.

'Let's not think about that now, Mrs Meredith,' the doctor in A&E had said. 'The important thing is that they got to her in time and it's looking like they'll only be keeping her in overnight.'

John had gone back to Cadwallader House once it was established that Grace would be okay.

'You've had a terrible day,' Elin had said to him, pulling on her coat. She'd hastily put together a few things for her grandmother – nightie, slippers, a washbag and a change of clothes. The poor thing would've only had her bathers on when they took her in. 'We'll drop you off on the way and keep you posted. Come over for your lunch tomorrow. Mum will want to see you.'

Once they'd seen him safely back to the home, Elin got in the car and they headed off for the hospital. Beca was in the front and Alys in the back. The atmosphere would've been hideous if Beca hadn't kept the chat going.

It was nearly nine o'clock by the time they were allowed to see her. 'Only two of you, I'm afraid,' said the nurse. 'It's hospital policy.'

'You and Beca go,' said Alys. 'I'll sit here and get to know my son-in-law.'

They headed off, following the nurse, but then Elin stopped. 'Actually, Bec, I think Alys should come. You don't mind, do you?'

'Course not. Nana? Mum wants you to go with her.'

Elin wanted to correct her, to say, *No, it's not that I want you to come with me, I just think you should.* But it sounded so churlish, so she said nothing, just gave a tight little nod.

Grace was in a side room. She looked remarkably good, considering what she'd been through. 'I am *so* embarrassed,' she said. 'Fancy them getting the lifeboat out to me. I'll never live it down!'

'Why didn't you tell us you were going swimming?' Elin asked, as she sat down on the other side of the bed from Alys.

'I don't know, bach,' said Grace, her voice a little weaker than usual. 'It was all a bit of a blur once John told me the news. I couldn't face going in there, seeing her—' And then she started to cry. 'Poor Cissie.'

'Oh Mum,' whispered Alys, taking Grace's hand. 'I'm so sorry.'

She looked over at Elin and motioned for her to pass the tissues from the bedside table.

Elin did so and said, 'Look, I'll ask if I can stay with you tonight. I can sleep on that chair, no problem. And then, all being well, you'll be discharged tomorrow.'

'As long as you pass your tests with flying colours!' said Alys, putting on a silly squadron-leader-type voice.

And Elin felt the bizarre sensation of envying her mother's humour, her ability to lighten a situation and to raise a smile, even in the direst situations. She always *was* good at doing that. And Lord knows they'd had some dire situations when she was little.

'You'll do no such thing,' said Grace, blowing her nose. 'A good night's sleep, that's all I need. What use will it do you, sleeping in a silly old chair? Tell me, how's John?'

'He's okay,' said Elin. 'Worried about you, of course.'

'Yes, well, tell him not to. We've got a funeral to plan. Got to give that sister of his a proper send-off. I've done a list here – hymns and whatnot. And there's a poem on there, R. S. Thomas. She always wanted that, did Ciss.'

'Blimey, Grama Grace,' said Elin, scanning the list, written in shaky but discernible handwriting. 'When d'you get a chance to write all this?'

Grace affected a hurt expression. 'Elin Matthews, since when have you known me to waste a single minute of my life? Four words – Devil, Work and Idle Hands. Now bugger off and let me sleep.'

Elin smiled, putting Grace's overnight things away in the side cabinet and checking there was plenty of water in the jug. Alys kissed Grace on the forehead and Elin noticed her hesitate as she did so. How many years since that had last happened, she wondered?

'Goodnight, Mum,' Alys said. And then, as if dusting off a phrase unused for so long it felt foreign, she whispered, 'I love you.'

Hearing Alys say it made Elin choke. She didn't know why. She should be feeling angry at her mother's presumption. It wasn't Alys's place to say things like that any more, she'd foregone that privilege decades ago. Elin should even be doubting that she meant it. But for some reason she believed her, even though she wished she didn't. Because life was so much easier when she didn't believe her mother.

'Night, Grama Grace,' she said. 'If you think of *anything* you need before tomorrow, you get them to call me straight away, okay?'

'Yes, ma'am!' said Grace, attempting a salute.

Alys and Elin made for the door.

'Oh, there *is* one thing,' she said, and they both turned.

'Anything. What is it?' asked Elin, smiling.

'Will you two sort yourselves out?'

'What?' Elin felt the awkwardness grow instantly in the room and she didn't dare look at Alys.

'When you get home now. Share a bottle of wine or something.'

'I don't drink!' said Alys.

'Don't you?' asked Elin, turning to look at her, shocked.

'No. Not for thirty years.'

'Bloody hell.'

'Well, have a cup of cocoa, then!' said Grace, sounding a tad irritated. 'Or a glass of orange squash. Anything – but just *talk*, will you? For God's sake, life's too bloody short.'

They both smiled politely and left the room, with no intention whatsoever of talking.

71

elin

She couldn't sleep. She'd opted to take Grama Grace's bed so that Greg could sleep in hers – he'd already announced he couldn't face driving home to Cardiff. When they'd arrived back from the hospital, they'd all been too tired to start fussing with bedding and sheets for the only remaining spare bed. There'd been such overwhelming relief that Grama Grace was all right that a night-time debrief over a hot drink or a family-bonding session seemed unnecessary and they'd gone their separate ways. Greg went up first, followed by Beca, who slunk off to her room. Alys had uttered a polite 'goodnight' before disappearing, and Elin was left alone to lock up.

Grama Grace's bed was exceptionally comfortable. *Why were we all so duped by duvets*, she wondered? Sheets and blankets were *so* much better, and she vowed that when she returned home, she would treat their bed – no, *her* bed – to an overhaul.

Her bed. Is that what it had become? Had Greg been sleeping in it whilst she was at Grama Grace's? She tried not to, but she couldn't help but relish the thought. He'd been so lovely tonight. So kind and gentle. The old Greg. Not some sad middle-aged idiot trying to be something or someone he wasn't. Maybe he did deserve another chance. Because what was the alternative? A life on her own? Did she really want that? She could hear all the feminist voices of protest in her head telling her that she didn't need a man to justify her existence, that he'd betrayed her trust once so he would do it again, that he didn't deserve someone like her, *blah blah blah*. But what a hypocrite she was! She was no better than him, not really. Infidelity was infidelity.

The truth was though, Kiwi gardeners and thirty-one-year-old hippy chicks aside, the absolutely unshakeable truth was that Greg, more than anything, was her friend. The other stuff – the sex and the romance and all of that – was a bonus: it was his friendship that she missed the most. That she needed the most, in fact. And if admitting that made her a traitor to the feminist cause, then so be it. She couldn't help what she felt.

Turning on to her side, she caught sight of the Perspex photograph cube on Grama Grace's bedside table and wondered how she might secretly 'borrow' it. For months now Elin had been collating photos from Grama Grace's life in order to scan and use them in a montage for the party. The party! It was just over a week away now. Surely the events of the past twenty-four hours wouldn't mean she'd have to cancel? She'd put so much effort into it, after all. No. It would be fine. It would cheer Grama Grace up, if anything. And John. The only fly in the ointment, of course, was that Alys would no doubt expect to be invited. *Bloody hell, that woman!* How could one person so single-handedly mess things up for everyone? Why did she have to come back? Shaking the thought from her mind, Elin switched on the bedside lamp and, in a bid to distract herself, picked up the cube of photos.

She'd never really looked at it properly before, not having spent a lot of time in her grandmother's bedroom – why would she? There was one photo of herself, aged about fifteen, blowing out candles on a birthday cake, and another from her graduation day with the four of them – her with Grama Grace, John and Cissie. Then a wedding photograph from her and Greg's wedding in 2003 – God, she'd been so happy that day. Next year would be their twentieth wedding anniversary – was she really going to throw all that away? She sighed and turned the cube to see a solo shot of Grace in bathers, wrapped in a towel on the Dylan's Quay seafront. The festive street decorations behind her suggested it must have been after she'd completed the Christmas Day swim – what year would that have been, she wondered, 2012 maybe? Elin shivered when she thought about Grace and her wild swimming. Surely after today she would consider knocking it on the head? There were two other photographs – one of Alys and Grace outside Swn-y-Môr, holding Elin's hand, bunting draped across the front of the house. Elin remembered it well – 1977, the Silver Jubilee. She'd have been six years old then. It was the only time she remembered visiting Dylan's Quay before things became really bad with Alys. In the photograph they are all smiling: Elin and Grace are waving Union Jacks, Alys is drinking champagne. Elin sighed and turned the cube to look at the final photograph. It was a two-shot of Grace and Cissie. Her heart lurched when she thought of poor Cissie. At least she was resting in peace now, away from the demons of dementia that had terrorized her more and more as time had gone by. There were no terrors or demons in this photograph, though: the two pals must have been at some kind of event, six or seven years ago, maybe. They were standing in front of a castle, and dressed in their 'Sunday best', as Grama Grace would call it, their arms thrown around each other's shoulders, looking pleased as punch. This was a *definite* for the party montage! Elin smiled and looked at the clock. Three thirty a.m. She was wide awake. Maybe a camomile tea would help . . .

72

alys

Alys was sitting in the dark, wearing a pair of Grace's pyjamas and nursing a hot drink, when Elin walked into the kitchen, switching on the light. 'God! I didn't see you there!' she snapped, nearly jumping out of her skin.

'I made myself some Ovaltine,' said Alys quietly. 'Little blast from the past.'

'We'll need to buy some milk tomorrow, there's hardly any left.' Elin began filling the kettle.

'Was that a dig?' asked Alys.

'No.' Elin hesitated then. 'Actually, yes it was. Look, Alys, what are you doing here? How long are you planning to stay, because—'

Alys interrupted her. 'I can't keep apologizing for who I am and what I did, okay?'

'*Keep* apologizing? I don't seem to remember you *ever* apologizing. Not once.'

'That's simply not true. You just never gave me the chance to do it properly.'

'Go on then, Alys—'

'Call me Mum, for God's sake!'

'No. I won't. Because I don't think of you as my mum.'

Alys shook her head and sighed.

'But carry on, *Alys*,' Elin said pointedly. 'Tell me how sorry you are. For dragging me up. For putting me in danger as a child. For neglecting me. For getting so off your face you nearly set our home on fire. For sleeping with so many different men I didn't know who I'd see eating breakfast of a morning – well, I *say* breakfast, that was a bit of a rare occasion when you remembered to buy food—'

Elin was on a roll, tears pouring down her cheeks as she hurled accusations at her mother she'd most likely wanted to say for thirty years. Alys could feel the colour drain from her face and she was suddenly so incredibly tired as Elin's rant continued.

'—tell me how sorry you are for being such an embarrassment that I could never bring friends home from school, so it was easier not to *have* any friends, or how sorry you are for dragging me all over Europe on a whim – *What an adventure we'll have, darling!* – because it suited you, or what about saying sorry for even *having me* in the first place! For getting pregnant by a married man who wanted nothing to do with you. Or *me*, for that matter—'

'That wasn't my fault—'

'Of course it wasn't. Nothing was *ever* your fault, was it, Alys? Never being there for me, that wasn't your fault, nor was forgetting to tell me about bras or boys or periods – nor was accidentally overdosing when I was eleven. That wasn't your fault either! WAS IT? ELEVEN YEARS OLD, ALYS! FINDING YOU OUT COLD ON THE BATHROOM FLOOR, HAVING TAKEN TOO MANY PILLS!'

The two women faced each other. Elin was shaking with rage and bitter resentment. Angrily she wiped her cheeks and turned back to the kettle.

The phone started ringing. They both ignored it.

Alys remained silent and still, terrified that any words would make it worse.

The phone stopped, the tears did not, the kettle boiled.

She watched Elin drop a camomile teabag into a mug, the little string and its label becoming swallowed up as she poured the hot water over it. Both hands against the work surface, Elin seemed to be holding on for grim life. Alys's head was spinning and she was fearful she would collapse in a heap. She tried to breathe deep breaths.

Then came a heart-wrenching wail of despair that rose from inside Elin, but sounded as if it belonged to someone else, or *something* else even.

Alys was overwhelmed by it – the primal urge to help her own child in distress.

And there it was – her hand on Elin's shoulder, so tentative yet so familiar.

Elin shuddered at the touch, but she didn't push Alys away. She turned, slowly.

And gave in.

Finally, gave in.

Letting her mother wrap her arms around her and hold her for the first time since she was twelve years old. Alys held her so tight. And began rocking her gently, whispering so quietly it was barely audible,

'I.

Am.

So.

So.

Sorry.'

When Beca ran into the kitchen, she was met by the sight of Alys and Elin in a mother–daughter embrace that looked for all the world like it happened every day. It was a sight she was about to destroy with what she was going to tell them.

'You didn't answer the phone,' she said, breathless.

They broke out of their hug and looked at her.

'What?' said Elin, looking dazed and drained and confused.

'It was the hospital,' Beca said. 'Grama Grace has died.'

73

beca

She'd cried for two whole days, even though, in a way, the week since it happened had been one of the loveliest of her life. There had been an air of gentleness in the house, a sort of sad calm. Her mum and Nana Alys kept laughing and crying together as they went through Grama Grace's things. They seemed more like very close sisters than confrontational mother and daughter now. Beca remembered a girl in school who'd had a sister eighteen years her senior. It was a bit like that, really. Except that Nana Alys acted more like the baby sister and Elin the big sister. Sometimes Beca found them annoying together – sometimes she even felt left out. But then she didn't begrudge them this new-found tight-knittedness – God knows they'd spent enough time apart. They kept finding out things about each other, sharing bits of information they'd missed out on over the years – things like Nana Alys's spiritual-enlightenment phase when she lived in Mexico, or the fact that Mum had done an MA when she was forty-two; how Alys had developed an allergy to aspirin and how Elin was really good on the cello.

Soozi had been lovely to her on the phone. Which was a double-edged sword really, because the kinder she was, the more Beca loved her.

'She was summin' else, your Gigi,' she said. 'Proper special lady.'
And Beca cried all over again. In fairness, Soozi had stayed true to
her word since she'd left, phoning or at least texting her every day,
telling her where she was on the tour and how it was all going;
who was a knob, who was sound, how receptive the audiences
were. And she'd always sign any message off with 'PS Heidi sends
her love' or 'Helga can't wait to meet you', which made Beca
laugh. The night before, on a crackly line from Munich, Soozi had
called her before the show. 'Listen, bird, we're in Stuttgart Friday
night, then no dates for ten days. So I'm coming home, okay?'

'For real? Sooz, that's amazin',' said Beca, unable to hide the
excitement in her voice.

'Of course. Gonna be there for you at the funeral, aren' I?
Hold your hand . . .'

'Actually, I might need more than that. Will you do me a
favour . . .?'

It was John who'd suggested a joint service. At first, Elin didn't
think it was 'appropriate' and Nana Alys had agreed with her.
Grace and Cissie were good friends, she said, yes, but since when
did friends share a final send-off? John had stayed silent on the
matter, and with hindsight, he'd been extremely patient in doing
so. And loyal. But the trip to register the deaths made them see
him in a whole new light.

As next of kin, he'd gone along to the town hall with the rest of
them – Beca, her mum and dad and Nana Alys. 'May as well kill
two birds with one stone,' her dad had said, and her mum had told
him off for being disrespectful. Although she did smile when she
said it. She seemed to like him again these days. And had even agreed
to put the divorce on hold. Maybe that's what death did to people.

When it came to filling out the forms, the registrar – a very tall
woman with a long face to match, asked about Grama Grace's
marital status.

'Widowed,' said Alys, nodding sadly at Elin.

'Actually . . .' interrupted John. And everyone looked at him.

'Look, I'm sorry, I really should've told you this before, but I promised I'd keep it a secret and I've never—'

'Oh my God, John!' exclaimed Elin. 'You were secretly married! You and Grama Grace!'

'I bloody *knew* it!' said Alys, as if she'd just solved a whodunnit mystery. 'But why didn't you say?' She smiled a teary smile, 'Good Lord! That makes you my stepfather!' And she tried to hug him, but he pushed her away, not unkindly.

'Wait, wait, no! You don't understand,' he said.

The registrar looked confused. 'So Mrs Meredith *wasn't* widowed. Is that what you're saying?'

'Yes, kind of . . . technically . . .'

'Take your time, John,' said Greg, gently.

'She was actually widowed *twice*.'

'Eh?' Elin looked at him, then at Alys.

'Your father's death meant she was widowed the first time, of course,' John explained to her. 'But the second time . . .'

Silence descended again as John tried to find the words.

Alys found them for him.

'Cissie,' she said, the realization hitting her.

'What?'

'She was married to Cissie. Wasn't she, John?'

There was a stunned moment when everyone took in what she'd said. And then Elin started on a rant – *How could they be serious? It just didn't make sense, Grama Grace had been married to a man and had a child, so how could she be a lesbian?*

'No offence, Beca,' she added, and Beca thought she was in some kind of black comedy. She pointed out that her mother was being a bit thick. 'Since when can't lesbians have babies? And loads of people get married to someone of the opposite sex and then come out as gay.'

'Oh, don't be so obtuse, Beca, you know what I mean. It just doesn't make sense that Grama Grace didn't say anything.' She'd then gone on to make things worse by asking John – quite insultingly – if he was 'losing his marbles'. Because you were a *couple*, John, remember? You were together for years!'

'No,' he said patiently. 'You just *assumed* we were. Everyone did. And we . . . well, we went along with the assumption. It was easier that way.'

John reached into his jacket pocket and pulled out a Manila envelope. 'Open it,' he said, handing it to Elin.

She did so and took out a marriage certificate. It stated that Grace Meredith had married Cynthia Rhiannydd Edwards on 5 April 2015 at Beaumaris register office, Anglesey. The marriage had been witnessed by John Edmund Jenkins and a Pennant Arthur.

'Who's Pennant Arthur when he's at home?' Greg asked.

John smiled at the memory. 'Just some poor fella we hauled in off the street to be the other witness!'

'My middle name is Rhiannydd,' said Alys, staring in shock.

'Oh yes,' said Elin softly.

'I thought it was you, John,' said Alys. 'All those years, I blamed you. When you came to my father's funeral and I saw how she looked at you—'

'She hadn't seen me for nearly twenty years, that's why.'

'And then when we moved to Dylan's Quay – I thought it was all because of you . . .'

And Alys began to weep.

'I loved Grace, Alys. I truly did,' said John, a sob catching in his voice. 'But as a sister, bach, nothing else.'

The registrar looked down. She was used to tears in her job. But her next appointment was due any minute and this family looked like they could be here a while.

'I was so awful to you all. So awful to my mother!'

'Mum, ssh now,' said Elin, reaching out and embracing her. This time it was Elin's turn to comfort. 'You weren't to know,' she soothed. 'You weren't to know.'

grace and cissie

1950–1968

74

October 1950

There is something about Sunday afternoons, Grace thinks, *that makes everything seem somehow otherworldly. Or perhaps it is just these particular Sunday afternoons.* They lie side by side on her bed, their clothes abandoned and the late-September sunshine shyly streaming through the nets. They are holding hands and Cissie's head is resting on Grace's shoulder, a blonde chaos of curls unpinned and free to roam.

'What do you miss the most?' whispers Cissie, basking in the gorgeousness of what they've just done, not wanting to disturb the sanctity of their afternoon together with the intrusion of loud conversation.

'So many things,' Grace whispers back, stroking her lover's arm. The softness of her flesh is like satin beneath her fingertips. 'The weather . . .'

'*Bien sûr!*'

'The wine . . .'

'*Mais oui!*'

'And sleeping. With you. With no care in the world.'

Cissie turns on to her side, her face close to Grace's now. She runs her finger along the profile of Grace's nose and across her lips. Grace teasingly takes it between her teeth and smiles.

'*Je t'aime*,' Cissie sighs, affecting a strong French accent, and they giggle and kiss. Again. Knowing that their weekly chance to be together is drawing to a close. Grace's mother will soon return from visiting a poorly aunt. As she does every Sunday afternoon. Grace's mother is a creature of habit. She operates like clockwork. And her habit grants them this liberty. To lie, side by side, without fear.

Grace and Cissie have been back in Wales for three weeks now. It's three weeks since their blissful summer in France came to an end. When they'd boarded *The Golden Arrow* at Victoria in May, they had done so as friends; when they'd boarded *La Flèche d'Or* at Paris in September, they had done so as lovers. And come home to Wales as lovers in secret.

When their journey began, they had each known privately, individually, how they felt about the other. Grace would say later, 'I knew the second you walked into the shop looking for tartan paint.'

'And I knew the second you promised to find it,' Cissie would reply.

They had known.

They had always known.

But they had not dared to share their feelings for fear of rejection – or, worse, repulsion. Both girls said that they would have contented themselves with platonic friendship and continued as they were, had that exquisite evening never taken place. 'I would have pined for you secretly for the rest of my days,' said Cissie. 'As long as I could have been in your company, then I could have lived with that.' And Grace confessed to feeling the same.

Neither Grace nor Cissie could say at what point the landscape had changed between them, at what point they had become braver or who had taken the first step. They just knew it had happened at a farmstead in Bordeaux at the end of the happiest evening, when they'd drunk a little wine, laughed long and sung loudly with their new French friends. They'd held hands walking home to their little hay barn of a room and had stopped to look up at the harvest moon. A silent moment of wonder and awe. Neither said a word, they just stared skywards.

Then lowered their gaze to look at each other.

Still holding hands.

Standing on the precipice of misunderstanding.

Where the potential lay for it all to come crashing down.

And then it happened.

Their most precious, delicate first kiss, bathed in moonlight, silently conveying a million words.

'*Dwi'n caru ti*, Gracie,' whispered Cissie.

'*Dwi'n caru ti, 'fyd*,' replied Grace.

And the alchemy of Love transformed their friendship that night.

'Why did we ever return?'

The question is rhetorical – they have pondered it time and time again since the day three weeks earlier when they boarded *The Golden Arrow* at Dover. Why did they ever surrender their life in Bordeaux, to come back to the darkness, the grime and gloom of post-war Britain? In their history of mistakes, returning to Wales ranks highest. And they will pay the price for decades to come. But for now they have this moment, this bed, the silkiness of each other's bodies, which they have both come to know so well, every curve and nuance, every sigh and sound, every pleasure. Oh, the pleasure.

And so lost are they in the pleasure that they do not hear the front door open and close below them. They do not hear the irritation in the voice of Grace's mother, who has had to return early because she is feeling unwell. They do not hear the footsteps on the stairs. And they do not hear the handle turn on Grace's bedroom door as it opens up to let in her mother and let out eighteen years of happiness.

But they do hear the words that fly at them.

Sordid.

Sick.
Perversion.
Evil.
Disgusting.
Shameful.
And *whores.*

They try to dress hastily, under fire, under a barrage of blows and abuse, attempting to dodge the slaps and the screams that come raining down upon them like the swatting of a spider or a mouse. As if the attack can somehow eradicate the beauty of what they have created. Of who they are. And who they always will be.

Cissie is crying. 'Go!' shouts Grace, urging her to escape, wanting to take on the pain for them both. Wanting to save her from this horrific indignity.

She hears the front door slam and faces her mother's rage. Humiliated. Shamed.

'You are an abomination!' her mother hisses. And the punch comes hard and fast across the cheek that only minutes earlier was being showered in tiny kisses.

75

November 1950

It is John who is their saviour. Dearest John, Cissie's gentle brother. Patiently he waits and watches the shop to snatch a moment when Grace is alone. Day after day, always Grace is in company. Her mother, Grace's self-appointed bodyguard, walks her to work each morning, meets her for lunch at one and collects her again at the end of her shift. Grace is never alone. But John knows that if he is patient, at some point she will be. And his opportunity finally comes. It is eleven o'clock on a Wednesday morning, two weeks after the 'discovery', the brutal, heartless discovery.

Where would they have been if it wasn't for gentle John? The kindly brother who does not judge, who only sees their love in all its tender glory. He is ready, he sits in the café across the road, waiting, waiting, and there it is: Mr Protheroe leaves his shop, merrily announcing that he will only be gone a short while. 'A short while' could cover anything from five minutes to a whole afternoon. But John only needs sixty seconds.

He is crossing the road, he is opening the door to the shop and he is inside, delivering his instruction: Sunday night, under the bridge at Maes Wen, Cissie will wait with him. But it is their only chance. Cissie will have left her family home – as will Grace – unable to ever return. And John will drive them both into the night and they will board another train and leave behind this cruel, evil world that knows nothing of love.

'You've only got one crack at this, Gracie,' he says.

'I will be there, whatever it takes,' she replies.

When Grace's mother collects her at the end of the working day, she has no notion, no speck of an inkling, that her daughter will shortly run away from home under cover of darkness. She has no idea how the prospect of escape has consumed her only child. All Grace's mother truly cares about is what other people think. She lives in fear of shame. Reputation comes before all: before happiness and certainly before love. Reputation is all. She cannot allow any whispers: there must be no rumours of shameful behaviour. Which is why she must watch her daughter's every move and never allow her sordid proclivities to rear their ugly heads again.

And Sunday is here. And Grace goes to chapel with her mother, and sits and listens to Reverend Jenkins as he loudly spouts the Word of the Lord, as he tells them all how they must live their lives, how God wants their remorse, their sacrifice and penance. He does not talk of love. But Grace doesn't mind. She sits in sombre, sober silence, her face hard and soulless. That's what she shows to the world. Not what is inside her heart. Not the unbridled joy, the counting down of the hours, the minutes, until she will be free.

Outside the chapel, her mother speaks to Mr Aneurin Meredith, the schoolteacher. They smile and share niceties, and her mother turns to Grace, inviting her to share niceties with Mr Meredith, too. But Grace declines. She has no niceties to share. And as they walk home, her mother berates her for being rude to the teacher. And Grace takes it all – because in less than twelve hours she will be free.

She can hear her mother snoring. She counts ten snores and then, overnight bag in hand, she creeps downstairs, knowing which steps creak and which are safe and soundless.

She turns the key; she turns the handle; she steps outside into the backyard and silently closes the door. It is a clear, crisp November night and the moon will show her the way. That blessèd moon. Passing the little row of shops, shuttered up now and closed, she feels safe in the moonlight and breathless with excitement.

She hears voices behind her, closing-time voices from the Lamb and Flag, a pub she knows a bit about: a pub which any decent chap would not frequent. Not a place where small glasses of pale ale are drunk in modest quantities at the end of a long day, but a place for those who are looking for a fight – the troublemakers, the trouble-seekers. She quickens her step, anxious to put as much distance as possible between her and the closing-time voices. Rounding the corner, she is relieved to see the street ahead is empty – no houses here, no angry voices, drunk on beer and lusting for a fight. She has half a mile to go. 'I'm nearly there,' she whispers to herself.

And from the shadows they step. There are two of them. 'What have we got here?' they leer and she tries to pass. But they do not let her.

'Only bad girls are out this time of night,' says one.

'Bad girls lookin' for trouble,' sneers the other, spitting on the ground in disgust.

'Let me GO!' she shouts when he pulls at her arm.

'Ooh, la-di-da,' he mocks and grabs her, this time round the neck.

She bites him hard. He yelps in pain.

And the other starts unbuckling his belt. 'When bitches bite, they need teaching a lesson,' he snarls.

She tries to run, but the other one is too fast for her. And the last thing she sees as her head hits the ground is the contents of her overnight bag – her soap case and face cream – rolling into the gutter.

76

December 1950

'And this is your *something borrowed*.' Her mother smiles and pins the marcasite brooch on to Grace's lapel. 'I wore it when I married your father.'

Grace doesn't reply. She's worried she might cry.

Her mother misreads the silence and, uninvited, begins to recite, like a schoolgirl chanting a skipping-rope rhyme, '*Something old, something new, something borrowed, something blue!*' The sound of her sing-songing jars, gauche and shrill in the sparseness of the bedroom. 'Let's look at you, then.' She turns Grace around and stands behind her as they both survey the reflection in the dressing-table mirror.

The outfit she's wearing looks faintly ridiculous. A simple skirt and jacket hurriedly put together in three days. Mrs Simpson from the draper's shop had sold them a few yards of grey tulle at a reduced rate. 'Not glamorous, I know,' her mother had said, cutting out the pattern on the kitchen table, 'but tulle is unrationed and beggars can't be choosers.'

That was only last week.

She had lain in bed three nights in a row, listening to the whirr and halt of the sewing machine as it floated up from downstairs, punctuated by an occasional curse. Grace's mother is not a natural seamstress, and the result of her efforts is an ill-fitting

two-piece suit that hides any hint of a waistline or bust or anything remotely bridal. The marcasite brooch glints incongruously
against a background of dishcloth dullness.

'You'll do nicely,' says her mother. And she squeezes Grace's
shoulders, as if divesting her maternal responsibility once and for
all. After today, her daughter will be someone else's concern.

The bruises are faded now, of course. The physical ones, at least.
Though the sickness Grace feels at the memory can still hijack
her whole body.

Her mother had quietly admonished her – sitting in that hospital ward, in hushed, harsh whispers so that none of the other
visitors could hear, she had told her daughter that it served her
right. What normal woman would be wandering the streets after
dark like that? There were bound to be men, she'd said. Bound
to be trouble. What was she thinking? Silly, foolish girl. And the
only attempt at consoling had been a feeble pat on the arm and
the offer of a glass of water.

She tells her to be grateful. That it all could have been so much
worse. 'If there'd been a child, on top of everything else,' says her
mother, with a sharp, disapproving intake of breath. 'Be grateful
at least for that.'

Be grateful.
Be grateful that you were found.
Be grateful to be alive.

Except she isn't alive. Not any more.

Her spirit died that night. Not because of what they did to her,
but because she never had the chance to explain to Cissie. To put
right the assumption that she'd changed her mind. And now it is
too late.

And when her mother invites Mr Meredith the teacher to tea
and tells her of their plan, she does not object. Because she no
longer cares about anything. Her spirit lives elsewhere. 'Soiled
goods,' her mother says, drying her eyes from the shame, whilst
Mr Meredith comforts her with a smile, telling her not to worry.

As if her mother is the victim in all this. Not her. Grace is just the troublemaker.

Outside the chapel, the minister is there to greet them. A solitary figure in his sombre suit, he attempts a smile. But jollity doesn't sit easily with the young Reverend Jenkins. '*Bore da,*' he calls out. 'We're all ready for you inside!' And he turns on his heel.

Grace falters. *Run!* says the voice in her head. *Go. Just do it.*

Sensing her reluctance, Grace's mother whispers, 'Come on, now. You know it's for the best.' And she tugs at her daughter's arm, leading her through the chapel door.

He doesn't turn to greet her. And for this she is grateful. She could not bear to see the deference in his watery eyes, the admiration and, God forbid, the lust. He is trying to affect an air of authority. She can tell this even from looking at his back. Poker-straight he stands, shoulders straining, desperate to conjure up the military aura that has always eluded him. Two world wars have shadowed his life and yet he's served in neither. She does not judge him for this, of course, but senses his shame. That he feels somehow diminished.

He is thirty-five years old.

She is barely eighteen.

The ceremony is mercifully short. And just like her bridal outfit, there are no frills. Perfunctory and pedestrian. The basic requirements fulfilled. Not how she'd imagined her wedding day would be. Slowly she writes her name on the register, as if signing her life away. As she does so, she thinks, *Where are you? What are you doing now?* And she bites her lip to stop the tears.

Back at the house – his house, *their* house now – a small luncheon has been prepared in the front parlour. Nothing fancy – as extravagant as food rationing will allow. But Grace is glad. She cannot face eating, cannot face living. Why did she not run?

The grandfather clock in the Bible-scented hallway marks time like a funeral drum, and for all the world they could indeed be at a wake and not a wedding. Mr Protheroe's fat fingers dance nimbly over the sparse array of sandwiches, before landing on corned beef and chutney. Cups and saucers slosh and rattle with tepid, weak tea. There is no sherry. This is not a sherry-drinking household. She has not married a sherry drinker.

Her husband. She steals a look at him now with his neat moustache and clean hands, a teacher of thirteen years who smells of coal-tar soap and Dettol. He clears his throat to speak and his tone is formal, as if addressing a school assembly. 'I should like to say something, if I may.' She hears the words that escape from his mouth, but she is not listening to them: she watches his lips, red and wet like strawberry jelly, and she closes her eyes against the sight.

She is thinking instead of soft, red wine and the vineyards of Bordeaux; the French sun kissing their faces as they pluck plump grapes from their stems, their fingers stained with sweet, dark juice, filling huge baskets by their feet. And then, with their morning's work done, how they sit in the shade of the vines, gorging on a picnic of strong local cheese, peaches and a little ham, if they're lucky. And they laugh – heady, girlish laughter, drunk not on the wine but on each other's company. And the adventure they are sharing. And the moments when time stands still and they stare, for what seems like a decade, deep into one another's soul. Happy, deliriously so, to be drawn in, swallowed up and consumed by love.

'. . . and may this form the solid foundation of our union, for many, many years to come.' Her husband's speech is over and Aunt Edna is tapping her teacup with an Apostle spoon, shouting 'Hear, Hear!' a little too enthusiastically.

Grace is hauled back into the parlour and the dread-filled present day. She watches Mr Protheroe drain his teacup and pick up his coat. Duty done, time to leave. He slaps her husband heartily on the back and turns his attentions to her. 'Now then, *Mrs*

Meredith.' She cringes inwardly at her new name. 'I don't want to see hide nor hair of you back in that shop till Tuesday, earliest,' he booms. 'You two lovebirds need a bit of a honeymoon – even if it's only here in Neath.'

'Get to know each other, isn't it?' says Mrs Joyce in agreement.

And suddenly the wedding party is dispersing, leaving the two of them alone.

Her husband closes the front door gently behind the final guest and they both stand in silence, teetering on the brink of this uncharted life together. Grace notes an unfamiliar kindness in his voice as he takes her hand. 'You will learn to love me, you know.' And she wonders if this is a command or an assurance. The skin on his fingers and palm is damp with nerves, a world away from the feel of the hand she would die to be holding now.

'I'd better wash the cups,' she whispers. And makes her way back into the kitchen. Her married life has begun.

77

October 1951

'It's a girl,' announces the midwife, over the lamb-like, newborn cries. She snips confidently at the umbilical cord, clamps the end with a peg, then scoops the baby up and on to the scales. 'She's a good weight. Eight pound two.' It's only a matter of minutes, but it seems like an hour before mother and baby are united – a whole host of functions and checks to be carried out first. Grace's pleas to hold her child are lightly admonished with a 'Hold your horses, you'll get your chance. We just need to give Baby a clean and then she's all yours. Have we got a name yet?'

'Rhiannydd.'

'Nice.'

'Well, it's what I want to call her, anyhow . . .' Her voice fades away, uncertain, weak now and desperate to hold this tiny mite in her arms.

The midwife finally hands her over, washed and wrapped in a crisp white linen sheet. 'There we are, go to your mam now, isn't it, cariad?'

Grace holds her and relishes the crying. The undisputable sign of life, of need. The sign that her baby has well and truly arrived. 'I would die for you,' she whispers. 'Cariadus.' She kisses her daughter's head.

The baby, eyes closed and tired from her momentous journey, quietens at her mother's touch, snuffles and settles to sleep.

He comes to visit the next day, wearing a new tie and a broad smile and carrying flowers. She's only finished feeding a few minutes beforehand and is eager to ensure she looks tidy, presentable. The thought of him seeing her in any state of undress distresses her. Their piecemeal intimacy had ended as soon as she'd discovered the pregnancy, and even on those prior occasions when he'd climbed on top of her in bed, he'd never seen her naked. So the thought now of his seeing her breastfeed fills her with utter dread.

He kisses her politely on the cheek. 'Well done, soldier!' he congratulates her, as if she's just won first prize at the chapel fête cake-making competition. 'Let's have a look, then,' he says. 'Let's see my little girl!' And he hands the flowers to a passing nurse with a cursory nod before bending over the bedside cot and staring in. He makes to pick her up and Grace tries to stop him. 'She's only just gone down.' But he ignores her, pulling back the satin-edged blanket and lifting the baby into his arms. Grace is surprised by the dexterity with which he does it, how easily he stands there rocking her. The epitome of a proud father.

'We shall call her Alys,' he announces. 'After my grandmother.'

'But I want to call her Rhiannydd. We discussed it.' She tries to control the alarm that grows in her voice.

'I know, but on reflection, I didn't feel it was right. So we shall compromise – and Rhiannydd can be her middle name, yes?'

He looks at her questioningly, as if offering her a choice in the matter. But of course he isn't. The decision has been made and to argue would be futile.

'We'll take a little trip next week to the town hall and register her. As a family, if you're feeling up to it, dear. Otherwise the two of us will go.' He coos at his daughter now, who is contentedly sleeping in his confident hold, revealing to Grace a side of him never hitherto seen. She longs to reclaim her baby from him. But he stands resolute, holding her tight, his ownership very firmly stamped.

'What do we say to that, then, little Alys, hmm?'

78

February 1968

seventeen years later

Grace is huddled into the corner of the shelter on Aberavon Promenade, wrapped in layers to protect her from the cold. The wind is icy, though nothing can cool her excitement. She pulls back the cuff of her navy leather glove to reveal her wristwatch. It is still early, too soon yet to worry that he won't come. Though that is, of course, a possibility. She has no way of knowing his intentions. She only knows that three days ago at the funeral, he'd clutched her note firmly in the palm of his hand. And she is here, as she'd said she would be.

On a brighter, sunnier day, this shelter with its wooden slatted seats and frosted glass panelling would make a perfect spot to sit idly and look out over the Bristol Channel, to watch the holiday-makers on Aberavon Beach building sandcastles and running into the sea.

'I brought an umbrella, though the rain's held off,' says a voice. And she turns, and there he stands.

'John,' she whispers. And they embrace for what feels like an hour. 'Come and sit down,' she says. 'I brought a flask.'

*

There's a slight hysteria between them for the first few minutes – disbelief that they have actually managed to meet.

'We should have done this eighteen years ago,' he says.

'Better late than never!' she jokes, trying to cover up the painful memory of that horrific night.

'We didn't find out what had happened,' he says. 'We just thought you'd changed your mind.' His face is sad.

'Don't,' she says gently, touching his arm. 'We've found each other again now, haven't we? That's all that counts.'

And she pours them two coffees from the Thermos.

'To old friends,' she says.

'And new beginnings . . . I hope.'

John goes on to explain how he and Cissie hadn't been able to go back once they'd left that night. And how they had both found work and taken two rooms in a house in Cardiff.

'Must have been dreadful,' says Grace.

'It was fine. Really, it was. And we weren't there for long. Cissie met someone, y'see. A nice chap. Sydney. Older than her, but very kind. And when they married . . .'

He looks away and she touches his hand. 'It's all right, John. It's what I expected.'

'Well, when they married, they bought this old house out west. Place called Dylan's Quay.'

'Sounds pretty,' says Grace.

'It's stunning there, Gracie, it really is. And it's not completely unconnected with why I'm here.'

Grace looks confused and listens as he shares what he has in mind.

'Look . . . When I saw your husband's obituary, it was like it was meant to be. The timing of the whole thing. I knew that your life circumstances would be very different now and it was a risk. I knew nothing about you or what you might think. I was basing everything on how life used to be, but it's been eighteen years – for all I know, your feelings could have changed . . .'

'My feelings have never changed, John,' she says firmly.

'I'm so glad,' he says, turning to her and smiling the broad smile she's always remembered. 'Cissie will be – well, I think she'll be lost for words.'

'I cannot wait to see her,' says Grace quietly, her eyes brimming with emotion.

'I know,' he whispers. 'And you don't have to.'

He leans over and gently taps the frosted glass at the side of the shelter. Grace is sure her heart has stopped. No. This cannot be happening. Can it?

She watches her walk tentatively around the corner.

And there she stands, swathed in a winter coat and scarf, her blonde curls dancing in the cold wind.

'Oh my darling, darling Cissie!' says Grace.

And they hold on to each other for dear life, with the grey Welsh waves crashing on the shore beyond them and the promenade deserted bar two passing dog-walkers, heads down against the cold and unaware that this most precious of overdue reunions is taking place just yardst away from them.

2022

79

alys

They walked to the church together. The three of them – Alys, Elin and Beca. Holding hands and dressed brightly. That's what Grace had asked for in the letter addressed *To my family – to be read in the event of my death*. It was found with a pile of other letters – dozens written by Grace over the years, *To Alys, wherever you are*. After Alys's initial shock at finding them, they'd been such a comfort to read. All stacked in date order, from July 1992 to the most recent, written less than a month ago. They helped fill the gaping chasm that had grown between them over decades.

The letter to the family was a practical instruction, written a couple of years previously, around the time when John had joined Cissie at Cadwallader House. It explained in detail what to do when she died – which solicitor held her will, where to find all her passwords and account numbers, and information about the house. She'd even told them how to locate the fuse box and stopcock and who supplied her gas and electricity.

Regarding my will, you'll see it's all laid out fairly simply, but I just want you to know a few things. I'm leaving everything to you, Elin, because you are the most sensible and most likely to be organized.

John and Cissie must be looked after; there is enough savings to take care of that, and if for some reason they live to be a hundred and ten, then you'll have to sell Sûn-y-Môr and get cash that way. But they must never, never go without. They are both incredibly precious to me.

Talking of Sûn-y-Môr, it's up to you what you do with it. Obviously I'd like to think that it will stay in the family, but I cannot insist on that. Dylan's Quay is a beautiful place to live – even if it's just for a few weeks a year, though you know my feelings about holiday homes!

With luck, I won't leave any loose ends or complicated problems for you to resolve. I wish with all my heart that I could see Alys again, but so far she's managed to stay away. If she does turn up, then Elin, you must look after her, too. Whatever you think of her, whatever she's done, she is still your mother. And I want you to tell her that I have never stopped loving her, just like I have always loved you and Beca.

I'm in danger of wittering now, so I'll sign off, but I'll leave you with this: I have had a good life, despite some ups and downs, and hopefully at the time of writing I've got a few years left in me yet. I have been blessed to have loved and to have been loved, too, and I hope I leave this world a better place. Please dress brightly at my funeral and remember me with a smile. Play some jazz, tell funny stories, but for God's sake don't be getting maudlin over me. Get on with your own bloody lives! There's still such a lot to do!

And with that she'd signed it with a flourish and a kiss.

When they arrived at the church, there was a crowd of people outside and Alys's first thought was that something had gone wrong. Greg and Soozi were there to meet them, having been charged with the task of looking after John and settling him in a seat at the front.

'What's going on?' said Elin. 'Why aren't they letting anyone inside?'

'They are,' said Greg. 'These are the people who couldn't find a seat.'

'It's absolutely packed, B!' said Soozi, grasping Beca's hand.

And Alys felt her knees wobble, thinking of the esteem in which the town held Cissie and Grace.

Today would have been Grace's ninetieth birthday. They could have chosen a different date for the funeral, but there was something satisfyingly symmetrical about having it today – as if Grace's life had come full circle. And since she had been such a practical person, they'd all agreed that Grace would not have wanted them to cancel the surprise party either. Even though ironically, had she been alive, she wouldn't have wanted to attend! But why waste all the hard work Elin had put into the organizing? 'Turn it into a wake!' Alys had said. She could see Elin's initial reaction was that the idea was somehow disrespectful, but it didn't take much persuasion to convince her otherwise. And so the booking at the Brookfield Hotel was upheld, with mourners at the service invited to join the family there afterwards.

They walked down the aisle, all three of them. Word had spread about the bright colours and the congregation was a mass of joy – blues, pinks, yellows, greens. There was even someone dressed as a parrot. Which made Alys laugh out loud and then cry. Her mother would've loved that, she thought. The church was bursting with love and celebration, a whole town gathered to bid farewell. The local male-voice choir, twenty-five strong, stood smartly in their blazers at the front of the congregation. A signal from the church door cued them to begin their rendition of 'Calon Lân' as the two elegant, identical wicker coffins, bestrewn with peonies and sweet peas, were carried to the front.

Much of the service was a blur. Neeta from the café read a eulogy to them both and Greg spoke on behalf of the family. Alys watched Elin smiling at him through her tears and she prayed they would sort things out between them. If there was one thing she hoped Elin had learned of late, it was that there is no rule book and sometimes you just have to work things out as you go along. *One day at a time,* she thought to herself.

She managed to keep it together till the end. But then the vicar threw a curveball. 'We're going to finish our service today,' he said, 'with a special piece of music composed by Grace's great-granddaughter, Beca.' He nodded at Beca, who stood and walked to the front. She'd told them she was going to do something in honour of Grace but had wanted to keep the details under wraps. *My granddaughter is a beautiful young woman,* Alys thought as she watched her beckon Soozi to join her. They exchanged a few words, and then Beca took her place at the grand piano. Alys knew that Beca could play, but so far hadn't heard her. There was so much she'd yet to discover about her granddaughter, and she prayed it wasn't too late for them to get to know each other properly.

There was a tapping on the microphone.

'Alrigh'?' asked Soozi, awkward and nervous, but stunning in a purple silk minidress and thigh-length boots. 'My name is Soozi Cole. I'm Beca's girl, I am.' And she looked over at Beca, who smiled back. 'Anyways, what it is, me an' her, we've been a bit of a double act, a duo, like – I mean, not any more, like, 'cos I'm tourin' now, off to Belgium tomorrow, I am, but you gets the picture.'

Alys suppressed a giggle at the non-sequiturs of Soozi's introduction and Elin leaned over, whispering, 'She's got an incredible voice, she really has.'

'And I gotta tell you all that that girl over there' – Soozi pointed at Beca, who went a deep shade of red – 'well, she's the dog's bollocks – she's incredible, she is.'

Alys laughed out loud. She *liked* Beca's girlfriend!

'An' she's found this poem. By some dead guy who her Grama Grace totally digged. And so did Cissie, like. Her beautiful wife. Anyways, she's only gone an' put this poem to music! And she sent it to me, an' my mind was well and truly fu—flippin' blown. And she asked me if I'd sing it today. For her Gigi. Who incidentally totally fuckin' rocked. Shit, sorry. Anyway, she's too shy to say nothin', aren't you, bird? But I tell you what, she fu—flippin' worshipped her. So this is for her. And for Cissie, obvs.'

And with that, Soozi nodded to Beca, who began playing the most moving, melodic piece on the piano, exquisite diminished chords and a mournful haunting jazz tune.

'It's called "A Marriage",' said Soozi, 'by R. S. Thomas.' And with that she began to sing.

> 'We met
>   under a shower
> of bird-notes.
>   Fifty years passed,
> love's moment
>   in a world in
> servitude to time . . .'

Alys reached over and held her daughter's hand, kissing it and whispering, 'What an astonishing mother you are, Elin, bach, to have raised such a wondrous person as Beca.'

Elin looked shocked by the praise, but beamed with pride. 'Thanks, Mum,' she whispered back. And Soozi continued singing.

> 'She was young;
> I kissed with my eyes
>   closed and opened
> them on her wrinkles.
>   "Come," said death,
> choosing her as his
>   partner for
> the last dance, And she,
>   who in life

had done everything
    with a bird's grace,
opened her bill now
    for the shedding
of one sigh no
    heavier than a feather.'

When the music finished, a hush descended. Beca walked over to Soozi and hugged her, then headed back to her seat, where she held her mother's hand.

'I am so proud of you,' whispered Elin.

And then a solitary clapping began, taken up by a second and then a third person, until the whole congregation was on its feet, giving a standing ovation, as Alys, Elin and Beca held each other tight in a three-generational hug.

EPILOGUE

grace

She wanders unseen and eavesdropping amongst the mourners. People are saying such lovely things. Her window cleaner tells John that 'Mrs M' was the kindest and funniest old lady he'd ever met and that he sometimes thought he liked her more than his own mam! John is putting on a brave face, bless him.

Darling John, it will get better, cariad.

Dolly Hughes from yoga is showing the manager of Cadwallader House an intricate love-spoon she's been given by Elin. They both admire the craftsmanship that has gone into it, especially the little addition Elin had made last week, before the funeral: a carved wooden heart bearing Cissie's name, attached to the 'daffodil' handle of the spoon by a copper loop. Grace has now forgiven her granddaughter for planning a surprise party against her will, and is just glad these keepsakes have not gone to waste.

Over on a linen-covered centrepiece table proudly stands a chocolate fountain. Grace watches Beca laugh as she dips a marshmallow under its flow, then offers it up to Soozi, who devours it, pelican-like, in one swift gulp. Others follow suit and nearby Elin looks on in delight. 'See!' she says to Greg. 'I told you it was a good idea.' He puts his arms around his wife and pulls her to him. 'Oh, shut up and come to Vienna with me,' he says, nuzzling her neck. 'Just for a weekend.'

Grace waits in hope for a positive reply. *Go on, Elin, bach, give it another chance, is it?*

And her granddaughter's bashful look says it all. As does the kiss she gives Greg in response.

Oh, you two will be all right.

Standing by the cake table in the corner, Neeta is showing off her baking prowess to Alys, who is peering at the marzipan version of herself stuck on to the side of this cake creation. 'It looks nothing like me!' she says, affecting indignation. 'My nose is *not* that big.'

'Yeah, well, it was a bit harder than I thought in the end,' replies Neeta defensively. 'And I didn't have a lot to go on, to be fair. I'd only met you the once!'

The cake is an overall triumph though, featuring, as promised by Neeta, all the significant others in Grace's life, but with the words 'Happy ninetieth birthday' replaced with 'R.I.P. Grace and Cissie'.

Only in Wales, thinks Grace with a smile. *Only in Wales.*

'So what's the plan with you, then?' Neeta asks Alys. 'You staying on in Dylan's Quay?'

You better bloody had! Took you long enough to come home, the least you can do is stay put!

'Yes, I think so,' says Alys. 'We're thinking of reviving Sŵn-y-Môr as a guest house.'

'Oh, that's a fabulous idea,' says Neeta.

Yes, it is!

'Well, it'll keep me out of trouble, and I can keep an eye on John if I'm here. I think Mum would approve,' says Alys.

Yes, she would!

'I know my daughter does.' Looking over to where Elin stands,

Alys waves and mouths, 'You all right?' Elin does a thumbs-up in return. It is an exchange Grace didn't think she'd ever witness.

Ah, my beloved girls.

There is a small stage at one end of the room where Beca has set up her keyboard and Soozi is testing her mic. They are about to perform again and there's a buzz of excitement in the air, a celebration not a wake. *Which is just as it should be.*

And the doors to the verandah are open.

And smiling just beyond them, waiting patiently in the sun, is Cissie.

Ready, my darling?

Ready, my love.

Grace walks towards her, taking one last backward glance before she reaches for her hand.

And they leave the party to carry on without them, just as Beca and Soozi launch into song.

Credits

Title and lyrics on pp. 192 and 193 from 'I'm Gonna Wash That Man Right Outa My Hair' from the musical *South Pacific*, music written by Richard Rodgers and lyrics by Oscar Hammerstein.

Lyrics on p. 259 from 'Abracadabra' by Steve Miller Band, written by Steve Miller.

Lyrics on p.260 from 'Another Brick in the Wall' by Pink Floyd, written by Roger Waters.

Lyrics on p. 311 from 'Respect' sung by Aretha Franklin, written by Otis Redding.

Extract on p. 85 from 'This Be the Verse' in *Collected Poems* by Philip Larkin. Copyright © Estate of Philip Larkin. Reproduced with permission of Faber and Faber Ltd.

Extracts on pp. 60 and 395–6 from 'A Marriage' in *Collected Poems 1945–1990* by R. S. Thomas. Reproduced with permission of Orion Publishing Group Limited through PLSclear.

Extracts on pp. 139 and 141 from *The Big Book* by Alcoholics Anonymous, written by 'Bill W.' (William G. Wilson) and others.

Acknowledgements

Writing *Love Untold* has been a journey and a half. And I am indebted to many kind people for encouraging me en route.

Firstly, I want to pay tribute to the readers of *Never Greener* and *Us Three*, whose positive feedback played a big part in my writing another book. *Love Untold* would not exist without you, lovely readers. And, of course, a big thank-you to all the booksellers and fans online, and across the independent book-shops, high-street chains and supermarkets.

I owe a huge debt of gratitude to my agent, Jonny Geller, whose guidance and support have, as always, been invaluable. Thank you, Jonny, for all that you've done – your calm wisdom and insights have been a blessing, as has your brilliant sense of humour. I am honoured indeed to know you and work with you. A big thank-you also to your colleagues at Curtis Brown, espe-cially the fabulous Viola Haydn, Ciara Finan and Sophie Storey; and to Kate Cooper and Nadia Farah Mokdad, who do such a brilliant job in translation.

My editor, Frankie Gray, is superb. Frankie, you supported me spectacularly on *Never Greener* and *Us Three,* but on *Love Untold* you have gone beyond the call of duty! It has been an absolute joy to work so closely with you on this novel and I cannot thank you enough for your brilliance. You are always astute, open, perceptive and responsive, and your patience and problem-solving are second to none. I marvel at your talent, I really do.

My thanks, of course, to the exceptional team at Transworld – my cherished publishers, led by the wonderful Larry Finlay, whose positive reaction to reading *Love Untold* bowled me over. Hugely appreciated is the work of the wonderful Alison Barrow and Vicky Palmer, who I always get excited to see, and after the Covid years of Zoom calls and screen chats, it's been fabulous to meet up again in the flesh. Thank you for doing such an incredible job on publicizing and marketing my books.

I also want to thank the lovely Hayley Barnes, Bill Scott-Kerr, Imogen Nelson, Tenelle Ottley-Matthew, Hana Sparkes, Emma Burton and Rosie Ainsworth, as well as my beady-eyed and brilliant copy editor Kate Samano, proof-readers Clare Hubbard and Sarah Coward, Beci Kelly for doing such a gorgeous cover design, the marvellous sales team – Tom Chicken, Emily Harvey, Laura Garrod, Louise Blakemore, Laura Ricchetti and Natasha Photiou – and the superb audio-book team: Alice Twomey, Oli Grant and Charlotte Davey. You all rock.

Much gratitude to those friends, authors and journalists who took time to read early copies, with special thanks to Nicola Merrigan and my sister Maria Cronjé for the very helpful notes and feedback. To my niece Nousha for patiently answering random questions from an old person to a young one, and to my nephew Isaak for pizza advice. *Diolch hefyd, i Aran Jones a Catrin Lliar Jones am helpu fi gyda'r Cymraeg!* And a big thank-you to James Corden, whose kindness knows no bounds.

To my brilliant family, thank you always for your love and support, especially to the newest addition, baby Frida, who lights up all our lives and whose smile conquers the world.

But most of all, thank you to my husband, David, who's been there for me throughout the process. David, your suggested solutions, humour, encouragement and love always buoyed up my spirits, especially when I found myself under flashback pressure!

Thank you for keeping me going through the difficult bits, and for sharing my joy when I got it right.

Although *Love Untold* is a work of fiction, I have taken some inspiration from my own life: for example, the town of Dylan's Quay is based on New Quay in Pembrokeshire, which I visited for the first time when filming *Who Do You Think You Are?* for the BBC. My ancestors hail from there and I have been back to visit several times since. It's a beautiful town. And I think the experience of filming there and discovering more about my maternal grandfather's family contributed hugely to my wanting to write something multigenerational. Also my lovely father, Richard, went to France in 1946 on *The Golden Arrow* and *La Flèche d'Or* to meet up with his penfriend, Pierre. He was just eighteen, the war had only been over a year and it was an achievement I didn't give him enough credit for when he first told me. Now I think what an extraordinary thing it was for him to do. I miss you, Dad. So many questions I wish I could ask you now.

And finally, unlike Beca, I never knew my great-grandmothers, but I like to think that the character of Grace has encapsulated the tenacity, optimism and inimitable Welsh humour of both my grandmothers, Gwen and Anita, as well as my dear mother, Hannah, to whom this book is dedicated. How blessed our family has been, to know such strong, inspiring women across the generations – those living and those who've gone on before us. They all make me very proud.

Ruth Jones is best known for her outstanding and award-winning television writing, most notably BBC One's *Gavin and Stacey*, which she co-wrote with James Corden and in which she played the incorrigible Nessa Jenkins. The 2019 Christmas Day special of *Gavin and Stacey* gained national critical acclaim, drawing an audience of over 18 million, winning a BAFTA for TV moment of the year and a National Television Award for Impact. Ruth also created and co-wrote Sky One's *Stella*, which ran for six series. Ruth has starred in several other television comedies and dramas.

Her debut novel, *Never Greener*, was chosen as WHSmith Fiction Book of the Year 2018, was nominated for Debut of the Year at the British Book Awards, was a Zoe Ball Book Club pick, and was a *Sunday Times* bestseller for fifteen weeks, three weeks at number one. Ruth's second novel, *Us Three*, was an instant *Sunday Times* bestseller in hardback and paperback and has sold almost a quarter of a million copies. Ruth was awarded a Comedy Women in Print Prize in 2020. *Love Untold* is her third novel.